THE WINDS OF CHANGE

THE WINDS OF CHANGE

"A Novel about the last 14 months of the
American Civil War"

RICHARD L. GUIDA

iUniverse, Inc.
New York Lincoln Shanghai

The Winds of Change
"A Novel about the last 14 months of the American Civil War"

iUniverse books may be ordered through booksellers or by contacting:

iUniverse
2021 Pine Lake Road, Suite 100
Lincoln, NE 68512
www.iuniverse.com
1-800-Authors (1-800-288-4677)

Certain characters in this work are historical figures, and certain events portrayed did take place. However, this is a work of fiction. All of the other characters, names, and events as well as all places, incidents, organizations, and dialogue in this novel are either the products of the author's imagination or are used fictitiously.

ISBN: 978-0-595-42308-8 (pbk)
ISBN: 978-0-595-67991-1 (cloth)
ISBN: 978-0-595-86647-2 (ebk)

Printed in the United States of America

This book is dedicated to my lovely wife, Dianne, without whose patience, understanding and encouragement this book would not have been possible.

CHAPTER ONE

Willard Hotel, Washington D. C.—March 8, 1864, 2:30 PM

A cold rain pelted the driver of the horse-drawn, covered carriage as an angry wind added to the man's misery. Inside the cab sat three military men and a twelve-year-old boy.

"Willard Hotel, sir," he said lifting the leather curtain to speak to the inhabitants inside.

Two men quickly exited. One ran for the canopy covering the entrance to the posh hotel, while the other sprinted to the front of the cab and paid the driver. Minutes later the third man exited the coach. A dark blue military poncho covered his clothes from the neck to the middle of his thighs. His light blue trousers rapidly became drenched below the knee as he patiently waited in the winter storm for the boy to exit. The top of his head was kept dry by a slouch hat. Water dripped down his back where the poncho and shirt parted.

"Hurry up, Fred, I'm not a duck," the man said in the tone of a doting father. Seconds later a brown haired boy exited the buggy. A military poncho covered his woolen gray suit. The man lifted his son and ran for the canopy.

The quartet entered the hotel and removed their raingear, unaware of the probing pair of eyes across the lobby watching the trios' every move. After waiting for almost four hours in the crowded lobby, the spy's vigilance had paid off.

"Colonel Rawlins, Colonel Comstock why don't you take Fred near the fire and warm yourselves while I check us in," said the third military man in a soft tone.

Three clerks stood behind the counter each focused on their paperwork as they checked in guests.

"May I help you?" asked a young man in his mid-twenties, without lifting his head.

"Yes, I would like two rooms and a suite please," the officer answered.

The clerk glanced up and quickly took note of the slender man who wore an ordinary private's overcoat but didn't carry a sword. His uniform had no gold braid and except for the rank insignia on his shoulders, an average person would mistake him for a private; not a Major General.

"Is it always this busy?" asked the military officer, his blue eyes framed by his long brown hair and full beard.

"It's usually busy, but not this much. Everyone is waiting for General Grant to arrive. We have officers who are looking for a command and businessmen who are seeking lucrative government contracts," replied the clerk. "They think he is going to end the war overnight. Grant is good, but I don't know if he is good enough to beat Bobby Lee. The war should have never occurred; it is a waste of time, money and men."

The Major General leaned forward and replied. "You sound like a person whose heart is with the South."

"I am the furthest thing from a Southerner. Don't get me wrong. I hope they are right and the General kicks Bobby Lee's ass. But if he becomes too cocky, he'll wind up like all the idiots that have come before him. Sir, I will stack my patriotism and love for the Union against any man's, including yours. I have been in every major battle in the East since this mess began. During the third day at Gettysburg I helped hold the center of our line against Pickett's charge. During the Rebs' retreat a minie ball nailed me in the knee. I lost my leg just above the joint. I spent five months in the hospital recuperating. Just as I was ready to return to the war, the morons at the War Department gave me this worthless piece of scrap iron along with my discharge."

The clerk reached into his pocket and removed a fancy military medal and showed it to the older man.

"That's the Medal of Honor; you should be proud of it. I apologize for upsetting you," said the man.

"It's all right, General, you didn't know," replied the desk clerk. "I don't have enough accommodations to honor your request. The best I can do is two rooms, one for you and the boy and the other for your aides. If this is agreeable, please sign the guest register."

"If that's all you have, I guess it has to do," answered the older man.

The younger man handed him the keys, "Rooms two nineteen and two thirty-two. Second floor and make a right."

The military officer nodded, turned and walked away.

"Holy shit, please come back!" shouted the clerk.

"I'm afraid I was mistaken ... I should have asked you your name before assigning a room," stammered the clerk. "Please ... forgive me ... for everything I said. I didn't recognize you ... General Grant. We have the Royal Suite reserved for you and ... two deluxe rooms for your aides."

"Thank you, young man. I appreciate your candor. What's your name, son?" asked the North's most successful General.

"Ronald Lyons," the clerk responded sheepishly.

Grant nodded, turned and walked toward the stairs. Once inside his suite he removed his overcoat and boots and sat on an overstuffed red floral easy chair. His son, Fred, occupied himself by sitting cross-legged on the floor reading the latest issue of Harpers Weekly Magazine. On the front page was a picture of his father looking very serious. Fred stared at the picture and then at his Dad, who was watching him intently with a smile on his face. The duo looked at each other for a full minute before the young man stood up and rushed to his father. The pair hugged. Ulysses S. Grant, the Victor of Forts Henry and Donelson, the Hero of Shiloh, the Conqueror of Vicksburg and the Savior of Chattanooga gave his son a kiss on the cheek. A knock at the door interrupted the peaceful moment between father and son.

"I'll get it," said Fred.

He opened the heavy, hand-carved oak door and in walked the General's aides, John Rawlins and Cyrus Comstock. Grant's facial expression changed to serious.

"What time is the reception?" asked Grant.

"It starts at seven o'clock," answered Rawlins. "We have about four hours. You haven't eaten since breakfast. Do you want to go downstairs and grab some supper or would you rather rest?

"I'm not hungry right now, maybe in a few hours. I think I'll just close my eyes and try to get rid of the pounding in my head. If the both of you are going to grab some supper, would you mind taking Fred?"

"Come on Fred, let's get something to eat. By the way, it's beginning to snow," responded Rawlins as he closed the drapes.

John Rawlins had the neighboring farm next to the Grants' when they lived in St. Louis. Through the years the two men had become close friends. Fiercely loyal he would go to any length to protect the General. Many of the duo's enemies described the aide's eyes as shark-like—black and lifeless.

White House, Washington D.C.—March 8, 7:00 PM,

Abraham Lincoln stood in front of the eight-foot sixteen pane window behind his desk in the Executive Office staring at the falling snow. The outdoor gas street lamps reflected off of the glimmering specs of white giving the evening a look of purity and tranquility. It reminded the former lawyer from Springfield, Illinois of happier times spent sledding with his sons Robert, Tad and Willie.

He took a deep breath and slowly let it out. The man who was leading the Nation during its most trying time missed his youngest son, Willie. Lincoln couldn't believe how fast the two years since his son's death from Typhoid had passed. Willie was his favorite. He remembered how he was called to a cabinet meeting the night of the boy's death. The Chief Executive often regretted not spending more time with his son during those last days. The death had severely strained the Lincolns' marriage. His wife still cried when she thought no one else was around.

Every time it snowed he thought of Willie and the snowmen they had built together outside his Law Office. *"No parent should ever have to outlive a son,"* thought Lincoln.

Tears slowly wove their way down his weathered face. Each time a casualty list was brought to him his heart would break feeling the grief of the parents. He knew he could end the misery and suffering by granting the South her independence; he also knew it would be the end of not only the Union but the Confederacy as well. The man had to remain strong in his resolve no matter what personal sacrifices it required.

Through the years he had alienated many powerful men in Congress. Three weeks earlier the Republican Leadership had approached the President with the strong recommendation he resurrect the Army rank of Lieutenant General. They assured him it would pass both Houses of Congress providing he promised to promote Grant to the new position and make him General-in-Chief of all the Armed Forces of the Union.

The idea had merit but Lincoln had reservations. Deep down he knew Grant had earned the promotion due to his numerous victories; however, every General he had ever met was pompous and arrogant. Even though he was an avid supporter of Grant he had never met the man. For the first time in three years Lincoln would have to take a back seat in running the war and trust his military subordinate.

A knock at the door startled the Chief Executive.

"Mr. President, the reception is starting. It appears to be a large crowd." said John Hay the President's personal Secretary and confidant.

Hay, a former newspaper editor, idolized the much maligned Leader of the Union. He couldn't understand how the Country didn't see the honesty, wisdom and integrity in the man. He stood helplessly by and watched the anguish on Lincoln's face when the reporters called him a "*despot*" and "*King Linkum*."

"It will make Mrs. Lincoln happy. She loves to be the center of attention. For the past year the crowds have steadily diminished. Last week we had only thirty people show up. She was heart-broken," replied the President buttoning his coat.

Confederate White House, Richmond, Virginia—May 8, 7:00 PM

Confederate President Jefferson Davis sat in his office peering over a large pile of telegrams from his Generals in the field. The most disheartening piece of paper lying on the desk wasn't a telegram but a small blood-stained note. In late February the Union had dispatched a small Calvary Brigade under the command of Brigadier General Judson Kilpatrick to raid the Southern Capital and to free prisoners of war held at Belle Island just outside of Richmond and Libby Prison in the heart of the city.

The raid had begun perfectly with the Union horsemen arriving at the outskirts of the city undiscovered. Unknown to the Calvary Commander, a Confederate spy named Benjamin Franklin Stringfellow working inside Washington D.C had sent word of the raid to Robert E. Lee who, in turn, dispatched his Calvary to intercept the Union raiders.

When Kilpatrick reached the Richmond City limits, he decided to split his force in half assigning his second-in-command and originator of the plan, Colonel Ulrich Dahlgren, to approach Richmond from the south while he assaulted it from the opposite end. The ambitious Brigadier General had just begun his attack when he noticed the Confederates had a formidable defensive line consisting of Calvary and Infantry hidden behind barricades of overturned wagons and bales of cotton. Losing his nerve, he retreated north abandoning Dahlgren.

Unaware his Commander had retreated, the Colonel attacked. His small band was quickly torn to shreds. Seeing his predicament as hopeless he ordered his men to cut their way out. Drawing sabers they attacked. Only a few were able to escape. Most lie dying or dead in the gutter of the cobblestone street. Among the dead was Dahlgren, a bullet through his heart. When the authorities searched the dead Officer's clothing, they found unsigned orders hidden in his wooden leg. They instructed him that after freeing the tprisoners he was to seek out the Confederate leadership and kill hem including the Southern President.

Davis, a former United States Senator and Secretary of War, was appalled by the order. The quick-tempered, sensitive, bull-headed former Plantation owner from Mississippi ordered his favorite General and friend, Robert E. Lee, to send a message across the 'no man's land' between the lines demanding an explanation from the Union's Army of the Potomac Commander, Major General George Meade.

The Southerners didn't have to wait long for an answer. Within twenty-four hours a reply from Lincoln and Meade was received denying issuing the order. Lee believed the men while Davis had his doubts.

The former Senator looked away from the scrap of paper and shook his head in disbelief. He knew Lincoln would go to any extreme to keep the Union together, but in his heart he hoped the man would not resort to murder.

He turned his attention to the Capital's most influential newspaper, *The Richmond Inquirer*. Picking up the paper he stared at the headlines. "*Grant Appointed Head of all Union Forces.*" The fifty-six year old, gray haired Rebel Leader's mind was racing from one thought to another.

Of the Union Generals, he disliked Grant the most. The hatred had nothing to do with the man being incompetent or immoral, he thought just the opposite. He knew the General was very skilled and, except for his occasional bout with the bottle, his scruples were beyond question. Unlike his predecessors he fought. He was low key, very calm and extremely focused. Glory didn't matter to the man from Galena, Illinois; it was the cause and only the cause which kept him going. He didn't back away from a fight. With Grant in command the winds of change were beginning to blow.

The North would throw its entire resources against the South. The Mississippian knew he must prepare his Country for a terrific storm and a way to survive its fury. Jefferson Davis' strategy was simple—do not give the Federals any substantial victories and the war-weary people in the Northern States would vote Lincoln out of office. His successor would, most likely, give the Confederacy her independence.

Davis wasn't worried about his Eastern Theatre of Operations. He had Robert E. Lee in command of the Army of Northern Virginia. The fifty-seven year old career soldier had given the South her only substantial victories. Several times he had approached the man about leaving the Army in the East to take command of the Confederacy's Western forces. Each time Lee's reply was the same—*"When I left the 'old Army,' I promised myself I would only draw my sword against the Union in defense of my State."*

The Confederate President had no other General of the Virginian's caliber for defense of the Western half of his Nation. Sidney Johnston was killed at Shiloh leaving a void no one had been able to fill. Albert Sidney Johnston had been Davis' senior at West Point. Throughout Jefferson Davis' life he had been in awe of the older Johnston. The two men had become close personal friends. The news of his friend's demise had put him in a severe depression that lasted a week.

The anguish he felt then was nothing compared to what he was now experiencing. Two weeks earlier his youngest son, Joseph Evan Davis, tumbled off the outside second floor balcony while playing and plummeted to his death on the cobblestone driveway. The entire South was in mourning for the boy. Sympathy ran high for the Chief Executive. Even his enemies were willing to bury the hatchet and start fresh with the combative, stubborn Mississippian. Unrelenting and unforgiving, he pushed away all attempts by his enemies to make peace.

His son's death plunged Davis deeper into his work. Often in his office sixteen hours a day, he became harder to deal with. Of all his Generals' only Robert E. Lee enjoyed the confidence and friendship of the Southern leader.

Davis stood and bent over stretching his back. It had been a long day. The severe pain on the left side of his face from his constant Neuralgia was beginning to subside. It had gone from a sharp stabbing pain to a dull throbbing. The man slowly walked out of his office and into his personal residence. His wife, surviving son and daughter waited patiently at the dinner table for him. The smell of smoked Ham, roasted sweet potatoes and peach pie greeted his nostrils as he entered the Dining Room. He walked to his wife, bent over and gave her a kiss on the lips.

"Sorry I'm late," he said softly as he walked around the table kissing each one his children.

"Sweetheart, rough day?" asked Varina Howell Davis.

The thirty-nine year old former Southern Belle from Natchez, Mississippi smiled sweetly at her husband.

"I think Lincoln is going to appoint Grant General-in-Chief. If I am right, Grant is going to hit us with everything he can muster. Things are going to get worse before they get better."

"Jeff, what are you planning to do? I don't know how much more the Country can withstand," said Varina.

"I'm not worried about Bob Lee. He will do whatever it takes to keep Meade in check. The problem is the West. I don't know if Joe Johnston has the stomach to hold the damn Yankees out of Georgia. He will give up ground rather than stand and fight. Our only hope is for Lee to keep Meade at bay and for Johnston not to give the Yankees cheap victories like he did on the Peninsular against McClellan. We must hold our ground until after the Northern elections. If we can do that, then, Lincoln will be voted out of office and we have our best chance at independence."

White House, Washington D.C.—May 8, 7:15 PM

Carriages were parked alongside the circular driveway leading to the Union White House. Drivers were huddled together in an open sided lean-to. A roaring fire blazed in the center of the structure as they struggled to keep warm. They smoked cigars while talking about the war. No one noticed the three Union Officers walking by.

Grant threw his half-smoked cigar onto the ground. The trio entered the foyer of the Executive Mansion. The entrance overflowed with people wanting to see the North's greatest hero. Weaving their way inconspicuously through the crowd they slowly inched toward the East Room.

Close to one hundred people packed the massive room. In the far corner a string quartet played a waltz as couples mingled. Union Officers talked with businessmen and their lovely daughters. Entrepreneurs pumped the military men for insider information while the men in uniform attempted to ingratiate themselves to the single women.

Grant looked at his companions and whispered, "Let the games begin."

Comstock looked at his boss with a puzzled, confused expression. The aide from Massachusetts was a staunch abolitionist who had been with the General less than six months. The amiable former lawyer had fit in well with the General's other aides especially John Rawlins.

Noticing the confused look on his subordinate's face, Rawlins leaned over and whispered to Comstock.

"The boss hates attention. He would rather go into battle without any weapons than face a crowd of civilians."

"Look everyone, here is General Grant," announced Lincoln.

"General Grant, welcome to Washington. May I present my wife, the First Lady, Mary Lincoln?"

"Nice to meet you ma'am," replied the humble General, bowing slightly at the waist.

"Mr. President and Mrs. Lincoln may I present my Chief-of-Staff, Colonel John Rawlins and my other staff member, Colonel Cyrus Comstock?"

The two men's faces became flushed with embarrassment as they shook hands with the President and the First Lady. They had expected their boss to be the center of attention, but it didn't cross their minds they too would be in the spotlight. Anyone who could not get to Grant would settle for the next best thing—his aides.

In the corner near the quartet a young woman no more than twenty-years old coyly flirted with an overweight, gray haired, Major assigned to the War Department. The older man with a pock-marked face enjoyed the attention of the five-foot, ninety-four pound female with cascading blond hair. She wore a lovely blue evening gown which completely covered her ample bosoms yet daintily exposed the top of her milky white shoulder. The couple glanced at the President and General then turned their attention back to each other.

"Do you know General Grant?" asked the woman demurely.

"Of course, I was with him at Shiloh," replied the overweight middle-aged man puffing out his chest.

"Was it as bad as the tabloids said?" inquired the young woman.

"The Rebs hit us hard. The first day we were almost pushed into the Tennessee River, but Grant kept his cool and the next day he launched a counterattack pushing the damn rebels all the way back to Corinth."

"What do you think of Grant as a General?" questioned the blonde.

"He's tough minded. The man's not easily ruffled. At Shiloh, he calmly sat on his horse smoking a cigar and watched our counter-attack. Minie balls were flying all around him, yet he sat their issuing orders. The man is fearless."

Meanwhile near the entrance of the East Room, Mrs. Lincoln continued to chat with General Grant.

"General Grant, you are alone. Where is Mrs. Grant?" asked the First Lady.

"Julia hasn't arrived yet in Washington. She is visiting friends in Baltimore. I had no idea she was invited. I wish she were here instead of me as I'm not one for parties. However; my wife, Julia, loves them and I love her so I go."

"Spoken like a true family man," replied Mary Lincoln. "With your permission, General, let me be her substitute for the evening?"

The First Lady liked the man. Unlike the other Commanders her husband had appointed, Grant had the humble qualities of a solider and respect toward his Commander-in-Chief.

Hooking her arm through his, Mary Lincoln escorted the hero around the East Room introducing him to all the influential people. Stopping at the Secretary of State, William Seward, the couple talked for fifteen minutes. The six foot, former New York State Governor had run against Lincoln for the Republican Party's Presidential candidate in eighteen sixty. Shortly after being appointed to the cabinet, the polished New Yorker soon realized the vast intelligence, resolve and political savvy the President possessed. A rough beginning had blossomed into a mutual respect and then into a deep friendship. Seward would support the President and anyone he chose to lead the Army. He was to Lincoln as Rawlins was to Grant.

Each person who met the shy General took an instant liking to the man. Everyone, that is, except Secretary of the Navy, Gideon Wells. The man from Connecticut was credited with transferring the Navy from an inferior force consisting of only a few ships into a mighty armada, capable of challenging Britain. With Welles at the helm, the Navy had successfully blockaded all Southern ports from Maryland to Florida and from Galveston to California. The Oceans and the Gulf were cut off. The Navy had greatly reduced the amount of supplies the South was receiving. Welles didn't see the difference between Grant and the others Lincoln had appointed.

The crowd began to become unruly in an effort to meet Grant.

"Mr. President," said Seward. "Maybe our guests will settle down if we allowed the General to stand on this sofa so everyone could see him. We could then form a reception line and allow everyone to meet him."

"Excellent idea," replied a smiling Lincoln.

"With all due respect, my boots are muddy," protested Grant.

"As your Commander-in-Chief I order you to stand on this sofa," replied Lincoln.

Mary Lincoln hid her smile with her hand fan. *"This man is truly humble,"* she thought as she watched the blushing General stand on the soft white and gold cushions.

"Grant, enjoy the moment. When you are done, please meet me in the Blue Room. Mr. Seward will show you the way," said the President.

For two hours he shook hands and made small talk. At the end of the line were the Major and the young woman.

"General, I don't know if you remember me?" asked the Major as he approached.

"Of course I do, Major Holt, how are you? I haven't seen you since the second day at Shiloh. Where are you assigned now?" asked Grant.

"I am at the War Department as an aide to General Halleck. Sir, I would like to present Miss Elizabeth Cardwell," answered Holt.

Grant smiled cordially and shook her hand. His arm felt like it was going to fall off. His hand was cramped and his throat was dry. He craved a cigar. As Holt and Cardwell walked away, he stepped down off the sofa. Seward silently escorted the trio to the Blue Room.

"How did it go?" inquired Lincoln.

"It was a circus," responded Grant.

Throwing his head back Lincoln let out a loud laugh surprising Secretary of War, Edwin Stanton. The Presidential advisor hadn't seen "old Abe" laugh so hard since just before Willie died.

"If you ever want to be President, you will have to get used to it," said Lincoln.

"With all due respect, sir, I am a soldier, I fight and win battles. My job is defeating the Southern Armies in the field. Your job is fighting the politicians. Hopefully you have no ambition to do my job because I certainly have none to do yours," replied Grant in a serious tone.

"Well said," interrupted the portly Secretary of War.

"Nice to see you again, Mr. Secretary," answered Grant.

"General, I asked you here to discuss your plans for defeating the South," said Lincoln in a serious tone.

"To begin with I wish you would not call me General," replied Grant. "You're my superior. My friends call me Ulysses or Ulys or Sam. I prefer Sam."

"Why Sam?" asked the Chief Executive.

"My friend at West Point, James Longstreet, nicknamed me that. He said my initials U.S. Grant stood for Uncle Sam Grant, henceforth, Sam," replied Grant.

"I will call you Sam if you call me Abe when we are in private," answered Lincoln. "I would like you to take Richmond. Be careful before you answer. Five other Generals assured me they could take that damn city and failed."

Grant peered at the Chief Executive. Reaching into his breast pocket he removed a six inch Cuban cigar. Striking a match he lit the brown tobacco stick carefully rotating its tip to ensure an even light. He took a deep drag and slowly exhaled.

"I can take Richmond, if you give me enough men. Abe, I just want you to know it will be a bloody and costly campaign. Lee will not yield ground voluntarily. He must be pushed off. Halleck will remain in Washington to handle my paperwork and I will be with the Army of the Potomac.

"With less men and material, the South has kept us at bay for almost three years. We have allowed them to do this by not having a coordinated effort in the East and West. The Army of the Potomac and the Armies in the West never simultaneously planned their campaigns. This allowed the rebels to shift men from the East to the West and vice versa. From this moment on all Armies will move as one. If a General fails to follow our orders, he will be immediately removed. We have no time to dilly dally. Except for protecting Washington, we don't have to protect any of our cities. Nature has taken care of that. The chances of Lee attacking New York or Chicago are remote at best."

Grant paused to let Lincoln, Stanton and Seward absorb what he was saying.

"On the other hand Lee has to protect Richmond and Johnston Atlanta. I could care less about those cities. The way to defeat the Confederates is to destroy her Armies in the field. I will go after Lee and Sherman will go after Johnston. At the same time Sigel will go after the rebels in the Shenandoah Valley while Butler assaults the enemy on the Virginia Peninsula. They have only one order—attack. Let Jefferson Davis worry about Richmond and Atlanta. I want Lee and Johnston. Only at Vicksburg did we win a city and capture an Army. Gentlemen, do you have any questions?" asked Grant.

Lincoln stared at the shorter man for a minute before answering.

"It makes sense. It is like the western way of hog-killing. Those not skinning can hold the leg," replied Lincoln.

Being raised in cities the Secretaries of War and State had a confused look on their faces, but nodded in agreement.

"Where do you suppose to get more men to replace those you anticipate losing in battle?" asked Stanton.

"Mr. Secretary, there are men on garrison duty in the Northeast which can be reassigned as combat troops. The rebels are interested in Washington, the chances of them attacking any city north of the Capital is remote. Consolidate these soldiers into a fighting Army and send their Generals home to await orders," replied Sam Grant puffing on his cigar.

"What makes you think the men you mentioned will follow your orders?" asked Lincoln.

"Mr. President, I am not worried about Billy Sherman, he will go into the depths of hell if I ask him to. If I keep Meade in command, he will be fine as I will be with him. The only weak links are Butler and Sigel. Neither has shown any real initiative or combat aptitude in their other roles. I know both have a great deal of political connections but if they fail, I will need your support in either firing or relieving them," answered Grant.

"You give me victories and you will have my undying support," replied Lincoln.

"I thought you would remain either at Culpepper or in Washington?" asked Stanton.

"Sir, I mean no offense in my next statement, but Washington is for politicians; the field is for Generals. I plan to move within the next sixty days. I need the roads to dry. Once again I must remind you, the butcher bill will be expensive," replied the General in a firm tone.

Lincoln looked at Grant and nodded. At last he had found a General who wasn't afraid to fight.

While Grant and Lincoln met in the Blue Room, Elizabeth Cardwell entered the lobby of the Willard Hotel.

"May I have my key please?" she asked sweetly.

Ronald Lyons handed the woman the key and watched her sashay away. Something was wrong with the young lady, but he couldn't put his finger on it.

Elizabeth Cardwell entered her room and removed her dress. Underneath the silk and crinolines was an Army Colt forty-five caliber pistol loaded with six shots. She removed her face makeup and stared into the mirror examining her face. Light colored stubble was beginning to show. She walked to her suitcase and reached under the lining of the luggage where she lifted up on a hidden tab in the center removing the false bottom. Underneath was a Confederate ciphering book and code wheel.

She took a key off the dresser and walked to the door separating the adjoining room. The woman unlocked it and entered the darkened room. She lit an oil based lamp and proceeded to the wash basin. She filled the receptacle with water, lathered up her face and shaved the stubble. She removed her under garments to reveal a male anatomy and put on a pair of trousers. He went to the writing table and composed a message to Robert E. Lee.

Benjamin Franklin Stringfellow was one the Confederates' most successful spies. The slightly built man had been turned down three times for active duty in the Southern Army until Jeb Stuart decided the man could provide a valuable service as a spy. Posing as a Dental Student he had become friends with many high ranking Union Officers. As a woman, he had access to areas and people a dental student did not. Registered under the name of Robert Cardwell he was Elizabeth's brother. No one would question the likeness. Union spy catchers had been trying to apprehend him for years.

CHAPTER TWO

Willard Hotel, Washington D.C.—March 9, 5:00AM

Grant woke at five sharp. He walked to a sleeping Fred, bent over and gave the boy a kiss on his cheek. The boy opened his eyes.

"What time is it?" asked the boy.

"It's still early; you sleep. I have business downstairs. I'll be back in a few hours and then we'll have breakfast. After we eat we'll go get your Mom and brothers at the train station," answered Ulysses.

Fred rolled over, closed his eyes and was soon in a deep sleep. Grant dressed and went downstairs. Sitting in the lobby smoking a cigar and drinking a cup of black coffee was John Rawlins.

"I'm surprised you're awake," said Grant feigning surprise.

"He's behind the counter," answered Rawlins ignoring his boss' comment.

"Good morning Mr. Lyons," said a cheerful Sam Grant.

"Is everything all right General?" asked Lyons.

"Everything's fine. Yesterday you said you wanted to stay in the Army. If that's still true, I'm here to ask you to join my staff effective this afternoon with the rank of Captain," replied Grant.

The man looked at the General for a few minutes then nodded.

"I have some business at the War Department. I want you to report to General Halleck at two this afternoon. He will get you settled in," answered the North's top General.

Grant turned and nodded to Rawlins. The black-eyed, ominous looking aide stood up and walked toward his chief. In the corner observing the entire scene was Stringfellow. Ten minutes after the duo left, he rose and headed to the War Department Building.

Grant and Rawlins entered the War Department building and walked up two flights of stairs to Henry Halleck's office. The Major General was Grant's former superior and enemy. Halleck's jealously bordered on hatred. The pair walked into the office without knocking. There was no love lost between the men. The bald, heavy-set Halleck was busy at his desk going over mounds of paperwork, which supplied the Union Army. Highly intelligent, his friends at West Point nicknamed him 'old brains'. The fifty-seven year old professional was an atrocious field commander, but behind a desk no one was better. The office was neatly organized. A fire burned in the pot belly stove in the corner. The drapes were open allowing in the morning sunlight. The window behind his desk was a quarter way up to allow in the fresh air.

Halleck looked up and spotted Grant standing before him wearing the rank insignia of a Lieutenant General. The older man stood and saluted. Grant returned the courtesy and sat down.

"Halleck, you have been trying to get me fired ever since we met. Because of you I almost quit the service. You are petty and small and have cost many a good officer his career. In spite of your short comings I have decided to keep you on. I will be in the field and I need someone of your caliber to keep the paperwork straight and keep our Armies supplied. I am willing to bury the hatchet and forget our past differences for the sake of the nation. Can you do the same?" asked Grant.

The older man stared at his new boss for a few minutes. He was surprised by the General-in-Chief's offer.

"I accept your generous offer and from this moment on I pledge my undying support. What will you have me do?" asked Halleck.

The two men shook hands and Grant lit a cigar. For the next hour he relayed the conversation he had with Lincoln and his strategy for the upcoming campaign. He would need Halleck's assistance in coordinating all the logistics.

Standing outside underneath the open window was Franklin Stringfellow. The spy listened intently all the while keeping a sharp lookout. He didn't take any notes. If questioned, he could claim he was taking his morning walk when he saw a suspicious person near the building and came over to investigate. If captured and searched any notes would be enough to incriminate him as a rebel spy. His fate would be a short drop from the gallows. After forty-five minutes he decided he had pushed his luck far enough and walked along Pennsylvania Avenue and hailed a cab.

"541 H Street," said Stringfellow.

During the short ride he wrote a message relaying Grant's plans of attacking several points at once.

Fifteen minutes later the buggy arrived in front of Mary Surratt's Boarding House. Unknown to Federal authorities the residence was frequented by rebel spies and sympathizers. Paying the driver, he climbed the stairs to the ten-room brick home and went to room three on the eastern corner of the first floor. He knocked twice, slowly counted to five then knocked once. He counted to five again and knocked three times. The door opened a few inches. The occupant peered through the opening and recognizing the rebel spy; silently motioned him inside.

"Get this message to General Lee," whispered Stringfellow handing the man a note.

Grant returned to the hotel later than he thought. The meeting with Halleck had taken several hours. Inside the room Julia Dent Grant was awaiting her husband's return. Fred was in the parlor playing with his brother and sister. Sam walked over to his wife of sixteen years and kissed her on the mouth. The couple had been introduced by his best friend, James Longstreet. The daughter of a wealthy plantation owner, Julia was not considered good looking; however, to Sam Grant she was the most beautiful woman in the world. When they were apart he was in agony. It was the long separations which first turned him to alcohol in order to cure his solace. Holding hands they watched their children playing.

Leaving Comstock in Washington, Grant and Rawlins left the Union capital in the late afternoon and headed south to meet with the Army of the Potomac's Commander and hero of Gettysburg, Major General George Gordon Meade. It was nearly dark when the duo arrived at the headquarters in Brandy Station.

In spite of the steady rainfall, Meade had organized a VIP reception for the new Commander. An honor guard of three hundred New York Zouaves dressed in baggy pants with red fezzes on their heads snapped to attention the moment Grant appeared. The original French Zouaves were considered the best fighting men in the world. When the war broke out, many units on both sides copied the famous uniforms. Many lived up to the honor, some did not. Fortunately for Meade, his Zouaves units were the cream of the crop.

"Company ... attention," commanded the young Zouave Captain in a loud firm voice.

Immediately they all snapped to attention, their backs straight and their chests out. Rifles were brought from a forty-five degree angle briskly to their sides.

"Company ... present arms," ordered the Captain.

Smartly the Union troops brought their muskets perpendicular to the ground with the trigger housing centered on each man's belt buckle and the bayonet pointed straight up. At the same time the regimental band played *"Rally Round the Flag."* Grant was impressed with the military bearing of the camp and Meade's respect.

The Commander of the Army of the Potomac was a West Pointer. Unlike his new boss he was a stickler for the rules. Against his will he was ordered to take command of the Army by Lincoln after the Union's disastrous defeat at Chancellorsville. He was in command less than a week when he fought against Robert E. Lee at Gettysburg.

After three days of combat, the Union troops were worn out. Meade rested his men instead of pursuing Lee's defeated Army. Lincoln and Stanton were infuriated with Meade's decision. The two politicians felt he had the perfect opportunity to destroy the Confederate Army and end the war.

Married with three children, the irascible Meade had a quick temper and an unforgiving nature. He could forgive a mistake but could not and would not forget a wronging. He took things personally and had a thin skin. The man was fiercely loyal to his family and friends.

"General Grant, it's a pleasure to finally meet you," said a patrician looking George Meade saluting.

"Thank you, General," replied Grant returning the salute.

"General Grant, I have assembled all of my Corps Commanders. They are waiting for you in my headquarters. After you have met with them, perhaps you and I could talk in private?" asked Meade in a respectful tone.

"Why don't you and I talk first," replied Grant.

Unknown to Meade, the General-in-Chief, with the urging of Lincoln and Stanton, was leaning toward replacing the Pennsylvanian, but had kept an open mind.

The two men walked toward the man's parlor of the Broward Mansion of Sycamore Plantation. Their boots resounded throughout the hallway as they stepped onto the hardwood highly polished floor. The Broward family had moved out of the main house and into a guest cottage. Staunch Southerners, the family had decided it was better to live in the guest house than under the same roof as Yankees. Losing a son at Gettysburg during Pickett's Charge, they hated all Yankees, especially George Meade.

The two Generals sat opposite one another. Grant lit a cigar and offered one to Meade. The Pennsylvanian refused.

"I know Lincoln and Stanton are upset with me. I also know with your being new to this theatre of the war, you may want to bring in Billy Sherman to replace me," said Meade.

Grant tried to stop him from going on, but Meade held up his hand and continued.

"Please, let me finish. Our cause is more important than any one man. If you feel you want to relieve me, then please do so. My only request would be to let me stay with this Army, even if it means commanding a Corps or a Division or even a Brigade. I still think I have something left to help our Country," said Meade.

A long silence followed as Grant stared into the Pennsylvanian's eyes trying to decide what to do. He had encountered many Generals during the war, but Meade was one of the few who put the cause above their own personal ambition. He was touched by the man's patriotism.

"George, I have no intention of replacing you. You have done an admirable job with this Army. Billy Sherman is needed in the West just as you are needed here. I will be with your Army for the entire campaign," replied Grant.

Meade extended his hand to his new boss as he rose from his chair.

"By this handshake, I pledge my loyalty to you, General Grant. I'll call in my officers so we may convene our meeting."

The brain trust of the Army of the Potomac entered the parlor led by John Rawlins. Each took a seat around Grant. The quiet man from Illinois watched each one intently as they entered.

"General Grant, may I present Major General Winfield Scott Hancock. It was Hancock's Corps which broke up Pickett's Charge. He commands the Second Corps," said Meade.

"Excellent job at Gettysburg, I understand you were wounded during Pickett's attack. How do you feel now?" asked Grant.

"Yes sir. A spent ball hit my saddle driving a nail into my stomach. I am fine and ready to resume the fight," responded the pale and sweating General of the Second Corps.

"Next is Major General Gouverneur Warren. It was Warren who at Gettysburg noticed Longstreet's forces attempting to flank our position at the

Round Tops and shifted some of our forces to meet the threat. He commands the Fifth Corps," said Meade.

"Well done," replied Grant shaking Warren's hand.

"My next Corps Commander is Major General John Sedgwick. His accomplishments in this Army are too numerous to mention. He commands the Sixth Corps."

"Pleased to meet you, Sedgwick," replied Grant shaking his hand.

Sitting in the corner by himself was a heavy-set, whiskered man.

"Gentlemen, as you noticed Major General Burnside is here. I have asked him to join us as his Ninth Corps will be a part of this Campaign. I know some of you dislike him because of the Fredericksburg debacle. He will have an independent command reporting directly to me. If anyone objects to this arrangement, let me know now," stated Grant in a firm tone.

Silence filled the room. After waiting a full minute for someone to voice any objections, Grant continued.

"Gentlemen, I want to know everything you know about the enemy and, in particular, General Lee. If you wish to smoke; please do so."

One by one the Generals spoke their minds on the mismanagement of the Army, beginning with McClellan and ending with Joe Hooker. Only Meade held their respect. Carefully choosing their words as not to diminish their new commander's victories, they told of the superiority of the Confederate Generals in the East as compared to those commanding in the West. The meeting continued until two in the morning.

Grant and Rawlins walked outside to discuss the results of what they had heard. The rain had stopped and smoldering pine from dying campfires filled the air with a sweet, smoky smell. Mixing with the coolness of early morning it was both invigorating and soothing. It was the time of the day Sam loved the most, peaceful and serene.

"John, did you notice the change in their voices when they spoke of Bobby Lee. It was like they were speaking of God," said Grant staring up at the sky.

Clouds lazily moved across the heavens occasionally blotting out the moon and casting an ominous shadow on the pair.

"For this Army to win it must lose its fear of Lee or the Country is doomed," said Grant.

The two friends walked back to the house. Rawlins went to his room while Grant bent over, picked up a stick and walked to a rocking chair on the porch. Sitting, he pulled his overcoat tightly around him. Reaching into his right coat pocket he withdrew a small pocket knife and began to whittle. It was a mindless way to keep his hands busy while his thoughts concentrated on the next steps of his plan.

Brandy Station, Virginia—March 10, 5:30 AM

Reveille sounded and the camp slowly came alive. Grant opened his eyes. Standing he stretched his muscles. He had been asleep less than an hour, but was refreshed. He stomped his right boot on the wooden porch bringing life back into his foot. When the tingling subsided, he sat back down and resumed his whittling.

Twenty minutes later he was joined by Meade and Rawlins.

"Sam, don't tell me you were out here all night. You're no good to the Country if you die of consumption," scolded the Chief-of-Staff.

"John, wire Halleck and tell him to put Ron Lyons on the next train coming here. George, I would like to borrow a horse and review the Army," said Grant.

"I have already issued orders to have our escort meet us here after breakfast," replied Meade.

"Just have the cook throw some bacon on a biscuit. I'll eat as I ride. No need for an escort," answered Grant.

The General-in-Chief rode through the various camps comprising the Army of the Potomac. He silently watched the men go about their business of cutting firewood, strengthening fortifications and close order drilling. They had the look of battle hardened veterans.

Soldiers looked up at Grant as he rode by. After seeing the General-in-Chief they all had the same thoughts. *"He doesn't look like much of a General. He might be good against the rebel Generals he faced in the West, but, wait until he meets Robert E. Lee, he'll high tail it back to Tennessee."*

Unlike their past Commanders he didn't make flowery speeches. His uniform had no gold braid. His overcoat was that of the common private. The slouch hat resting on his head contained no embroidery. The man didn't carry a sword or a pistol. Except for the shoulder straps indicating his rank no one would ever suspect him of being the highest officer in the Union Army.

A little after noon the trio returned to Meade's headquarters for lunch with all of the Corps Commanders and their Chiefs-of-Staff. In the middle of the noon day meal, Ronald Lyons, the former Federal Sergeant turned hotel desk clerk turned Union officer, appeared at the doorway of the dining room sporting a newly issued blue uniform replete with Captain's bars and a wooden leg courtesy of the War Department.

"Ah, Captain Lyons, please pull up a chair and join us," said Grant looking at the young man.

"Captain Lyons has recently joined the General-in-Chief's staff. You will be seeing a great deal of him," said Rawlins.

Each of the Officers around the table stood and introduced themselves. After lunch Grant and his two aides adjourned to the parlor.

"Corporal, I want another guard here with you and the two of you will post from across the hall," ordered Grant.

Once inside the room, the General looked at the pair and motioned them to sit down.

"Ron, your timing couldn't have been any better. It was good you met the Corps Commanders as they must be able to recognize you. Remember the lunch meeting and who was in attendance as it may someday save your life. I want you to go behind the rebel lines and bring me back information about Lee's Army," said Grant.

The General paused for a few seconds, reached into his breast pocket and removed a cigar.

"I want to know how Lee has his Army positioned. Bring me back every piece of information you can gather, even if it's rumor or gossip. If you are caught, the rebs will hang you. Here's a pass to get you through our lines. Use it only when you have to," said Grant as he lit his cigar.

"Sir, when do you want me to leave?" replied Lyons smiling.

"You leave tonight. Rest here and keep out of sight. The less people in camp who recognize your face, the safer it'll be for you. Tomorrow I leave to visit Billy Sherman. I'll be back in three weeks. I would like you back in five." answered Grant.

Orange Court House, Virginia—March 10, 8:00 PM

Confederate General Robert E. Lee sat in the parlor of his temporary head-quarters. A huge fire roared in the fireplace adding additional light to the dimly lit room. Candles intermixed with whale oil lamps burned throughout the room. The gray-haired, gray bearded, slightly balding slender Virginian was bent over his desk reading the Northern newspapers' reports on Ulysses S. Grant. The fifty-seven year old Lee had spent his entire adult life in the Army.

Many of the men he now faced in battle were his friends. He couldn't bring himself to refer to them as enemies.

Married thirty-three years to the granddaughter of Martha Washington he was a devoted family man. His three sons were serving the Confederacy. His oldest son Rooney was a Brigade Commander in Jeb Stuart's Calvary. The second oldest, George W. Lee, was on the military staff of Jefferson Davis while his youngest son, Robert, was serving in the Army's artillery as an enlisted man.

He removed his glasses and rubbed his eyes. Years of living outdoors along with the stress of command and the failing health of his wife was taking a toll on the South's finest General. His stomach had become sensitive causing him to eat only bland foods. Lately he had been experiencing severe chest pains leaving him gasping for air and light headed. He ignored the advice of his Surgeon to turn command over to a subordinate and take a much needed rest.

Studying the Confederate battlefield reports and Northern newspaper articles, he pieced together a profile on his newest foe. Grant was not a flash in the pan. He earned his stars with victories. Each battlefield report read the same. The Union General hit hard wearing his enemies down. On his desk was Stringfellow's report, however, he needed to know more about the man and not the General.

"Grant is going to leave Halleck to do the paperwork while he stays with Meade. He is smart not to make too many changes. He is going to be tough, but he must have a weakness," whispered Lee out loud.

A knock at the door silenced the Virginian.

"Enter."

A thinly built man in his mid-twenties opened the door, walked in closing it immediately behind him.

"General, you sent for me?" asked Channing Smith.

"Channing, take a seat. Have you seen this article in the *New York Herald* about Grant," asked Lee turning in his swivel chair and handing the younger man the newspaper.

"Yes sir, I have read it. I think Horace Greeley is full of shit. He doesn't know a damn thing about Grant except what he reads in his own newspaper," replied Channing Smith.

"I agree that's why I need to know more about the man. I want you to infiltrate Grant's camp and report back to me and, only me, what you have found. I have to know where he is going to hit us, when he is going to attack and with how much force. Get me any information you can about Grant even if it's rumor or gossip. In each rumor or point of gossip there is always a hidden truth," said Lee.

"Sir, I leave tonight," answered the young Captain.

Smith had no sooner left the parlor when the General's Corps Commanders arrived. They all had seen the young man leave and knew he had been sent on another mission behind enemy lines. They also knew better than to ask Lee what it was.

One-legged Lieutenant General Richard Ewell hobbled into the parlor. Commanding the Army of Northern Virginia's Second Corps the forty-seven year old battle-tested man from Washington D.C. was a fierce fighter. He had served with distinction at the First Manassas. Seriously wounded in the leg during the battle of Groveton he had been laid up for almost three months before returning to duty. Leading a Division, he was quick to act. However, as a Corps Commander, he was often hesitant and unsure.

Following Ewell was the quick-tempered and impetuous Lieutenant General Ambrose Powell Hill, Commander of the Army's Third Corps. The five-foot seven inch man from Culpepper, Virginia was one of the most feared Corps Commanders in the Southern Army. His attacks against the Federal forces were always ferocious and bloody. Extremely frail, he often fought while in pain from a reoccurring urinary infection.

Behind Hill was the Commander of Lee's Calvary Corps, Lieutenant General Jeb Stuart. The thirty-one year old cavalier was bold and reckless. His boldness often earned him accolades from the Southern press and the admiration of the ladies. Headlines were like food to Stuart. The more he got the more he craved. There was no mistaking the man on the battlefield. He rode a large black horse while his uniform had gold braid midway up his arms and he wore a hat with a large plume.

"Gentlemen, I've asked you all here to discuss the upcoming spring campaign. As you know, Lincoln has made another change in command appointing Grant his General-in-Chief. Our resources in Washington inform me Grant has decided to make his headquarters alongside Meade's. This means he'll command the Army. We must be prepared for a long and bloody year. What do you know about our new adversary?" asked Lee.

"Everything I can gather on the man indicates he is not the type of person to be underestimated. Sidney Johnston, Braxton Bragg and John Pemberton didn't think much of his ability and he defeated each one of them," answered Stuart.

"In the "old army" he had a reputation of being a drunkard. I will tell you this, I never knew a drunkard who could analyze the ever changing tides of a battle with such clarity. In the war against Mexico he was twice cited for bravery. He is usually calm and speaks little. He keeps his own council. The man is not known to be impetuous," added Ewell.

"From letters I received from friends who are officers in our western army I know that when he strikes, he will use all of his available forces. The man will come after us and wear us down. He will hit and continue to strike until we are too weak to resist. The man is not an egotist. In my opinion he is the most dangerous enemy we have ever faced," said Hill shaking his head.

After three hours of discussion, Lee rose. His blue eyes turned a steely cold gray; the lines in his face grew taut. His entire face took on the look of a warrior.

"When Grant moves, we must hit him with everything we have and destroy him before he annihilates us," said Lee in a determined voice.

Rapidan Mills, Virginia—March 11, 1:30 AM

Hidden in the thick trees of the Wilderness, Channing Smith sat on his horse on the southern bank of the Rapidan River. An icy wind blew behind him. Dressed in a Union Officer's Calvary uniform the spy gently nudged his horse forward. The chestnut mare hesitated at first. It didn't want to get wet anymore than the rider did. Smith had taken the horse from the Army's corral. He picked it because it looked strong and had a US brand on its rump. Everything he had with him was Federal issue.

The forty-five degree water stung his legs as he crossed. Once across he would change into a dry uniform. The wind rattled the trees masking the sounds of horse and rider. The fierce wind blew into the faces of any sentries posted on the northern bank, impairing their vision.

Five miles upriver Ronald Lyons donned the civilian clothes of a farmer and waited patiently on the northern bank of the Rapidan. Earlier in the evening he had appropriated a rubber poncho from Rawlins. The spy had cut it into long strips and had tied the lengths around his legs and waist to prevent them from getting wet. The wind struck him in the face causing his eyes to involuntarily flutter. He glanced up at the moon and waited for the large cloud to pass in front temporarily blocking the light. He nudged the spotted mare without a brand forward and into the river. His invention had worked. His clothes were as dry as the Sahara sand. He wished he could say the same for his horse, which shivered from the cold.

Lyons proceeded south through the thickets, his eyes darting in all directions in search of rebel Calvary or sentries. He had gone three miles when he spied movement in the trees to his right. The spy's heart raced as he instinctively reached for his revolver.

Fighting his training and his natural reaction to defend himself, he continued his journey. Posing as an innocent southern farmer, he had nothing to fear. Brandishing a pistol would blow his cover and get him hung. Suddenly movement burst from the brush and bounded away with lightning speed. His startled horse instinctively reared. Breathing a sigh of relief, he watched three deer sprint away.

Dawn broke giving birth to a warm sunny day. It was a typical March. One moment it was snowing and the next the sun shone brightly in a cloudless sky. Reaching the Old Richmond Road he changed direction and headed north into the heart of Robert E. Lee's Army. It was nearly noon when he was surrounded by Confederate Calvary.

"Where're you headed?" asked a young Lieutenant barely eighteen years old.

"Benning's Brigade," replied Lyons calmly.

"What's your business?" inquired the rebel officer.

"I've come to see my brother. I caught a minie ball at Round Top. We both joined together and I promised my mother when she was lying on her death bed that I would always take care of my brother, Samuel Ridley. He's a good solider but he isn't the smartest of the litter," answered Lyons.

The young officer glanced to his left at a balding heavy-set Sergeant in his mid-thirties seated on the horse alongside Lyons.

"What Division and Corps were you and your brother in?" asked the older man drawing his pistol.

"Hood's Division of Longstreet's Corps," responded Lyons without hesitation.

"You have any identification?" asked the Sergeant.

"Just my discharge papers," replied the spy reaching into his pocket.

He handed the Sergeant forged discharge papers given to him by Rawlins.

"That's me, Joseph Ridley," said Lyons pointing to the name on the paper.

"He appears to be all right, Lieutenant," said the Sergeant.

"I don't think Longstreet's Corps is back from Tennessee yet, but you're welcome to ride ahead and find out. Go straight up this road and you'll run into Early's Division; they may know. Good luck, Mr. Ridley," answered the officer.

Meanwhile across the Rapidan River, Channing Smith rode among the Union troops observing their movements. Every so often he would stop, dismount and walk toward a group of Federals to chat.

Just before noon he made a wrong turn and found himself at Grant's and Meade's headquarters. He dismounted and slowly walked his horse through the campsite. Aides were busily setting up a table for the Generals' lunch. The thought of killing Meade and Grant crossed his mind but he knew if he drew his pistol he would be dead before he could squeeze off his first shot. Both Generals had handpicked bodyguards who carefully eyed any strangers.

Meade exited his headquarters followed by his staff and sat down at the table. Glancing up he saw Channing watching the group and motioned the spy to join them.

"Where are you coming from, Captain?" asked Meade.

"I was inspecting our picket lines along the Rapidan, made a wrong turn and wound up here," answered Channing innocently reaching for a slice of beef.

"Which unit are you assigned?" inquired the General's Chief-of-Staff Andrew Humphreys.

"Ninth Corps, First Rhode Island," replied the rebel spy.

Unlike the Confederate troops which identified their units by their Brigade and Corps commander's names, Union soldiers were taught to identify themselves by their units numbered designation.

Satisfied with the answers Humphreys turned his attention Meade. The conversation at lunch became a cornucopia of information. The rebel learned of Grant's departure in the early morning to meet with Sherman in Chattanooga. He learned the disposition of the Union forces and which Generals commanded what units.

CHAPTER THREE

United States Ford, Virginia—April 18, 11:00 PM

Spring rains flooded the Rapidan River causing it to overflow its banks. Lee intensified the Calvary patrols of the fords in anticipation of the renewal of the fighting. Channing Smith had returned from his journey into the depths of the enemy with vital information.

Lyon's watched as the rebel Calvary patrol passed, their attention on the northern bank of the Rapidan. In spite of the flooding, he decided to cross the swollen United States Ford. Reaching the northern bank he wove his way through the thick woods purposely avoiding the main thoroughfares.

Six hours later he rode into Grant's camp. Rawlins was the first to spot him. The Chief-of-Staff calmly walked over to the spy.

"We were getting worried about you," said Rawlins. "I'll take you to the General and have breakfast brought to you."

The pair entered the back of the house. Stopping in the kitchen, Rawlins gave orders to the cook to bring some breakfast and coffee to Grant's parlor. The men proceeded to the large parlor the General was using as an office. The pocket doors were open. Seated at an immense desk peering over maps was the General-in-Chief. Crumbled papers containing discarded plans littered the floor.

"Sam, look who I found," said Rawlins.

Grant glanced up. His eyes were bloodshot from long hours of logistic planning.

"Ron, damn glad to see you, boy, what information have you brought me?" asked Grant smiling.

The spy returned the smile as Rawlins closed the doors and sat in an easy chair next to his friend. Grant lit a cigar, took a deep drag and slowly exhaled.

"Well what have you found out?" asked Grant again.

"Lee's Army is spread out over twenty miles. Ewell's Corps is guarding the Fredericksburg portion of the Rapidan River line while Hill's Corps guards the river near Libertyville. Longstreet's Corps is in reserve at Gordonsville. Jeb Stuart's Calvary is filling the gaps in the line with roving patrols," replied Lyons.

Grant nodded taking it all in. His mind was already beginning to formulate a plan.

"All told, Lee has around seventy-two thousand men at arms. They are well rested and in good spirits. Everywhere Bobby Lee goes his men cheer him. He doesn't understand why. Rumors around his headquarters say the old man's health is failing. Even if it's true, he still looks like he has plenty of fight left in him," said Lyons.

Thirty minutes into the briefing there was a knock at the door. Rawlins opened the pocket door to let the cook in with breakfast. The spy relayed tales of narrow escapes and making friends with men of Hill's and Ewell's Corps as he searched for his alleged brother.

Three hours later the meeting adjourned and Grant gave the spy the remainder of the day off. With Lee's Army spread out he would maneuver the Army between Ewell and Hill splitting the Confederate Army in half. Meade's Chief-of-Staff, Andrew Humphreys, had devised such a plan and had presented it to Grant three weeks earlier. Not knowing the strength and disposition of the enemy at the time, he hesitated to approve it. Now he was ready to proceed.

There were only two drawbacks. First, the Federal troops would have to march through the roughest, most unforgiving piece of land in Virginia the locals called the Wilderness. Joe Hooker had tried the same tactic a year earlier and Lee had sent him back across the Rapidan with his tail between his legs. Second, Meade's Army numbered nearly one hundred and twenty thousand men with two hundred and fifty cannons and four hundred and twenty-six supply wagons. A force so large is impossible to conceal and moves slowly. If the rebels consolidated their forces and hit the Union men while they were crossing or still in the Wilderness, Grant would be defeated.

Parker's Store, Virginia—May 4, 9:15 AM

Lee sat in the parlor of the home he was using as his headquarters and peered over a map of Northern Virginia. Calvary patrols reported heavy Union activity in the Wilderness. The Confederate General issued orders to his Corps Commanders to be ready to move at a moment's notice. He had to make sure of Grant's true line of march before he committed his Army. The long winter's inactivity was over.

Just before ten Jeb Stuart rode into camp followed by a three man bodyguard. The flamboyant Cavalier removed his large plumed hat as he entered the home. His sword hung menacingly atop a bright red sash. The horseman's silver tipped spurs announced his arrival.

"General Lee, sir, my men report Hancock's Corps is crossing at Ely's Ford. Warren's Corps is at the Germanna Ford with Sedgwick's Corps close behind. The enemy has a gap between their Corps of nearly six miles," said Stuart.

"So, Grant is moving through the Wilderness. The dank, slick, moss-covered forest floor will force those people to move slowly. The denseness of the forest will make it almost impossible for Meade to use the full weight of his Army and artillery effectively. If we can consolidate our forces quickly, we may be able to defeat those people before they can unite. General Stuart, the Almighty has once again favored us," answered Lee.

"Colonel Taylor, please come in here and bring my order book," said Lee.

Moments later the young, brown-haired twenty-three year old aide was in the make-shift office.

"Colonel Taylor, send the following message.

> To: Generals, Ewell, Hill and Longstreet. Grant is crossing the Rapidan. His Army is separated into two wings. Hancock is headed toward Wilderness Church while Warren and Sedgwick are crossing at the Germanna Ford. My orders are to consolidate. Ewell will march east on the Orange Pike Road and take up a position to attack Warren. I will be with Hill's Corps marching east on the Orange Plank Road and will unite with Ewell. Longstreet is to follow Hill. Stuart's Calvary will screen our movements and protect our flanks. No attack is to be commenced until all of our forces have been united. We must crush Grant in the Wilderness.
> Signed,
> Robert E. Lee
> Commanding General"

Wilderness, Virginia—May 5, 4:30 AM

The sound of reveille filled the air as the rising sun broke through the clouds and Sheridan's Calvary broke camp. The bandy-legged Commander of the

Union's Cavalry was assigned the task to hide the movements of the main Army by sending his horsemen well in advance of the infantry. They would encounter the enemy first. If the enemy seemed to be in force, Meade and Grant would have the option of either sending the Cavalry infantry support or move the Army by another route.

Colonel Preston, Commander of the Union's Third Vermont Cavalry Brigade sent out an advanced party of twelve troopers to scout ahead of his main column. He had fought against Jeb Stuart's well-trained Cavalrymen many times and he wanted no surprises.

The sweet smell of honeysuckle filled the men's nostrils as they rode through the forest. The soft earth deadened the sound of the horses' hooves. Suddenly, the sound of carbine fire and the return report of muskets broke the stillness. The advanced party had run into the enemy. Out of the woods ahead burst a rider galloping as fast as his mount could muster on the slick forest carpet. Reining hard, his horse skidded to a stop in front of the thirty-five year old Colonel.

"Sir, the woods are alive with rebs. Captain Alworth reports at least a Brigade or more. They charged, but we held our ground. The Captain says he needs help now," panted the rider.

"Bugler, sound formation ... Lieutenant Brannan pass the order in columns of three ... troopers draw sabers ... forward!" shouted the Colonel.

Three hundred men in blue advanced slowly toward the shooting. They rode a half-mile when they met up with the remnants of the advance party. Alworth had them dismounted and dug in behind fallen trees. The rapid fire Spencer repeating rifles had given the small detachment a fighting chance. Preston quickly surveyed the situation and determined he was outnumbered at least four-to-one.

"Lieutenant Brannan, send word to Colonel Chapman we are engaged against a strong detachment of Cavalry and are in need reinforcements immediately. Also send word to General Warren of our situation," said the Colonel as he and his men dismounted.

The smell of honeysuckle was quickly replaced with the stench of sulfur from gunpowder. The stillness of early morning was replaced with the dull sounds of lead projectiles striking the vulnerable flesh of men and their mounts. Cries of pain and anguish filled the air as men and horses lay dead and dying. Preston's men slowly fell back as the numerical advantage of the enemy took its toll. Hope of being reinforced was beginning to fade when Chapman, with the remainder of the Cavalry Brigade, arrived on the scene.

Quickly they dismounted and added the weight of their repeating rifles to Preston's firepower. The tables had turned. The Confederates retreated as Chapman and Preston pushed the gray-clad horsemen back two miles. Chapman halted the advance and ordered his men to dig in. Both Colonels knew if they pushed too far from their main body, they ran the risk of becoming completely isolated and could either be surrounded or cut to pieces.

The four-hour skirmish died down as the Northern Cavalrymen dug in. All was quiet. Men on both sides rested. Those who had water drank it and shared with those who did not.

Three miles away Union General Charles Griffin reported to General Warren that his skirmishers had been in contact with Confederate forces under Ewell. Knowing Grant's orders not to engage the enemy until out of the Wilderness, he requested further clarification.

Warren was stymied. Preston and Chapman had pushed the enemy Cavalry back two miles and were now digging in. Griffin had uncovered Ewell's unsupported Corps. He knew he should attack but orders were orders. He forwarded the information to Meade and waited for instructions. Within fifteen minutes Meade and his staff were at Warren's headquarters.

"Well Gouverneur, it appears you have made contact with the enemy. It also appears that if you were to attack now with Sedgwick in support you both could destroy Ewell before Hill or Longstreet could reinforce him. Am I correct?" asked Meade in a cheerful tone.

"Yes, sir, you are correct," replied Warren, his face turning red with embarrassment.

"Then, General, I would advise you to order your entire Corps to attack the enemy without delay. I will send orders to General Sedgwick to put his Corps in support of yours. I will also send orders to General Hancock to halt his march in the event you need further support," answered Meade.

While Warren and Meade discussed the situation, Confederate General Richard Ewell made careful preparations not to engage the enemy without orders from Lee. Subsequently, he sent couriers to Lee who was with Ambrose Hill's Third Corps. He reported he had discovered the enemy's Fifth Corps isolated and unsupported. If he struck now, he might be able to destroy the enemy while they were still in the Wilderness.

As Generals on both sides decided on their next course of action, the Cavalry was already in a fight. While Preston and Chapman were fighting the Southern Cavalry seven miles away, Lieutenant Colonel John Hammond's

Fifth New York Cavalry Brigade engaged Confederate infantry near Hancock's position.

Shortly after dawn, Hammond's advance party had run into infantry skirmishers. The contest quickly escalated into a full battle. For five hours the Fifth New York held its ground before slowly retiring toward Hancock's Corps.

The Confederate Cavalry Brigade which Preston and Chapman ran into belonged to Confederate Brigadier General Thomas Rosser. Known for his courage and cunning, the twenty-eight year old Texan had earned a well-deserved reputation as a fierce fighter.

While Chapman and Preston dug in, Rosser, reinforced by another Brigade of Cavalry, struck the tired Union troops. The Federals put up a brief struggle and then fell back. At first the withdrawal was orderly; then the Northerners began to panic as Rosser's horsemen aggressively pursued their retreating foe. The Confederates quickly recovered the lost two miles and then some. Chapman's and Preston's Commanding Officer, Brigadier General James Wilson, seeing his men in full retreat, ordered his reserve forces forward to stop the rebel onslaught.

The battle seesawed back and forth for six hours. The ground was covered with blood and severed human limbs intermingled with dead and wounded bodies. At times the men fought hand-to-hand slashing each other with sabers and Bowie knives. By four in the afternoon Wilson had stopped Rosser's advance.

Grant paced back and forth outside his tent. A thick blue cloud of smoke circled his head as he feverishly puffed on the three-inch stub of his cigar. Reports had been coming in since six in the morning. First the report from Hammond of engaging enemy infantry followed by Preston's and Chapman's report about engaging enemy Cavalry. Then there was the report from Meade about ordering the attack on Ewell. Suddenly the reports stopped coming.

Nearly four hours had passed without a word. The only sound he heard was the Cavalry battles. If Meade would not order the attack, he would.

"Colonel Comstock, take down the following and copy General Meade.

> *To: Major Generals Griffin, Wadsworth, Wright, Getty and Hancock.*
> *You are, hereby, ordered to attack along the turnpike without further delay and without concern to your flanks. General Wadsworth will push forward a heavy line of skirmishers followed by a line of battle. Attack the enemy at once and push him. General Griffin will also attack. Do not wait for him, but look out for your*

own flanks. General Getty will move out promptly to the Orange Plank Road and drive the enemy back. General Wright will advance his Division on the Robertson Tavern Road and be ready to support Getty. General Hancock will move up the Brock Road to the Orange Court House Plank Road and attack the enemy infantry engaged by Hammond's Fifth New York Cavalry.
Signed:
U.S. Grant
General-in-Chief"

Leaving Comstock behind to direct Burnside; Grant, Rawlins and three aides mounted their horses and rode to Meade's headquarters a half mile away. When they arrived, they saw Meade seated on his horse on a knoll overlooking Warren's Corps.

"Damn it, Humphreys, I swear if Warren doesn't move out within the next thirty minutes, I will have him replaced," shouted Meade as he pounded one of his fists into the other.

"Hello General," said Grant. "What seems to be the delay? I thought you ordered Warren to attack hours ago."

Before Meade could answer, Warren appeared looking haggard.

"Damn it, Warren! "What the hell is the delay?" shouted an angry Meade.

"Sir, General Griffin holds the center and he has refused to move requesting more time to reconnoiter the ground in front of him," replied Warren.

"Griffin knows the damn ground. It is the same ground Lee used against us under Hooker. You tell Griffin to move out or I'll remove him and bring him up on charges of cowardice in the face of the enemy," answered Meade in a cold tone. Warren saluted and rode away.

Within fifteen minutes Griffin was on the move. His men moved slowly but deliberately through the thick tangled underbrush. The sound of smashing twigs and crushed leaves broke the dead silence of the peaceful countryside as the twelve thousand two-hundred and fifty-four men of Griffin's, Wadworth's and Crawford's Divisions marched toward the enemy. Fallen trees and irregular terrain instantly brought confusion among the regiments as squads intermixed with companies of other battalions and battalions intermixed with regiments of other Divisions. In certain areas the men were able to advance thirty abreast; while in others they would have to separate and go single file in order to pass.

Officers lost contact with their units and organized new commands as they reassembled with other Union soldiers. It was this type of confusion Lee had counted on and Grant had hoped to avoid. Neither Commander could afford to allow an opportunity to slip through their fingers. Both armies were split and both Commanders thought they had the advantage.

As the Federals advanced, each soldier knew every step they took brought them closer to the enemy and the chance of dying or worse. At least with death it was over. Being wounded was being doomed to a life as a cripple with the constant physical pain of the wound and the memories of war.

On the other side of the forest Ewell waited for the boys in blue to come into the range of his guns. Although ordered by Lee not to bring on a full engagement, he knew that if attacked, his Commander would want him to defend and defeat the enemy. The Southern Corps Commander had his men well hidden just inside the tree line behind fallen logs and natural deep depressions in the earth.

Griffin's Division exited the forest first. In front of Griffin's men was a half-mile clearing called Sanders Field. On the other side of the field were Ewell's hidden rebels. Stopping to take a breath, the men fixed bayonets, realigned their companies and resumed the advance. Brigadier General Romeyn Ayres' New York Brigade led the charge on Griffin's right. Drawing his sword and waving it over his head then pointing it toward the far end of the field the thirty-nine year old New Yorker gave the order to charge.

Quickly the men crossed the field pushing Confederate skirmishers before them. A hundred yards from the far end of the field the men in gray suddenly disappeared as they entered a gully. Ayers' men followed and pushed them up and out of the depression. The New Yorkers were hot on the heels of the retreating gray coats. The blue-clad Brigade exited the gully and saw the skirmishers head into the woods. They quickly followed. It was like lambs being led to the slaughter. Ayers and his men were twenty yards from the tree line when the Southern Brigades of George Steuart, Leroy Stafford and James Walker opened fire. Instantly the sound of two thousand muskets filled the air. It was quickly coupled with the dull thud of projectiles striking flesh. The New Yorkers tumbled like autumn leaves in a windstorm.

Blood splattered over the ground and on the men next to the wounded as the northerners attempted to continue the attack in spite of being in the middle of a deadly crossfire. Men pitched backward throwing their weapons in the air as the force of a minie ball ripped through their bodies.

Seeing the first wave falter under the heavy musketry and cannon fire from the tree line, Colonel David Jenkins formed his New York Zouaves, some of which served as Grant's honor guard, and moved them forward into the maelstrom.

While the second wave advanced they noticed the Union cannon had finally arrived and were returning fire on the Confederate artillery. The wave began the attack at a slow walk and then, as they approached the gully, they broke into a trot.

The Confederates now focused on Jenkins and the second wave. Men stepped over and on their fallen comrades as they tried to break the Confederate line. The smoke of the volleys temporarily screened the combatants of both sides. The stench of sulfur and gunpowder stung their nostrils. Men's faces were sweaty and black from biting off their gunpowder charges. Those who reached the Confederates were quickly killed, wounded or captured. Ayers' Brigade was being cut to pieces. Among the dead lying at the base of the Confederate log fortifications was Colonel Jenkins.

While Ayers' Brigade attacked the Confederate left, Griffin ordered another Brigade under Brigadier General Joseph Bartlett to strike the center of the Confederates' line. Bartlett quickly ordered his regimental Commanders to spread out and not to attack until they were all in position. He would hit the enemy as a united Brigade and not individual regiments. Bartlett decided to swerve his Brigade to the left of the enemy using the gully as cover and enter the woods unseen by the Confederates.

Bartlett's men marched through the dense underbrush. Hearing the sounds of Ayers' Brigade being cut to ribbons they quickened their pace. Experience told them Ayers' men couldn't take much more punishment. The only way they could help their friends was to draw the Southerners' attention.

A half-mile into the woods Bartlett spotted a Confederate Brigade under Brigadier General John Jones. The Union General waited until his men were in position before giving the command to charge. Instantly, a thousand men sprang from the forest and pitched into Jones' Brigade. The charge and force of the attack had completely surprised the troops in gray.

Neither side had a chance to reload as the men plunged into one another using whatever means they could find to kill. There was no thought of wounding someone or taking them prisoner. The soldiers on both sides knew they must kill in order to survive. Gone were all the human qualities of reason and compassion. Some used bayonets to pierce their opponent's body while others swung their ten pound muskets using them as clubs to bash the enemies' skulls.

The attack raged on for thirty minutes when the outnumbered Confederates gave way. Trying to rally his men, Jones took off his hat and placing it on his sword he waved it above his head.

"Virginians, rally round me," shouted the Brigade Commander.

No sooner had he spoken the words when he was struck down. A minie ball through his heart ended his life. Seeing the Confederates break, Bartlett's men quickly pursued the retreating enemy. Without waiting for the supporting troops of other Brigades, his men pushed forward a half mile. Suddenly, the pursuers were face-to-face with fresh Confederate troops.

The tide of battle once again turned. Now Bartlett's men were outnumbered, outflanked and outgunned. The weary men in blue tried to stand their ground but were easily pushed back leaving their dead and wounded behind. Ewell's center was again in tact.

While Griffin's men attacked the Confederate left and center, Brigades under Major General Wadsworth attacked the Confederate right. Like Bartlett and Ayers they too enjoyed a temporary success. Wadworth's men pushed Ewell's Corps deeper into the woods. It quickly became apparent to Ewell that his entire right flank was in danger of breaking. Ewell sat on his horse and watched the escalating battle when a courier came to an abrupt halt in front of the General.

"General Doles reports the enemy is attempting to flank his right. He also wishes me to report that he and Generals Battle and Daniel will hold the center and the extreme right, but if the Yankees get around their right, they will be forced to withdraw," panted the courier.

"Inform Generals Doles, Battle and Daniel they must hold their position against all hazards and help is on the way," replied Ewell in a high pitched voice.

Ewell spurred his horse and galloped at break-neck speed toward his reserve Division under Major General Jubal Early. He hadn't ridden very far when he spotted Early's second-in-command, Brigadier General John B. Gordon, and reined his horse hard sliding to a stop two inches from Gordon's knee.

"General Gordon, our right is in danger of being turned. Please take your Brigade and form them on the right of General Doles. You must push the enemy back! I will hurry reinforcements to you as fast as I can find them," said an excited Ewell.

Gordon quickly ordered his men forward. It would take the young General from Georgia thirty minutes to get his men into attack position. Unaware of Gordon's presence, the Union troops proceeded to push the outnumbered Confederates.

Suddenly, the sound of a thousand rifles exploded to the left of the Yankees. Wadsworth's men were now caught in a deadly crossfire between Doles, Daniel and Battle's Brigades in front and Gordon's Brigade to their left.

The Southerners poured volley after volley in the surprised blue coats. After a few minutes the men in blue broke and ran for the safety of the rear. The rebels pursued only to the point where they reconnected with their center. Both sides were spent.

Seven miles away Major General Winfield Hancock had his men moving to the sound of battle. He had heard the Cavalry in combat and his experience told him they had encountered more than just enemy mounted units. By the sounds of the battle and reports from Hammond, he had correctly surmised he had found the Army of Northern Virginia's Third Corps.

Hill and Hancock's men had faced off against each other many times in the past. They both knew each other well. Hill's attacks were fierce and furious. Hancock's were determined and steady. They were both highly respected by their men and their Commanders.

Hancock ordered Getty's Division to take the lead and to reinforce Hammond's men while he rushed the rest of the Corps forward in support.

Moving through the dense underbrush took time. Getty stopped every thirty minutes to realign his men. Even though Hammond's men were only three miles away, it took Getty over four hours to reach the Cavalry and ready his men for a counter-attack.

The Union General watched the dismounted Cavalry stubbornly give ground while his men prepared to ambush the rebels. The General from Washington D.C. had his men hidden in the trees waiting to pounce.

Confederate General Harry Heth led his Division forward unaware of Getty's surprise. Slowly the men in gray pushed their adversaries back. Suddenly from their right, the forest burst forth with the sound of two thousand firing muskets. It was quickly followed by the grunts, groans and cries of the wounded. Men fell instantly to the ground, some dead or wounded others just scared. Pieces of wood flew in all directions as projectiles missed their targets and splintered trees.

Less experienced soldiers would have turned tail and run, but these were Heth's men of A.P. Hill's Corps—experienced and hardcore. They quickly reformed and pressed their attack.

"Major Anderson, please ride to General Hill and inform him I have encountered Federal infantry in force. I believe it is Hancock's Second Corps.

Tell the General unless I'm immediately reinforced, I shall be forced to retire," said Heth, his face covered in sweat.

Hill was seated on his horse talking to Robert E. Lee when the courier from Heth arrived. Since Hill was not feeling well and possibly would be unable to command, Lee decided to ride with Hill and his men.

The two Generals listened intently as the young aide relayed the day's happenings. Anderson told the older men how Heth's Division had pushed back dismounted Cavalry, but out of nowhere Federal infantry ambushed them.

Without hesitating, Hill issued orders for the rest of the Corps to engage the enemy. Lee watched in silence as Hill took charge of the battle in his front. This was the second time Heth had brought on an engagement against the Commanding General's wishes. The first time was at Gettysburg and now in the Wilderness. Lee had hoped to wait until Longstreet was up before attacking Hancock. Grant had stolen the initiative.

Sensing the danger of being overwhelmed, Heth pulled back a half-mile and dug in. This was as far as he was willing to go. If he went further, he would endanger the entire Third Corps. He had to hold his position until either relieved or killed.

Hancock pressed his men forward even though not all of his troops were up yet. Getty attacked Heth's front while Hancock ordered his other Division Commanders, Birney and Mott, to strike the flanks.

Getty's troops moved forward through the dense underbrush. Brigades became intermingled; regiments couldn't see more than twenty-five yards. The Federals had to fight the rebels as well as a terrain which prevented them from using their full advantage of superior numbers. Heth's men patiently waited for the Federals to enter the clearing directly in front of them. The men in blue were sitting ducks. They fired one volley and charged but were repulsed. Getty's men reformed and charged again. Four times they attacked and four times they were repulsed. Seeing that dislodging Heth's troops was impossible, Getty's Brigades Commanders ordered their men to lie down and fire at the enemy. The assaults had turned into a fierce firefight. Heth's dug-in men had the advantage. As one regiment ran low on ammunition, it was immediately replaced by another and sent back to the rear to be re-supplied.

Getty sat on top of his horse and directed his men. Next to him were his two aides, Majors Roland and Long. They begged him to either dismount or move. Bullets struck the trees beside him and the ground underneath his horse, but he ignored their pleas. The man from Washington D.C. glanced at his pocket watch. It was five-thirty. His men had been fighting for over six hours. Birney and Mott's Divisions should have attacked an hour ago.

"Major Roland, please find General Birney and find out when he is going to attack. Major Long, please locate General Hancock and inform him I'm almost out of ammunition. My reserves have been committed and I must be reinforced or I'll be forced to disengage," said Getty.

He didn't have to wait long for his pleas for help to be answered. Sensing the danger, Hancock had ordered his other Division under Brigadier General John Gibbon forward to relieve Getty's men. Gibbon was also very familiar with A.P. Hill and his tactics. They were classmates and friends at West Point. By six o'clock Getty's men were in the rear and Gibbon's Division now took on Heth's battered Confederates.

As Gibbon's men traded places with their Corps mates, Mott's Division had worked its way around Heth's right flank and was preparing to attack. Mott's men slowly made their way through the thick forest. They moved to the sound of the gunfire. When they were within six hundred yards of the Confederate position, the trees to their front suddenly spit forth thousands of projectiles striking the Yankees point blank in the face.

A.P Hill noticed Heth was able to hold his own against the attacks but that the flanks were unprotected. He ordered his other Division under Major General Cadmus Wilcox forward to protect the exposed sides.

Wilcox's surprise stopped Mott's advance dead in its tracks. Union soldiers were cut down as they tried to deploy and return fire. Mott's men quickly dove behind trees and into gullies and returned fire. Hancock's front had turned from a battle to a slugfest.

CHAPTER FOUR

Wilderness, Virginia—May 5, 7:30 PM

Night fell and the firing ceased. Tired soldiers welcomed the dark and the rest it would allow.

Grant returned to his headquarters and sat in front of the campfire. He looked down and picked up a stick. Reaching into his pocket he pulled out a pocketknife and began to whittle. All around him aides raced back and forth preparing battle reports and supper for the General.

John Rawlins cautioned the aides not to approach the General. He knew that when Grant whittled, he was deep in thought. Rawlins saw it at Shiloh, Vicksburg, Chattanooga and now in the Wilderness.

The Commanding General's thoughts were suddenly interrupted by a commotion less than fifty yards away. Grant rose and summoned his aide, Horace Porter.

"Horace, what's all the fuss about?" inquired Grant.

"Sir, Brigadier General Alexander Hays' … body … he was killed about two hours ago … leading his Brigade," replied the young assistant, visibly upset.

Grant's body started to shake as he fought to keep his composure, his eyes filled with tears as he stared at Porter, a look of disbelief on his face. Turning he walked from the campfire into the darkness. When he was sure he was far enough that no one could see or hear, he gave in to his emotions.

He and Hays had been friends for over twenty years. They were roommates at West Point and graduated together. They fought side-by-side in the war with Mexico. Grant didn't have a great deal of long time friends. Most had abandoned him after he left the military for private life. He remained close to only three people from his academy days: Simon Buckner, James Longstreet and Alexander Hays. He defeated Buckner at Fort Donelson. Since then Buckner had refused to talk to Grant. Longstreet was now against him fighting with Lee's Army. Only Hays had stayed with the Union. Although close to Grant, he never asked any favors or special treatment.

Thirty minutes went by before Sam Grant emerged from the darkness and re-joined his staff at the dinner table.

"General Rawlins, report please," said the Commander

"Sir, General Hancock holds the Brock Plank Road. He reports that due to the terrain, he was not successful in throwing his entire Corps against the enemy. He does report that he has Hill's Corps pinned down. They were trying to join with Ewell, but he prevented the link up," answered Rawlins.

"Hancock's a good soldier. I have no doubt he handled his Corps correctly, please continue," interrupted Grant.

"Yes, sir, Warren, however, was less successful. His Corps had some success but his attacks were not coordinated properly and they were driven back to our original lines."

"Thank you, John. Colonel Comstock, any word from Sherman?" asked Grant.

"Yes, sir, we received a telegram from him this morning. Due to heavy rains in Northern Georgia, he is unable to move on the third as planned. He will have his troops on the move tomorrow morning. His scouts report the rebs are well dug-in but he feels confident he will move Joe Johnston out of his stronghold," replied Comstock.

"I have no doubt that Sherm will do his duty. Colonel Porter, what news from Butler?" asked Grant.

"Sir, General Butler reports his men have landed on the Virginia Peninsula. He will begin his march on Richmond tomorrow," responded Porter.

"Very good, but let's watch Butler. He would rather be President than a General," replied the Commanding General.

"John, any word from Fritz Sigel?" inquired Grant.

"Sir, General Sigel reports that he is moving his Corps against Breckenridge. He expects to be engaged tomorrow," responded the Chief-of-staff.

"Let's watch Sigel. Like Butler, he's more afraid of losing a battle than fighting one. Gentlemen, tomorrow will be a very busy day so I suggest all of you plan to go to sleep early," replied Grant as he rose from his chair and walked toward the campfire.

Approaching the fire, he noticed Meade sitting on a chair warming his hands.

"General Grant," said Meade rising.

"George, please keep your seat, if we both get up and down every time we see each other, we'll be tuckered out by the end of the war. How long have you been waiting?"

"Sir, I arrived about a half hour ago. I saw you were busy with your staff so I decided not to interrupt," answered Meade.

"Nonsense, George; the last time I looked, your uniform was the same color as mine. If I can't trust you at my table, then I can't trust you to lead my Army and, sir, I trust you completely. In the future, feel free to join my table at any time. Are we clear on that?" replied Grant.

"Yes, sir. I heard your aides give their report of my Army's activity for the day. It's very accurate. I'd like to say that your aides are all very professional; they leave their opinions out. They report only the facts. I can't tell you how unusual that is."

"They're staff, it's not their place to criticize an officer in the line. That privilege I reserve for the two of us. We both know how fast a battle can shift sides. They don't," replied Grant.

"George, I'm satisfied with the results of today. Our only failing was that we couldn't throw our entire Army against Lee. I would like to have Hancock attack Hill at four-thirty tomorrow morning before Longstreet arrives. I have ordered Burnside to force march tonight and place his Corps between Warren's and Hancock's Corps. This will link our line together and give us the ability to strike Lee with everything we have. Burnside's men will strike Hill in the flank while Sedgwick's Corps will strike Ewell in the flank. This evening I'd like the men to rest as much as possible. Also, I would like you to send out scouting parties to find our wounded and bring them into our lines. Our brave boys have suffered enough."

"General Grant, I'd like you to reconsider moving Hancock at four-thirty. I would like to delay the attack until six."

"Request denied, I want to hit Hill before Longstreet arrives, but I'll revise my orders to five," answered Grant.

Granted waited until everyone left and then walked to where Hays' body lay waiting to be shipped home. Removing the blanket from the face, Grant touched his friend's hair.

"Alex, I'll miss you. The Army will prevail without you, but in my heart there will always be an empty place. May God take you to his bosom for you were a good man, a good soldier and a good friend," whispered the General-in-Chief.

Lee's Headquarters—Same day

A few miles away Robert E. Lee sat by a campfire surrounded by his aides.

"Colonel Venable, any news from General Longstreet? What is the report from General Ewell? What does General Stuart report?" asked Lee.

"Sir, General Longstreet reports his Corps should be up by ten tomorrow morning. General Ewell reports he has repulsed Warren's and Sedgwick's Corp but it was with a great loss on our side. His men are now refitted and, with some rest, he feels he can hold.

"General Stuart's Cavalry has been heavily engaged throughout the day. He says Hancock's Corps is in front of A.P. Hill. He estimates Hancock's strength to be about twenty-five thousand. He reports Burnside's Ninth Corps of fifteen thousand is in reserve four miles behind Hancock," replied the aide.

"Good report. Tomorrow Longstreet will be up and we'll hit Grant with everything we have. Colonel Marshall, please draw up an order for my signature to General Ewell. Tell him I wish his Corps to remain on the defensive but if the opportunity arises for him to attack; I wish him to do so and to do it with all of his forces. He is to hold nothing back," answered Lee.

"Major Venable, find General Stuart and tell him I wish him to attack the enemy right flank at first light. His attack must make Grant think I am trying to get around his right. When Grant shifts Hancock's Corps to parry the thrust he'll create a gap between Hancock and Warren and we'll strike through the gap," said Lee.

While the aides quickly went about their assignments Lee walked to A.P. Hill's tent. The younger General was lying in his cot in obvious pain. When he heard his mentor's voice he struggled to rise.

"Ambrose, please stay. How are you feeling?" asked Lee in a fatherly voice.

"I'll be ready tomorrow morning. What are your orders for tomorrow?" inquired Hill in a low raspy voice.

"General Hill, it's my desire that Wilcox and Heth's men dig in and wait for Longstreet. He'll be up shortly after daylight and will strike the gap between Warren and Hancock," answered Lee.

The two Generals continued to talk for another hour before Lee retired to his tent. The Commanding General took off his overcoat, stretched his back, and then sat at his writing table to compose a brief telegram to the Confederate Secretary of War.

"To: James A. Seddon
Secretary of War
From: Headquarters, Army of Northern Virginia
May 5, 1864 11PM
The enemy crossed the Rapidan yesterday at Ely and Germanna Fords. Two
Corps of this Army moved to oppose him. Ewell's by the old Turnpike and Hill's
by the Plank Road. They arrived this morning in close proximity to the enemy's
line of march. A strong attack was made upon Ewell, who repulsed it capturing
many prisoners and four pieces of artillery. The enemy, subsequently, concen-
trated upon Hill who, with Heth's and Wilcox' Divisions, successfully resisted
repeated and desperate assaults. A large force of Cavalry and artillery on our
right flank was driven back by Stuart's Cavalry under Rosser's Brigade. By the
blessing of God, we maintained our position against every effort until night,
when the contest closed. We have to mourn the loss of many brave officers and
men. The gallant J.M Jones was killed and Brigadier General Leroy A. Stafford,
I fear, was mortally wounded while leading his command with conspicuous
valor.
Robert E. Lee
Commanding General
Army of Northern Virginia"

When he finished the dispatch he called for Venable, handed him the telegram and then the old soldier lay on his cot and instantly fell asleep.

Wilderness, Virginia—May 6, 4:00 AM

Hancock and his men were awake at four o'clock. Forty-five minutes later
they were in position waiting for the appointed jump off time. The Corps
Commander, mounted on his huge black horse, rode across his line making
sure everything was in readiness. Behind him rode his three aides.

Seeing an old friend, he reined his horse. Leaning over he extended his
hand.

"General Birney, is your Division ready to wreck A.P. Hill's Corps?" asked
Hancock.

"Yes, sir, my Division will do its duty. However, you must take caution and
not expose yourself as you did yesterday. This Army cannot afford to lose its
best Corps Commander," replied Birney.

"David, there comes a time when a Corps Commander's life isn't worth a
tinker's damn. I can't and won't lead from the rear. May God keep you safe,
my friend," answered Hancock as he rode away.

At precisely five o'clock Birney commenced the attack followed by the rest of Hancock's Corps. At first the resistance was sporadic as the guards alerted their sleepy comrades. Within minutes the gunfire escalated to a deafening tone as fourteen thousand Confederate muskets repeatedly fired at the approaching enemy. Forty thousand Union muskets answered the challenge. Men on both sides fell to the ground, dead or wounded.

Hancock rode along his lines accompanied by George Meade's most trusted aide, Lyman Bostick. He sent several of his aides to different portions of the battlefield with orders to align his troops. They would no sooner return and were ordered out again. Hancock was slowly moving his men toward the right flank of the enemy occupying the area where Burnside was to be. The fiery General would not wait for Burnside. He was determined to break Hill before Longstreet arrived on the scene.

For two hours the struggle seesawed. Unlike the previous day, he noticed the Confederates were played out while his men were refreshed. At first only a few individual Confederates withdrew, but the constant hammering had its effect as Hill's entire Corps began to slowly evaporate.

"Damn it, Lyman! Tell General Meade that if Burnside was here like he was supposed to be two hours ago, we could have destroyed all of Hill's Corps," shouted Hancock above the din of battle.

"General Hancock, I don't know what happened to General Burnside. What do you wish to report to General Meade?" asked Bostick.

"Tell General Meade I am pushing Hill's Corps and that the rebs are played out. Longstreet has not yet arrived on the battlefield," sighed Hancock.

Robert E. Lee and his staff sat on their horses watching Hill's Corps' slow withdrawal become a wholesale retreat. With Hill sick in his tent, Lee assumed direct command.

"Colonel Marshall, rally as many men as you can and have them meet me at Pogue's artillery batteries. We'll make our stand there. Send a courier to General Longstreet informing him the situation is desperate," said Lee in a calm voice, just before spurring his horse toward Pogue's position.

"General Pogue, raise our flag as high as you can. You, sir, are the rallying point!" shouted Lee as he reined his horse, Traveler, to a stop.

"What are your cannon loaded with?" asked the commanding General.

The young officer looked at Lee, saluted, and immediately gave the order to raise the flag.

"General Lee, my cannons are armed with double loads of canister," answered the young officer.

"Excellent, the spread of the ball bearings when the canister is fired will give those people a surprise when they come. They will think they have charged into hell," responded the Army Commander.

Moments later retreating Confederates broke out of the woods with Birney's men hot on their heels. Seeing the Southern Stars and Bars ripping in the wind they changed direction and ran toward their flag. Approaching, they saw their beloved Commanding General sitting calmly on Traveler beckoning them toward him.

"General Pogue, wait until our boys reach that slight depression fifty yards in front of us and then fire your weapons," ordered Lee.

Pogue pulled the lanyard of his cannon. It was quickly followed by the roar of 19 artillery pieces. Deadly projectiles flew toward the retreating Confederates and their pursuers. The flying lead flew harmlessly over the men in gray missing them by a few inches and struck Birney's men. Those struck by the ball bearings were thrown backward ten feet from the force of the shotgun-like blast.

Crouching, Hill's men continued their run for Lee and safety while Pogue's men quickly reloaded and fired again. As the rebs made their way toward the rallying point, Marshall returned with an additional three hundred men, giving Lee a total of eight hundred defenders. The Southern icon was determined to hold this point until either Longstreet arrived or he was killed.

Birney's men withdrew into the tree line and returned fire. Lee, ignoring the danger, reassembled his force and personally directed their counter-fire. Suddenly he heard shouts behind him. Turning he saw the advance troops of Longstreet's Corps.

"WHAT BRIGADE IS THIS?" shouted Lee.

"GREGG'S TEXAS BRIGADE, FROM LONGSTREET'S CORPS," shouted back Brigadier General John Gregg.

Lee breathed a sigh of relief. The Texans were his shock troops. In every major battle these men never failed him.

"Sir, I am glad to see you. I wish you to give those people the cold steel. They will stand and fight all day and never move unless you charge them," replied Lee, his eyes ablaze from the heat of battle.

"Yes, sir," replied Gregg.

"ATTENTION, TEXAS BRIGADE, THE EYES OF GENERAL LEE ARE UPON YOU. FORWARD MARCH!" shouted the thirty-six year old Brigadier General.

As the men passed Lee, they raised a cheer. Some shouted they would charge hell itself for Master Robert. Lee rose in his stirrups, uncharacteristically removed his hat and swung it above his head. Then, turning Traveler, he rode toward the front of the forming battle line. Bullets swarmed all around the gray-haired soldier. Seeing that their Commander was intent upon leading the charge, the Texans stopped and surrounded the Commanding General.

"LEE TO THE REAR; LEE TO THE REAR!" they shouted in unison.

A leathery-faced sergeant grabbed Traveler's reins and began to lead him to the rear. Lee tried to grab the reins from the sergeant, but it was futile.

"We must push those people back!" said Lee.

"General, please retire. My Texans and I will push those people back. We've never let you down," replied John Gregg.

Lee retired to a grassy knoll two hundred yards to the rear where he watched Longstreet ready his Corps for a massive counter-attack. From his new vantage point, the Commanding General could observe the entire line in this part of the battle. His battle blood was up. He hadn't experienced this kind of adrenalin rush since he was a young officer in the war with Mexico. His aides were dismayed. They had never seen Lee so worked up. His face was red, his eyes were ablaze and his lips were pursed. He had the determined look of a warrior.

Major Venable of the General's staff approached Longstreet and relayed what happened with the Texans. Hearing the story and how Lee was determined to lead the attack, he rode to his Commander and friend.

"General Lee, I understand you're intent on directing this part of the field. If that is the case, then, with your permission, I will retire. This Army cannot afford to lose the both of us," said Longstreet.

The Virginian stared at the burly Georgian. He knew his "old warhorse" was right. He turned his horse and rode another two hundred yards to the rear to watch his faithful subordinate begin the counter-attack.

'Old Pete,' as he was called by his friends, was at his best when the situation was dire. Time and time again he had turned the tide of battle. He was instrumental in Lee's victories during the Seven Days Battles, Second Manassas and Fredericksburg.

While he admired Lee and the leadership he had brought to the Army, he was one of the few on either side who saw his Commander as a man with human frailties and not as a human "God."

Twenty minutes later Longstreet gave the order to attack. Bugles sounded and the air was filled with the dreaded "rebel yell" as the Army of Northern

Virginia's First Corps shouted at the top of their lungs and plunged forward toward their blue adversaries. Veteran Union troops had heard the yell before and it was always followed by a fierce charge. It was a sound which, once heard, was hard to forget.

Birney's men fired into the on-rushing Confederates repulsing their attack. Longstreet reformed his men and struck again. Once again the Union men held their position. Longstreet would not be denied their position and continually hit the beleaguered defenders. The constant hammering by the rejuvenated Southern troops took its toll and the men in blue slowly retreated.

Now it was Hancock's turn to sweat. The Union Corps Commander rode along his lines steadying his men. Burnside had not yet arrived. He was now facing Hill's and Longstreet's Corps.

For the next four hours the battle seesawed. Men on both sides lay on the forest floor either dead or dying. When one side attacked, the other side would lie down and pile the dead bodies in front of them using their fallen comrades as protection against the enemy bullets. Artillery on both sides fired blindly into the woods crashing down trees in the hopes of them falling on the enemy. The artillery rounds started small fires as they struck dried kindling or fell into beds of dry leaves. The fires were quickly extinguished, but their smoke added to the confusion.

Longstreet rode to Lee's position and briefed the Commander of the results of the past four hours.

"Sir, we have pushed Hancock back to his original position of this morning, but he has thrown up breastworks. If I can have two Brigades from General Ewell, I know I can push him back across the Rapidan River."

"General Ewell reports he is hard pressed by two Federal Corps and cannot spare anyone. Apparently General Grant decided to use his entire force across our front preventing me from reinforcing any part of our line. General Longstreet, we must find a way to break Hancock's line. He's the best they have. If we break him here and now, then Grant has no choice but to pull back across the river," replied Lee.

"General Lee, I disagree. The only way to have Grant cross the river is by destroying his entire Army. I know the man personally. If he has only one regiment left, you can count on him attacking and, most likely, inflicting a great deal of damage," answered Longstreet shaking his head.

The two men continued to plan strategy when Longstreet's Chief Engineer, Major General Martin Smith, came galloping up the hill. His horse was foamed and covered in sweat from being ridden hard.

"General Lee, General Longstreet, I've been scouting the Union position and I've found a way around their left flank. It is unguarded and is in the air. I've found an old railroad cut which will shield our men's march. We can use the cut to circle around Hancock and hit him in the rear," panted the middle-aged officer.

"General Lee, with your permission I would like to take advantage of this opportunity," said Longstreet.

Lee nodded in concurrence as Longstreet called for his Chief-of-Staff, Moxley Sorrel.

"Colonel Sorrel, I would like you to take "Tige" Anderson's Brigade, "Scrappy" Mahone's Brigade and "Billy" Wofford's Brigade and follow General Smith. He will lead you to the unprotected left of Hancock's Corps. Once our men are in position, they are to attack holding nothing back. The assault must be swift with continued pressure brought against the Federals. At the same time, I'll lead the balance of the Corps in a frontal assault. Together we'll destroy Hancock's Corps. Are there any questions?" asked Longstreet.

"No, sir," replied the faithful subordinate.

"General Lee, I shall take my leave and ready my command. We must be ready to strike when we see the enemy's left roll up," said Longstreet wiping the sweat from his brow with his hand.

"God has granted us a divine opportunity to destroy those people. I caution you, General, not to expose yourself needlessly. Your bravery goes without question, but I've noticed you are taking needless chances. This Army and our cause cannot afford to lose you, sir," answered Lee as he shook the Georgian's hand.

Hancock steadied his men. He noticed the attacks had slowed. Instead of being vigorously pursued, they appeared to be diversions. Experience taught him that the enemy was up to something, but he was too busy to worry about what Lee had in store for him. The morning had gone better than expected in spite of the fact that Burnside had not yet arrived. He sat on his horse trying to ascertain the enemy's next move when he was joined by Colonel Porter of Grant's staff.

"Good afternoon, General Hancock, General Grant has sent me to find out how it's going in this portion of the line," said Porter.

"Colonel, you may report to the General-in-Chief that we had them on the run. However, Longstreet arrived and has pushed us back to our original position of this morning. Tell the General not to fret. I'll hold my line with or without Burnside," replied Hancock with a determined look in his eyes.

It took Moxley Sorrel forty-five minutes to move around to Hancock's left. The railroad cut had hidden the Confederate movement. Longstreet's trusted aide peered over the depression and saw that the Union's left flank was indeed in the air. Normally, the end of the line would be responsible not only to watch their front, but to bend its line back on an angle to protect against a flank attack.

Sorrel watched as the Federal's kept a vigilant eye toward its front unaware of the enemy on their flank. The Confederate officer looked at Smith and gave the nod to begin the attack. Instantly the Southern troops let out their famous rebel yell and charged the unsuspecting Union troops.

The defenders turned and fired an un-aimed volley which flew harmlessly by the attackers. The Confederates pitched into the startled Federals. The fighting became hand-to-hand. Men used their rifles as clubs. Fingers clawed faces; blood dripped into men's eyes. The boys in blue gave it their all, but the surprise was too great and the rebel movement too swift. Men sprinted for the rear; their enemy hot on their heels.

A quarter of a mile away; Wadsworth saw the break. He turned his remaining Brigades toward the charging enemy and sought to rally his men to stop the charge. When his retreating men were clear, the Union General ordered the remaining Brigades and artillery to open fire.

The sudden hail of lead striking the unsuspecting Confederates had its effect. The Southerners stopped, regrouped and charged again. Wadsworth, put up a stubborn resistance when suddenly, grabbing his chest, he fell to the ground mortally wounded. Seeing their beloved Commander fall, the Union troops broke in a panic.

Hearing Sorrel's assault, Longstreet commenced his attack while Hill's Corps entrenched. The assault would be like an anvil and a hammer. Longstreet and Sorrel being the hammer and Hill the anvil.

From his position, Robert E. Lee watched his troops push the men in blue back. He watched with pride as Longstreet galloped up and down the line urging his troops forward. His "old warhorse" was at his best during a battle. Longstreet smelled victory and was not going to let it escape.

Hancock directed his Division Commanders to hold their ground against the frontal attack, unaware his left flank had caved in. Longstreet attacked with everything he had. The men of the Union held their ground. Suddenly, the remnants of Wadworth's Division appeared on their left with Sorrel's rebels close behind.

Hancock shifted his reserve Brigade facing them toward Sorrel's attackers. He would fight on two fronts at the same time. His men were seasoned veterans, they would not break.

"Colonel Porter, please ride to General Grant and inform him that my left has been rolled up; but we hold. Ask him to find General Burnside and order him to my aid," said Hancock calmly as bullets flew all around him.

Wilderness, Virginia, Grant's Headquarters—May 6, 2:00 PM

Grant sat on a stump on top of a knoll whittling. From his vantage point he could observe Warren and Sedgwick's Corps. He watched as both Corps struck Ewell's entrenched positions. The attacks seemed uncoordinated. Instead of hitting with their entire force, they were piecemeal. He knew the terrain prevented a full-scale attack. He hoped the attacks would prevent Ewell from reinforcing Hill and Longstreet.

The General-in-Chief looked up from his whittling when he heard Horace Porter gallop into camp. The young aide ran to the Commander and informed him of what had happened to Hancock. The messenger was highly excited and was waving his arms all about. His action quickly drew a crowd.

"This is terrible, if Hancock is forced to retreat, then our campaign is doomed," rambled Porter.

Grant listened intently and calmly. Turning to his other aides, the General quickly issued orders

"Colonel Comstock, please find General Burnside and hurry him along. Tell him the Commanding General wants him to move in support of Hancock. Colonel Porter, please ride back to General Hancock and tell him he must hold on and fight with what he has on hand. Major Arnold, please ride to Generals Warren and Sedgwick and tell them to press their attacks with more vigor. If we can force Ewell back, maybe Lee will dispatch some troops from in front of Hancock to Ewell's aid," said Grant.

The General-in-Chief watched his messengers leave and resumed his seat upon the stump. While he whittled his mind was racing. He was anxious, but not worried. He had faith in Hancock. But where the devil was Burnside?

Wilderness, Virginia, Hancock's front—May 6, 3:00 PM

"General Longstreet," called Micah Jenkins as he approached the older General.

Jenkins was the Corps Commander's favorite officer. The twenty eight-year-old from South Carolina had been with Longstreet since the beginning of the war. Graduating first in his class from the South Carolina Military Academy, Jenkins had worked his way up from Captain to Brigadier General. His bravery and common sense at Manassas, the Seven Days Battles, Second Manassas, South Mountain, Sharpsburg, Gettysburg, Chickamauga and Knoxville had earned the young man a warm spot in Longstreet's heart. The older man looked upon Jenkins as a younger brother.

"Yes, General Jenkins," replied Longstreet.

"Sir, we have pushed the Yankees back to their original lines, but they have entrenched and are giving us heavy resistance. When I saw you riding by, I thought it would be an opportunity to brief you on the current situation. Having done that, sir, I'll return to my Brigade," said Jenkins.

"General Jenkins, please ride with me, I wish to make a reconnaissance of the Federal position we flanked. Bring your Brigade with you, perhaps we can find a new way to get in the rear of Hancock's troops again."

The two men, along with their staff and Jenkins's Brigade, followed the path of Sorrel's little force. They left the cut and rode along a deer path many called a road, talking amiably. Suddenly, Longstreet fell from his horse. Blood flowed out of his throat. The road was peppered with bullets. Jenkins' men dove to the ground and started to aim their rifles into the forest.

"FRIENDS!" shouted the staff members. "DAMN YOU, WE ARE FRIENDS."

Instantly the firing stopped. Staff members leaped from their horses and ran toward the fallen General. Jenkins sat erect on his horse issuing orders. A few moments later he too was on the ground. Still shouting commands the young man from South Carolina did not realize no one was listening. A bullet had entered his brain causing delirium, within thirty minutes he was dead.

Moxley Sorrel sprinted to Longstreet's side. Holding the General's head in his arms, he stared into the burly Georgian's eyes. Lee's "old warhorse" looked up at his aide and, turning his head away from Moxley, blew the bloody froth from his mouth.

"Moxley, tell General Field … to take command of the Corps. Notify General Lee I have been shot … and must leave," said Longstreet in a raspy voice.

The staff of both Generals took hold of Longstreet. They placed him on a blanket. Using it as a stretcher, they carried their fallen chief to the rear. Six men from Jenkins' Brigade did the same for the mortally wounded man.

The small group had gone less than a quarter mile when General Lee met them. Dismounting Lee called for an ambulance and knelt next to his comrade-in-arms.

"Pete, I pray you will return to me and that God the Almighty will not take you from us," said Lee in a soft, gentle voice.

The Georgian looked up at his friend and once again blew the bloody forth from his throat and informed the Commanding General of the disposition of his and Hill's Corps and his plan to press the attack.

Lee stood, looked at the men around him and issued orders. Once again he was in direct command. Longstreet's men were scattered throughout the area. He had no choice but to consolidate his forces and then strike Hancock. For the next few hours the Commanding General rode among his men readying them for an attack against the hard-pressed Union forces. At the same time Hancock used the lull to strengthen his position.

At four o'clock Lee ordered an attack along the entire line. The Southern men surged forward but were easily repulsed. The Confederates reformed and struck again. Once again the results were the same—a repulse.

"Colonel Taylor, please ride to General Anderson and tell him he has command of the field and that he is to press the attacks. I'm going to ride to General Ewell and see if he can pull some of the pressure off of First Corps," said Lee.

Wilderness, Virginia—May 6, 6:00 PM

Lee arrived at Ewell's headquarters and found the one-legged Corps Commander sitting by the campfire talking to Jubal Early and John Gordon. From the looks on the men's faces it was apparent he had interrupted a heated discussion.

"Gentlemen, General Longstreet has been severely wounded and, I fear, may die. His command has recaptured our lost ground, but is facing overwhelming forces. Is there anything you can do to relieve pressure on that portion of the field?" asked Lee

"General Lee, I'm afraid there's nothing we can do. We're being heavily pressed ourselves and it's all we can do to hold our own. I wish ..." replied Ewell.

"Excuse me, sir, the Union right is in the air," interrupted Gordon. "My engineer and I found a path which would let us circle around the enemy undetected ..."

"General Lee," interrupted Early. "General Gordon has been here three times with the same story since nine this morning. He is mistaken. The enemy right is not in the air. Their troops are hidden from view because of the forest."

"General Early is mistaken, sir, I have personally completed a reconnaissance not more than an hour ago and nothing has changed. Neither General Early nor General Ewell has reconnoitered the area. The right is still in the air. General Lee, with your permission I can have my troops ready to attack within thirty minutes," responded an irritated Gordon.

Lee's gray eyes turned stone cold as he glared at both Ewell and Early. If Gordon was right, then both Ewell and Early had cost the Army of Northern Virginia a once in a lifetime opportunity to destroy Grant's Army. With both flanks in the air he would have ordered a joint attack, which would have sent Grant and his men reeling back across the Rapidan River.

"General Gordon," said Lee. "Please make preparations for your Brigade to attack. General Early will give you another Brigade to join with yours. You'll be in command of that section of the field and of both Brigades. General Ewell will have his entire Corps ready to move in support as soon as you roll up Grant's right flank," said Lee in a disgusted tone.

Ewell and Early looked at Lee, their faces turning crimson from the admonishment they just received.

"General Ewell, send a courier to General Anderson and to Colonel Taylor that I'll be directing operations from this portion of the field for the balance of the day."

Wilderness, Virginia, Grant's Headquarters—May 6, 6:45 PM

Grant sat by his campfire talking to Meade and Rawlins. Aides busied themselves in preparing supper for the Generals. Darkness was beginning to set in. An eerie silence swept over the Wilderness. It was as if someone had turned a switch to off. The Union Army had survived another day.

Suddenly the boom of Confederate artillery broke the silence, quickly followed by the rebel yell. Gordon had started his attack. Within fifteen minutes couriers arrived at Grant's headquarters bringing news of the attack and the subsequent roll up of the Union left. Some reported the entire left was captured and that Generals Warren, Sedgwick, Seymour and Shaler along with their commands were now guests of Robert E. Lee. Grant quickly sifted through the reports separating fact from fiction, exaggeration from truth. He turned to Rawlins.

"John, please send word to Warren to push his reserves forward in support of Sedgwick," said Grant calmly.

No sooner had Grant ordered his reserves in when a Brigadier General burst through the woods and galloped straight toward the General-in-Chief.

"General Grant, this is a crisis. I know General Lee's methods well by past experience. He will surely throw his entire Army between us and the Rapidan cutting off our supplies and retreat," panted the young General his voice shaky.

"I'm so tired of hearing of what General Lee is going to do to us. Some of you officers think Lee is going to magically do a double somersault and wind up on both our flanks and in our rear all at the same time. Return to your command and start to think of what we're going to do to General Lee," retorted Grant in a terse voice.

Cannon balls began to land all around headquarters as Babcock of the General's staff galloped into camp, dismounted and calmly walked to the commanding Generals.

"Sirs, I have just returned from the breach in our lines. The reserves are going in and General Burnside has sent two Brigades to assist and Warren has sent a Division. Sedgwick has rallied his Corps and is making a stand. Generals Seymour and Shaler have been taken prisoner with about three hundred of our men. Both Warren and Sedgwick feel they can hold and the crisis shall pass within an hour," said Babcock calmly.

Grant nodded and slowly walked away. From his vantage point he could see the fireworks display as the muzzle flashes from rifles and artillery roared and thundered lighting up the darkness with bright yellow flashes.

The General looked at his watch. It was eight o'clock. Gordon's attack had been going on for an hour and fifteen minutes. The Confederates were unable to effect the break-through they had hoped for. As the General watched the exchange of fire, he noticed a red glow intermingled with the flashes of yellow. The increased artillery use on both sides had caused the dry leaves and timber to catch fire. The Wilderness would soon be ablaze.

Wilderness, Virginia, Ewell's front—May 6, 8:00 PM

Lee and Ewell watched Gordon's men drive the Yankees from their position. The initial success was better than anticipated. "*If only Ewell would have lis-*

tened to Gordon and had attacked earlier in the day they could have rolled up both of Grant's flanks," thought Lee. Darkness and the billowing smoke from the fires hindered the Confederate advance. Seeing his faltering troops, Lee quickly surmised that nothing more could be accomplished and ordered Gordon to halt the attacks and dig in where he was.

"General Ewell, convey my compliments to General Gordon for a job well done. I am going to return to my headquarters. I will send over your orders for tomorrow before midnight," said the tired Commanding General.

"General Lee, you're welcome to spend the night at my headquarters," replied Ewell.

"Thank you, General, but there's much that I must attend to before morning," answered the exhausted Commander.

Lee turned his horse and, along with his small escort, started on the thirty minute ride back to his headquarters. He had a great deal to think about. Only he knew how bad Grant's attacks had crippled the Confederate high command. Two promising officers, Jones and Jenkins were dead while another talented officer, Leroy Stafford was dying.

Experienced Brigade Commanders like John Pegram and Harry Benning were seriously wounded. Powell Hill was so sick that Lee could not count on him for full service and Ewell seemed to be plagued by indecision. The worst of all was the wounding of Longstreet. If the burly Georgian died, there was no one Lee could turn to for advice. The best he could hope for was Longstreet's return, but he knew it would be at least three months before he would have his "old warhorse" back. A year ago he lost Stonewall Jackson in these very woods; now Longstreet

Lee had to pick a replacement for Longstreet and if Hill was too sick to continue, he had to pick a replacement for him also. Early was the Senior Division Commander in the Army of Northern Virginia and should be given command of Longstreet's Corps. The irascible General had made so many enemies within Longstreet's First Corps that his success in leading those men would be doubtful. Dick Anderson was the Senior Division leader in First Corps and had always performed admirably. He was well thought of by the men. He had to weigh his options before morning.

Arriving at his headquarters just before nine, he slowly dismounted and walked to his tent for some much needed rest. The chest pains had returned.

"General, I'll have some supper brought in for you," said Major Venable as Lee approached his tent.

"No thanks, Major, just have the cook bring me a few biscuits. Please ask Captain Channing to come to my tent."

"Sir, you must keep up your strength. Mrs. Lee would never forgive me if I let you starve to death. I'll have the cook bring some beef with your biscuits," answered a concerned Charles Venable.

Ten minutes later the cook appeared at Lee's tent carrying a plate of boiled beef, baked potato and two biscuits. The servant gently set the plate on the folding table and silently exited. The smell of the food sparked the General's appetite; he hadn't eaten all day and hadn't realized how hungry he really was. He'd just finished sopping up the last of beef gravy with the second biscuit and had popped it into his mouth when Channing appeared at the entrance of the tent.

"You sent for me, sir?" asked the solider spy.

Lee looked up. The Captain's uniform was stained with mud and blood. He had taken part in the Calvary battle.

"I need you for another mission. Are you up for it?" asked Lee.

"Yes, sir!" came an enthusiastic reply.

"I need you to cross into those people's lines and scout around. I have to know what Grant is going to do next. Is he going to retreat or stay and fight? Stay as long as you need in order to get me the information. Try to find out how many casualties he has, particularly among his officers," said Lee as he unhooked his belt and sat on his cot.

"Consider it done, sir," responded Channing as he saluted and left the General.

Wilderness, Virginia, Grant's Headquarters—May 6, 10:00 PM

With the close of fighting for the night, Grant sat by his campfire and peered over a map of Northern Virginia. He realized fighting in the Wilderness was a mistake. He had to break out of the forest and into the open in order to use his superiority in numbers. In the distance he could hear the cries of the wounded as the fires burned them alive. The popping sound of bodies bursting open as the gas inside expanded until the skin could no longer contain it mixed with the screams of the wounded.

The smell of burning flesh filled the air. If anyone ventured out to help the wounded, enemy snipers would add their name to the causality list. In spite of his reputation for being uncaring, the Union General-in-Chief hated to see suffering. He would prefer to see more enemy prisoners taken and less dead. He knew the dead would not be able to rebuild the Country after the war.

It was well after one in the morning before Grant decided to go to bed. His plans for the next day had been made and orders issued. He would not retreat. His orders to all Commanders, *"dig in and wait for Lee to attack."*

CHAPTER FIVE

Wilderness, Virginia—May 7, 5:30 AM

A steady drizzle masked the dawn as a low-hanging fog hugged the ground making it impossible for the combatants to see more than a few feet. Men on both sides were edgy firing blindly in the direction of any sound in front of them. Channing Smith cautiously crossed into the Union lines. Three times he was shot at, but the wildly aimed rounds sailed by harmlessly. Just before seven o'clock he arrived at Warren's headquarters and mingled with other staff members as they prepared breakfast.

Warren approached the table at seven-thirty and invited his staff to join him. Recognizing Channing as the aide at Meade's and Grant's headquarters, he invited the young man to join them.

"Gentlemen, yesterday we damaged Lee pretty hard, but he gave as good as he got. The Army needs to be consolidated and re-supplied. Grant's orders are to hold our present position and wait for Lee to attack. I want you all to be ready to ride at a moment's notice," said Warren as he chewed a piece of cooked salt pork.

As breakfast was ending, Horace Porter arrived at Warren's headquarters.

"Colonel Porter, welcome. Would you care for some breakfast or coffee?" asked Warren shaking the aide's hand.

"Sir, orders from General Grant," replied Porter handing the Corps commander a sealed envelope.

Warren opened the envelope and read its contents to his staff.

> *"To: General's Warren, Hancock, Burnside, Sheridan and Sedgwick.*
> *Beginning at eight p.m. tonight Warren's Corps will pull out of the line move behind Sedgwick and Hancock's Corps and make all possible haste for Spotsylva-*

nia Court House. Sedgwick's Corps will proceed after Warren's men have passed, followed by Burnside's Corps and lastly Hancock's Corps. Warren is to be at the Courthouse no later than dawn and is ordered to entrench and take no offensive action until joined by the rest of the Army. Sheridan's Calvary Corps will guard our flanks against any attack by Lee.
Signed,
Ulysses S. Grant
General-in-Chief"

As darkness fell, Channing Smith slipped back to the Confederate lines and raced to Lee's headquarters. The rebel pickets heard Warren's Corps moving and assumed the Yankees were retreating. All along the line the word was spread that the Yankees were retreating.

Lee sat in his tent and peered over the rough-hewn maps of the area. Reports from Ewell and Hill's Divisional Commanders stated Grant was retreating. Lee disagreed. It didn't fit Grant's character or past performance to retreat after only two day's conflict. The General peered over the maps trying to decipher what his adversary was planning.

"What the hell is Grant doing?" wondered Lee out loud.

"He's moving to Spotsylvania. Warren's Corps is to move first followed by Sedgwick, Burnside and Hancock. Sheridan is to guard the flanks," replied Channing Smith.

Lee looked at his spy, smiled and turned his attention to the maps.

"Well done, Channing. Grab some coffee as I may need you later on this evening."

The pair's conversation was interrupted by the arrival of Lee's senior commanders.

"Gentlemen, it has been reported that the Union troops are pulling out of their breastworks," said Lee.

"Yes, sir," interrupted Ewell. "I think Grant has had enough and is high tailing back across the Rapidan."

The other Generals nodded in agreement.

"General Grant is not retiring. Based on everything I have read about him and based upon a lengthy conversation I had with General Longstreet before he was wounded, this Union General will fight it out as long as he has one man standing. We must not confuse him with Hooker, McClellan or Burnside. Smith has just informed me that Grant is moving his Army around our right flank and is heading for Spotsylvania Courthouse," answered Lee.

"Sir, if Smith is correct and Grant is changing direction, what makes him think the Yankees are headed for Spotsylvania Courthouse?" asked Jubal Early.

"Because, gentlemen, Smith said it and it makes sense. If Grant gets control of Spotsylvania, then he has placed his Army between us and Richmond. He knows I must attack him on a ground of his choosing. It is what I would have done if I were in his place.

"General Anderson, your First Corps is the nearest to Spotsylvania. I would like you to move your men out of the line at three o'clock in the morning and force-march them to Spotsylvania. Time is of the essence. You must beat Warren there. In the meantime, come dawn and if Generals Ewell and Hill find those people have left their front; they are to immediately move to Spotsylvania. General Stuart will take one Brigade and personally ride ahead to try to hold Grant in place until the infantry arrives. The rest of his Calvary will guard our flanks," said Lee.

"Sir, how are we supposed to beat Warren to Spotsylvania? From our position there is only one road to the courthouse. Moving that many men will surely clog it up," said Ewell.

"In anticipation of Grant's move, I ordered General Pendleton, with a pioneer Corps, to cut a road through the Wilderness to Spotsylvania yesterday. General Early, you are here because in the event General Hill is unable to perform his command functions you will assume command of Third Corps. Therefore, it's necessary for you to know the battle plan," replied Lee.

"Gentlemen, if there are no questions, you may rejoin your commands."

The brain trust of the Army of Northern Virginia left the Commander's tent leaving the aged warrior alone with his thoughts. His head ached and the pains in his chest were back. He didn't know how much longer his strength would hold out. He knew the cause needed him. His State needed him. Lee's entire life had been devoted to serving others. First his bedridden mother, then his fragile wife and always his Country. He loved the United States. He didn't believe in slavery or secession but he loved his State of Virginia and he would defend her to the death.

Wilderness, Virginia, Anderson's front—May 7, 9:00 PM

Dick Anderson looked at the terrain surrounding his men. All around him fires were raging out of control. Smoke choked his men and blocked their vision. The Corps Commander examined the newly constructed road. He found it narrow and lined with stumps. The going would be slow at best. Without informing Lee, he pushed up his departure time to midnight. While on the march he would rest his men ten minutes every hour.

As Anderson waited until midnight, Warren was already on the move. At first the Union men assumed they were retreating and the thought of abandoning the fight aggravated them. They knew they could beat Lee if they were only given the chance. After an hour on the march they realized they were headed south and not north. The spirits of the men in blue were suddenly lifted. Grant was not retreating, he was flanking Lee. The Union General-in-Chief sat on his horse and watched Warren's Corps as it pulled out of the line. As the men passed and recognized their commander, they began to cheer wildly. Grant … Grant … Grant. At last they had a General who was going to let them fight.

Spotsylvania Court House, Virginia—May 8, 5:00 AM

Dick Anderson's men were one mile from the Courthouse when they heard the sound of musket fire. A courier came galloping up the road. Seeing Anderson he reined his horse to a stop and gave him an unsealed dispatch from J.E.B. Stuart. The message was addressed to Lee. Since it was unsealed, the newly appointed Corps Commander read it.

> *"General Lee,*
> *At dawn this morning I encountered enemy infantry advancing on Spotsylvania Courthouse. I have dismounted my men and have been able to hold my ground.*
> *I am in need of infantry and artillery support if I am to hold this position.*
> *I estimate the enemy to be two Divisions, but every minute more are appearing.*
> *Respectfully,*
> *JEB Stuart"*

Anderson took out a pencil and underneath Stuart's name wrote.

> *"General Lee,*
> *My Corps shall be at the Courthouse within fifteen minutes.*
> *Respectfully,*
> *D. Anderson"*

Anderson handed the message back to the courier and gave orders for his Corps to move at the double quick.

JEB Stuart rode along his line encouraging his men. He knew he had a tiger by the tail. Although outnumbered at least four-to-one the Cavalry Commander held the high ground. Stuart had beaten Sheridan's Cavalry by a scant ten minutes. The Federal horsemen attempted to push Stuart's men from the high ground but the Southerners had used their time advantage well by quickly throwing up a breastwork made up of fence rails; repulsing the assaults.

As Sheridan's men reformed, they were joined by the lead elements of Warren's Corps. The fence rail breastwork was two hundred yards away across an open field. Behind the rails were Stuart's outnumbered Cavalry. Behind Stuart's men, coming up fast, Warren saw the lead elements of Anderson's Corps. Without waiting to form ranks, the Federal Commander gave the order to fix bayonets and charge. The men in blue took a deep breath and sprinted up the hill toward the rails.

"RUN OR ELSE THEY WILL BEAT YOU HERE AND ALL WILL BE LOST!" shouted Stuart to Anderson's men.

The race was on. Like their Northern counterparts, the men in gray took a deep breath and with their last ounce of strength sprinted up the hill from the opposite direction arriving moments before the Federals and opened fire on the attackers.

The hand-to-hand fighting was savage. Gone was all sense of humanity. This was combat at its ugliest. Minutes became an eternity. After an hour of continuous combat the Federals were driven from the breastworks.

Warren watched his men stagger back and decided to halt the attacks and wait for the rest of the Army. His Corps had been badly mauled. Sedgwick was on his way with three rested Divisions. When he arrived, the Federals would resume the attack. For the balance of the day, Warren waited while on the other side of the field Anderson waited for Ewell. At four o'clock Sedgwick arrived. The two Generals conferred for fifteen minutes before resuming the assault.

On a ridge overlooking the Union forces, Grant, Meade and Rawlins sat on their horses and anxiously watched their Army attack. It was too little too late. Anderson's Corps, now reinforced by Ewell and Hill easily repulsed the Union troops.

Grant watched the sun set over the battlefield putting the end to another day of bloodshed. Lee had won the race for Spotsylvania by minutes. The Union General-in-Chief had Lee where he wanted him—in the open. Now he could take his time and probe Lee's defenses for a weakness.

"John, please send a message to the Secretary of War informing him that we met Lee in the Wilderness and after two days of heavy fighting, we have moved the battle to Spotsylvania. Also inform him that I have sent our wounded to the rear and they should be arriving shortly. I have also sent the supply wagons back to be re-supplied and returned here. Inform him that I plan to fight it out here if it takes all summer," said Grant as he lit a fresh cigar.

CHAPTER SIX

Dalton, Georgia, Confederate lines—May 9, 10:00 AM

Confederate General Joseph Eggleston Johnston dismounted his horse and joined his three Corps Commanders. The four men watched as the valley below slowly filled with bluecoats. The slender, fifty seven-year-old Virginia-born Johnston was loved by his men. A West Point classmate of Robert E. Lee, the two had been life-long friends. Their fathers had fought together under George Washington during the American Revolution. Unlike his classmate, Johnston had fallen into disfavor with Jefferson Davis for disputing his rank in the Army. Johnston felt that since he had held a higher rank in the Union Army than Robert E. Lee, he should have been ahead of Lee on the South's seniority list.

On Johnston's right stood Lieutenant General William Hardee. Nick-named "old reliable" by his Commanders, the fifty-three year old Georgian had abandoned a long and respectable career in the Union Army to join the South. When he was the Commandant of Cadets at West Point, he wrote the textbook "Rifle and Light Infantry Tactics." His strategies were used by Line Officers on both sides. Along with 'Stonewall' Jackson and James Longstreet, Hardee was considered by many on both sides as the finest Corps Commander in the Confederacy.

On Johnston's left was Lieutenant General John Bell Hood. The thirty-three year old Kentucky resident was considered by many as the fiercest Division Leader the South had. He lost the use of his right arm due to wounds sustained while charging up Little Round Top at Gettysburg. He lost his left leg while leading a charge on the second day of the battle of Chickamauga.

To the right of Hood stood Johnston's Calvary Commander, Major General Joseph Wheeler. The twenty-eight year old Georgian had served the

South faithfully from the beginning of the war. Wounded three times, he was a fierce fighter and extremely loyal to his Commanders.

"Gentlemen, below us are the Federal Armies of the Cumberland, Tennessee and Ohio. These armies are lead by extremely brave and resourceful men. In addition, it appears that Hooker's Corps of the Army of the Potomac has reinforced them. Don't be lulled into complacency. Sherman will first probe our positions and when he feels he has discovered a weakness, he will hit us with everything he has," said Johnston in a respectful tone.

"General Johnston, who do you think is more dangerous, Grant or Sherman?" asked Hood.

"They are both dangerous and aren't easily rattled. In my opinion, Sherman is more patient and that makes him better than Grant; which also makes him more deadly. Gentlemen, let's double-check our position and make sure we've left nothing to chance. Our only hope of defeating Sherman is if he attacks us here. General Wheeler, I want your Cavalry to patrol all of the gaps and passes and let me know if anything happens on our flanks," replied Johnston his eyes focused on the sea of blue below.

"General Johnston, wouldn't my horsemen best serve you if we circled behind Sherman and cut his supply lines?" asked Wheeler.

"I thought of that, however, the Union supply lines are very well protected. Furthermore, I feel it would be a waste of time and horseflesh to attempt such a maneuver. I'd rather fight Sherman now when our men are fresh and rested than thirty days from now when the heat and the strain of being so close to the enemy takes its toll," answered the Virginian. "My philosophy is that time is an ally only when used to your advantage. Delaying this contest only strengthens the enemy. They can get more reinforcements, unfortunately, our manpower is already severely strained."

In the valley below, Sherman sat on his horse and watched as Thomas and Schofield deployed their men. Everything was going according to plan. By noon both Union Generals would be in place to begin their attack. He could feel Johnston's eyes upon him. The red-haired Union General knew his Confederate counterpart could observe his every move. He hoped he had Johnston's full attention and that his third Army, the Army of the Tennessee under the command of his protégé James McPherson, was able to circle around the aged Virginian. By attacking the southern stronghold front and rear, Johnston would be compelled to either fight or be starved into submission.

Dalton, Georgia, McPherson's front—May 9, 2:00 PM

James McPherson, the thirty-six year old West Point graduate from Ohio, rode at the head of his Army. The handsome, bearded McPherson was the favorite of not only Sherman; but Grant as well. Normally fast moving and hard hitting, the young General was taking his time. He knew his task was important. He wasn't going to mess things up for himself or his mentors.

"General," the scouts have just returned and report that Resaca is not defended," said Major Higgins, the twenty-one year old Chief-of-Staff.

"Major, send a courier to General Sherman informing him that I'm almost clear of Snake Creek Gap and am pushing onto Resaca," replied McPherson.

The Union Army of the Tennessee was a half-mile from the end of the gap and two miles from the Georgia city when they encountered Confederate infantry.

"Major Higgins, send word to my Corps Commanders to deploy their men in a line of battle. I want General Howard's Corps in the center; Dodge's Corps on the left; Logan's Corps on the right; with Hazen's Division in reserve for support."

It took the veterans less than forty-five minutes to deploy. General O.O. Howard was at the head of his Corps as they opened the attack. The full-bearded, thirty-four year old, one-armed General from Maine graduated West Point with J.E.B. Stuart and Custis Lee. Deeply religious he was given the nickname, "the Christian General."

As Howard approached the Resaca road, he noticed formidable breastworks blocking his approach. Pinching his knees inward Indian style, he stopped his horse. Turning in his saddle he gave the order to charge. Without hesitation Howard's lead Division of five thousand men broke into a run toward the fortifications.

Twenty-five yards from the breastworks the Confederate infantry opened fire. Four thousand muskets spit fire and flame into the faces of the onrushing bluecoats. The Southerners quickly reloaded and fired again. The second volley stopped the attackers in their tracks. The third volley caused them to retreat.

With Howard's Division in retreat, the Southern defenders shifted their position to the Union right and repeated the scene; this time against Logan's Division. The result was the same—a Union retreat! The width of the Gap prevented McPherson from throwing his entire Army against the defenders. After two hours of trying to force an opening, the young Army Commander halted his attacks and pulled his men back to the entrance of Snake Creek Gap three miles back and dug in. He sent another message to Sherman stating he had encountered sizeable resistance and was forced to retreat.

At the same time, Southern Brigadier General, James Ganty, sent a courier to Joe Johnston, informing him of McPherson's attacks. Ganty led the advanced division from Polk's Corps out of Atlanta. While marching to Johnston, he noticed McPherson's skirmishers moving through the Gap. Ignoring orders he deployed his four thousand men and defended the back door to Resaca; thereby, saving Johnston and his Army from a surprise attack.

When Ganty's messenger arrived at Johnston's headquarters, the slender Virginian wasted no time ordering John Bell Hood to take three Divisions and reinforce Ganty. Hood was to assume command and wait for Polk; while Johnston waited to see what Sherman was planning.

Sherman read McPherson's second dispatch, shook his head in disbelief and turned to his Chief-of-Staff.

"McPherson has over twenty-five thousand men. He should've been able to sweep away any resistance. Tell him I'm sending him two Brigades from Hooker's Corps and that, come dawn, he's to attack whatever is in his front. Thomas and Schofield will demonstrate at Johnston's front," said Sherman in disgust.

The night passed slowly for Billy Sherman. It was three in the morning when he gave up trying to sleep and went outside. The crisp mountain air invigorated the worrisome General. He enjoyed the solitude of the early morning before the camp became alive. In less than three hours his men would, once again, be engaged in battle and his headquarters buzzing with excited couriers. The red-haired General stopped, lit a cigar and looked up at Johnston's formidable position. Campfires glowed in the darkness. He thought of his wife and five children at home and to happier moments when he was the Superintendent of the Louisiana State Seminary of Learning and Military Academy. He loved Louisiana and the South. Many of the friends he had made in Georgia and Baton Rouge were now his enemies.

Suddenly his mind snapped back to the present.

"Why should I attack when I can still flank him out of his stronghold?" asked Sherman out loud as he sprinted for his Chief-of-Staff's tent.

"Major Hitchcock, wake up!" said an excited Sherman.

"General, what can I do for you, sir?" asked the tired Chief-of-Staff.

"Major, wake our couriers and have them report to my tent immediately. I need to call off McPherson's attack."

The sun slowly rose in the east as Sherman met with his two remaining Army Commanders. The three men sat in front of the campfire drinking coffee as Sherman briefed them on his change of plans.

The Commander of the Army of the Cumberland, stoic George Thomas, sat on Sherman's left. The large heavy-set, Virginia-born career soldier was estranged from his sisters and cousins for staying loyal to the Union. At Chickamauga, while his peers ran, Thomas and his Corps alone held the entire Confederate Army at bay, saving the Union Army under the command of William Rosecrans from destruction.

Commander of the Army of Ohio, John Schofield, sat on Sherman's right. The West Point graduate had a reputation of being an excellent staff officer and extremely loyal. It was this loyalty to both Grant and Sherman which earned him a chance to command an Army in the field.

"Gentlemen, Johnston has discovered our flanking movement. By this time he has reinforced his forces at Resaca. I can only surmise that he's ordered Polk from Atlanta. His position on top of Buzzard's Roost is very formidable and I won't waste lives trying to dislodge him. Therefore, at midnight Schofield will move out of his trenches and join McPherson at Snake Creek Gap. George, your Army will spread out and keep Johnston occupied. If he moves to parry our thrust, you'll hit him while he's on the march. With any luck, come the thirteenth, we'll have Johnston caught between our two forces and he'll have to either surrender or be annihilated," said Sherman lighting a cigar.

Spotsylvania, Virginia, Union lines—May 12, 3:45 AM

Grant sat on his horse waiting for the predawn attack to begin. He lit a cigar, inhaled deeply and slowly exhaled as he turned to his Chief-of-Staff and best friend, John Rawlins.

"John, I wonder how Sheridan's doing? I only let him take his Cavalry on a raid to Richmond yesterday in the hopes of getting Jeb Stuart out of my hair for a while. Jeff Davis will be clamoring for Lee to send Stuart after Sheridan to protect Richmond. If he can defeat Stuart, then Lee's Army will be blind to our movements," said Grant as he took another drag on his cigar.

"Sam, I'm sure 'little Phil' can defeat him," replied Rawlins

"If I live to be a hundred, I'll never forget the look in Meade's eyes when he stormed into my tent and wanted to have Sheridan shot for insubordination," said Grant laughing.

"What happened?" asked Rawlins leaning forward in his saddle.

Apparently our hotheaded Cavalry Commander called Meade a pompous jackass who hadn't the slightest inkling of how Cavalry should be used. He told Meade that if he let him take his Cavalry to Richmond, he would not only draw Stuart away from Lee, but would defeat the Southern Cavalry Commander," replied Grant with a huge smile on his face.

"What did you tell Meade?" asked Rawlins.

"I said that I'd let him go as Sheridan generally knows what he's talking about," answered Grant.

Sam Grant removed his pocket watch, lit a match and looked at the time.

"In fifteen minutes all hell is going to break loose."

Winfield Hancock sat on his horse next to the artillery battery that was to signal the beginning of the assault. Once again, his Corps was chosen to lead the attack. Two days ago the Union had some success in breaking Lee's line at the center. The unsupported Union troops led by Colonel Emory Upton had accomplished a breach at dusk, but were counter-attacked by both Ewell and Early's Corps. The greatly outnumbered Union troops were forced to withdraw.

Lee used the lull in fighting to his advantage by fortifying his position. Using the natural lay of the land he deployed his men in the form of a mule shoe with the curved end pointing toward the Federals.

Sedgwick's death from a sniper two days earlier along with yesterday's heavy rains prevented Grant from following up on Upton's success. Today would be different. Horatio Wright was placed in command of Sedgwick's Corps. The predawn gave promise of a clear day with moderate temperatures. Grant was going to assault the same spot where Upton attacked. This time instead of attacking with three thousand men, he was going to use fifty thousand.

Hancock looked at his pocket watch then at the battery Commander and gave the order to fire.

Instantly the Union troops started across no man's land between the lines. The grass was wet and slippery, but at least they were out of the cursed Wilderness. Step by step the men in blue drew closer to the Confederate breastworks. The dark uniforms of the Union troops hid them well in the blackness of the predawn. In less than twenty minutes the sun would be up making them completely visible.

Southern soldiers strained their eyes to find their human targets. The lack of light played tricks on their eyes. They could hear the Federals coming but couldn't see them. John Gordon, mounted on his huge black mare, rode along his line.

"OPEN FIRE!" Gordon shouted.

"GENERAL, FIRE AT WHAT? WE CAN'T SEE THEM!" shouted back a young Colonel.

"YOU DAMN FOOL, THERE'S SO MANY YOU DON'T HAVE TO SEE THEM TO HIT THEM. FIRE AT THE SOUNDS AND AIM LOW!" yelled back an angry Gordon.

Instantly the entire Confederate line opened fire. The dull thud of minie balls striking human flesh filled the air. The survivors continued forward breaking into a run. Seconds later a second Confederate volley added more casualties. Blood rapidly saturated the green meadow.

The determined Federals continued forward like men possessed, their only thought—to breach the Confederate defenses.

Before the defenders could fire a third volley, Hancock's men were over the breastworks and were in hand-to-hand combat with Ewell's men. The battle escalated into a full-scale free-for-all. Once again, all humanity disappeared. It was survival of the fittest. Sabers were drawn and flailed about stabbing and slicing flesh. Those who did not have a saber drew Bowie knives or bayonets and wielded them about. Others used their muskets as clubs and bludgeoned their adversaries or used their hands, feet and teeth to obtain victory.

For three hours Hancock's men battled with Ewell's Corps. The Confederates slowly gave ground as fresh Union troops from Wright's Corps poured over the breastworks. Both Generals ordered their men to spread out to the left overlapping the defenders' right.

Gordon saw the flanking movement and called for his courier.

"Tell General Early he must come up now or else the day is lost. Tell him we're engaging two Union Corps and it appears a third is advancing to widen the breach," panted Gordon.

Leaning forward Gordon grabbed the youthful courier and whispered.

"Ride like the wind."

Robert E. Lee arrived at Gordon's side within minutes of the courier leaving. Seeing the Commanding General, the Division Commander stopped.

"General Lee, it appears Grant has hit us with everything he has. They've ruptured our line. Stewart and Johnson's Divisions have been overrun. I've ordered my Division into the breach. We temporarily halted their advance when a fresh Union Corps entered the fight. I've sent a courier to General

Early asking him to bring his Corps forward," said Gordon as he fought to remain calm.

"Very good," replied the older General.

Lee turned to Charles Venable, a look of fire in the General's eyes.

"Colonel Venable, please send a courier to General Heth and tell him to bring his Division up. Then ride to General Anderson and inform him of the breach of our lines and tell him to bring his Corps forward and strike those people in the flank and to hold nothing back. He must move quickly or else the day is lost," said Lee in a stern voice.

Sitting on Traveler, the Southern icon watched as Early's men entered the melee. Slowly the tide of battle shifted in favor of the Confederates as Hancock's and Wright's tired troops started to give way.

Both of the Union Corps Commanders were in the thick of the action, yelling commands and directing troops. They were both not more than a hundred yards apart when Hancock noticed Wright grab his arm and double over. Instantly aides were at the side of the fallen Corps Commander.

"Leave me alone damn it! Go back to your posts!" shouted Wright.

A dark-haired Captain, not more than eighteen years old, approached the wounded General

"General, my place is here, but your place is in the rear of this Corps directing us."

Wright was seething. His battle blood was up. Nobody was going to order him from this field. He looked at the Captain and noticed blood flowing down the Captain's leg.

"Captain, you're wounded. You should return to the rear," answered Wright.

"No, sir, my duty is here with my men," replied the youth.

Wright looked at the officer and smiled

"Son, that is precisely why I must remain. Your duty is to your Company; while mine is to my Corps. Let us return to our duty."

Taking heart from Wright's refusal to leave the battlefield, his Corps rallied and slowly pushed Early's and Ewell's Corps back.

Seeing his Army once again being forced back, Lee rode to the front of his troops. Out of the corner of his eye Gordon noticed his gray-haired idol approaching the danger zone. If Lee died, so would the Army of Northern Virginia. Gordon spurred his horse forward and grabbed Traveler's reins and pulled hard. A small group of men gathered around the two Generals.

"General Lee, you must retire and get us fresh troops. My men and I will halt the enemy," said Gordon as he nodded to the crowd for concurrence.

"These men are Virginians and Georgians and have never failed you," said Gordon.

"NO, NO WE WILL NOT LET OUR GENERAL DOWN. LEE TO THE REAR! LEE TO THE REAR! GENERAL, WE WILL DRIVE THEM BACK!" shouted the crowd.

Refusing to move, Lee glared at Gordon and the crowd for a full five minutes. A tall Sergeant from one of the Virginia regiments brazenly walked up to the Commanding General, grabbed Traveler's reins, turned the horse around and led Lee to the rear. The South's number one soldier jerked the reins from the Sergeant and without saying a word rode back two hundred yards to direct the fight.

On the other side of the battlefield Grant sat on his horse and watched as Hancock's men supported by Wright's Corps pushed the Confederates back. He anxiously watched as Lee counter-attacked driving both Hancock and Wright's men back across the curve of the "Mule Shoe" and over the breastworks. There the Union troops made a stand refusing to be pushed back any farther. Only the log breastworks separated the two armies. Men stabbed at each other through openings in the logs. Muskets were fired at point blank range into the faces of the foe. Some took their muskets, attached their bayonets and used them as spears. The wounded were trampled and the dead were used as shields.

Turning to Meade, Grant inquired.

"General Meade, shouldn't Warren's Corps have been engaged by now?"

Sir, General Warren is still assembling his Corps for the attack on the enemy left," replied the Pennsylvanian

"General Meade, please inform Warren that if he doesn't attack within the next fifteen minutes I'll have him relieved of his command," answered an agitated Grant.

Meade saluted and rode away to personally hurry Warren along.

Grant turned to Rawlins.

"I hate to have to talk to Meade that way. He's a good officer and a loyal patriot, but at times he's too cautious. Can't he see that Warren must attack in order to relieve pressure on Hancock and Wright? At times I...."

Grant was interrupted by a courier from Burnside. The Union Commander read the dispatch and then looked at Rawlins.

"General Burnside's attack against the Confederate extreme right flank has failed. He's moved his Corps within musket range and is now engaging in a long-range duel with the enemy."

The two men continued to talk when Rawlins pointed to the battlefield. Grant watched as Warren's men aggressively attacked the Confederate breastworks. Although Lee had pulled men from Anderson to assist Gordon, the Confederate position was still formidable.

Anderson waited until the Union troops were within two hundred yards before ordering his artillery to fire. At once fifty-two cannon balls tore into the attacking formation creating gaping holes where men once stood. Limbs were ripped from bodies and torsos cut in half. The artillerymen quickly reloaded and fired again with the same devastating effect. After the third artillery volley, the Southern infantry joined in. Instantly the air was filled with eight thousand muskets balls tearing into Warren's brave men. The men in blue continued their assault but were cut down before they could reach the breastworks.

After two hours, Warren called off his infantry attack, but he wasn't through. He ordered his artillery to keep up a steady cannonade against the enemy in their front. If he couldn't break their defenses by assault, he would batter them down.

Even though Warren and Burnside had been repulsed, both Hancock and Wright refused to give up the fight. Hour after hour men continued to kill and maim each other. Both sides were played out. The fighting continued with no food or water for over ten hours. It was now two in the afternoon and the bright sunshine had given way to a steady drizzle. Ignoring the weather change, Hancock and Wright ordered every man they had including their reserves, into the fight.

"IF WARREN AND BURNSIDE WILL NOT FIGHT, THEN THEY SHOULD SEND US SOME HELP!" shouted Hancock to his aide.

Observing the shifting tides of the battle, Grant was thinking the same thing.

"John, inform Burnside and Warren to each send a Division to both Wright and Hancock," said Grant in a disgusted tone.

Lee noticed Grant's shifting of troops and turned to his Chief Engineer, Brigadier General Martin Smith.

"General Smith, please retire from this field and make me a new breastworks running east to west across the center of the Mule Shoe. I'm afraid General Grant will use the full weight of his Army to expand his break-through. If he succeeds; then all is lost. You must hurry your work along for I'm afraid our boys are almost played out," said Lee in an anxious tone.

Smith saluted and rode away to accomplish his orders. The head of Lee's Engineer Corps was considered the best engineer in the Confederate Army. It was rumored he could build a breastwork out of matchsticks and make it so strong a cannon at point blank range could not penetrate it.

Lee rode forward to inspire his men to hold. Suddenly, Traveler reared up on his hind legs as a cannon ball soared beneath its stomach.

Seeing the near catastrophe, the soldiers began to shout again.

"LEE TO THE REAR! LEE TO THE REAR!

Some of them left their posts and encircled the General in an effort to protect him with their bodies.

Looking down at his men, the General shouted above the din of battle.

"IF YOU WILL PROMISE ME TO HOLD OR DRIVE THOSE PEOPLE BACK I SHALL RETIRE."

"WE WILL! WE WILL!" shouted the men in return.

Darkness descended on the battlefield, yet, unlike other battles, it brought no relief. Men, senses now numb and their eyes with a far away gaze went through the motions of killing each other. It was after one in the morning when the orders came from Lee to withdraw. Many of them had been in battle since four the previous morning. Neither side was willing to quit. Slowly the Confederate troops backed away. Even more slowly the Union troops advanced forward. It was two in the morning when the last of Lee's men entered their new defenses. The battle had raged non-stop twenty-two hours. Hancock and Wright's men hastily threw up breastworks to protect them against a counter-attack and went to sleep—too tired to eat.

Hancock made sure his men were bedded down for the night before he lay down on his poncho to grab a few hours' sleep.

Seeing his men push forward and the battle ending, Wright called for his surgeon and had his wound attended. He inquired about the wounded Captain and was told he had been killed in the final assault.

Lee removed his sword, sat on his cot, picked up the dispatch that he had read just before leaving for the battlefield and re-read it. He ran his right hand through his hair, shook his head and let out a loud sigh.

"General Robert E. Lee
Commanding General of the Confederate States of America's Army of Northern
Virginia.

Dear General Lee,
I find that I must be the bearer of grave news. Yesterday afternoon at a cross roads near Yellow Tavern, General Stuart and his command encountered and fought against enemy Cavalry under the command of Philip Sheridan. During the battle, Major General Jeb Stuart was mortally wounded. He died during the night.
Respectfully yours,
Wade Hampton
Major General Army of Northern Virginia"

Tears filled the General's eyes.

"He was like my own son," whispered the old man.

He lay down on his cot and closed his eyes his thoughts carrying him back to when he first met Stuart on the Plains of West Point. Stuart, a young cadet, and Lee, the Superintendent.

The young, future officer became a regular at the Lee residence as Stuart and Lee's nephew, Fitzhugh, became close friends as well as classmates. After graduation from West Point, Stuart served under Lee in Texas and later was the older man's aide at Harper's Ferry when they captured John Brown. The young man's future seemed destined to be linked with his superintendent.

Washington, D.C—May 13, 7:00 AM,

Union President Abraham Lincoln was having coffee in his office when Stanton walked in.

"Good morning, Mr. Secretary. How are you?" asked Lincoln.

"Mr. President, I'm fine. As a matter of fact, I'm more than fine."

"YOU HEARD FROM GRANT DIDN'T YOU!" shouted an excited Lincoln springing from his chair.

"What does our General have to say?"

"Mr. President, it isn't much. It appears Grant is a man of few words. He says he fought Lee in the Wilderness and has pushed south and is now in front of Lee at Spotsylvania Court House. He states he needs supplies and Lee is well entrenched and ..." said Stanton.

"And, he wants more men to continue the campaign," interrupted Lincoln.

"Well, sir not exactly, perhaps you should read it for yourself," responded the portly Secretary of War.

Lincoln grabbed the dispatch, sat down, put on his glasses and began to read. He broke out into a big smile when he read the last line. "I propose to fight it out on this line if it takes all summer." The President slapped his right hand against his knee and let out a shout of joy.

"Alleluia, Stanton, we have ourselves a General who fights. Give this dispatch to the newspapers. I think the whole nation will rejoice with this news from Sam Grant," replied a happy Lincoln.

"Mr. President, I have Congressman Elihu Washburne waiting outside. He's been with Sam since the opening of the Campaign. I thought maybe you would like to speak with him," responded Stanton.

"Yes, Edwin, I'd like to speak with him. Please show him in."

Stanton escorted in the Congressman. Elihu Washburne was Grant's political benefactor. It was Washburne who first recommended Grant to the President to lead an Illinois Brigade and to be appointed a Brigadier General in 1862. It was Washburne who defended Grant when others in the Army were trying to get rid of him. Finally, it was this same Congressman who made the recommendation to Lincoln that Grant be appointed Lieutenant General of all the Union Armies. The slightly graying Congressman from Lincoln's home State entered the office.

"Good morning, Mr. President. General Grant sends his warmest regards," said Washburne as he took the seat offered by the President.

"Eli, tell me all about the campaign—leave nothing out. The fate of the entire Nation rests on Sam Grant," responded Lincoln.

Washburne told Lincoln and Stanton all about the past nine days. He told the pair about crossing into the Wilderness and the fierce fighting and Grant's refusal to retreat. He relayed the gallantry of Hancock and the stubborn defense made by Sedgwick. Lincoln's eyes grew sad when he heard about how hard Grant had taken Hays' and Sedgwick's death. The President felt sympathy for the man who had to order his friends to their death. He admired Grant for his willingness to fight and how he had taken the initiative away from Lee by shifting the campaign from the Wilderness to Spotsylvania.

Richmond, Virginia—May 13, 9:00 AM

While Grant rested and Washburne briefed the President, Confederate President Jefferson Davis was meeting with his Secretary of War, James Seddon, reviewing the latest dispatches from Lee.

"Mr. Seddon, it appears the Federals have engaged us on four fronts simultaneously. They have forced Lee out of the Wilderness and have been in constant contact with the Army of Northern Virginia for nine straight days," said Davis

"Mr. President, Grant doesn't appear to be the type who's going to give up easily. I think the only way to make him go away, is to completely annihilate his Army. It seems to me if he has only one soldier left standing, he would order him to attack," replied Seddon.

"James, I'm not worried about Grant, but I am concerned about Lee's latest dispatch. He's never sent me such an urgent request for reinforcements. The man has always fought with what he has. His loss in senior officers is staggering. Do you realize he has none of his original senior Commanders left? Lee is asking for reinforcements and I don't know where to get them," answered a frustrated Jeff Davis.

"Mr. President, General Lee suggests that maybe we can strip some forces from the coastal defenses and send them to him," responded Seddon.

"James, please meet with your staff and see which troops we can spare from our coastal defenses without jeopardizing our shipping lifeline," replied a tired Jeff Davis.

CHAPTER SEVEN

Resaca, Georgia—May 14, 6:00 AM

Sherman successfully disengaged from Johnston's front and moved the bulk of his Army through Snake Creek Gap and was now at the outskirts of Resaca. Sensing Sherman's move, Johnston shifted his Army during the night and occupied a defensive position protecting the Georgia city.

The sun had just crossed over the top of the mountains casting a dark shadow on the Union troops. Like an omen of evil it hid the men in blue from their Confederate foes. At six o'clock a lone signal cannon boomed its command to commence the assault. The weather favored the men of Lincoln's Army. The temperature was mild, the air crisp and clean. The slippery red Georgia clay had dried making the footing firm.

William Hardee's Corps held the Confederate center with Hood's Corps on his right and Polk' Corps on his left. Hardee, the battle-hardened former instructor at West Point, rode along his lines on his jet black mare, Midnight.

"Steady men ... hold your fire ... wait until you have a good target ... remember to aim low as your rifles will lift upward when you shoot," commanded Hardee.

John Palmer, the former Congressman from Illinois and political ally of Abraham Lincoln, led his Corps from Schofield's Army straight toward Hardee's center. When he was within a hundred yards of the breastworks, Palmer turned toward his men.

"MEN OF THE UNION—ATTACK!" shouted Palmer.

The Federals sprinted toward the entrenched men in gray quickly followed by the remainder of Schofield's men. Hardee gave the command to open fire. Instantly the air was filled with minie balls while a gray cloud of smoke hung over the firing rebels.

Palmer's men recoiled, took a breath and charged on. This time the minie balls were joined by grape and canister from Hardee's artillery. To the onrushing soldier they didn't know which was worse. The grape was two cannon balls linked together by six-foot iron chain. When fired from the cannon, the cannon balls would separate stretching the chain ripping apart anything in its path. Canister was like a huge shotgun shell containing ball bearings instead of lead shot. When fired from the cannon, the canister would split open and the ball bearings would spread out to a killing radius twenty feet wide. They were both designed to stop an infantry attack. Once again, Palmer's men recoiled and recovering they surged forward.

At the same time, Thomas watched intently as Union Major General Gordon Granger led the Fourth Corps into battle against Polk's dug-in troops followed quickly by the remainder of Thomas' Army. It was Granger who had ridden to Thomas' rescue during the battle of Chickamauga.

Granger coolly led his men into a hailstorm of leaden projectiles. As men fell wounded or killed, others would advance and take their place. Time and again Thomas' Army was pushed back only to rebound and move forward.

On the Union left it was the same as McPherson's Army slammed into the stubborn defenders of Hood's Corps, but were unable to breach the Confederate lines. After three long hours, Sherman called a halt to the attacks and asked his Army Commanders to join him for a strategy session. He was not yet done for the day.

As the attacks died down, Joe Johnston summoned his Corps Commanders for a strategy session of his own. He had made Sherman pay dearly. Even though he wished Sherman would leave; he knew better.

"Gentlemen, Sherman has been probing our defenses. He hopes to draw us into the open and then use his superior numbers to destroy us. We must be aggressive in defense and cautious in the advance," said Johnston.

"General Johnston, if Sherman withdraws after a probe, shouldn't we follow in pursuit? We can then use their withdrawal to our advantage. I know General Lee used this tactic very successfully in the East," suggested Hood innocently.

Johnston glared at the crippled Corps Commander. Hood had struck a nerve. Even though Johnston and Lee were good friends, they were rivals. It was Lee who replaced Johnston as Commander of the Army of Northern Virginia after he was wounded at the Battle of Fair Oaks. The rivalry was all on Johnston's part. Both Generals were loyal to the Confederate cause, but their tactics were different. Lee favored the advance, while Johnston favored defense.

"General Hood, General Lee is very successful, however, the terrain is different in Virginia and Sherman is a better General than Grant. To attack now will only mean disaster for this Army. We must stay on the defensive and wait for the right time to attack," replied Johnston fighting to remain calm.

Across the battlefield Sherman met with his Armies' commanders.

"Johnston has repelled us on all fronts. Hitting him straight on is a mistake as he is too strongly entrenched. Therefore, I'd like Thomas to engage Johnston in the center of his line. George, I just want you to demonstrate against his defenses. Use Palmer's Fourth Corps in the advance supported by the Twenty-Third Corps from Schofield's Army.

"James, when Palmer and the Twenty-third are fully engaged, I want you to order Logan's Fifteenth Corps around Johnston's left flank. Their orders are to take the hill overlooking the railroad bridge. Once Logan takes the position, he must hold it against all hazards.

"John, at the same time your Army will assail Johnston's right occupied by Hood's Corps. Hooker will be in support."

Sherman's commanders gave him a surprised look. He was going to hit Johnston on all sides at the same time. The coordination would be difficult given the terrain. Sherman wasn't finished.

"Mac, while all this is going on, I want you to send a Brigade ten miles downriver. They're to build a pontoon bridge and cross the Oostanaula. This will place us in Johnston's rear. His supply lines will be threatened and he'll be forced to abandon Resaca. With Resaca in our hands, it will mean the fall of the industrial city of Rome."

Sherman knew the movements would be difficult, but he trusted his commanders and their men.

Resaca, Georgia—May 14, 2:00 PM,

Hardee watched in disbelief as Palmer's Corps began their advance. He couldn't believe Sherman was actually going to attack his position. He rode along his line instructing his Brigade Commanders to wait until the Union troops were within range.

Unknown to his adversary, Palmer ordered his Corps to stop just out of musket range. He dressed his line and ordered his skirmishers forward followed by the rest of his men. Slowly the Union forces advanced, firing as they walked. It was an attack but it was very slow in developing. Palmer was doing his job. He was occupying Hardee while the rest of Sherman's command carried out their roles.

Then, without reason, Palmer decided to change the demonstration into a full attack. Unsupported except for the Twenty-Third Corps he ordered his men forward at a run. The boys in blue broke into a run and surged forward with wild abandon. Five thousand Confederate muskets answered the charge. Lead projectiles filled the air. Smoke from the guns partially masked the defenders. When they were less than fifty yards from the Confederates, Palmer's men gave up and withdrew. They back pedaled two hundred yards until they were out of range, caught their breath, reformed and charged again. Four times they attacked and four times they were repulsed.

As Palmer's men withdrew for the last time, Schofield ordered Howard and Hooker to begin their attack against Hood's position. The Union men started at a brisk walk. When they were within a hundred yards of Hood's position, they broke into a run. As with Palmer's attack; it was quickly repulsed. Bloodied, but determined, the men of Schofield's Army reformed and charged again only to meet the same results. Sherman's plan was working. He was keeping Johnston's army occupied with meaningless assaults.

Hardee, Polk and Johnston watched Hood's men protect the Army's flank. It was as if they were watching a play. They watched in awe as projectiles tore into flesh and ripped apart limbs. Hood was handling his Corps with great professionalism.

Suddenly the scene shifted. The three Generals watched in disbelief as Hood ordered a counter-attack against the retreating Federals. The Confederates were outnumbered with no hope for success.

Angrily, Johnston turned to Polk.

"General Hood will have to answer to me for this. Mark my words he will ruin this Army by his rash behavior."

The Confederate Commander quickly called for a courier.

"Take this order to General Hood immediately. He is to abandon his attack before he's destroyed," said an angry Johnston.

Polk turned to Johnston and whispered.

"I'm afraid that by the time the courier reaches Hood it will be too late."

"You're right Leonidas, but I had to do something," replied the Virginian lowering his head in disappointment.

Hood's men fired a final volley as they left their entrenchments and pursued the retiring blue coats. After fifty yards they stopped, loaded their weapons and fired at the retreating Union troops. The air was filled with the smoke of ignited gunpowder followed by the fierce rebel yell as the pursuit continued.

A hundred yards away, the men of Hooker's and Howard's Corps were attempting to reform when the projectiles struck. The survivors looked up at the charging Confederates and retreated further. Officers pleaded to no avail with their men to hold their ground as the Federals sprinted for the rear.

Hood had learned his lessons well from Stonewall Jackson and Robert E. Lee. His mentors had shown him on several occasions that if you charge a retreating enemy before they can regroup, you can escalate an orderly retreat into a panicked rout.

Johnston and Polk watched in disbelief as Hood's Corps pushed the Federals back. They watched in awe as the Federals orderly retreat rapidly escalated into an undignified dash for the rear. The Union flank was in danger of being rolled up.

Hood watched his men with pride as they pushed the enemy back.

"Our boys are grand. Now all Johnston has to do is press our advantage and victory is ours," said Hood to his aide.

Hooker and Howard were alarmed by the fierceness of Hood's counterattack; however, they had held back a sufficient reserve force specifically in the event of this scenario. In addition, Sherman had ordered Schofield to be prepared to support the duo if the need arose. The Union troops had gone almost a mile when they noticed reinforcements arriving. The reserve force formed a horseshoe with the open end toward the charging Confederates.

The unsuspecting, unsupported Southern troops, caught up in the heat of the chase, unwittingly rushed into the middle of the horseshoe. Gunfire erupted on three sides of the surprised butternuts. Hood's battle-tested troops knew better than to stay. Quickly they sprinted back to the safety of their entrenchments. The Union troops pursued the retreating Confederates, but stopped just out of gunshot range. Order returned to Sherman's left flank.

Hood's mood turned from elation to fury as he watched his men's rapid withdrawal. Before he could say a word to anyone, Johnston's courier arrived ordering Hood to abandon the attack. The crippled General stared at the courier. Fire blazed from Hood's eyes, his body shook as he fought to control his temper.

"Inform General Johnston his orders have been obeyed," said Hood.

"If only General Lee was in command. He would've given me the support to break Sherman's lines. If only the Almighty could duplicate Lee," thought Hood as the courier rode away."

No sooner had Hood's men settled back into their entrenchments than the air was, once again, filled with the sound of musketry. Johnston looked to see where the sound was coming from. There was no attack in front of Hood,

Hardee or Polk. The sounds were coming from the extreme Confederate left and rear. He soon realized the earlier attacks were just a ruse to hold attention. The Virginian reeled his horse around and rode to the sound of the guns.

As he galloped to the sound of the battle, he quickly surmised Sherman was attempting to take the hill overlooking the railroad. If successful, the enemy would hold the high ground. He knew he must retake the hill before the Federals could move artillery into position and shell the exposed Southerners.

Polk, coming to the same realization as Johnston, ordered a counter-attack. It was a suicide mission for the Confederates. Up the hill they charged and down the hill they retreated. The incline, coupled with the amount of firepower from the Union troops, made short work of the Confederate attacks. Six thousand Yankees stubbornly held the hill. After two hours of constant combat darkness set-in putting an end to the day's bloodletting.

A worried Joe Johnston returned to his headquarters to contemplate tomorrow's action. He sat in his tent alone and reflected on the day's events. The wily Virginian peered over a map of the terrain trying to find some way to flank Sherman. After several futile minutes, he came to the conclusion that Hood should attack at first light. He would support Hood with a Division from both Polk's and Hardee's Corps. He issued the orders and then lay down on his cot to grab some sleep. It had been a long day.

An hour later he was awakened by the loud voice of a courier halting his mount. "Is General Johnston here?" inquired the young rider.

"The General has gone to bed," replied the guard at the tent flap.

Before the courier could respond Johnston was outside.

"I'm General Johnston, what news do you have?"

The young man saluted. "I have an urgent message from General Wheeler. My orders are to wait for a reply, sir."

Johnston opened the dispatch and shook his head in disbelief. He re-entered his quarters.

> *"General Johnston, Yankees are at Lays Ferry 12 miles south of your position. It appears to be at least one Division. They are making preparations to cross in the morning. I shall delay as them long as possible, but do not have enough men to prevent it. Please advise me as to your wishes.*
> *Your obedient servant,*
> *Joe Wheeler"*

Joe Johnston grabbed a pencil and wrote underneath.

"Hold the enemy on their side of the river. Help is on the way."
Joe Johnston"

Emerging from his tent he handed the message to the young courier.

"Ride as quickly as you can to General Wheeler and give him this reply."

The young man jerked the horse's reins hard and sped off. No sooner had Wheeler's courier departed than another courier came bounding into camp. This time it was an urgent message from Polk informing the Commanding General that the blue coats had moved long-range artillery on top of the high ground. From their position, the Union troops could easily shell the railway and turnpike bridges endangering their line of retreat.

As he was digesting Polk's report of bad news, another courier arrived. This one from Hood. The Texan reported Union troops had left Dalton and had reinforced Schofield.

Johnston peered over the maps and decided on a new plan. He cancelled Hood's attack and decided to wait for Sherman to make the next move. He then ordered Hardee to send Walker's Division to Lays Ferry to prevent the enemy from crossing.

At the same time Johnston ordered his engineers to ride to Cassville and prepare defensive fortifications. If Walker couldn't stop the Federals from crossing, he would have to abandon Resaca.

While Johnston reacted to the news his couriers brought him, Sherman met with his Commanders to plan their strategy for the fifteenth. The five men, including Hooker, sat at a makeshift table. The red-haired Sherman sat at the head. To his right were McPherson and Schofield. Opposite them, sitting by himself, was George Thomas. Directly across at the foot of the table sat the arrogant Hooker.

Candles flickered in the cool mountain air. The smell of Georgia pine had replaced the stench of sulfur. Darkness covered the horror of the day's battles. The stillness of the night was pierced with the cries of the wounded as surgeons amputated mangled limbs.

"Gentlemen, today's attacks were not wasted. We've taken the high ground overlooking the railroad. Mac, we must reinforce those men tomorrow. Joe Johnston will attack the hill with everything he has. We must hold the high ground at all costs," said Sherman in a tired, determined voice.

"I want you all to dig in and wait. If Johnston attacks, we'll smash his Army. Mac, have you heard from Sweeny? Has he crossed the river yet?" asked Sherman.

The Army of Tennessee Commander looked at his mentor and cleared his throat.

"I received a courier from him just before leaving my headquarters. He's found a ford in the river and is about 12 miles south of Resaca. He plans to start crossing at first light.

The five men talked through the plan many times, making slight modifications as different scenarios were discussed. At one in the morning, the meeting broke up and the Generals returned to their commands.

Resaca, Georgia—May 15, 5:00 AM,

Joe Johnston paced back and forth like a caged lion. On one hand he was hoping Sherman would attack his well-entrenched troops, while at the same time he was praying Sherman would not use the advantage of the high ground. The Union General had again outflanked him. The red-haired Federalist had stolen the initiative.

Across the battlefield William Sherman also paced, a thousand thoughts rambled through his mind, but only one reoccurred. Why hadn't Johnston attacked? Sherman would have bet everything he owned the Virginian would have followed up on Hood's success the previous day.

The sun climbed higher in the sky as the morning wore on. Sherman was growing impatient. If Johnston wouldn't attack him, he would modify his plan and strike first.

The Federal Commander stopped pacing and went inside his tent to write out his orders. He would have McPherson open fire on Johnston's rear from the high ground. When Mac started his bombardment, Thomas would advance against Hardee who was holding the center of the Confederate line. When Thomas' attack was at its peak, both Hooker and Schofield would attack the enemy right flank held by Hood. At the same time McPherson would hit Polk's troops holding the Confederate left. If Johnston reacted the way he hoped, the rebel Commander would pull troops from both his flanks to support Hardee's defense. With the flanks weakened; McPherson, Hooker and Schofield should be able to collapse Johnston's Army from the sides.

A half hour later Sherman emerged from his tent; handed his orders to his Chief-of-Staff and watched as couriers sped out of camp. The Union General placed a cigar in his mouth, lit it and took a deep drag. As he slowly let out the smoke, he glanced down at his pocket watch. It was nine-thirty. He set the time of McPherson's bombardment for eleven and Thomas' attack for eleven fifteen. By a quarter to twelve the entire Army should be engaged.

At precisely eleven o'clock McPherson's cannons on top of Railroad Hill opened fire on Johnston's reserves. Supply wagons were thrown six feet in the air as the Union long-range artillery found its targets. Tethered horses bucked in all directions pulling on their bindings in an effort to escape. Teamsters fought to control the fear-filled beasts. Shrapnel flew in all directions tearing into man and beast as ammunition wagons exploded.

As the men on Railroad Hill created havoc on Johnston's reserves, Thomas' troops stepped lively across the no man's land between the lines. Hardee's men were well fortified and protected. When the Federals were within a hundred yards, the Confederates opened fire. The air was instantly filled with objects of death and destruction as the Southern infantry and artillery opened fire. Huge gaps were torn in the Union lines. The attackers recoiled. Quickly they reformed their lines and pressed forward.

Throughout the remainder of the morning Johnston received messages from his Corps Commanders. Hardee was being pressed by Thomas, but felt he could hold. Hood had easily repulsed Hooker and Schofield. McPherson had temporarily pushed Polk back, but the Corps Commander put in his reserve troops and pushed McPherson back to his original lines.

By noon the Union attacks had died down. Sherman realized Johnston was too strongly entrenched. He would have to flank the Virginian out of Resaca. Success now hung on what happened at Lay's Ferry.

At one o'clock a courier arrived at Johnston's headquarters and reported Walker was approaching Lay's Ferry. No blue coats were in the vicinity. The reports of a crossing at the Ferry were untrue.

Johnston stared at the message for a few minutes and then called for two couriers.

"Sergeant, ride back to General Walker and tell him to return to this Army at once," said a frustrated Johnson.

Turning to the second courier, he continued.

"Tell General Hood the Commanding General wishes for him to attack as soon as practical. Tell him I believe the earlier repulses along our entire line have seriously weakened the enemy."

Within an hour Johnston heard the sound of Hood's signal cannon. The attack had begun. It started brilliantly. Hood's men drove back Hooker and Schofield's men easily. Neither Union General had believed the Confederates would dare to attack. They neglected to dig in. Hood's attack had caught them flat-footed. In spite of Sherman's warnings, his subordinates had ignored him and now were paying the price.

Resaca, Georgia—May 15, 1:30 PM,

Couriers from Schofield and Hooker arrived at Sherman's Headquarters requesting reinforcements. Before the commanding General could issue orders, another courier arrived; this one from George Thomas.

"General Sherman," panted the young Sergeant. "General Thomas wishes me to report that Hood has attacked Hooker and Schofield and has driven them back a half-mile. He's ordered his reserves forward in support and they should be hitting the rebels in their flank within a half-hour."

"Tell General Thomas, well done."

Turning to the other couriers he said, "Ride back to your Generals and tell them they must hold a while longer—reinforcements are on the way."

The couriers had just ridden away when another courier rode briskly into camp; this one from Sweeney's Headquarters. The horseman reined his lathered mount to an abrupt halt.

"General Sweeny wishes to report his Division along with Kilpatrick's Cavalry have successfully crossed the Oostanaula River at Lay's Ferry as ordered. He's ordered his men to take an hour's rest and then proceed north to Resaca."

Sherman smiled at the officer. He had Johnston just where he wanted him.

"Captain, this is the best news of the day. Rest for an hour, grab a fresh mount and return to General Sweeny with my compliments. Tell him to press forward at all possible speed."

The red-haired Union Commander returned to his tent and began making plans to capture Johnston and his Army. He no longer worried about Hood's attack. Thomas knew what had to be done. Sherman concentrated fully on the maps on the table in front of him. His fingers traced lines around Resaca and the surrounding towns. He took a pencil and paper and sketched out his plan. He would no sooner finish, then, crumble the paper and throw it to the ground. His mind worked at a feverish pace.

The sudden boom of Thomas' artillery startled him. He had forgotten about the impending attack. The sound of rifle fire was quickly added to the cannonade. A mile away Hood's men were being ripped to pieces by the flank attack.

Hood quickly realized he was outnumbered, outflanked and outgunned by the Federal buzz saw. The fierce Confederate General ordered a withdrawal before his Corps was annihilated or captured.

The sun was beginning to set when Sherman's Commanders arrived at his headquarters. Thomas was the first to arrive.

"Excellent work today, George," said Sherman.

The reclusive Commander smiled and went inside. Hooker and Schofield arrived at the same time. McPherson a few minutes later. The men sat inside the tent. The front flap was up to allow in the cool night air. The smell of burning wood from the campfires filled the air.

"Gentlemen, earlier today I received word from Sweeney. He and Kilpatrick's Cavalry have crossed the Oostanaula and are in Johnston's rear. The Confederates must either fight on two fronts simultaneously or retreat. It is my opinion that tonight Johnston will retreat. He'll fall back toward Atlanta following the railroad.

"Mac, I want you to take your Army and proceed toward Lay's Ferry. You're to cross the Oostanaula and unite with Sweeney's Division. You're then to march north toward Johnston's Army. You are to leave at three in the morning."

Sherman lit a cigar and turned to Schofield.

"John, at sunrise I want you to feel Johnston's right. If he's there, you're to wait until Mac hits him and then strike hard. If Johnston has abandoned his front, you're to push through Resaca and proceed to Field's Ferry. You're to cross the Oostanaula at Field's and proceed south in pursuit of the rebs. I'm going to detach Hooker's Corps from George's Army in support."

The always calm Thomas sat back in his chair and watched intently as Sherman took a deep draw on his cigar, then slowly let the smoke flow out of his mouth. The red-haired General turned toward the Virginian.

"George, I want your Army to be the main pursuer. Mac and John will be covering your flanks. You are to closely follow Johnston. At sunrise I want you to feel the rebs center. If they are still there, I want to hold off attacking and wait until Mac is engaged. I want you to send two regiments to the high ground to replace Mac's troops. From their vantage point, they'll be able to see when Mac attacks. Make sure they have some signalmen. Once you receive the signal Mac is engaged, you'll attack. If you discover Johnston is gone, you're to begin your pursuit."

The Generals stood and peered over the map spread on Sherman's table. They repeated the plan just to make sure that they each fully understood their roles and those of their counterparts. In spite of whatever differences they had, their ultimate survival depended on each other. After an hour, they adjourned and had supper together.

Sherman was awake early the next morning. Soon after sunrise reports began to arrive from Schofield and Thomas that Johnston had withdrawn and they were in pursuit.

CHAPTER EIGHT

Spotsylvania, Virginia—May 18, 5:00 AM

Grant sat on his favorite horse, Cincinnati, waiting for the attack to begin. Knowing he needed to reinforce his decimated Army, he left a skeleton crew to guard the coastline and ordered the remaining heavy artillery units to Spotsylvania. The eight thousand replacements were a welcome sight to Meade and his Generals, in particular Hancock, who needed fresh troops the most.

As the sky brightened, the replacements were about to get their first taste of combat. Grant had decided not to push another attack at the "Mule Shoe". Instead he opted for a flank attack. For two days he shifted troops from the "Mule Shoe" to Lee's right. The Confederate Commander countered by shifting his forces to parry the thrust.

Assuming Lee had stripped his troops from their previous position, he had Wright and Hancock secretly double-back hoping to catch his adversary flat-footed.

The reinforcements had arrived in time to join the assault. Hancock rode along his line. He was going to throw the Divisions of Gibbons and Barlow against Gordon's Division while Wright was going to throw the Divisions of Ricketts and Neill against Rodes Division. The Union front stretched a half-mile across and a mile deep.

When Hancock reached the end of Gibbon's Division, he was met by his peer and friend, Horatio Wright.

"Good morning, Win" said Wright. "How're you holding up? I was told that your Gettysburg wound is acting up."

Hancock looked at the goateed General from Connecticut.

"Thank you for asking. My wound was giving me some trouble the past few days, but it seems much better now. I'm glad the damn rain has stopped. It's going to be tough enough to cross this field without having to worry about slipping on our asses in the mud."

"Win, if Grant is right and Lee has only scattered remnants of Ewell's Corps in this section and we take the 'Mule Shoe', then Lee is finished. We'll have him flanked on the right and rear.

"Horatio, we've both been fighting Lee since the Peninsula Campaign and we both know the old man isn't going to be fooled so easily. I have faith in Grant and, so far, he has led us admirably; but this time he's mistaken," answered Hancock.

Slowly the early morning darkness gave way to the new day's dawn. The eastern sky began to brighten. The shadows of the enemy entrenchments started to take form. Union artillery commenced its pre-attack barrage, quickly followed by the infantry assault.

Men in blue surged forward across the open field they had dubbed "Hell's Half Acre." Veterans and replacements marched side-by-side. For the artillerymen converted to infantry, it would be their first time in combat. Only time would tell how well they would withstand the rigors.

John Gordon watched the Union assault as he rode among his troops urging his men to hold their fire until he gave the order. He and Rodes had decided to let the Federals come well within range before giving the order to open fire.

Hancock watched intently as his men closed in on the Confederate line.

"If there were rebs in the trenches, their artillery would have begun to fire by now," thought Hancock.

Abruptly the air was filled with the lead of two thousand projectiles as the Confederate Generals gave the order to open fire. Artillery rounds joined the musketry of the infantry. Huge gaps were torn from the ranks of the attackers as men were felled by exploding cannon shells and bullets. The cries of the wounded were mixed with the sound of the battle. The stench of disemboweled men was intermingled with the odor of gunpowder.

Hancock's and Wright's men recoiled. Quickly they reformed and charged again. Once more they were repulsed. Again they reformed and charged with the same result. After an hour, Grant halted the bloodletting. He would rest his men and try another tactic.

As a disappointed Grant rode back to his tent he noticed a young, wounded officer sitting with his back against a tree. Bloody froth blew from the man's mouth as death approached. He was shot in the chest. Grant dismounted and walked toward the dying man when a Union courier galloped by. Mud from the courier's horse splashed into the face of the wounded man. A pitiful look of pain appeared on his face as if to say, "what else can happen."

Seeing Grant approaching the man, Horace Porter, quickly dismounted, sprinted to the youth and wiped the mud from the man's face. He looked up at Porter, smiled and then died.

"General, he is out of his suffering now."

Grant's eyes became moist.

"Find me that courier. I want his damn hide. Don't come back without him."

The two men remounted and rode away, Grant to his tent and Porter on his quest.

The Commanding General was in a foul mood. His disposition didn't improve as he entered his tent. Seated at his desk was John Rawlins.

Rawlins was the only man, with the exception of Sherman, who would dare approach the General when he was in this mood.

"I heard it didn't go well today. I have some telegrams here that are not going to improve your day or mood. Do you want to see them now or would you rather wait?" asked Rawlins.

"Hell, John. Just tell me what's in them," replied a dejected Grant.

"The first is from Franz Sigel. He said he's outnumbered and is retiring from the Shenandoah Valley to regroup his forces and plan his strategy."

"I'll plan his next move! Wire Halleck and tell him to relieve Sigel from command and to replace him with Hunter. Sigel is a political General. I hope Lincoln won't give me grief on this issue."

"I don't think it's going to be a problem. The next telegram is from Stanton giving you permission to do just that. I also have a telegram from Banks in Louisiana. It pretty well reads the same as Sigel's. Have to regroup, etcetera," replied Rawlins.

"Wire Halleck and ask him to remove Banks and replace him with Canby. I like Banks, but war is no place for sentiment. Banks is also a political appointee. I hope Lincoln agrees with this one."

"Sam, once again the Secretary concurs. The last telegram is from Butler. He reports that he's been driven from Drewy's Bluff outside of Richmond and he has regrouped at the Bermuda Hundred on the Peninsula. He also reports that Beauregard is now in charge of the Richmond defenses."

"Leave Butler in place, he's too influential. When the time is right, I'll remove him. With Butler bottled up by Beauregard, it means Lee will soon be receiving reinforcements."

Grant sat on his cot and rubbed his temples. He had a bad headache.

"Well, John, the only way to counteract Lee's reinforcements is to retake the initiative and drive him back toward Richmond. Inform Meade I expect Lee to attack us either later today or early tomorrow morning. I want all of our men to be ready—especially those in the rear."

The two friends' conversation was interrupted by a familiar face, Ronald Lyons.

"Colonel Comstock said you wanted to see me," said Lyons wiping his brow.

"Ron, I have another mission for you. I want you to leave camp tonight and head south. I plan to drive Lee toward Richmond and I must know what to expect. These maps are shit. Take your time and report back to me when you've gathered sufficient information. I must know how many troops the rebs have around Richmond and on the Peninsula," said Grant.

"General, consider it done," replied Lyons wiping his brow.

"Are you all right?" asked Rawlins. "You seem to be sweating."

"Just a cold," answered the Captain coughing.

"You take care of yourself, young man," admonished Grant.

"Will do," responded Lyons as he saluted and left the tent.

"John, please leave me now. I must plan my next move," said Sam Grant softly. "Make sure no one disturbs me."

White House, Washington D.C.—May 18, 4:00 PM

Abraham Lincoln sat at his desk dictating a letter of thanks to Pennsylvania Governor Andrew Curtin for his support of the Administration. Across from him sat his trusted private Secretary, John Nicolay.

The slender thirty-two year old, dark-haired Nicolay was a newspaper editor when he first met Lincoln in 1854. The two men became instant friends. When Lincoln was elected President, he had asked the young man to be his private secretary. The Chief Executive often took the younger man into his confidence and was able to relay his fears for the Country, the Army and his own hidden feelings without worrying they would find their way into print.

Seated next to Nicolay was Lincoln's assistant private secretary, John Hay. Like Nicolay, Hay was slender and young. Only twenty-six years old, he had also earned Lincoln's confidence.

The President had just finished the letter when the three men were joined by Secretary of War, Edwin Stanton.

"How are you today, Edwin?" inquired the President in a jovial tone.

"Fine, Mr. President, thank you for asking. Sir, I have some dispatches we should go over in private," replied the portly Secretary of War sitting down on the overstuffed sofa.

Hay and Nicolay left the room.

"Mr. President, have you seen Horace Greeley's latest editorial in the New York Herald?"

"I haven't had the chance. What does Mr. Greeley say now?"

"He writes that you have led the Country to ruin and you should not run again for President. He continues his diatribe for two columns. Mr. President, have you decided what you're going to do?" Are you going to run again? The convention is only a few months away."

"Edwin, I have pondered long and hard on that subject. At this time I just don't know. A week ago the people were happy about Grant forcing Lee backward. Then they found out the cost of victory in the Wilderness was sixteen thousand men killed and wounded. That was quickly followed by the additional loss of seventeen thousand men killed and wounded at Spotsylvania. If we don't have a decisive victory indicating the end is near before the convention, not only won't we win re-election, but in my opinion, our Republican Party may be doomed. Perhaps Greeley is right."

"No, Mr. President, he isn't right," interrupted Stanton. "A lesser man would have given in by now and let the Union be dissolved. Sir, you are the right man for the job. Whatever your decision is, I want you to know I am behind you one hundred percent."

Spotsylvania, Virginia—May 19, 4:30 AM

Lee awoke early in the morning feeling better. His mood was bolstered further when a courier arrived from Ewell reporting that during the night Hancock's Division had abandoned their position. If Grant was retreating, he must act now. He decided to send Ewell's Corps around the left of the enemy while leaving a single Brigade from Rodes Division to hold Warren in place. Ewell was to screen his movements by using the woods as cover; then strike Grant's columns while they were on the move. When he was fully engaged, Early, commanding A.P. Hill's Corps, would attack in support. Anderson, commanding Longstreet's Corps, would remain in reserve ready to take advantage of any opportunity which presented itself. The aged Commander calculated that if Ewell was to leave within the hour, the attack would begin between four-thirty and five in the afternoon.

A mile away Grant issued orders to move the remainder of his Army to the left toward Richmond, forcing Lee to leave his trenches and either attack or move between him and Richmond. Yesterday's attack convinced him Lee's position was too strong.

Throughout the day, Grant busied himself with business outside of Spotsylvania. He read Sherman's telegram explaining how he had outflanked Johnston from two formidable positions losing only three thousand four hundred men and was now in hot pursuit of the retreating rebels. He smiled as he put the message down. Grant was rapidly coming to the conclusion that if the Union was going to win the war, it would be up to Sherman and him to do so. He would use his other Armies as diversions to keep Jefferson Davis from reinforcing Lee and Johnston.

It was nearly five o'clock in the evening when Grant finally finished his correspondence. His staff had prepared an early dinner for the General. They knew, with the Army about to move, tomorrow would be a long day. As the General began to eat, he heard the sound of gunfire. He quickly sprang up and called for Horace Porter.

"Colonel Porter, please ride to General Meade and have him dispatch as many troops as necessary to check the enemy advance. Find out what is going on and report back to me. I think Lee is trying to turn our left flank. If that's the case, then tell General Meade that Hancock is to cut off the enemy lines of retreat. I will send Comstock to Burnside to do the same. Colonel, you must stress to the line officers that we have a unique opportunity to destroy or capture a good portion of Lee's Army."

Rodes and Gordon had slipped their Divisions between Hancock and Burnside's Corps and crossed the Ny River undetected. The Confederate Generals took their time so as not to raise any dust or commotion, which may alert the Union troops. After crossing the Ny they came upon the Union supply wagons staged at Harris's farm. It was guarded by only a Division. Taking a page from Stonewall Jackson at Chancellorsville, the two young Confederate Officers aligned their men quickly and quietly. When they were ready, they attacked simultaneously.

The Union troops were an untested heavy artillery Division stationed around Washington under the command of Brigadier General Robert Tyler. This would be their "baptism under fire." Many hoped it would not be their last. The six-foot, balding, former West Point graduate from New York quickly placed his men in a defensive line. Although outnumbered and untested, the former artillerymen held their ground.

It was a slugfest as the men in gray crashed into the men in blue with no trenches to protect either side. Fighting was hand-to-hand. Men on both sides fought with animal savagery biting and clawing to survive.

The Battle raged for a half hour when fresh troops from Hancock's Division arrived pushing the Confederates back. Gordon rode to the front of his Division. Waving his sword he rallied his men, stopping the counter-attack. With the Federals temporarily in check, Gordon and Rodes slowly retreated with Tyler and Hancock's men in pursuit. Four hours later the men in gray were back within the safety of their trenches. The attack had cost the Union nine hundred men killed and wounded. Lee's misreading of Grant's intentions had cost him thirteen hundred troops which he could not easily replace. The Union General-in-Chief was disappointed he had not been able to bag the rebs. He postponed the movement around Lee until tomorrow deciding to let his men rest.

Cassville, Georgia—May 19, 5:00 PM

Sherman eagerly pursued Johnston. Convinced his adversary was preparing a strong defensive position at Kingston, he ordered all his Commanders to proceed with all possible speed. They mustn't give Johnston time to dig in.

The wily Confederate General, realizing Sherman had divided his Army into thirds, decided to divide his Army into two parts. He would place Hardee's Corps at Kingston and have them spread out to make them appear to be the entire Army. Hardee's orders were simple. Hold Thomas and McPherson in place. At the same time Hood's and Polk's Corps' were to wait in the hills and forests around Cassville. When Schofield's isolated Army passed, they were to hit him hard. Their orders were simple. Destroy Schofield!

Johnston waited at his headquarters near Kingston for news of Hood's and Polk's attack. The morning passed without any reports. He sent his Chief-of-Staff, John Mackall, to see what was going on.

While Schofield marched unexpectedly into the deadly ambush, a Brigade from Joe Hooker's Corps assigned to guard the Union left flank, had gotten lost. Being the advance of the Army, the Brigade had taken a wrong turn in the dense Georgia forest. They followed roads and trails not on any map in hopes of rejoining the Army. The Brigade Commander knew his Division Commander, Daniel Butterfield would have a big chunk of his hide and whatever was left would be sent to Hooker. If anything remained of his hide after Hooker, it would be sent to Schofield and maybe even Sherman.

Hood waited patiently as Schofield's unsuspecting Army came into view. The crippled Corps Commander turned to his Chief-of-Staff and spoke in a low whisper.

"Shoup, they haven't a clue what's going to happen to them in less than an hour."

"You're right, General. They haven't even put out a guard on their left flank, it's in the air."

"As my poor dead friend Stonewall Jackson would say, Providence has smiled upon us. It is the exposed left which we'll hit. Schofield has marched his Army to destruction or surrender," replied Hood smiling.

While the two men discussed the upcoming battle, a courier galloped behind them and reined his horse hard.

"General Hood," panted the excited courier. "Federals have been spotted in our rear."

"Where?" asked the Corps Commander.

"They're on our right marching north to take us in the rear. It's at least a Brigade from Butterfield's Division. They'll be here in less than a half hour," replied the courier.

"Shoup, send couriers to our Division Commanders and have them pull back to our line of defense. Send another courier to General Polk explaining our change of position and why," ordered Hood.

Mackall reached Hood as he was changing his position. The Corps Commander explained the reasons why he cancelled the attack. Johnston's Chief-of-Staff galloped back to the Army Commander to inform him of the sudden change in developments.

Johnston's temper flared.

"That's hogwash! Polk's Cavalry would've spotted any damn Yankees in our rear. Hood overreacted! We've lost a golden opportunity to cripple Sherman. If we continue to fail to take advantage of opportunities offered to us, we lose this campaign."

The Virginian issued orders for Hardee to disengage from Thomas and march to Cassville. He would make a stand there. His men were tired. In less than four days Sherman had pushed them south thirty-two miles. Everyday was filled with skirmishing as Union advance troops collided with the Confederate rear guard.

Schofield was surprised when his advance companies reported rebels in the woods to their left. He was even more surprised when he heard they were breaking camp. The General sent word to Sherman of Hood's position and cautiously advanced his men in battle formation.

Sherman received Schofield's message at the same time he was informed by Thomas, that Hardee was abandoning Kingston moving east. The red-haired Commander quickly surmised his adversary was consolidating at Cassville and ordered Thomas and McPherson to follow the Confederates.

Johnston had chosen a wooded ridge southeast of Cassville to make his stand, while Sherman chose a ridge northeast of the hamlet. Townspeople sought refuge outside the small village as artillery rounds from both sides screamed overhead. Occasionally a shell would fall short increasing the panic of the civilians.

As the moon rose over Cassville, Johnston called a council of war. For three hours the Senior Officers argued about what to do next. Johnston and Hardee wanted to fortify their current position and wait for Sherman to attack, while Hood and Polk favored retreating.

"Gentlemen, for three hours we have debated the pros and cons of our situation. It is obvious that neither Generals Hood nor Polk like this position. If I can't have concurrence, I have no other choice but to order a withdrawal. Their lack of confidence would be ultimately transmitted to their men making resistance to Sherman's attacks a risk," said an irate Johnston.

"Sir, I feel you're doing both Polk and I a disservice. You're the Army's Commander and if you feel we are wrong, then it's your duty to override our opinions. Let me state for the record, at no time ever in my career as a soldier did I do anything to sabotage or circumvent my Commanding Officer's orders. At Gettysburg, I disagreed with Longstreet's orders to attack the Devil's Den. He said orders were orders and they came from General Lee. Sir, I did my best to take the position and lost the use of an arm in the process. I resent the implication," responded an angry Hood.

"General Hood, I really don't care about your opinion or outrage. If you wish to resign from this Army, you may. But in my official report I'll cite whatever reason influenced me the most."

The adopted Texan glared at Johnston, eyes full of fire. He bit the inside of his check as he struggled to maintain his composure. The tent was filled with tension. After several minutes Hood retorted.

"General Johnston, I'll not resign my commission. I've fought for the cause just as hard or harder than any man in this room and I'll not be shuffled off or forced to resign. Now, sir, if you would please give us your orders."

"Gentlemen, your orders are to abandon our trenches, move through Cassville, cross the Etowah River and take positions at Allatoona. We must move swiftly so we can fortify before Sherman follows. Hood's Corps is to leave first, followed by Polk's. Hardee's men will be the rear guard. If there are no questions, you're dismissed."

Hood glared at Johnston as he left the room. Both men would do their duty, but the closeness needed for success between a Commander and his direct subordinates would never be there again.

Sherman woke to find the Confederates had abandoned their lines during the night. Johnston had stolen another march on the Ohioan. He rested his men while he waited word from his Cavalry Commander to tell him where Johnston was headed. Within two hours he received word that his adversary had withdrawn to Allatoona.

While a young Lieutenant, Sherman was assigned to this region of Georgia. He knew it better than most of the Confederate Commanders. He knew the mountain passes surrounding Allatoona afforded his adversary a distinct advantage. He sat in his tent and contemplated his next move. He had no choice but to flank Johnston out of position; however, before he could start another flanking movement, he would have to resupply his men. Food and forage were low.

North Georgia was heavily wooded with very few large farms or plantations. Johnston's Cavalry had taken or destroyed most of the crops or livestock. The rural population feared the Confederate Cavalry almost as much as they did the Union horsemen. Sherman had counted on some food and forage coming from the countryside. The Virginian was going to make it as uncomfortable for the Ohioan as humanly possible. Sherman's thoughts were interrupted by the arrival of his Chief Engineer, Orlando Poe.

"You sent for me, sir?" inquired the thirty-two year old. It was Poe's defenses which stymied Longstreet's attack on Knoxville the previous November. The five-foot ten-inch, engineer from Ohio had become a favorite of Sherman.

"Ah, Poe," replied Sherman looking up from his maps.

"I want you to take your engineers along with a Brigade of Infantry and go back to Resaca to repair the railroad bridge Wheeler's Cavalry destroyed. This must be accomplished within two days. Supply trains from Chattanooga are stuck at Resaca and cannot proceed to us. The men are in need of food and the animals forage."

Poe stroked his beard, thought for a moment and answered.

"General, I have just the men for the job. Colonel Wright has a Brigade which consists entirely of rail repairmen. We'll have the bridge rebuilt and supplies rolling to you in no time."

With Army business completed, he turned his attention to personal matters and wrote a letter to his wife, Ellen. He was worried about her. They were expecting their sixth child. Although healthy, Ellen had difficulty in the delivery of the Sherman's fifth child. The couple were devoted to each other. She stood by her Willie when he left the Army to enter Banking. She stood by him when he volunteered for active duty at the beginning of the war. She supported him after the first Battle of Bull Run when the newspapers called him insane. The woman knew him well tolerating his stubbornness, his irritable nature and his bouts of depression. Like his friend Grant, Sherman drew his strength from his wife.

Altoona, Georgia—May 20, 5:30 PM

While Sherman wrote to his beloved Ellen; Hood, a bachelor, sat in his tent fuming at Johnston's comments. If the statements weren't bad enough, the petty Johnston told the citizens of Cassville that Hood was to be blamed for his abandoning the town. Normally not political, the Texan had decided to fight fire with fire. While recuperating from his wounds at Gettysburg, he had a chance to meet Jefferson Davis and his cabinet. The unmarried General quickly became the darling of Richmond Society. After his wounding at Chickamauga he found himself back in Richmond and in the city's inner circle. The Confederate President often visited the crippled General. The two men grew close. Hood admired Davis' bearing while the President liked the General's aggressiveness on the battlefield.

Hood wrote Davis and informed him how Johnston should have continued the attacks at Resaca, and how Johnston should have assailed Sherman at the beginning of the campaign. The Corps Commander closed the letter stating he doubted Johnston would ever take the offensive. The die was cast.

Spotsylvania, Virginia, Hancock's Corps—May 21, 11:00 PM,

With the threat of Lee's attack now over, Grant issued orders for Hancock to depart his trenches after dark. The General from Pennsylvania mounted his horse and headed toward the North Anna River thirty-four miles away

Hancock reached into his inside pocket and pulled out a note from Grant. He read it and smiled.

> *"My dear General Hancock—I wish to commend you for your gallantry. Your coolness under fire has been an inspiration for many of us. As you are aware, we are once again by-passing Lee's defenses. I am also convinced Lee will not attack unless he sees an opportunity. Your Corps is going to give him that opportunity. I'm going to create a gap in our movement of ten miles between you and the remainder of the Army. I tell you this so you will be on your guard. With Lee in the open and you on the defensive, I know we'll finally destroy the Army of Northern Virginia. Your Corps will be the anvil and the rest of the Army the hammer. God be with you—U.S. Grant."*

Replacing the note in his breast pocket he turned his thoughts to his wife and to happier times. Amelia Hancock was an Army wife. She had followed her husband from one outpost to another. Wherever they lived she made their house a home. During his career she became friends with the very men who were now fighting against her husband. Two of their closest friends, Dick Garnett and Lo Armistead were killed attacking Hancock's Corps at Gettysburg. Of all the deaths, she took Armistead's the toughest. It seemed no matter where the Hancocks lived, Lo would either already be there or would join shortly. Through the years she came to think of Lo as a younger brother. The three had become a family.

It was mid-afternoon when Hancock called for his men to fall out and rest for two hours. In an effort to bait Lee he put out a thin picket line and had his men dig shallow breastworks. He knew Lee wouldn't bite if he offered too inviting a feast.

Ten miles away Grant rode with his staff.

"General, there appears to be a huge gap between Warren and Hancock," said Porter. "Should I send word to Hancock to withdraw back to us?"

"No, Colonel. Rather than have Hancock withdraw, maybe we should speed Warren up a bit," replied Grant.

Continuing southward, Grant became perplexed. He couldn't understand why Lee had not attacked. Little did he know that his adversary was sick and confined to bed rest. Lee's chest pains had returned along with stomach cramps and diarrhea rendering him weak and tired. With Hill still sick in bed, command of the Army of Northern Virginia fell to its Senior Corps Commander, the indecisive Richard Ewell. Heated discussions took place at Ewell's headquarters on whether or not to attack Hancock's isolated Corps. Gordon and Early favored attack—Anderson favored a watch and wait posture stating that Grant was no fool and it was a trap.

Even though ill, Lee had surmised from his Cavalry reports what Grant's objective was and ordered his Army to the North Anna twenty-eight miles away. Once again, the race was on.

Richmond, Virginia—May 22, 3:30 AM

Jefferson Davis sat at the conference table in his office peering over telegrams from Georgia's Governor, Joe Brown. The Governor complained about Johnston's constant retreats and requested that the Virginian be replaced. Although political enemies, both men knew their fate rested on the other. With the exception of PGT Beauregard, Johnston was Davis' only choice. He disliked Johnston; but hated Beauregard. The only option the Southern Chief Executive had was to leave Johnston in place and encourage him to be more aggressive.

Another telegram sat on the President's table, this one from A.P. Hill, caused him the most worry. Although sick in bed, he heard from reliable sources that during the campaign Lee had recklessly exposed himself to enemy fire on several occasions. The soldiers had to forcibly remove him to a place of safety. Lee's loyal subordinate requested Davis to order the Army Commander be more cautious stating that if something were to happen to the Virginian, it would be a blow from which the Army and the Confederacy would never recover.

Davis agreed with the ailing Hill and wrote a simple note to his friend.

> *"My Dear General Lee,*
> *It has been brought to my attention that on several occasions during the recent campaign, you have recklessly exposed yourself to enemy fire. Our cause has lost many a good General; at Shiloh we lost Sidney Johnston; at Chancellorsville we lost Stonewall; at the Wilderness, Longstreet was grievously wounded; at Yellow Tavern we lost Stuart.*

The Confederacy can afford to lose its President, but cannot afford to lose its most beloved Army Commander. It is from you, Robert, that the South draws her strength. My dear friend please, for our sake, do not expose yourself needlessly. Your friend always,
Jefferson Davis"

CHAPTER NINE

North Anna River, Virginia—May 23, 7:00 AM

Hancock arrived at the River and saw the Confederates had dug-in. The Union General quickly surveyed the enemy works. He noticed the rebels had not yet finished their breastworks on Telegraph Hill across from Telegraph Bridge. He decided to take the bridge and hit the Southerner's unprotected flank.

He threw his entire Corps against the rebels. The southerners put up stiff resistance, but being outnumbered, they were forced to withdraw. The Union troops pursued their retreating foes for a mile before they ran into the rest of Anderson's and Ewell's Corps. Undeterred, Hancock's men smashed into the breastworks. After fifteen minutes of savage hand-to-hand combat, the Union troops withdrew three hundred yards and dug-in to wait for the rest of their Army.

A mile to the west Burnside's Corps crossed the North Anna at Ox Ford and ran into Confederates. Lee had placed a portion of Hill's Corps in an inverted "V" with the point of the "V" separating Burnside from Warren. Using the terrain to his advantage the Southern Army had split the Union forces in half enabling it to destroy Grant's Army piecemeal.

A.P. Hill watched Warren's Corps with interest trying desperately to ascertain the size of the isolated enemy Corps.

"Sergeant Tucker, ride to General Wilcox and tell him to attack the Federals in his front. Tell him Heth will be in support. Then ride to Heth and tell him it's my orders that he's to support Wilcox in the attack," said Hill.

Confederate Major General Cadmus Wilcox had performed well in all the battles the Army of Northern Virginia had fought and had earned Hill's respect. The forty-year old, slightly balding, thin West Point graduate was extremely loyal to Hill and would, without question, do whatever was ordered.

He quickly called for his four Brigade Commanders and issued orders. They would hit the Federals from the front and the side. Two Brigades would attack crossing two hundred yards of open ground, while one Brigade would move through the woods. The fourth Brigade would hit the Federals from the side. Since Heth's Division was already flanking the Federals, Wilcox assumed they would strike the right and rear of the enemy.

Warren's troops took their time digging in; unaware of the danger awaiting them. Men laughed and joked. The men were relaxed as they worked; there was no sense of urgency. They were feeling cocky, after all, they had pushed Lee from the Rapidan River sixty miles south to the banks of the North Anna.

Without warning the Southerners attacked. Men dove for their weapons and tried to fire, but the rebels were too fast. First one Union Brigade broke for the rear; followed by two others. Wilcox's men pursued the men in blue like a hound pursuing a fox. The Brigades had gone a half-mile when they passed through the rest of Warren's Corps. The men in the rear parted ranks to let their comrades through. When the last man was safe, the remainder of the Corps opened fire, stopping the attackers. After the first Union volley, the sky became black. Lightning flashed across the horizon giving an eerie hue to the second volley as the Confederates returned fire. Warren was not going to be pushed back. He ordered his entire Corps to fix bayonets and charge. Seeing the glistening steel of 8,000 bayonets surging forward at a run, the outnumbered Southerners made a hasty retreat. Rain poured down in violent torrents turning the ground into a muddy quagmire. Lightning struck trees causing them to crash heavily to the earth. The Confederates slipped and slid in their escape. Those falling were quickly captured and would sit out the remainder of the war in a Northern prisoner of war camp.

Once back inside their entrenchments, Wilcox rode to Harry Heth's headquarters.

"Harry, what the hell is wrong with you!" shouted Wilcox. "How come your men didn't support me?"

"Cad, we did support you!" retorted an angry Heth.

"Horseshit!" yelled Wilcox. "Your men marched like they were on their way to a picnic. I saw them myself. They weren't even in a line of battle! You arrogant ass, you butchered my men. Mark my words, this is not the last you shall hear of this!"

A mile away Robert E. Lee met with A.P. Hill. Lee, still weak and unable to ride, commandeered a buggy and was driven to the Confederate position.

"General Hill, why did you not do as Jackson would have done, thrown your whole force against those people? You would've driven them back," said an agitated Lee.

Hill idolized the older man and would not answer for fear of losing his temper. He knew the rebuke was due more to the General's ill health than to the way the battle was fought.

Lee walked back to his buggy shaking his head.

"General Hill, for the first time since assuming command of this Army, I have been forced to relinquish the initiative to the enemy. Grant is sapping the strength of this Army. We have the desire, but not the muscle. Even with the eight thousand five hundred reinforcements we received today, we are too weak to hit Grant head on. We must be ever vigilant for an opportunity to destroy him piecemeal and when it occurs, we must strike a hard blow."

The next morning, Grant rode to the front with Hancock and Meade at his side. The three men watched intently through the heavy rain as the enemy continued to strengthen their fortifications. Logs were felled during the night and placed in front of the trenches. The last log was raised allowing the defenders to shoot through without exposing themselves. Fifty yards in front of the entrenchments were sharpened stakes pointed toward the attackers. Unseen by the Union Generals was the telegraph wire strung in front of the stakes to make the attacker trip and become impaled. The war was changing. No longer was it a conflict based on chivalry. It had become a total war with no quarter given. The niceties were gone.

"Looks like General Lee has been busy," said Meade in a calm tone.

"Many men will be lost if we try to take that position," replied Hancock grimly.

"Gentlemen, I've no intention of attacking Lee. His entrenchments are too strong. He'll consolidate his artillery on half his line and, with a Brigade of infantry support, be able to hold half of us at bay while he throws his entire Army against our two isolated Corps. When those Corps had been annihilated, he'll then destroy the other half." replied Grant.

"Sam, what makes you think he is planning to do that?" asked Meade.

"Because, George, it's what I'd do." replied the General-in-Chief. "I don't like having our forces split. We'll wait until the rain stops and the roads dry; then we'll move around Lee and force him out of his fortifications. In the meantime let them dig and wear themselves out."

As the moon rose and the rain stopped, a familiar face greeted Grant's headquarters. Sheridan had returned from his raid. Although the railroads he destroyed would soon be back in operation his mission was successful. Stuart was dead along with his faithful Brigadier General James Gordon, third cousin to Ewell's Division Commander, John Gordon. The myth of the Confederate Cavalry being invincible had been laid to rest.

Over dinner Grant teased Sheridan. Even the stoic Meade joined the fun. The Cavalry Commander took it good-naturedly.

"Well done, Phil. Come to my tent tomorrow morning and I'll have orders for you. George, can you join me in my tent now?" asked Grant.

The two men entered the tent and sat down on the folding chairs.

"George, I want to start off by saying how much I appreciate your indulgence when I go directly to Hancock or Warren. Sometimes I become too impatient. I apologize for that," said Grant as he lit a cigar.

"Sam, I know you don't jump the chain of command to embarrass me. So I don't perceive it to be a slight. As I said when we first met, preserving the Union is the only thing that matters," answered Meade.

"George, I called you in here to discuss the next phase of our campaign. In three days I plan to move our Army around Lee and will try to take Richmond from the southeast. I'm sending Sheridan's Cavalry in advance of our infantry. He'll screen our movements and scout what's in front of us. As usual Hancock's men will be in the lead. I have also ordered Butler to send us two Corps from his Army of the James. This will bring our strength up to one hundred thousand men. Butler will stay on the Peninsula with two Corps to hold Beauregard in place."

"Sam, I think the plan is good," replied a wide-eyed Meade. "I think the Army of Northern Virginia is hard pressed for replacements. I don't believe Lee is strong enough to defeat us, but we must be careful not to give him an opportunity to hurt us."

"I agree," answered Grant nodding. "George, my duties have spread me too thin. I'd like to place Burnside's Ninth Corps under your direct command."

Meade stared at his Commander for a few minutes before speaking.

"Sam, Burnside has seniority over me. According to Army regulations, I should be reporting to him."

"I don't give a damn about regulations. He'll be ordered to place himself and his command under your jurisdiction. It will take me a few days to issue the orders and break the news to Burnside."

The two men continued to talk for another hour before calling it an evening.

The rain continued to pour in southern Virginia. It was as if God was washing away the bloodshed of the past three weeks. Grant sat in his tent waiting for the weather to break; writing a letter to his wife and children. He put his pen down and listened to the rain patter against the canvas of the tent. He wondered how Lyons was doing.

Dallas, Georgia—May 25, 4:50 AM

Sherman, with his men rested and re-supplied, renewed his campaign by avoiding Allatoona and headed instead for Johnston's main supply depot at Dallas. Schofield protected the Armies' left flank while at the same time he was responsible to hold Johnston's Army in place at Allatoona. McPherson protected the Armies' right flank, and was to strike the town from the west. Thomas would drive straight through cutting off Dallas from the north. Sherman hoped to quickly take the depot before the rebs could destroy it. Once it was taken, he would turn McPherson and Thomas east to support Schofield. He knew once Johnston discovered he had lost Dallas, he would strike the isolated Schofield. Sherman intended to move rapidly, but cautiously.

The Union General issued his men each twenty days' rations and sixty rounds of ammunition. He knew from his younger days that this part of Georgia was densely wooded with very few useable roads. His men would have to fight nature, the rebs and the hot Georgia sun. The Union troops' heavy woolen uniforms were great during the Spring, Fall and Winter; but in the hot Southern summer they sapped a man's strength. In contrast, the Confederates cotton uniforms were great during Spring, Fall and Summer but were no good during the winter.

Black smoke blotted out the rising sun of the twenty-fifth as men from Joe Hookers Corps rushed forward to put out the fire on the bridge spanning Pumpkin Vine Creek. Wheeler's Cavalry had set the bridge on fire to slow their advance. For two hours the men fought the blaze, finally extinguishing it and resuming their march.

Joe Hooker sat ramrod straight on his large white stallion watching his men as they passed. His erect posture, military bearing and muscled physique gave anyone who didn't know him the impression that they were in the presence of a strong military man. His ego surpassed his ability to lead, while at the same time it made him enemies with his superiors, peers and subordinates. "Fighting Joe", as the newspapers nicknamed him, was taking no chances putting his most able-bodied Division Commander, John Geary, in the lead.

Geary had been with Hooker in the East. Before coming West to help raise the siege of Chattanooga, he had fought in every major battle of the Army of the Potomac. The six-foot six-inch, Brigadier General from Pennsylvania hated Hooker. He thought "Fighting Joe" was more interested in headlines than he was in winning the war. He confided to his staff on several occasions that Hooker had more hot air then a blast furnace.

Two miles from the bridge, Geary's lead Brigade encountered Wheeler's horsemen. The Union troops quickly formed for battle and moved forward. The rebels fired two quick volleys and rode away. The Brigade cautiously moved in pursuit with the rest of the Division close behind. Throughout the morning and into the early afternoon the scene repeated itself time and again.

Suddenly, Geary's lead Brigade ran into a strongly dug-in Brigade of rebel infantry. The battle-hardened Commander ordered his entire Division forward. The Union troops marched through the woods with its tangled underbrush, passed into a clearing and then rushed without any cover up a slight upgrade to the entrenched enemy. The denseness of woods made a flank attack impossible. Geary hoped to carry the position by sheer force of numbers. Much to his surprise his men were easily repulsed. Geary reformed his Division and attacked again. After his second repulse he sent word to Hooker for reinforcements.

Within thirty minutes Hooker had his entire Corps up. He met with his Division Commanders. He deployed his Corps in the woods for the attack; Geary's Division would be in the lead with Williams' Division on his left and Ward's Division on his right.

At precisely three o'clock, Hooker gave the order for the attack to begin. The men in blue moved out of the woods. When they entered the clearing, they broke into a run toward the enemy entrenchments less than two hundred yards away.

Standing behind the breastworks, Confederate Major General Alexander Stewart watched the enemy approach. The forty-three year old Stewart was well liked by his peers and superiors. He was a loyal officer who avoided political frays that were common among the General officers in the Southern Army of Tennessee. A West Point graduate of the class of 1842, he resigned from the Army in 1845 to teach mathematics at Lebanon University in his home state of Tennessee.

Hidden behind the breastworks were twenty-four cannon supported by five thousand infantry. The artillery was loaded with grape and canister. Stewart had used only four cannon and one thousand men in repulsing Geary hoping to draw more Yankees into his trap. Once the blue-clad troops were well into the clearing, he gave the order to fire causing maximum damage to the northern invaders.

Hooker and Geary had underestimated the size of the enemy force; it wasn't a lone Brigade nor was it just Stewart's Division. It was Hood's entire Corps. Supporting Stewart on the left was Stevenson's Division and on the right was Stephen D. Lee's Division. The supporting units could be easily and quickly moved to repel any breach in the line should Stewart request assistance. The Union men paid dearly for their Commanders' error.

The Union line recoiled from the initial surprise, reformed and continued its advance, firing as they walked. When they were within fifty yards of the Confederates, the Union troops had enough and retreated back into the woods. Geary's men were badly bloodied. Hooker ordered Williams' Division to assume the lead supported by Geary and Ward. Fifteen minutes later the attack continued ending a half hour later with the same results. Hooker was determined to take the position and ordered the attack renewed, this time, with Ward's Division in the lead. For two hours the men in blue attacked and were repulsed. At five o'clock the Union troops with Geary's Division, once again, in the lead resumed the attack. Abruptly, the sky darkened and lightning flashed across the horizon. The heavens opened sending a downpour of water on both the attacker and defender. The ground instantly became slick as water and blood mixed causing the attackers to slip and slide their way to the enemy position. The men in the trenches were suddenly up to their knees in mud making reloading and moving about difficult and tiring. The fighting continued for another hour.

Suddenly the dark clouds vanished, the rain stopped and the sky became a mixture of bright orange and dark blue as the sun set behind the mountains. Realizing further attacks were useless, Hooker ordered his men to entrench within the tree line.

Sherman remained with Thomas as Hooker's battle reports arrived throughout the afternoon.

"General Sherman, I think Hooker is mistaken. I'm sure he has a bigger force opposing him than he realizes," said George Thomas.

"According to Hooker, he's facing a part of Stewart's Division of Hood's Corps," replied an agitated Sherman

"Billy, by the sound of the gunfire, it appears to be more like a full Division than a Brigade," interrupted Thomas.

"George, I would have to agree with you. I'd bet my eyes that he's facing Hood's entire Corps. Johnston is probably already at Dallas and Hood is protecting their right flank. George, let's hurry your Army forward so by tomorrow morning we'll be in a position to see what old Joe Johnston has in store for us," answered Sherman.

Throughout the night Sherman had his Armies on the move. The late rising of the moon, mixed with the denseness of the woods, made going slow.

At midnight Sherman decided to call it a day and bedded down on the ground next to a log. It was a fitful night as the Commander tossed and turned. It was well after three when he finally fell asleep. His repose didn't last long. At five-thirty he was awakened by a courier from Schofield. The Commanding General recognized the Sergeant.

"Good morning, Sergeant," said a sleepy Sherman. "What news have you brought me today?"

"Good morning, General. I only deliver them. I don't read them" replied the courier.

Sherman opened the dispatch. It wasn't from Schofield. It was from Jacob Cox. Schofield was hurt. While riding to Sherman last night, the Union General was struck in the head by a low hanging branch and knocked unconscious. Being the Senior Division Commander, Cox had assumed command and wanted to know if Sherman had any orders for him.

"Sergeant, inform General Cox he is to link up with Thomas' Army and cover our left flank. He is not to engage the enemy until ordered," said Sherman.

As the courier left, Sherman's aide, Henry Hitchcock, approached and handed him a cup of coffee. The two men were talking when another courier arrived, this one from McPherson.

"General Sherman, I have a message from General McPherson," said the young rider.

The two men looked at the courier waiting for the message. The seventeen year old was intimated by the volatile Commander. He had heard rumors about how Sherman's temperament could change at the blink of an eye.

Losing patience Sherman finally blurted out, "Well, son, what's the message?"

"General McPherson reports he has arrived at Dallas, but that the Rebs are entrenched. We probed their defenses but we didn't find any weakness. The

General says Hardee's entire Corps is in Dallas. He wishes to know what his orders are," stammered the messenger.

"Tell General McPherson to dig in and not attack. I'll send him further instructions later in the day. In the meantime, I'd like him to continue to probe the enemy position for weakness and if he finds one, he may use his own discretion," responded Sherman.

At ten o'clock Thomas arrived at Sherman's make-shift headquarters. The two men talked for over three hours. Thomas informed his Commander that Hooker had been well bloodied and they had been correct. Hooker had taken on Stewart's Division supported by Hood's entire Corps. The Union troops had been bloodied but not disheartened. Hooker's men had nicknamed the Confederate position at New Hope Church, "the Hell Hole."

The morning of the twenty-sixth found Joe Johnston up early personally inspecting his lines. At first he was nervous about Hood's position, but after yesterday's repulse of Hooker's Corps he was again confident he could hold Sherman in place.

Everywhere he rode, he was greeted with cheers. In spite of being pushed back, he had the love of his Army. They knew he truly cared about them. His inspection revealed what Sherman had feared, there was no weakness in the entrenchments. The Virginian and his subordinates were tightly compacted in a five-mile span from Pickett's' Mill to Dallas. Hardee, protecting the Confederate left, was well fortified at Dallas while Polk held the center and Hood the right. Johnston was content to stay where he was and let Sherman wreck the Union Army by attacking the Southern positions.

It was after five in the afternoon when Johnston returned to his headquarters very satisfied with what he saw. His positions were strong, maybe a little too strong. If Sherman remained true to the strategy, he would try to flank Johnston. The question was—which flank would Sherman attempt the turn?

After much internal debate, the Virginian had come to the conclusion his adversary would try to flank Hood's position. The terrain around Hardee's area was too open for a flanking movement. McPherson would have to circle at least ten miles to be out of sight. On the other hand, Hood's area was surrounded by dense forest and rocky outcrops. Schofield could easily skirt around Hood undetected and hit him in the flank or rear. Johnston ordered Hardee to dispatch Cleburne's Division to Hood.

Nicknamed the "Stonewall of the West," Patrick Cleburne was considered by most of the men and officers in Johnston's Army as the best Division Commander. It was Cleburne who held Sherman in check during the battle of

Chattanooga. Born in Ireland, the thirty-six year old had served three years in England's prestigious Forty-First Regiment of Foot. The aggressive Irishman believed in throwing as much lead at the enemy in the shortest period of time. He personally trained his men to aim, fire and reload quickly. While the average infantryman could aim, fire and reload three rounds per minute; Cleburne's men could, in the same time span, reload six rounds.

Across the battlefield Sherman spent the day inspecting his lines and meeting with his Generals. He concluded Johnston was too strongly entrenched for a frontal assault; therefore, he would have to strike at his flanks. After talking to Hooker and Cox, he decided to reinforce Hooker with Howard's Corps and have Howard lead the attack against Hood's flank while Cox would stand by ready to assist if needed.

The rising sun brought the promise of a beautiful spring day. The temperature was sixty degrees with a breeze blowing. The going was slow and tedious as the men in blue made their way through the dense Georgia pine. They frequently rested to allow stragglers to catch up.

The day wore on as Howard continued his trek toward Hood. Being unfamiliar with the area, he had gotten lost twice in the dense woodlands. While Howard marched, Sherman paced back and forth in anticipation of hearing either the sounds of battle or word from Howard that he was in Johnston's rear.

"Hitchcock, I want you to ride to General Hooker and ascertain if Howard put his troops on the march yet. They should have been engaged by now. If Hooker tells you they are on their way, have him send some riders to Howard and find out what in the damn hell is going on," said an anxious Sherman.

It was after four when Howard's men reached the edge of the woods. Facing them was Cleburne's Division; well entrenched and rested.

The one-armed Union Commander ordered Woods' Division to lead the attack. Massing his men in a compact formation, he threw the entire weight of his Division against Cleburne's extreme right. Once the enemy right was turned, the rest of Howard's Corps would join the assault and together they would roll up Hood's entire Corps. In theory, it should work like a fine watch, but this wasn't a classroom.

Woods' men calmly walked out of the tree line and into a clearing. When they were within one hundred yards, Cleburne gave the order to fire. At once the Confederate position seemed to erupt into flames as a thousand muskets fired simultaneously filling the air with deadly projectiles. The defenders quickly reloaded and fired again and again. Woods' men kept their forward movement in spite of the maelstrom they had entered.

The going was slow as men stepped gingerly over their fallen comrades. Unlike Geary's attack, the enemy had no artillery to assist them. This would be man against man. After a half hour of punishment, Woods' men withdrew back to the safety of the forest and were instantly replaced by another Division; who fared no better. Howard continued to throw men against Cleburne's well-entrenched fortifications. Those who did not want to risk being killed while retreating; lay prone and using their fallen comrades as protection returned fire. Howard's men continued firing well into the darkness. As the moon rose, the tired men in blue caught in no man's land, crawled back to the safety of the Federal lines.

Realizing the Federal troops were digging in and those caught between the lines were fruit ripe for the picking, Cleburne ordered an attack against the unsuspecting Northern soldiers. Resistance was light and the Southern General easily scooped up three hundred prisoners.

While Cleburne marched his prisoners to the rear, Joe Johnston was holding a council of war to decide his next course of action. Hood stood on Johnston's left his weight supported by crutches. Hardee and Polk were on the Commanding General's right. The four men stared at the map on the table in front of them as Johnston explained his plan and asked for the opinion of the others. All of the men favored attacking Sherman's flanks. They felt the repulses had surely demoralized Sherman's men.

Johnston agreed and ordered Hardee to probe his front opposite McPherson. If successful, Polk would join in the attack followed by Hood. It was after one in the morning when the Generals returned to their respective commands. Dawn was a scant five hours away and orders had to be distributed.

CHAPTER TEN

Eight miles north of Haws Shop, Virginia—May 28, 5:45 AM

Phil Sheridan had his Cavalry on the road at dawn. His orders were simple. Keep Robert E. Lee from discovering Grant was on the move again. Sheridan's men were to push aside any of Lee's Cavalry or infantry, which might be in the way of Hancock's march.

Sheridan rode at the head of his First Division under the command of Brigadier General Alfred Torbert. The converted Infantry officer had earned Sheridan's confidence almost instantly. He had fought in every major engagement of the Army of the Potomac earning the praise of all his Commanders. Torbert had the finest Brigade Commanders in all of Sheridan's Corps. His first Brigade was commanded by a young General named George Custer and his second Brigade was commanded by Thomas Devin. It was Devin's Brigade which helped hold back Heth's Division on the first day of the battle of Gettysburg.

There was no way for the seven thousand Union horsemen to conceal their movement. The sound of the hoofs striking the hard ground and the clanking of metal sabers carried quite a distance. Sheridan put patrols on his flanks to prevent surprise attacks. During the entire morning, they only encountered a few Confederate Cavalry patrols and these were easily brushed aside. At eleven o'clock Sheridan rested his men and horses.

"Well, Torbert, it looks like the rebs aren't expecting us. I think old Grant has finally surprised Lee," said an enthusiastic Sheridan.

"Phil, I've fought in every major engagement from Bull Run until now and in all my engagements there has been one common element ... always be on the alert—when you least expect it—Lee will strike," responded Torbert.

"Well, I hope Lee does strike. We outnumber him and with Grant in command, we'll out General him," answered Sheridan smiling.

Meanwhile, at Lee's headquarters, the Southern Commander began to receive reports from those brushed aside Cavalry outposts that Grant was again on the move. The "gray fox" of the Confederacy wasted no time.

"Colonel Marshall," called Lee.

Almost instantly the young aide appeared. After serving with Lee for almost three years, the youthful officer had learned to anticipate his Commander's needs. He was always close enough to immediately respond, yet far enough away to allow the General his privacy.

"Yes, sir?"

"Colonel, send a courier to Generals Hampton and Fitzhugh Lee and inform them Yankee Cavalry are on the move toward Hanover Town. They're to engage and stop those people. They have to buy me time to get ahead of Grant," said a pensive Lee.

Jeb Stuart's death had left a void in the command of Lee's Cavalry. The burly Wade Hampton had earned Stuart's confidence; but, then again, so had the Commanding General's nephew, Fitzhugh Lee. Both men were smart, aggressive fighters. Both were seasoned veterans. The Commanding General couldn't decide who should replace Stuart, so he split the command.

By eleven-thirty in the morning, the Southern Cavalry was on the move. Fitzhugh and Hampton conferred for a few minutes and decided they would block Sheridan's path at Haws Shop.

A little before one o'clock in the afternoon the Union advance scouts encountered the Southern Cavalry. Sheridan wasted no time. He immediately ordered his men into attack formation. Drawing sabers, the Union horsemen slowly rode toward the enemy three hundred yards away. The men in blue kept their alignment as if on parade. The ground was relatively flat with a slightly rising incline running from south to north favoring the defenders. A cool breeze blew into the faces of the attackers. The sun shone brightly, it was a perfect day to die.

The seasoned veterans of Hampton and Fitzhugh waited patiently. The horses pawed the ground in anticipation of the impending battle as their riders fought to hold them back. The adrenalin rose in both man and beast. When the Union men were within one hundred and fifty yards, the Southern Cavalry drew its sabers. The sound of metal swords being drawn from their scabbards increased the anxiety of the horses.

At one hundred yards both sides spurred their mounts and charged. Seconds later the air was filled with the high pitched sound of metal striking metal as the men on horseback danced a waltz of death. Heads were gashed. Necks were sliced open. Blood spurted from open wounds. Unlike a gun battle where men were often killed a distance away, the battles on horseback were up close and personal. The rider had to fight their adversary while at the same time controlling their mount. Very often those unfortunate enough to be knocked from their horse were trampled to death by friend and foe alike.

The men on both sides fought like demons disregarding their personal safety. First the Union men would retreat, catch their breath and charge again. Then the Confederates would retreat a short distance, catch their breath and resume the battle. Casualties mounted as each side attacked and counter-attacked. For two hours the battle rocked back and forth. The Confederates slowly retreated to their second line of defense in the woods behind them. The cavalrymen dismounted and fought like infantry. The Southern combatants poured a continuous volley of lead at the attacking Northerners.

Sheridan's men attacked, reformed and attacked again. After three bloody hours, the Union men put up their own breastworks and the conflict took yet another turn. The men in blue would not attack but would use their carbines to return fire. It was now a battle of trenches.

As darkness settled in, the Confederates broke contact and, using the blackness as a curtain, withdrew unmolested leaving the field to Sheridan's men. The battle had raged for seven hours.

Dallas, Georgia—May 28, 5:00 PM

McPherson started to move his men out of their entrenchments to circle around Thomas and Schofield and strike Hood's extreme flank. Seeing the men in blue on the move, Hardee attacked. McPherson's men dove back into their trenches. For two hours the Confederate's attacked, reformed and attacked again. It was like leading lambs to the slaughter. The Southerners were cut down before they got halfway to the defenders as McPherson's men poured out a continuous hailstorm of lead.

When one Brigade ran out of ammunition, it was replaced by fresh troops and sent to the rear to be re-supplied. Once they were restocked, they went back to their positions and relieved the troops who had relieved them. For two hours McPherson shifted troops in and out never giving the rebels a moment's rest. While the battle raged, he sent word to Sherman of the attack and waited for further orders.

Sherman smiled when McPherson's courier arrived and he read the message. He'd been waiting for this news. Unfortunately, it was only against McPherson.

North Anna River—May 28, 9:15PM

"General Early, as you are aware, General Ewell has been very ill these past few days. He's been unable to lead his Corps. I am ordering General Ewell to Richmond to recuperate. While he is recuperating, I would like you to take command of the Second Corps," said Lee.

"I'll do my utmost not to disappoint you," replied Early.

"I want you to know you have my fullest trust and support," responded Lee somberly.

"General Early, we must be ever ready to strike a blow against Grant's army before it gets to the James River. If it gets there, it will become a siege and then it will be a mere question of time."

"Sir, my Corps and I will be ready,"

"Our Cavalry has captured some prisoners and, upon questioning them, they've confirmed what I thought. Grant's Army is indeed on the move south. I intend to intercept here at Totopotomoy Creek a half mile north of Shady Grove. I want your Corps there by morning. Hill's and Anderson's Corps will join you by mid-morning."

Near Totopotomoy Creek, Virginia—May 29, 4:30 AM

Dawn found the Federals on the move south with Hancock's Corps once again in the lead and Wright's Corps in close support. The two Generals rode side by side for most of the morning.

"Well Wright, it looks like "old Grant" is trying to draw Lee out into the open," said Hancock wiping the sweat from his brow.

"I agree, but old Bobbie Lee is too smart to be suckered in. He knows we outnumber him three-to-one," responded Wright.

"Lee will wait for Grant to make a mistake—then try to exploit it," replied Hancock.

It was just before noon when Hancock's advance Brigade encountered entrenched Confederates. Lee had once again blocked Grant's army. Using the natural lay of the land, the Southern Commander had his men dig in on the south side of Totopotomoy Creek. He used the Creek as a natural barrier between him and the invaders. The Union men would have to cross the Creek and then attack across open ground a hundred yards.

Hancock's men dug in and waited for orders from their Commander. The last time they faced a position this formidable was at Fredericksburg.

Within minutes Wright and Hancock were at the scene. The two men surveyed the situation and both came to the same conclusion. It would be suicide to attack.

"Win, I'll place my Corps on your right and wait for orders," said Wright shaking his friend's hand.

"Agreed, but be careful. I see only infantry," answered Hancock.

A short time later Grant and Meade arrived.

"General Meade, what're your orders?" inquired Hancock.

"General, I'd like you to make a reconnaissance of the area to your front. I'll send orders for Wright to do the same. Burnside's Corps will be up soon and will be placed between you and Wright. This way he can support either of you should the need arise. Don't attack unless the situation changes. I don't want another Fredericksburg," said Meade.

Hancock saluted and issued the appropriate orders. Grant turned his horse and rode along his line. He watched the men entrench. When they noticed their unimposing down to earth General-in-Chief; they cheered. The quiet man doffed his hat in response. In spite of losing forty thousand of their comrades, the Army loved their Commander. They were his and he was theirs.

Night descended upon the combatants in southern Virginia as Grant sat in his tent and read telegrams from Sherman and Hunter. He was disappointed that Sherman had to break off contact with Johnston to, once again, re-supply his Army.

At the same time Hunter, who replaced Sigel, had reorganized his Army of the Valley and was marching on the Confederate Army under "Grumble" Jones.

The often-melancholy Jones was a fierce fighter. His attacks were always brutal giving no quarter. He was a favorite of Jeb Stuart until he made the mistake of disagreeing with the late Cavalry General in front of others and was quickly banished to the Valley.

On the other hand, the sixty-two year old Hunter was a stern disciplinarian and a fierce fighter. A West Point graduate, he believed in total war wanting the South to pay for its insolence.

After reading the telegrams, he turned his attention to his current situation. Lee had again strongly entrenched his Army between Grant and Richmond inviting the Union Commander to attack. He agreed with Meade and would not foolishly waste men in a headlong attack. He'd ordered Sheridan to probe Lee's flanks. If any of the probes found a chink in the Confederate armor, they were to attack at once and not wait for the rest of the Army.

He decided to bait Lee into the open by splitting his Army. He would send Warren's and Wright's Corps across the creek and dig in. Burnside and Hancock would be held in reserve. If Lee did not attack, then the Federals would swing to their left cross the Chickahominy River and be between Lee and Richmond.

Grant realized his supply lines were becoming too long. They would need to be shortened, so he issued orders for his engineers to build a wharf and supply depot at the small hamlet of White House less then ten miles away.

The Union General-in-Chief exited his tent and walked to the fire. Sitting down on a log by himself, he picked up a stick and began to whittle. His thoughts turned to Lyons and he wondered how the young man was faring. He had sent him on an extremely dangerous mission but, nonetheless, an important one.

Rawlins walked toward the General and sat next to him.

"Are you alright, Ulys?"

"I'm fine, John … it's just that …" Grant hesitated.

"Just what Ulys?"

"It's just that sometimes I feel like I've got the entire weight of the world on my shoulders. I know in my heart we can defeat Lee and Sherman can beat Johnston. I'm worried that if Lincoln is defeated at the polls, we'll not have time to finish what we have begun."

"Ulys, the election is five months away and a lot can happen during that time. I think you're just tired. It's been a long day and a busy month. As far as having the weight of the world on your shoulders, I've got news for you. You do! The entire fate of the nation is riding on your strategy. If you fail, then Lincoln loses the election and the South wins her independence."

Grant looked into Rawlins' eyes, excused himself and went into his tent to grab some much needed sleep.

Across the battlefield, Robert E. Lee sat with Jefferson Davis and discussed the situation. With Lee's Army a short nine miles from Richmond, the Confederate President had decided to visit his favorite General. Davis relished the times away from Richmond. On several occasions he thought of resigning the

Presidency and taking over command of Johnston's Army. The South's Chief Executive loved the military and the thrill of combat. His sense of duty kept him in his present job. He was elected—he will serve.

The two men were joined by General P.G.T. Beauregard. It was Beauregard who fired on Fort Sumter and defeated the Union forces at the first battle of Bull Run. At the beginning of the war, the General from New Orleans was very popular with the Southern people and the President, himself. However; after his victory at Bull Run, the General had begun to take full credit for the victory and didn't share the glory with Joe Johnston, who arrived in the nick of time with reinforcements. He openly criticized the Davis administration on how they were conducting the war. The President immediately banished the Creole General to the Western theatre as the second-in-command to Albert Sydney Johnston.

When Sydney Johnston was killed during the first day of the battle at Shiloh, Beauregard assumed command and was, subsequently, beaten by Grant. After the loss, he was then sent to the coastal defenses in South Carolina. While in South Carolina, he constantly submitted plans directly to Davis detailing how the South could defeat the North. Each plan called for more men, arms and talent than the Confederacy could provide. Beauregard remained in the Carolinas until Butler landed on the Virginia Peninsula and, having no choice, Davis ordered him back to Richmond. Although outnumbered two-to-one, he had managed to bottle Butler up into a small area of the Peninsula called the "Bermuda Hundred."

"Mr. President, the Army of Northern Virginia has suffered greatly during this campaign. Grant has used his superior advantage in numbers to constantly hammer this Army. He knows I must defend Richmond and he's free to maneuver anywhere he desires. This gives him the advantage. I've lost thirty-seven percent of my General officers."

Lee reached into his front pocket and pulled out his reading glasses and a list of names. Solemnly, Lee read the names out loud.

"Micah Jenkins, Junius Daniel, George Doles, John M. Jones, Leroy Stafford, Abner Perrin, James B. Gordon and Jeb Stuart all killed. E.M. Law, Henry Benning, Harry Hays, Robert Johnston, John Pegram, James Walker, John Cooke, James Lane, Samuel McGowan, Edward Perry, Henry Walker and James Longstreet all wounded and lost to this Army at this time. Edward Johnston and George Stuart are prisoners of the Union, while Dick Ewell is too ill to continue the fight and has been ordered to Richmond."

Lee paused and looked up at the President. He could see the look of shock and pain in the Chief Executive's eyes. Davis knew the cost had been high; but, until this moment, hadn't realized the true picture. Lee had done what a General was supposed to do, fight with what he had on hand.

"Mr. President, if I don't receive reinforcements immediately, I'm afraid Grant will get around this Army and take Richmond. It is my opinion that Grant is withdrawing troops from Beauregard's front and bringing them here to reinforce Meade," finished Lee in a tired tone.

"Mr. President, General Lee is right. Butler has sent some troops to Grant, but they don't number more than four thousand. This still leaves Butler with thirty thousand men. If I dispatch troops to assist General Lee, then I run the risk of being overwhelmed myself and Richmond will fall from the south. I truly sympathize with General Lee and the current condition of his brave Army, but I don't see how we can risk my Army for his," replied Beauregard respectfully.

"Mr. President, there's no way General Grant is going to allow Butler's men to be wasted. Butler will be ordered to send a large number of his troops to Grant," rebutted Lee.

"Gentlemen, I see both your points and while my initial feeling is to support the Army of Northern Virginia, I must defer to General Beauregard's opinion and not pull troops from him at this time. However, General Lee, if you should receive proof that Butler's Army or a good portion of it is being withdrawn, then you'll notify me immediately and you will be reinforced. General Beauregard, should the time come for the issuing of those orders, I will expect them to be carried out without hesitation," said Jefferson Davis

Totopotomoy River, Virginia—May 30, 11:00 AM

Warren sent Crawford's Division across the river and had them dig in. He ordered the rest of the Corps to cross further downstream out of sight of the enemy. The lack of resistance to the crossing made the Union General nervous. The hair on the back of his neck stood on edge. Being live bait did not appeal to the experienced Commander.

When the Union Army did counter-attack, they would be joined by twenty thousand fresh troops from Butler's Army of the James. Lee was right. Grant had ordered Butler to dispatch General William Farrar Smith and his Corps to White House Landing and then onto Meade.

Butler was eager to get rid of the argumentative Vermont-born General. The West Point graduate was considered by many to be an excellent engineer. He was creative and energetic. His primary weakness was his inability to keep his opinions to himself. After the battle of Fredericksburg, he sent a letter directly to Lincoln criticizing Burnside. Later he did the same thing regarding Rosecrans and now Butler.

Jubal Early sat on his horse and watched as Crawford's men crossed the creek unsupported by artillery. The new Commander of the Confederate Second Corps stroked his beard and smiled. This was the opportunity Lee was waiting for. It was too good to be true. He must attack. He would first probe the Union lines with one Division and if they were successful he would follow-up with the rest of his Corps.

By noon, Early had his Corps out of their trenches marching toward Crawford. In the lead was Major General Robert Rodes. The thirty-five year old Virginia Military Institute graduate had been in every major battle of the Army of Northern Virginia. He was Early's most experienced Division Commander. Rodes had his men in battle formation a little before one in the afternoon. When all was ready, he gave the order to charge. The Confederates let out their famed rebel yell and sprinted toward the Union lines.

Crawford's men let loose a volley sending a thousand projectiles of death towards the men in gray. The Confederates were unaffected and continued their assault. The Federals quickly reloaded and fired again. The second volley sent the battle-hardened veterans of Rodes Division to the ground. They immediately returned fire continuing their advance in leaps and bounds. First one Brigade would race forward twenty yards and drop to the ground. They would cover the second Brigade as it raced forward to their position. Then the two Brigades would lay down covering fire while a third Brigade raced forward. When all the Brigades were together, they would do it all over again. This time, however, the last Brigade would be the first and so forth. Slowly the rebels advanced and slowly Crawford's men retreated, drawing the unsuspecting attackers further into the trap. Grant's plan was working.

At three in the afternoon Crawford's men, with their ammunition almost gone, ran for the rear. The men in gray quickly pursued their game for a half-mile when they ran headlong into the rest of Warren's Corps supported by Wright. Both Wright and Warren had moved their Corps along with their artillery across the river unseen. A deadly volley halted the Confederate attack. Before the attackers could regroup, the Union troops counter-attacked. Rodes' men scampered back to their lines.

John Gordon was preparing to join in the attack when he saw Rodes' men in full retreat. The Division Commander formed his men into a defensive position and fired upon the pursuers. This slowed the charging Federals; but didn't stop them. Gordon's men fired two more volleys and joined Rodes' men in full retreat.

Early's Corps was in danger of being completely destroyed. Warren and Wright were not giving the rebels a chance to regroup. It was now a foot race to see if the Confederates would make it back to their lines before the Federals caught up with them. Early had acted on his own initiative and had not told his fellow Corps Commanders, Anderson and Hill, what he was doing. He hadn't performed any reconnaissance of the area before attacking. His rashness had jeopardized the remainder of Lee's Army.

Noticing Early's men leaving their positions, Anderson ordered his reserve Brigade into the vacated space. If Early was successful, then the Brigade could easily join in the attack. If the assault failed, they would be able to cover the retreat.

Noticing Early's men in full retreat Anderson gave the order for the Confederate artillery of both Early's Corps and his own to fire at the pursing enemy. Within minutes a hundred cannon spit forth flame, smoke and lead. Shells exploded in the middle of the attackers. Limbs were blown from their bodies; heads were ripped from the necks as the bursting artillery rounds performed their deadly task. The shelling continued for fifteen minutes before the Union Generals ordered a halt. Grant's plan had partially worked. He had badly mauled Early's Corps, but failed to draw out the rest of Lee's Army.

Campfires dotted the night sky as both Armies settled into their evening quarters. Grant sat by the fire whittling. A few minutes later he was joined by Rawlins.

"All right if I sit, General?" asked the trusted aide.

"Of course, sit down. We almost had them today. I thought for sure Lee would swallow the bait."

"Well, he did chew on it for a while," replied Rawlins. "I do have some good news. Smith's Corps has disembarked at White House and will be with us by first light tomorrow."

"That's good news. Instead of having him march here, issue orders to have him march to Cold Harbor. I've decided to move the Army there. Sheridan's Cavalry is to leave for Cold Harbor at first light. Wright's Corps is to wait until dawn and then move to Cold Harbor to reinforce Sheridan. I'll keep

Warren and Hancock here to keep Lee's Army in place. I want the enemy to think we are all still here."

Why Cold Harbor?" asked Rawlins.

"Cold Harbor is the key to the campaign. From there I can strike either North Carolina or Richmond. It's the crossroads to the James River. If Lee deprives me of Richmond, then I shall strike for North Carolina," replied Grant as he whittled.

Across the river Robert E. Lee sat in his tent with A.P. Hill. The red-haired fiery Corps Commander was fully recovered. He was the last of Lee's original Lieutenant Generals. Not noted for his tact or his strategic ability, he was a fierce fighter whom Lee had come to depend upon.

"General Hill, I've just been informed by our scouts General Grant has been reinforced by Smith's Corps. They tell me he now has an additional sixteen thousand men and another hundred Cavalry, not to mention, sixteen more cannon.

"Earlier I sent a telegram to the President requesting he immediately order Beauregard to send me Hoke's Division and any other reinforcements he can. I told him failure to do so will result in disaster for this Army and our cause," said Lee in a worried tone.

The young Corps Commander was startled by Lee's choice of words. In two years and countless skirmishes and battles, he had never heard Lee use the word 'disaster' in relation to the Army of Northern Virginia.

"About an hour ago I received a telegram from President Davis. He has ordered Beauregard to send me Hoke's entire Division. I've ordered them to Cold Harbor. I think General Grant will move his Army to Cold Harbor. From there he can strike either Richmond or Petersburg.

"In addition to Hoke, I've ordered Early's and Anderson's Corps to Cold Harbor. When General Grant arrives, he'll be met by over two thirds of this Army. General Hill, I need you to hold Grant's Army in place here. I want you to feign an attack by making a heavy demonstration. I'll order General Anderson to reinforce your Corps with a Brigade from his Corps," finished Lee.

Richmond Virginia—May 30, 9:30 PM

Ron Lyons hobbled into a tavern on Eleventh Street across from the City Hall. "Beer," said the spy to the burly bartender.

"Five dollars," barked the man.

"Isn't that a bit steep," replied Lyons throwing a five dollar Confederate Note on the bar.

"Shit, you call this piss, beer?"

"You're lucky I don't serve you piss," retorted the man taking the note and walking away.

Lyons stood at the bar sipping his beer when a short pudgy man approached him.

"How come a strong strapping lad such as you ain't in the Army?" asked the man in a loud, high-pitched voice.

Heads turned toward the pair as the other patrons looked at the spy suspiciously.

"What business is it of yours? How come a fat son-of-a-bitch like you ain't in the Army?" shot back Lyons.

"Young man, I am in the Army. My name is Captain Archer and I'm assigned to General John Winder's Secret Service to catch spies and deserters. Which one are you?" asked the rotund man seriously.

Slowly the men in the Tavern moved toward Lyons.

"I'm neither, you fat bastard," answered Lyons sternly while raising his pants to reveal a wooden leg.

"Lost the leg at Chickamauga under Hood and spent three months in the hospital in Atlanta before being discharged."

Lyons reached into his pocket and showed the man his discharge signed by none other than Robert E. Lee.

"I recognize the old man's signature," shouted one of the men in the back.

"I was courier for Lee until I lost my arm at Chancellorsville. That's Lee's signature all right," shouted another.

Soon others shouted their validation of the document. Archer stared at the paper for five minutes before handing it back to the young man.

"No hard feelings I hope. What brings you to Richmond?" asked Archer apologetically.

"I was looking for my brother. I was told he was at Almhouse Hospital, but they have no record of him," said Lyons.

"Give me his name and I'll try to track him down," replied Archer in a softer voice. In the meantime, let me buy you a drink. Bartender, some good beer for my young friend."

CHAPTER ELEVEN

Cold Harbor, Virginia—May 31, 12:00 PM

Riding at the head of the column Sheridan noticed Fitzhugh Lee's Cavalry Division occupying the cross-roads. Quickly he assembled his men into attack formation. Torbert's Division led the attack while Gregg's Division guarded the left flank. The horsemen in blue galloped toward their dismounted counterparts.

The Confederates opened fire toppling many of the charging enemy from their saddles either dead or wounded. Sheridan reformed and charged again. Once again the stubborn defenders held on. For three and half hours the Union troopers attacked repeatedly and were repulsed.

"Where the hell is Smith?" shouted an irate Sheridan in frustration.

"Sir, the scouts report General Smith and his men are nowhere to be found," answered an aide.

"Ride to General Gregg and tell him that at precisely four o'clock he is to pitch into the rebs flank."

Turning to another aide Sheridan continued.

"Ride to General Torbert and tell him to pull his men back. He is to rest and refit and at precisely four o'clock he is to throw everything he has against the rebs."

A strange silence took over the battlefield as Sheridan prepared his men for an all or nothing assault. Fitzhugh Lee paced anxiously knowing his men were played out. Ammunition was low and his casualties were high. He was desperately in need of reinforcements.

At precisely four o'clock Gregg's men hit the unsuspecting defenders. Fitzhugh Lee had no choice but to face half his command to his right to stave off the new assault. No sooner had he repositioned his men than Torbert attacked the tired defenders from the front.

George Armstrong Custer led the frontal assault. Twenty-five yards from the Confederate breastworks he was suddenly splattered with blood. His horse reared on its hind legs and collapsed dead. Seeing their Commander go down, the Brigade faltered. Custer immediately leaped to his feet and gave the order for his men to dismount and continue on foot. The men in blue stormed the breastworks. The fighting quickly escalated to hand-to-hand combat. Steel met steel as sabers clashed. Flesh was ripped open, blood and limbs littered the landscape.

While Custer's men, supported by the rest of Torbert's Division fought with Fitzhugh's men, Gregg and his Division stormed the hastily made breastworks in their sector. Slowly the Confederates gave way contesting every yard. For two hours the battle at the cross-roads raged.

Fitzhugh glanced over his shoulder and saw the lead Brigade of Hoke's Division advancing. The southern Cavalry Commander ordered his men to fall back to the infantry. Seeing Fitzhugh's men retreating in haste, the foot-sore infantrymen assumed a retreat had been ordered and broke for the rear.

Sheridan initially ordered a pursuit of the enemy, but with darkness rapidly descending and realizing his troops were strung out he quickly countermanded the order. Riding the battlefield he came to the conclusion that given the size of his force the cross-roads were untenable. He sent a courier to Meade and Grant informing them of his decision to pull back and dig in.

Grant and Meade sat in front of a campfire discussing the campaign and what Lee might be up to. The duo agreed to move Wright and Warren out in support of Sheridan and leave Hancock to hold Lee in place.

The Generals' conversation was interrupted by arrival of Sheridan's courier.

"Sir, General Sheridan reports he has routed Fitzhugh Lee's Cavalry along with Hoke's supporting infantry. He has taken the crossroads ..."

Grant jumped to his feet and clapped his hands together in a rare demonstration of emotion.

"At last we have stolen a march on Lee," said an elated Grant.

His elation was abruptly ended by the courier.

"Sir, General Sheridan has determined the crossroads are untenable and he is pulling his men back," stammered the courier

Before Grant could answer Meade blurted out.

"Ride back to General Sheridan and tell him he is not to pull back, he is to hold those cross-roads at all costs. Tell him Wright's Corps is moving to reinforce him as we speak."

The messenger looked at Grant who nodded in agreement. The young man saluted and departed.

Robert E. Lee sat by the campfire outside his tent listening to his nephew's courier on how he was forced to abandon his works and how Hoke's command had broken.

"Return to Fitzhugh and tell him Anderson's and Early's Corps are on their way and in the morning I will move my headquarters to Shady Grove Church. His orders are to dig in and wait for their arrival."

Lee watched the courier ride away into the darkness and then turned and entered his tent.

"Colonel Marshall I need my rest please make sure no one disturbs me unless it is an emergency," said a tired Lee as he closed his tent flap.

Alone inside his tent Lee lifted his bloodshot eyes skyward and began to pray.

"Almighty Father, please make me a wiser Commander so I may destroy those who have invaded my State. This war has cost too many lives. I beg thee strengthen my men and deliver us from those people who wish to vanquish us. You have seen fit to take Longstreet, Stonewall and JEB from me your will be done but please, Father, I implore you give me victory over General Grant."

Cold Harbor, Virginia—June 1, 5:25 AM

The sun shone brightly giving every indication of another hot humid day. Sheridan paced back and forth behind the breastworks his men had thrown up during the night. He stationed himself behind Custer's Brigade. He knew if there was action, the "Boy General" would be in the middle of the fight.

Sheridan patience was growing thin. He was promised reinforcements. Wright and his Corps should have been on the scene hours ago. He watched as Confederate reinforcements filled the Southern ranks. At eight o'clock Anderson's Corps attacked followed by a Division from Early's Corps, along with Fitzhugh's Cavalry. For the first time during the entire campaign, the men in gray outnumbered their blue-clad counterparts.

The air was quickly filled with smoke as thousands of projectiles flew across the open field. Most of the rounds struck the ground or trees while some found their human targets. More often than not, multiple rounds hit the same target. The gray ranks slowly melted, but still they advanced.

Anderson's and Early's artillery fired on the defenders causing them to duck their heads. Unfortunately, Sheridan only had a few cannon to return fire. He ordered them to concentrate on the rushing infantry. The Southerners were within twenty yards of the Union position when they were suddenly blown skyward. Wright's Corps had arrived. The Union General had ordered his artillery to unlimber and to fire on the men in gray closest to the Union breastworks, while his infantry filed in next to Sheridan's Calvary.

"General Sheridan, sorry for the delay but this cursed country is damn confusing in the dark. My men will overlap Anderson's men and fire into their flank," said Wright.

"General Wright you and your men are a most welcome sight," replied a relieved Sheridan.

After fifteen minutes of enduring a punishing crossfire Anderson ordered a retreat. The Union position was now too strong to be stormed. Once again, a unique opportunity had slipped through the Army of Northern Virginia's fingers. Corps Commanders on both sides dug in and waited.

Lee and Grant arrived on the battlefield at the same time. Quickly they both assessed the situation and decided to wait for the rest of their Army.

Night descended upon the battlefield. Grant sat by his campfire reading dispatches. Hunter was moving to engage Jones in the Shenandoah. Sherman was refitting his command and would soon be ready to again move against Johnston. He read the New York Herald and the Chicago Tribune.

"Good evening, Sam. Anything interesting in the papers?" asked John Rawlins.

"After reading this trash, I understand why Sherman and Meade hate reporters. Horace Greeley is the best man in Lee's Army. He is calling for the Republicans to dump Lincoln for the fall elections. The piss brain wants Chief Justice Chase for President," answered a disgusted Sam Grant.

"Nobody ever accused Greeley of being smart. In my opinion he is a few logs short of a full cord," replied the Chief-of-Staff smiling.

Grant stared at his friend in amazement. Rawlins seldom, if ever, told a joke.

"I am worried about the President. Doesn't the Country know he is our only hope for victory," said Grant.

"Ulys, why don't we let Abe worry about the politics and you concentrate on Lee. What are your orders for tomorrow? General Meade will be expecting them," responded Rawlins changing the subject.

"Speaking of Meade where is he?" inquired Grant.

"General Hancock's Gettysburg wound has flared up again. Meade went to visit him," answered John Rawlins.

"Inform George that I would like the Army to test Lee's line tomorrow. The results of the probe will determine our next course of action."

Across the battlefield, Lee met with Hill, Anderson and Early. He issued orders for the Army to dig in and to wait.

"Gentlemen, tomorrow General Grant will probe our lines and if he finds a weakness, he will attack. Depending on when he finds our weak spot, the attack will either be tomorrow in the afternoon or around dawn the next day. I want our men to spend the night and most of tomorrow fortifying our position. I also want us to leave a small gap between Hill and Anderson's Corps. I don't want to make it too obvious or else Grant will suspect something. I want to bait Grant into attacking and when he does, we'll destroy his Army."

As the sun rose bringing life to another day, Meade had patrols probe the Confederate lines. Each one reported the same thing. All day riders came and went from Meade's headquarters. There was no weakness in Lee's lines. Grant became more anxious as the day wore on. He had to do something for Lincoln. At six o'clock in the evening Meade arrived at Grant's headquarters.

"Good evening, General," said Meade.

He could immediately tell Grant was in no mood for niceties.

"Well, Meade, what have you discovered?" asked an anxious Grant.

"A half-hour ago one of our engineers discovered a small gap between Hill's and Anderson's Corps. My staff officers are of the opinion that we have discovered a chink in Lee's armor ... but I am not so sure," answered George Meade.

The Commanding General turned away and stared into the campfire, stroking his stubble of a beard. After a few minutes he turned back to his Army Commander and replied.

"I agree with you George. Your staff is incorrect. Lee wanted us to find this gap and attack him there. He probably has the bulk of his Army positioned so that he can destroy us when we strike the gap. That would mean he is weak across his entire line and come tomorrow we will hit everywhere at once. Hancock is to attack the right. Wright and Smith are to assault the center while Warren strikes the left. Sheridan's Cavalry will hold the bridges across the river and be in reserve. I want the attack to begin at four-thirty in the morning."

Meade stared in astonishment and began to protest, but the look in Grant's eyes told him any disagreement would be futile. A rapid change in the weather seemed to be a sign from heaven that Grant's orders were wrong as lightning flashed across the sky followed by thunder and a sudden downpour.

"General Grant, with your permission I will retire and issue the appropriate orders," replied a melancholy Meade.

As Meade rode to Hancock to deliver the orders in person he noticed the soldiers with their coats in their laps. They appeared to be sewing the holes and tears in their uniforms. As he rode closer he noticed the men, in anticipation of an assault, had written their name, address and next of kin on slips of paper and were sewing them inside their coats. If they were killed, they hoped someone would notify their next of kin of their demise.

Cold Harbor, Virginia—June 3, 4:30 AM

Without saying a word, Grant and Meade rode in the predawn to a hill less than a mile from Lee's lines. The time had come for the Union forces to break Lee's defenses. The rain ended as the sun began to rise. Union buglers blew the charge. Brigade and Division officers shouted to their respective commands to move out. Federal troops emerged from their shallow rifle pits like the dead rising from the grave. The wet and mud-soaked Union men formed ranks and with a firm and determined step advanced.

They had gone one hundred yards when they were greeted by the high pitched screams of minie balls and the loud boom of artillery shells bursting overhead and among them. It was like a volcano had erupted. Large chunks of dirt mixed with stones flew into the air as the Confederate artillery fired round after round. Huge gaps instantly appeared in the Union formations as men were mangled by the instruments of destruction.

In spite of the heavy fire from the rebel trenches, Grant's Army kept its advance. The air was completely filled with minie balls. The men in blue leaned forward, like a person walking against a fierce wind. They were determined to take Lee's fortifications. When one Brigade was decimated, it was quickly replaced by another as Division and Corps Commanders threw more men into the maelstrom.

Hancock watched in despair as his Corps was being slaughtered. He was filled with mixed emotions. On one hand he felt sadness; on the other he felt pride at the courage of his Corps.

Wright and Smith watched their respective Corps become decimated and were experiencing the same emotions as their peer.

Union artillery quickly responded to the Confederate challenge. Gun carriages flew through the air as the Yankee gunners found the range. Fireworks lit up the early dawn sky as the artillery rounds struck ammunition wagons.

Grant bit down hard on his cigar. His army was being destroyed in front of his eyes.

"General Meade, issue orders to stop the attack. Let's get our men out of there."

Grant turned his horse and rode back to his tent to plan his next move.

On the Union right, Burnside and Warren had captured Early's advanced rifle pits, and prepared to move out against the main entrenchments when they received Meade's orders.

Across the battlefield Lee sat on his horse and watched his men repulse the Union troops. He felt pity for the fallen Union soldiers, yet at the same time he was proud of his men. He was also disappointed Grant had cancelled the attack.

When Grant arrived back at his headquarters he was greeted by Lyons. The young man couldn't have arrived at a better time.

"Ron, what have you got for me," said Grant dismounting and walking rapidly to his tent.

The General-in-Chief entered his tent and motioned Rawlins and Lyons to follow. The three men sat down.

"Tell me what you found out," said Grant anxiously.

Lyons took a breath and started to cough. Regaining his composure the young man replied.

"The rebs want you to think Richmond is an empty shell, but it isn't. They have enough reserves and militia to hold you in check until Lee arrives with his Army. Petersburg is lightly defended with no more than five hundred men. Mostly boys and old men. Beauregard is concerned about Butler and is concentrating on him. There is a disagreement between Lee and Beauregard. With you stopping the prisoner exchanges, the South is in dire straits for replacements. General, I recommend you move on Petersburg."

Lyons began to cough; blood spilled from his mouth. Rawlins reached out and grabbed the man as he fell face forward toward the ground.

"He's burning with fever. Guard!" shouted Rawlins.

Instantly, Horace Porter and two of the General's bodyguards sprinted into the tent.

"Take Captain Lyons to my surgeon and stay with him. Report to me hourly on his condition," ordered Grant.

When Grant and Rawlins were alone, the man the press had nicknamed the Conqueror of Vicksburg put his face in his hands and then ran his hands backward through his hair.

"If I live to be a hundred years old, I will always regret ordering this morning's attack. I should have known better. As God is my witness, I shall never make that mistake again," said Grant his eyes beginning to well with water.

Rawlins listened quietly as Grant described the carnage in detail. The General was disheartened but not broken. Three hours later Grant stood and looked at his Chief-of-Staff. Rawlins saw a look of determination once again in his friend's eyes.

"John, I must be left alone to ponder my next move. Please post a guard in front of my tent."

CHAPTER TWELVE

Washington, D.C., White House—June 8, 10:00 PM

Abraham Lincoln sat behind his desk in the Executive Office. The grandfather clock in the hall gonged ten times. The Union President rose and walked into the outer office. Seated at a small writing table was John Hay.

"John, any word from the convention?"

"None, sir, they should be about halfway through the balloting. I don't expect we will hear anything until around midnight. Senator Cameron and Secretary Seward feel you should win the party's nomination on the first ballot."

While the two men talked, they were approached by portly Edwin Stanton.

"Edwin, what brings you out this time of night?" inquired Lincoln.

"I am waiting for the party's convention results," replied the weary Secretary of War.

"Any word from Grant?" asked Lincoln.

"None, sir, you know Grant; he won't trust the telegraph lines. We'll know what he's doing when we read it about in the papers. He has ordered Halleck to send every available pontoon bridge he can lay his hands on to City Point," answered Stanton.

"It sounds like our General is planning a new movement. I wonder what he is going to do next," said the President.

Before the three men realized it, the grandfather clock chimed one time. The men heard a courier enter the main foyer asking for the President. The butler escorted the man to the trio.

The young man had sandy hair. His uniform blouse was a dark blue, while his trousers were a lighter shade of the same color. It was obvious he had just been issued the uniform a few days earlier. He handed the President a telegram, saluted, did an about face and departed without saying a word.

Lincoln looked at his two companions, shrugged his shoulders and read the telegram out loud. A smile quickly spread across his face; but was instantly replaced with a frown.

"Gentlemen, the Republican Party has nominated me on the first ballot. It was a unanimous vote," said Lincoln dryly.

"Congratulations, Mr. President, I ..." began Stanton.

The President held up his hand and stopped the Secretary in mid-sentence. "There's more. The Party has not nominated Hannibal Hamlin as Vice President. According to Cameron and Seward, the Party feels McClellan will be the Democratic Party nominee and, in order to defeat him, we need someone from a Border State to get the Border States' electoral votes."

"Who are they suggesting? Sir, Hannibal Hamlin has been an excellent Vice President and a loyal and supportive sponsor of your Administration," replied John Hay

"Tomorrow morning they are going to nominate Senator Andrew Johnson from Tennessee as Vice President. They feel he also will win by a unanimous vote," answered Lincoln.

"Either way, this is a victory for you. Three months ago, we only had fourteen states voting for us, now we have all of them," responded a happy Stanton.

"We still have to win in November and unless General Grant and his armies win a major victory, I will be a one-term President. Gentlemen, I bid you both a good-night. I must tell Mrs. Lincoln of our victory. She will be delighted," answered Lincoln as he walked to his bedroom.

Over the next few days the President received telegrams of congratulations. Abolitionists reveled in the party's choice. In Middletown, Connecticut a clergyman hung a sign from his door quoting Genesis 22:15 *"The angel of the Lord called unto Abraham out of heaven a second time."*

As much as the Republicans lauded over Lincoln's victory, the Democrats were vicious in their attacks of the President. *"The New York World"* called Lincoln an ignorant, boorish, third-rate backwoods lawyer. *"The Chicago Times"* wrote that Lincoln was a pompous ass. *"The New York Tribune"* called the President indecisive and easily influenced by the Washington cabal.

The President was a strong Republican while the Vice President was a war Democrat. The ticket was united except for Andrew Johnson. He never sent

Lincoln a telegram of congratulations, nor did he receive one. It was a marriage of convenience—not love.

Washington, D.C., Soldier's Home—June 11, 9:00 PM

Lincoln entered the Soldier's Home, which was the fancy name given to a hospital used for recuperation of the Union wounded. The Home was located on the Arlington plantation once owned by Robert E. Lee. In 1863 the Union had foreclosed the estate for non-payment of taxes. It was decided the massive plantation would be a burial ground for Union dead and the Lee Mansion would be a hospital.

The President walked the wards stopping at every bed and talking with the soldiers. John Nicolay accompanied the Union's Chief Executive. At the end of the tour the two men stepped outside on the front porch. Torches lit up the long bridge leading from Arlington to Washington. In the distance gaslights lit up the streets of Washington. The cool night air and the chirping of crickets gave the semblance of calm and tranquility. Lincoln leaned against a marble pillar and looked down.

In his hand he held a telegram from Grant. He read the message, sighed and in a soft, low voice said.

"Mr. Nicolay, General Grant reports Hunter has won a great victory. The Shenandoah is ours once again. Confederate General "Grumble Jones" is dead and his Army in disarray. He also reports Sherman is again on the move and he anticipates a renewal of the contest with Lee and Johnston forthwith."

Lincoln was tired of war. His eyes became misty as he resumed his statements.

"I was half hoping Lee would surrender and this terrible conflict would be ended. How sleep the brave; who sink to rest. By all their Country's wishes blest and women o'er the graves shall weep where nameless heroes calmly sleep."

While Lincoln reflected on the horrors of war, Benjamin Stringfellow rode the streets of Washington making mental notes of the strength of the garrisons occupying the forts around the Capital City. He was surprised on the lack of manpower.

Pine Mountain, Georgia—June 12, 5:30AM

Joe Johnston peered through his binoculars and watched the blue wave slowly approach. To his right stood Leonidas Polk with Hardee on his left. To

Hardee's left John Hood sat on his horse. The four men were mesmerized by the size of Sherman's Army.

A cold rain whipped across the mountaintop as Johnston pulled the binoculars from his eyes. The wet, icy blast penetrated the flimsy rain ponchos of the quartet sending a chill up their spines.

"Must be at least a hundred thousand," said Johnston in a business-like tone as Union artillery punctuated the General's statement.

"Looks like he's going to try to turn us again," replied Hardee.

Puffs of white smoke dotted the countryside as Sherman's long-range cannons fired repeatedly.

"I agree. Unfortunately, we haven't the men to meet the threat and we must slowly fall back," responded Johnston.

"When would you like us to move our ..." said Polk.

He never finished the sentence. While he was speaking a cannonball hit the ground three feet in front of Johnston. Striking a small boulder it careened to Johnston's right and struck Polk in mid-sentence ripping his head from his body. Blood spurt two feet into the air, the bulk of it landing on Johnston. The head hit the ground with a resounding thud. The body stood rigid for a few minutes then collapsed. A look of surprise was on the dead man's face. Aides raced to the fallen officer. Gently they lifted him, placing the head inside the poncho, and took him to the rear.

"Make sure ... his body is properly ... cared for. Telegraph the President ... and inform him of General Polk's death. They were close personal friends," stammered a shaken Johnston.

The three men turned their attention back to Sherman's forward movements, each pretending not to be affected by the sudden loss of their comrade. Their conversations continued in a calm manner, discussing their retrograde movements. They decided to wait until dark and then slip away.

"Jeff Davis isn't going to like us falling back," said Hardee.

"The President can remove me anytime he sees fit. I will not jeopardize this Army to satisfy him," replied Johnston defiantly

They continued their strategy session until another cannon ball struck Hood's horse shearing off the front legs of the animal. Hood pitched forward and landed painfully on his backside as his mount fell forward in agony. Another aide rushed forward, helped the General up, while another dispatched the crippled horse with a pistol shot to the head.

"Gentlemen, I think we should move to another position," said Johnston mounting his horse.

Cold Harbor, Virginia—June 12, 1:00 PM

Grant sat in his headquarters' tent as the rain continued to fall. In spite of the weather, he decided to begin a turning movement. For the past nine days his Army had laid opposite Lee. It was an obvious stalemate. The last assault had cost the Union over seven thousand casualties. Half were dead the other half lay wounded in the no man's land between the two Armies. Meade pleaded with Grant to ask Lee for a truce to retrieve their wounded. The Union General-in-Chief stubbornly refused. Under the rules of war, the party which requests a truce is considered to be the loser and Grant refused to concede anything to Lee.

At night Union squads of two or three ventured under the cover of darkness to retrieve their wounded comrades as rebel sharpshooters laid in wait ever vigilant of any moving shadow. Three days after the battle, Grant finally acceded to Meade's request for a truce under the provision that it came from Meade. Of the thirty-five hundred men trapped between the lines only forty were found alive. The rest had died of exposure, lack of water or bled to death.

"General Grant," said a courier interrupting Grant's thoughts. "General Sheridan instructed me to report that last night he was engaged by Hampton's Cavalry. We put up a struggle and then darkness ended the conflict. This morning when I left, he was preparing for battle. He estimates the enemy force to be five thousand."

"Ride back to General Sheridan and instruct him to keep Hampton occupied. He must buy me time," replied Grant staring at his maps.

Quickly he wrote orders to Meade.

"General Meade.
Tonight, under the cover of darkness, Warren will pull out of his position. He is to march to Malvern Hill leaving Brigades along the way to protect the rest of the Army's approach to the James River. At Malvern Hill he is to entrench. Wright and Hancock are to spread out and cover Warren's vacated position.
Once we receive word Warren has entrenched; Hancock, Burnside and Wright will move out. Hancock is to march to Wilcox's Landing where boats will be waiting for him and his Corps to cross the James. Burnside and Wright will cross the James via the pontoon bridge, which our engineers should have finished by the time they arrive. Smith's Corps will move to West Point on the York River and board ships that will take him south of the Bermuda Hundred. Once his force has landed he is to march to Petersburg.
U.S. Grant"

Based on the information provided by Lyons, Grant decided to bypass Richmond and take the important railroad junction at Petersburg. It was Richmond's lifeline with the rest of the South. It was from this town that the Richmond-Petersburg Railroad supplied the Confederate capital and Lee's Army. Also running through Petersburg was the Weldon and Petersburg railway, which brought supplies from the deep South, while the Southside railway linked the Confederate capital with the North Carolina coast.

The maneuver was extremely risky. If Lee discovered what Grant was up to, the "silver fox" of the Confederacy could destroy the Union Army while it was on the move and very vulnerable. Secrecy and rapid movements were essential to the success of the plan. Never before had anyone constructed a pontoon bridge across such a rapid, wide river. If all went well, his Army would be across the James and in Petersburg before the sixteenth.

On the other side of the battlefield Lee was meeting with his Commanders. Early sat directly across from the Commanding General, next to Early sat Hill and next to Hill was Anderson. The aged Virginian looked across the table at his brain trust. They were the best men he could muster to command.

"Gentlemen, as you are aware, Grant's strategy of attacking the South at many different points simultaneously is working. We can no longer afford to weaken one part of our Country to support the other. Each Army must stand on its own. I think we can safely assume Grant will not ask for quarter nor will he give any. This became obvious when he refused to seek a truce at Cold Harbor. He has the same belief I have. That to be a successful Commander, you must love your Army and be willing to sacrifice a part of it to save the rest."

Lee paused and looked down. In his right hand he held a telegram from Bragg in Richmond.

"Gentlemen, 'Grumble Jones' is dead and his Army routed. Hunter has burned the Virginia Military Academy and is now ravaging the land. The Shenandoah is our breadbasket. We cannot lose her."

"General Lee, tell us what you want us to do and we'll do it," responded Hill.

"I propose to send General Early to the Shenandoah along with the entire Second Corps," answered Lee.

Early's eyes widened, he hated this cat and mouse game with Grant. This was his chance to reward Lee's trust in him. The confirmed bachelor was strange and irascible, but he was a fierce fighter.

"General Early will take his Corps out of the trenches tonight under the cover of darkness and circle around Richmond through the mountains and defeat Hunter. When Early leaves, I want Hill and Anderson to spread out their men so Grant will not know we have reduced our force"

After the conference the Generals left Lee's tent. He called out to his aide that he wished to retire and would not like to be disturbed. The South's finest soldier undid his sash and sat at his portable desk and wrote a letter to his wife.

> *"My dear Mary:*
> *I have received your several notes, but have not had the opportunity to reply to them. I am glad you have our friend, William Carter, with you. I hope you will take good care of him and soon make him well. We require everyone in the field we can get. I presume they have suffered everything at Hickory Hill and Uncle Williams. Indeed I have heard that the enemy has taken everything from them. It is lamentable in the extreme. You must thank the kind ladies for the nice bread. Tell them their remembrance of me is more comforting than their rolls and loaves. Little Sallie, I understand, had to run off to North Carolina to get rid of her beaux. What is she going to do now? I must write and thank Mr. Jackson for the pieces of cotton. I do not require nightshirts. You had better keep them for day shirts, which I may require after a while. I saw nephew Fitzhugh and our youngest son, Rob, yesterday. Fitzhugh was with his Cavalry command while Robert was with his artillery battery. Young Robert is still refusing an officer's commission and says he will earn what he gets. They were both marching from one end of our Army to the other in anticipation of another movement by Grant. My pen will not mark and I must stop. Give love to my daughters. How are the little cormorants? I hear they eat everything before them. I am glad their appetites are good. I hope you are doing well. I am well again, thank God. May He in His infinite mercy keep you all under the shadow of His wings.*
> *Truly and constantly,*
> *Robert"*

Cold Harbor, Virginia—June 14, 8:00 AM

Lee sat with his staff eating breakfast when A.P. Hill rode up. Dismounting, he saluted the Commanding General and approached. By the way he was walking; it was obvious the diminutive Corps Commander was still in pain.

"Good morning, General," said Hill.

"What brings you out this morning, Ambrose?" asked Lee as he dipped his biscuit in gravy.

"Sir, Grant and his Army are gone. I sent out a few men on patrol. They rode for a mile in all directions and found nothing," replied Hill

"I thought Grant would move. He doesn't like a stalemate. The question is—where did he go?"

The Commanding General leisurely paced back and forth while he pondered his enemy's options. After ten minutes he stopped.

"Colonel Marshall, ride to General Hampton. At the same time I would like Major Venable to ride to General Lee. Tell them the Commanding General is ordering them to send out patrols in all directions and find Grant's Army. I must know where he is headed. Make all possible speed, I fear he his headed for Richmond; but I can't move until I'm sure," said Lee.

The Confederate General turned to Ambrose Hill.

"General Hill, I wish to borrow Sergeant Tucker. I would like him to ride to General Anderson and inform him I'm sending out Cavalry patrols to ascertain where those people have moved. He must have his Corps ready to move at a moment's notice."

Throughout the day Lee waited for news of the whereabouts of his foe. Riders came and went all with the same story. *"No sight of the enemy."* At four in the afternoon a rider galloped into camp. He reined his horse hard forcing its hind legs to buckle.

"Sir, General Hampton reports that our patrols encountered a Federal Corps dug-in from Cold Harbor to Malvern Hill. We tried to penetrate their lines, but were turned back by Sheridan's men. General Hampton is of the opinion the enemy is trying to take Richmond from the south," panted the courier.

No sooner had Hampton's messenger reported than another arrived.

"Sir, General Lee reports that, according to our spies at White House Landing, a large detachment of Federals left the landing about nine last night. They were headed up the York River. They overhead a few officers talking about sailing to Washington," said the winded courier.

The Commanding General quickly dismissed the Washington rumor. The information seemed to validate Hampton's theory the enemy could be heading up the York and around the James to take Richmond from the south. He couldn't commit himself until he was certain of where Grant was headed. For the first time, Lee was stymied.

Meade rode with Hancock to the James River. The two friends talked politics—Meade, the Republican and Hancock, the Democrat. Both men liked the President and were elated with his nomination. Meade favored Lincoln's re-election. Hancock, favoring Lincoln also, was torn between his close personal friendship with McClellan and what was good for the Country.

As darkness descended, the two Generals watched as the Second Corps marched aboard their transports. In less than five hours they would be across the James and be disembarking at Windmill Point. After a few hours of rest, they would march due west and join Smith's Corps already enroute to Petersburg. The two friends said good-bye. Hancock led his horse onto the transport, while Meade galloped back to Grant and the rest of the Army.

Grant was up early on the morning of the fifteenth. He was in a good mood. Everything was going better than planned. Hancock had crossed the James. Smith was enroute to Petersburg. The massive pontoon bridge would be finished by mid-afternoon. Tonight under the cover of darkness, he would pull Wright's Corps out of the line in support of Warren and have them cross followed by Warren and Burnside. He would cross with Burnside's Corps. By tomorrow, Smith and Hancock would take Petersburg. With Hunter in control of the Shenandoah Valley and Meade in control of Petersburg; Richmond would be starved into submission.

At Cold Harbor Lee paced back and forth. He had no idea where Grant was. The Cavalry screen was effective. Hampton's and Fitzhugh's Corps were kept busy chasing Sheridan, while the Commanding General's son, Rooney Lee, with two thinly spread out Divisions continued to search the countryside for the Union Army.

He would wait until noon. If he didn't have a definite word of Grant's whereabouts by then, he would move his Army south—but where?

While he was pondering his next move, Colonel Charles Marshall interrupted.

"Sir, a telegram has just arrived from President Davis."

"Please read it aloud," requested the Army Commander in a distracted voice.

> *"General Lee, have you been able to ascertain the whereabouts of the enemy? If not, should you not issue orders to General Early to return to you and let the freeing of the Valley wait?*
> *Respectfully,*
> *Jefferson Davis*
> *President of the Confederate States of America"*

Lee stopped his pacing and, turning to his young aide, dictated a reply.

"To his Excellency,
I don't know where Grant is or where he is headed. I think he is headed south. I
am issuing orders for this Army to move to just below White Oak Swamp. From
there the Army can protect Richmond in two directions while at the same time we
can support Beauregard at Drewy's Bluff. It is my opinion Early should proceed
with his current mission.
Your most obedient servant,
Robert E. Lee
Commanding General
Army of the Northern Virginia CSA."

Having finished his dictation, Lee issued orders to Hill and Anderson to move south.

Richmond, Virginia—June 14, 5:30 PM

Confederate President Jefferson Davis sat at his large conference table in his Executive office. On the highly polished table lay four telegrams. The first was Lee's reply. While concerned about Grant's disappearance, he had full faith in his friend.

The second was from Beauregard. The Creole General was requesting reinforcements stating he thinks Grant is heading for Petersburg. Before he could send an order to Lee to abandon Richmond and head for Petersburg, he would need definite proof. The movements could be a diversion.

The other two telegrams were from Joe Johnston. The first one informed the President of the death of Polk; while the second one stated he was, once again, forced to retire.

"Every mile Johnston retreats boosts Lincoln's chances of re-election. The only hope for the Confederacy was for Lincoln to lose in November. For that to happen, Grant must be kept out of Richmond and Sherman out of Atlanta. Why can't Johnston see this?" thought Davis.

His thoughts were rudely interrupted by the sound of cannon fire.

Davis raced to the porch outside his office. The sounds were coming from east of the city. He cocked his head to the left then to the right in an attempt to ascertain where the bombardment was coming from. He had no idea Hill had run into Wrights Corps, which was screening Grant's movements. At the same time, Anderson had run into Warren's Corps.

Neither of the Southern Corps Commanders knew the other was engaged and both requested reinforcements from the other. Anderson and Hill sent couriers to Lee stating that they had each found an isolated Corps. If they could be reinforced, they could destroy it.

Davis listened to the cannonade north of the city. A few minutes later it was joined by the sounds of an artillery battle southeast of the city. He was as confused as Lee.

Petersburg, Virginia—June 15, 6:30 PM

While Wright and Warren kept Lee's men busy, "Baldy Smith" and his entire Eighteenth Corps, consisting of sixteen thousand men, were at Petersburg preparing to attack Beauregard's twenty-two hundred defenders.

The Southern General positioned his men across a ten-mile defensive line heavily supported by cannons. An additional thirty-two hundred men four miles away were keeping Butler's fifteen thousand Union troops pinned down at the Bermuda Hundred. At Petersburg there was one defender for every twenty-four feet of trench. To fill in the gaps, the Creole General had sticks placed in the entrenchments which were painted to look like muskets. On top of the sticks he placed a hat. He made it look like he had twenty-two thousand troops and not twenty-two hundred. In addition, he had his men cut down trees, paint them black to look like cannons and place them on wagon axles.

His defenses weren't without teeth. He had fifty-five square shaped forts interlinked by six-foot high breastworks twenty feet thick. In the forts he placed a combination of fake and real cannons.

In front of his breastworks there was a dry moat six feet deep and fifteen feet wide. In the moat Beauregard had placed fallen trees with the branches sharpened on all sides. Infantry entering the moat would be under fire with no protection.

Additionally, the Confederate General had his men clear the ground a half-mile in front of the works giving them a clear field of fire. The defenses appeared to be formidable and would be if he had troops to man them.

The Federals arrived in front of Petersburg at noon and had spent the next five and half hours preparing to attack. Smith personally surveyed the Confederate defenses looking for a weakness and found none. Duped into thinking Lee had reinforced Beauregard and knowing Hancock and the Second Corps were on their way, he decided to wait.

Meanwhile Hancock sat on his horse swearing up a storm. The normally calm Union Commander was in a foul mood. His Gettysburg wound was still causing him severe pain. He would have preferred to ride in the ambulance where he could lie down; but with the chances of a battle at any time, he felt it was his duty to be at the head of his Corps.

The Second Corps was across the James River by dawn. Hancock rested his men until ten. As he prepared to move them out, he received orders from Grant to wait for supplies. The Corps Commander was not happy with the delay and began cursing like a mule driver. He had plenty of supplies.

Minutes turned to hours as Hancock and his Corps waited for the supplies they didn't need. The Corps Commander dismounted and walked to his ambulance. His aides had found an icehouse nearby and commandeered some ice. They had him unbutton his heavy wool coat, lift up his shirt and placed the frozen water on his wound. The coolness helped relieve the pain. After a few hours he had enough. It was past two o'clock and still no supply ships.

"Enough is enough! We march on Petersburg!" shouted Hancock exiting the ambulance.

Hancock mounted his horse next to his friend, John Gibbon; their civilian scout joined the two Union Generals. Within a half hour the Second Corps was on its way. For three hours the Union men marched along unfamiliar roads. This was the furthest south the Army of the Potomac had ever come. Their maps were useless and outdated. At five o'clock Hancock halted his men and questioned their guide. He quickly ascertained the man was lost and called for his aide.

"Colonel, change clothes with this so-called guide and ride ahead to that farmhouse over there on the horizon. Tell the occupants you are with Lee's Army and need directions to Petersburg to help Beauregard."

An hour later the Colonel was back with the directions. They had missed the Petersburg turnoff and marched two and half-hours out of their way. At best, they wouldn't be with Smith until after eight o'clock.

"Baldy" Smith paced back and forth at his headquarters. It was six-thirty and still no word from Hancock. The sun was beginning to set and with it any chance of breaking the Petersburg line. He had no choice but to attack.

"Major Hamilton," said the Corps Commander.

"Yes, sir," replied the young officer with military efficiency.

"Send a courier to Generals Hincks, Martindale and O'Neill. Inform them that at precisely seven o'clock, they are to attack the rebels in their front as we discussed earlier. Hincks' Colored Division is to lead the attack and will be supported by Martindale's Division on the right and O'Neill's Division on their left."

Hincks readied his men for the attack. The woods would conceal their movement for fifty yards. Once they cleared the forest, success was dependent upon how rapidly they moved. The Division Commander was not new to combat having fought in every major battle with the Army. Wounded twice, he was known for his bravery and his abolitionist feelings. He was a perfect choice to lead the inexperienced Negro soldiers.

Earlier in the war, Jefferson Davis issued orders to treat the officers of black troops not as prisoners of war, but as insurrectionists encouraging slaves to rebel against their masters. As such they were to be shot while the black troops were to be considered runaway slaves. If their masters were identified, they would be returned. If no master claimed them, they would be sold at auction with the proceeds going to the Confederate government. Instead of discouraging the Union troops, it only served as an incentive for the officers and men of any colored division to fight harder.

At precisely seven o'clock Hincks and his men stepped out of the woods and sprinted across the clearing. Artillery shells of canister burst into the ranks thinning the charging blue line; minie balls whizzed through the air. Some passed harmlessly by, while others struck their human targets. Approaching the moat, Hincks ordered two of his three Brigades to provide covering fire while the third entered the moat and dismantled the Confederate defenses. The Union Division Commander wasn't about to let his men become helplessly trapped in the moat. As the Brigades covered their comrades, Hincks noticed resistance was light.

In less than ten minutes, the Union troops were through the moat and had taken the first of the Confederate defensive positions. Hincks reorganized his men and proceeded forward pressing the attack. Seeing his line breached, Beauregard ordered a full retreat. Slowly the men in gray gave way.

Like a slalom skier they weaved back and forth keeping in between red stakes planted in the ground. The heat of battle blinded the attackers as they ignored the stakes and rushed straight for their retreating foes. Suddenly the air was filled the sound of explosions. Men in blue were blown skyward, their bodies violently ripped apart. The attackers stopped and looked around. The explosions weren't from cannons. A look of confusion spread across many of their faces.

Hincks had faced this type of warfare before in 1862. He and his men had run into a field of buried land torpedoes. The sunken, concealed artillery shells were primed to explode when stepped on. He had two choices, return the way they came or proceed forward. Since he wasn't exactly sure when they entered the field or which way they had come, he opted to run the gauntlet of explosive devices and ordered his men to run forward. Once again bodies were flung skyward their limbs raining down on their comrades. Within five minutes Hincks Division cleared the mine field and stormed the empty breastworks. He passed the order to dig in and prepare for a counter attack. Ten minutes later "Baldy" Smith and his staff arrived at the front.

"Edward, well done," said the Corps Commander climbing down from his horse.

"Thank you, sir. In less than two hours we captured five enemy works, twelve cannon and one hundred sixty prisoners," replied a sweating Hincks.

"Excellent, most excellent; in total the Corps has captured seven enemy works, sixteen cannon and three hundred prisoners. This news will please General Grant," answered Smith.

"Sir, the enemy has buried land torpedoes along the entire field. I have lost twenty-three men to those damn things. Seventeen killed and six severely wounded."

"Damn rebels. They'll stoop to any means not to lose this war. Use the prisoners to locate and remove the devices. They planted the damn things and I don't give a damn if they all get killed removing them."

"Sir, resistance was light. I don't think the rebs are heavily reinforced. I'd like permission to take my Division forward and press the attack. We can smash their defenses and be in Petersburg before midnight," said Hincks.

"Permission denied. I have heard General Lee has reinforced Beauregard. We will wait until Hancock arrives then; if he orders the attack, we'll have fifty thousand men to hit the rebs."

"Sir, we don't need Hancock. Let me take two Brigades and attack," pleaded Hincks.

"Request denied. Hold your position and wait further orders," retorted Smith.

Hancock arrived at Smith's headquarters just before eight in a foul mood. His temper flared as he relayed his delays to his peer. The General from Vermont listened patiently waiting for the Second Corps' Commander to calm down.

"Win, we have taken the first of the Confederate defenses. My men are in position to press the attack if you order it," said Smith.

"Baldy, I'm not familiar with the field; therefore, I'll place myself under your command until morning when I can inspect the ground before us. What are your orders?" asked Hancock.

"Win, I've a bad feeling about pressing the attack. I think Lee is waiting further down the road with his entire Army and would like nothing better than to destroy two of Grant's Corps. We'll wait for Burnside and then hit him with sixty thousand men across his entire front," replied Smith.

The two Commanders inspected the placement of Smith's Corps and agreed Hancock's Second Corps would take a position to the left of Smith's men. When the sun rises, the Southern Commander would be facing fifty thousand Union troops. When his men were in place, Hancock retired for the night. His Gettysburg wound continued to bother him. At the same time Smith, who was suffering from malaria, decided it was time to retire and be fresh for the next day's contest.

While Hancock and Smith slept, Grant was peering over maps at his new headquarters on the James River, City Point. Located less than a half day's ride to Petersburg and less than an hour ride from the Bermuda Hundred; it was central to both locations. The wharves on the James River provided more than adequate depth for the Navy to unload supplies or for troop transports to unload reinforcements or, if the need ever arose, to send reinforcements north.

CHAPTER THIRTEEN

Petersburg, Virginia—June 16, 4:00 AM

Beauregard woke before dawn with a feeling of impending doom. During the night Hoke's and Ransom's Divisions from Lee's Army arrived and were positioned in the trenches, bringing the total number of defenders to fifteen thousand.

As the sun rose, he saw his worst fears had come true. Smith had been reinforced. The Cajun General estimated forty thousand Union troops were now facing him. Without hesitation he wired Richmond that he now faced Smith's and Hancock's Corps. There should be no doubt of Grant's intention to take Petersburg and not Richmond. The General from Louisiana sent a courier to Lee informing him of the situation.

On the other side of the field, Hancock and Smith rode among the Union troops inspecting their own entrenchments as well as reconnoitering Beauregard's defenses. They looked impregnable; however, the two men were not deterred.

"Baldy, I would like to probe their lines for weakness and then decide where we should strike. Burnside should be here by noon. We'll wait for his men before commencing the attack."

"I concur, Win."

City Point, Virginia—June 16, 9:00AM

Grant sat outside his tent smoking a cigar when Meade arrived. The General-in-Chief walked over to his faithful subordinate, reached up and shook his hand. Their conversation was brief.

"George, I want you to pull Warren out of his trenches and march him to Petersburg. I'd like you to ride to Petersburg and take command there," said Grant.

Meade turned to his Chief-of-Staff and issued the orders. Couriers immediately sped away to deliver the instructions.

The Commander of the Army of the Potomac saluted and rode away. For the first time since the campaign began, Meade would have independent command without Grant breathing down his neck. He would make the most of his temporary independence.

Meade arrived at Petersburg at the same time as Burnside. He immediately met with his three Corps commanders. He ordered Burnside to place his troops at their left flank putting Hancock's Corps in the center and Smith's men on the right flank. The attack would commence precisely at three o'clock. The repositioning of almost sixty-five thousand troops would take time and Meade wanted to make sure it was done right.

Meade rode with Hancock as the pair inspected their lines. Sweat poured down the Corps Commander's face. By the expression on his face, it was obvious he was in a great deal of pain. Normally steady in the saddle, he would periodically wobble back and forth. Unseen by anyone blood and puss were oozing down the General's leg into his calf high boots.

"Win, are you ok? You look as pale as milk. Perhaps you should sit this one out and let Birney lead the attack?" asked a concerned Meade.

"I'm fine. It's just this blasted heat. I can lead my Corps."

At three o'clock the attack began. It slowly developed as the coordination between the Union Corps was lacking. Their attacks were disjointed preventing them from taking advantage of their superior numbers. They outnumbered the defenders five-to-one. For some unexplained reason Smith and Burnside did not begin their attack at the same time. Even Hancock did not use his full Corps. He opted instead to send only two Divisions keeping the third in reserve.

The Pennsylvania General's Corps met with slight success pushing back the defenders a few hundred yards. Using his advantage of short interior lines, the Creole defender shifted the majority of his forces to parry Hancock's thrust. No sooner had he stabilized his center than Smith attacked the left. Leaving a skeleton force to keep Hancock's Corps in check, the Southern General shifted the majority of his troops to meet the new threat of Smith's attack. Once again the defenders were fortunate. Smith's men were stopped before any serious breach in the line occurred.

With the majority of his forces engaged against Smith, there was only a small force available to stop Burnside. The southerners were pushed back losing six hundred men, five cannon and one mile of breastworks.

Darkness descended upon the battlefield as Beauregard made plans to defend against the attacks he knew would continue the next day. He had been fortunate. He knew if the Union forces had attacked across the entire line at the same time, his force would have been either captured or killed and Petersburg taken. He held strong ground on his left and center, but with Burnside a mile in his works on the right, his entire position was in jeopardy. His defenses now looked like an inverted "L". He sent a telegram to Lee.

> *"To: General Robert E. Lee*
> *Whereabouts of the rest of Grant's Army is unknown. Hancock and Smith are in my front. I believe Grant is moving to this place. Can you not reinforce me immediately?*
> *P.G.T. Beauregard*
> *General CSA"*

With no immediate hope of reinforcements, he pulled his men back to a third line of defense.

City Point, Virginia—June 16, 10:00 PM

"Ulys, we've had one hell of a day," said Rawlins lighting a cigar.

"I'm pleased with today's results. The majority of the Army is across the James and by tomorrow, the entire Army will be across the river. Lee still doesn't know where we are. By midnight tonight, Warren will be at Petersburg. Wright has been diverted to assist Butler. I think we did well crossing a great river and attacking Lee in the rear before he is ready for us," answered Grant.

Rawlins nodded his head in agreement.

"Any word from Sherman?" asked Grant.

"His latest telegram, received this morning, states he was pushing Joe Johnston back; but the rain was making the movement slow. He said Johnston appeared to be moving to Kennesaw Mountain. McPherson, Schofield and Thomas are in close pursuit."

"Any news from Hunter in the Valley?" asked the General-in-Chief.

"He reports he has left Lexington and is headed for Lynchburg. He also reports that he burned the Virginia Military Academy," replied Rawlins.

"Why in the world would he burn the Academy? It poses no threat to us." responded a perplexed Grant.

"He felt it would go as a lesson to the rest of the South."

The two men shrugged their shoulders in disbelief and continued their conversation for another hour before the General decided to call it an early night.

While Grant slept peacefully, Meade was awake making plans to continue the attacks. He decided to use Warren's fresh troops to extend his flank. Meade had just retired for the evening when a courier arrived from Hancock saying that Hancock was too ill to take the field and he was temporarily turning command over to Major General David Birney. Meade shook his head in disappointment.

"Birney is a good soldier, but he is no Hancock," thought the Commanding General.

Petersburg, Virginia—June 17, 5:45AM

At dawn Burnside ordered his Corps forward. In the lead was his senior Commander and personal friend, Orlando Willcox. The two men had graduated together in 1847 from West Point. Willcox's men had to cross a hundred and fifty yards of open ground carefully stepping over telegraph wire strung low to trip an assaulting force. Small pits two feet deep were filled with sharpened stakes and camouflaged with dirt. Beauregard's men had made sure that, if an attack came from Burnside's front, the Union men would pay dearly.

Confederate cannon boomed dotting the dawn-lit sky with small, white puffy clouds of smoke. Within seconds leaded projectiles sailed overhead whistling their tune of death. The high-pitched sound sent shivers down the attackers' spines. Ignoring their fear; they continued forward.

Halfway across the open field, explosions blew some of the attackers skyward as they entered a torpedo field. Drawing his sword backward and then bringing it forward up over his head in a slow moving arc, Willcox shouted at the top of his lungs for the men to charge.

At once his Division broke into a run. Yelling, they surged forward. The Southerners had their "rebel yell"—a high-pitched shrill. The Northerners had their "Yankee grunt," a lower pitched version of their foes' yell.

When the First Division was about out of the torpedo field, the Confederate infantry opened up sending hundreds of leaden missiles toward their human targets. Men continued to fall, but the hard-bitten veterans of the

Ninth Corps kept moving forward. Within minutes they were over the Confederate breastworks. Defenders either fled to the next defensive line or were captured. Burnside's men pushed the Southerners back a mile before they ran into Beauregard's reinforcements. The Creole had shifted men from the center of his line to meet Burnside's threat.

Willcox's orders were simple. If he was successful, he was to send word to the Corps' Second Division to attack in support. The Commander of the Union Ninth Corps Second Division, Brigadier General Robert Potter, anxiously awaited the signal to attack.

Potter's men were seasoned veterans. They watched as the cannon balls ripped gaps in the Union line. All eyes in the second Division were fixed on Willcox's men. Patiently they waited for the order to attack. Willcox, caught up in the heat of battle, assumed Potter would see his Division was successful and join the assault. Unfortunately, the smoke from the artillery and musket fire hid the Union success from its support. Hancock's Corps under Birney were idle; unaware he had started forward. The entire Union front was in a state of confusion. For the remainder of the day, Meade tried his best to get his troops organized for a coordinated attack, but was unsuccessful as Beauregard shifted his rag-tag force from one threatened point to another.

As the sun began to set in the west, Meade finally had his Army organized and at precisely seven o'clock Birney struck the Confederate center with his entire Corps. At the same time, Burnside ordered Potter to attack in support of Birney. When the Union troops linked with Willcox's dug-in Division, the entire Union left would continue forward and straighten its line.

Beauregard swallowed hard as he watched fifty thousand men start their assault. His artillery immediately opened with canister. Aligned slightly to the left and behind Birney's lead Division, the men of Potter's Division could only see a portion of the enemy breastworks. Like his peers, the Division Commander was in front of his troops.

Seeing Birney's troops break into a run toward the enemy works, Potter drew his sword backward and then in a slow arc brought it forward and shouted, "CHARGE"! The men in the second Division, giving the "Yankee grunt," broke into a run toward the enemy breastworks. They were more fortunate then their friends in the Ninth Corps' First Division. They encountered no torpedoes.

By eight o'clock the Union Army had straightened its line and linked up with Willcox's Division driving the defenders back an additional mile. Watching his line crumbling, Beauregard ordered his reserve Brigade under the command of Brigadier General Archibald Gracie to counter-attack.

Gracie, the former New Yorker whose father and brothers were a political presence in New York City, had made his home in his adopted state of Alabama. The thirty-two year old West Point graduate drew his sword and led his men in a desperate attack. The sun had just set when Gracie's undermanned Brigade of seven hundred smashed into Birney's entire Corps. The savagery of the attack coupled with the blackness of night caused the Union men to halt and dig in.

With no reserves left and his men close to exhaustion, Beauregard let his men rest until midnight. At the strike of twelve, he pulled his tired defenders back a mile. Working in shifts they used bayonets and tin cups to dig a new defensive line.

When he arrived at his headquarters, the nearly exhausted General was handed a telegram. Turning to his aide he dictated a response.

> "*To: General Robert E. Lee*
> *All quiet at the present. My troops are exhausted. Without strong reinforcements, Petersburg cannot be held much longer. It is reported that Grant is on the field with his entire Army.*
> *Signed,*
> *P.G.T Beauregard*
> *General Commanding Petersburg*"

Beauregard's telegram was received at Lee's headquarters at one in the morning. The telegraph operator personally brought the dispatch to Lee's Chief-of-Staff, Colonel Walter Taylor, who was fast asleep. Dismissing the operator, he read the note. Sitting up, he cleared the sleep from his eyes. He had a decision to make. Taylor knew Lee had a long, tiring day and needed rest. At the same time, he knew the importance of the news. He was in a quandary. Running his fingers through his thinning brown hair, the young aide rose from his cot and, fixing his uniform, left to wake Lee.

"General Lee, sir," whispered Taylor trying not to startle the older man.

"What is it, Colonel?" answered the General in a tired tone.

"Sir, an urgent dispatch from Beauregard," replied a drowsy Taylor.

"Come in, Colonel," responded Lee.

Taylor entered the General's tent. Lee was fully dressed and wide-awake. It never failed to amaze the Chief-of-Staff how the Army Commander always seemed to be dressed, ready for battle and wide awake. He handed Lee the telegram. The Commander of the Army of Northern Virginia smiled as he read it. At last he knew where his adversary was. The speculation was over.

"Colonel, wake Major Venable and the couriers; this Army moves immediately to Petersburg," ordered Lee.

Petersburg, Virginia—June 18, 4:00AM

Meade issued orders for an all out assault across the entire line to begin precisely at dawn. He proudly watched his Army form for the attack. The sky began to slowly brighten going from black, to dark blue and then to a lighter shade of blue as the sun neared the horizon. He took a deep breath and watched the sun peek over the skyline.

At once a hundred Union cannon spit forth their deadly message. Huge chunks of debris were thrown skyward as the projectiles struck the enemy breastworks. The artillery continued to shell the enemy position for fifteen minutes before the infantry began to move. The men in blue rushed forward. Resistance was non-existent. Unknown to Meade and his Commanders, Beauregard had abandoned the trenches and was repositioned a mile to the west.

The empty trenches confused the attackers. They weren't used to taking abandoned works. The Union Commanders wasted no time. They quickly had the troops dig in and fortify their position against a potential counter-attack. While their men strengthened the position, reconnaissance parties were sent to locate the Southerners.

It was mid-morning before Meade found Beauregard. The Union General rode to the front line for a personal inspection. He was not pleased with what he saw. Beauregard had made a new and shorter defensive line. The crafty Confederate General had his men dug in from the Appomattox River south to the Jerusalem Plank Road—a distance of ten miles. He clustered his artillery closer together to provide a more powerful punch. In spite of the defenses, Meade ordered Birney, Burnside and Warren to attack.

At exactly twelve o'clock, the Army of the Potomac commenced its assault. Unknown to Meade, Lee arrived with Anderson's Corps. They now faced thirty thousand dug in Confederates.

Arriving in Petersburg at eleven o'clock; Lee, being the senior General, assumed command making Beauregard his senior deputy. The Confederate Generals watched as the Union artillery traded blows with its Confederate counterparts. Ammunition chests on both sides were blown into the air. Artillery horses screamed in pain as exploding shells ripped into their flesh. It was a typical pre-assault, artillery dual. After thirty minutes of sparring, the Union infantry crossed the no man's land between the two lines.

Birney's second Corps led the assault with the other Corps in support. For the first fifty yards everything went smoothly. The enemy artillery was silent. There was no musket fire. A hundred yards from the gray-clad defenders the entire enemy line fired a devastating volley. Thirty thousand muskets rained havoc on the attackers as the leaden missiles hurled through the air. Some struck their human targets with an all too familiar dull thud. Others sped by harmlessly, while still others whizzed by the attackers so close they heard the bee-like buzzing sound and felt the heat of the bullet racing by.

Switching to canister, the artillery joined the musket fire. The Union men were bloodily repulsed. Meade gave orders to reform and hit the defenders again. Fortunately for the Army of the Potomac, Grant had arrived and had witnessed the bloody repulse.

"George, you may want to reconsider the attack order. Lee's position is stronger here than it was at Cold Harbor." suggested Grant."

Meade nodded in agreement and cancelled the order. The two Generals would rest their men and plan for a different way to take Petersburg. Seven weeks of continuous fighting had taken its toll; the Army was played out. Corps by Corps the veterans were slow in responding. Since the beginning of the campaign in early May, the original Union Army of the Potomac had lost seventy-five thousand men killed, wounded or captured. The veterans were rapidly disappearing.

Grant retired to City Point to plan the next phase of the campaign. Across the battlefield Lee and Beauregard argued about what to do next. The Cajun General wanted to attack Meade's right flank recovering his lost works. Lee agreed the plan had merit but also knew his men were worn down. The constant attacks by Grant had taken its toll. They needed rest and he needed to reorganize his tattered command structure.

Shenandoah Valley, Virginia—June 18, 1:00 PM

General David Hunter formed his men for an assault against the beleaguered troops of "Grumble" Jones' Army of the Valley. With Jones dead and his men demoralized Confederate Major General John Breckenridge assumed command and reorganized the broken Army. He had his men dug in just outside of Lynchburg. The town was in the foothills of the Blue Ridge Mountains, a scant twenty miles from Richmond.

Hunter had marched his men from Piedmont in the northern Valley sixty miles south to Lynchburg leaving in his wake a path of desolation and despair. The Union Commander burned houses, barns and needlessly killed livestock. He was determined to make the Valley residents pay for their support of the rebels. Unknown to the Union General, the defenders had been reinforced during the night by the arrival of Early's Corps from Lee's Army.

At two o'clock all was ready. Hunter gave the order for the attack to begin. The countryside was well suited for a defensive action. The Federals would have to cross two hundred yards of open ground.

Learning from Lee, Early had the defenders dig four-foot trenches and then place a log on top of the trench. Leaving a one-foot gap to look and fire through, the defenders then placed another log on top.

When the Federals were halfway across the field, Early's artillery opened fire tearing huge gaps in the formations. Hunter quickly realized that Breckenridge had been reinforced and ordered the attack cancelled. Fearing a counter-attack, he ordered his retreating soldiers to dig in and wait for further orders. The chances for wiping out Breckenridge had passed.

Later in the evening Hunter met with his Corps Commanders, Generals Crook, Sullivan and Averell. The three subordinates were battle-tested Commanders who had served the Union faithfully since the beginning of the war. Unfortunately, none of the three were considered forward thinkers.

After three hours of debate, they all agreed to pull their men back ten miles to the Blue Ridge Mountains and use the mountain's terrain to establish a strong defensive line should Early pursue.

The next morning Jubal Early and John Breckenridge woke to find Hunter had abandoned his position. Reports from local residents indicated the Union Commander was headed for the Blue Ridge Mountains and, perhaps, to the Federal stronghold of the new Union state of West Virginia.

Jubal Early wasted no time and ordered a pursuit. Taking a page from Grant's playbook, he would stay in constant contact with his enemy.

CHAPTER FOURTEEN

City Point, Virginia—June 20, 8:00 AM

Grant and his staff waited on the wharf as the passenger steamer tied up. It had been two days since Hunter's withdrawal. Early pursued the retreating Federals like a wolf after a flock of sheep. When Hunter stopped to dig in, the Confederates attacked before his defenses were complete.

The Union General-in-Chief was not overly concerned with Hunter's withdrawal. There were plenty of troops in the Valley to deal with Early. His concern was with the steamer. Yesterday he had received a telegram from the President that he was on his way to City Point to meet with the General.

Aboard the ship Lincoln waited in his cabin with John Hay. The President was nervous about the meeting.

"Mr. Hay, the last General I visited a in the field was McClellan and I was treated most coldly. I don't know if this is typical of field Generals or if it was just McClellan."

"Mr. President, the reason why McClellan was your only visit was because "Little Mac" was the only General, next to Grant, who was in command long enough to warrant a visit," replied Hay.

Lincoln looked at his secretary and smiled as the duo left the cabin.

Seeing Lincoln on deck, Grant called the honor guard to attention. At once the military men snapped a salute. The Union Chief Executive was both surprised and pleased with the honor. He stopped and nodded in acknowledgement. Grant then gave the order for parade rest and approached the President.

"Welcome, Mr. President, how was your trip?" asked Grant offering his hand.

Taking the General's hand, he shook it warmly.

"Last night we had some rough seas and, I am afraid, I'm more of a land lubber than a sailor. My stomach did not hold down my supper," answered Lincoln.

Grant turned to Horace Porter and asked him to run to the cook and have breakfast prepared for the Chief Executive.

Lincoln was surprised and pleased at the respect and consideration he was being given. He assumed he would be treated as an outsider; a meddler who was not welcome and had no right to interfere with military men. Instead it was just the opposite.

Grant introduced the President and his secretary to his staff and then left their aides to get acquainted. The two most powerful men in the Union walked to the General's tent. They sat and talked while Lincoln ate his breakfast. It was an easygoing, light conversation.

"General Grant, you should be proud of yourself and your men. You have accomplished more in seven weeks than all my previous Generals combined," said Lincoln as he popped a biscuit into his mouth.

"Thank you, Mr. President, but the praise goes to the Nation and not to me," replied a humble Grant.

Lincoln liked Grant's humility. Unlike other military men he had met since the war began, his humility was genuine. His dress was that of a regular private. His uniform didn't have gold braid or epaulets. It was a regular issue Union uniform and if it weren't for the shoulder straps indicating his rank, he would be mistaken for a private. The General wore no sash or sword. He was a soldier's soldier.

Grant explained the campaign's results, thus far, and what his plans were for the future. He explained to the President that Hunter was in retreat in the Valley and will link up with Sigel. Together they would keep Early in the Valley. He went on to tell his boss how Sherman was preparing to attack Johnston at Kennesaw Mountain and that two weeks of constant rains had kept Sherman from bringing on a battle. Grant expressed his full faith in his subordinate and that he was keeping Johnston from sending reinforcements to Lee. After the briefing, he showed Lincoln a map of Petersburg.

"As you can see, Mr. President, Petersburg is the key to Richmond," said Grant.

Lincoln's untrained military eye tried to see what Grant saw, but couldn't. Observing the bewildered look on the President's face; Grant explained.

"Petersburg is the railway hub in which Richmond and, subsequently, Lee receive supplies from the rest of the South. There are five major Confederate railway lines, which all converge in Petersburg."

Grant patiently pointed each one out to the Union's Chief Executive.

"There is the City Point Railroad used to bring supplies from the James River to Richmond through the rail hub. We now control that railway and its source of supply is gone for Lee. This leaves the Norfolk-Petersburg railway, which brings supplies from Norfolk to Petersburg; we semi-control that one. Then there is the Weldon-Petersburg railway, which brings supplies from the Deep South through the Carolinas to Petersburg. Then there is the Petersburg-Richmond railroad, which sends the supplies to Richmond. Finally, there is the Southside Railroad which brings supplies from the western part of the Confederacy to Petersburg."

The General-in-Chief paused, took a drink of water, looked at the President and then continued the briefing.

"Then there's the Jerusalem Plank Road, which is the major source of supplies for wagon travel. By taking Petersburg we force Richmond to fall."

Lincoln stared at the map. Grant had explained his reasoning for fighting at Petersburg clearly. Unlike other military men, the General didn't talk down to the President. He explained his reasons in everyday terms.

"General, I see why Petersburg is so important; but I have two questions. First, why didn't my other Generals see this? The second question; what is your plan to take Petersburg?" asked Lincoln.

"The answer to your first question is I don't know. Regarding your second question, my plan is to extend our lines southward, slowly stretching Lee's line. Eventually his line will be spread so thin, it will break like yarn stretched too tight. This morning I have ordered Hancock's and Wright's Corps southwest to attack and take the Norfolk-Petersburg Railway, the Jerusalem Plank Road and the Weldon Railroad," answered Grant as he lit a cigar.

Lincoln looked at his General.

"Your plan is very practical and I can see its success. What do you need from me?" inquired the President.

"Mr. President, I need two things of major importance. First, I will need more men to make sure I don't stretch our lines to the breaking point and Lee does to me what I intend to do to him. Secondly, you will need to get yourself re-elected. This semi-siege will take time and this Army needs a Commander-in-Chief that will stay the course."

Lincoln was totally surprised by Grant's second request. The first item was the same with every Commander the Union had; however, unlike the previous Generals, at least Grant had a plan and proved to the President he was worthy of his support.

"General Grant, I'll get you your men; however, I'm afraid your second request is up to the American people. The people in the North are getting tired of the war and my popularity has waned. I know in my heart that, come November, I will be defeated."

"Mr. President, you're mistaken. You are more popular than you think; especially with the Army. Would you like to take a ride and see our men?" asked Grant.

Once again, Lincoln was surprised. No other field General had ever offered an inspection. Although he had personally known Grant for only a short while, he liked the man. The feeling was mutual.

Grant ordered his favorite horse, Cincinnati, saddled. The bay-colored mare was huge, over seventeen hands high. A combat veteran, the horse didn't shy or buck with the sounds of battle. It had a steady, gentle gait. The mount would compliment the Chief Executive's tall stature without making him look awkward. The General would ride his second horse, Jeff Davis. Slightly smaller at sixteen hands, the horse was more skittish than Cincinnati. Grant, being an excellent horseman, could easily handle any mount in the Army.

On the way to Petersburg the two men had a friendly chat. They were fast becoming friends. They visited Meade's headquarters. The Commander of the Army of the Potomac explained to Lincoln the disposition of the enemy forces and where the Union troops were located. After the briefing, the trio went to visit the ailing Hancock.

The Corps Commander lay in his cot. When he saw Grant and Lincoln, he tried to raise himself; but the pain in his stomach was too intense. The President put his big hand on Hancock's shoulder and told him to lie still.

"General Hancock, I know I sent you a letter thanking you for your service at Gettysburg, but I would like to thank you now, in person, for your service not only at Gettysburg but for all you have given during this terrible war," said Lincoln shaking Hancock's hand.

"Thank you, Mr. President," replied the Corps Commander in a tired voice.

It always pained the President to see men suffer; especially those who had served so faithfully. Blood oozed from the wound. Bone fragments from his pelvis had worked their way down, reopening the wound.

The trio stayed with Hancock for an hour. Seeing the melancholy look on Lincoln's face, Grant suggested they visit Hincks' Division, which had been the first to take the enemy works. The three men mounted and rode at a leisurely pace. The day before, the Division had been pulled out of their advanced position and been brought to the rear for a rest. As the three men approached the resting Division, Grant and Meade slowly fell behind the President. The pair knew the reaction the President would receive from the colored troops.

At first the colored men didn't recognize the Chief Executive.

Suddenly someone in the crowd shouted.

"Praise the Lord it's Mr. Lincoln himself."

Instantly the President was surrounded. Some shook his hand or kissed his boots while others shouted words of praise. The outbreak of spontaneous emotion from the troops greatly affected the man who had freed the slaves. It was the first time the Chief Executive had seen the effects of his Emancipation Proclamation.

Hearing the shouting of the men of Hincks' Division, the neighboring white units ran to see what was causing all the commotion. When they saw it was the President, they began to chant.

"Lincoln … Lincoln … Lincoln. Three cheers for the President. Hip … hip … hooray. Hip … hip … hooray. Hip … hip … hooray."

The sound of ten thousand men cheering him almost brought the Illinois politician to tears. The men who were doing the fighting, dying and suffering were clearly in support of their President.

While Lincoln was with Hincks' Division, the men of Wright's and Hancock's Corps were engaged in a deadly battle for the Weldon Railroad.

Informed of the movement of Union troops to the southwest, Robert E. Lee moved A.P. Hill's Corps to intercept the men in blue. Hill wearing his famous red shirt waited in the woods west of the Jerusalem Plank Road with his men, ready to ambush the Federals as the passed.

The battle-weary men in blue marched southwest unaware of the lurking danger. Seven weeks of continuous combat had taken its toll. Their eyes were dark and sullen. Bags with black circles had formed under their eyes. For many, their hair had begun to turn prematurely gray. They hadn't bathed since just before entering the Wilderness. Many were lice infested.

Hill and his Corps waited patiently two miles west of the road for their unsuspecting foes to come within range. He was back to full health. The aggressiveness had returned. His men saw it and were inspired. They had the old Hill back.

The Federals crossed the Jerusalem Plank Road and entered the dense forest. The road twisted and turned without reason. They instantly became entangled in a mass of confusion as they desperately tried to keep their formations. Unaware of the terrain, the two Corps became separated creating a gap between them of almost a mile.

Seeing his opportunity, Hill unleashed his men. One Division attacked Wright's men head-on, while the other two hit Birney's Corps in the flank. The Confederate attacks were savage and brutal giving no quarter. The veterans of Birney's Corps faced their left to meet the threat; but it was too late. The Federals put up a brief struggle and then broke for the rear leaving twenty-four cannons to the enemy. The men in gray turned the guns on the retreating men in blue. Seventeen hundred Federals surrendered rather than die.

With Birney's Corps in retreat, Hill turned his attention to Wright. The Union Commander was holding his own when, suddenly, he was struck in his right flank forcing his men to fight on two fronts. Unlike their peers, the men of Wright's Sixth Corps gave as good as they got. For two hours the combatants traded blows neither able to gain a distinct advantage over the other. The Federals began to run low on ammunition. Wright pulled his artillery back followed slowly by his infantry.

Birney rallied his men a mile west of the road and had them dig in. It was useless to move them forward. They would fight well enough on the defensive; but while their minds said attack, their bodies wouldn't respond. He sent word to Wright he had rallied his men and had established a defensive line a mile behind him.

Wright passed orders to his men to fall back slowly by Brigade. One Brigade would lay down covering fire, while a second Brigade raced back a hundred yards to establish a hasty defensive line and lay down covering fire. The first Brigade would fall back a hundred yards behind them. Using this method the Union Corps Commander was able to extricate his force without serious loss in men or equipment.

When they approached Birney's line, the men broke for the rear and took cover behind their peers. Seeing the Union men race away; the Confederates, smelling victory, charged after them, unaware of the dug-in men of Birney's Corps. A shower of flying lead abruptly stopped the rebels. The Confederate

Commander saw the Federals were well entrenched and decided not to waste lives. He accomplished what Lee had wanted and saved the railroad.

As darkness descended, Hill sent word to Lee that the Weldon Railroad was safe; however, Grant now occupied the Jerusalem Plank Road. Lee read the dispatch and sitting on the edge of his cot, raised his eyes to heaven and thanked God. The Confederacy was still alive. The Virginian quickly surmised Grant's plan and knew he was powerless to prevent it. His worst fears had come true. Three weeks earlier he told Jubal Early that if it ever became a siege, it would only be a matter of time before Lincoln's Army would win.

Lincoln sat in a camp chair near a blazing campfire. Grant sat next to the President. All around the fire the staff officers sat and listened to the Chief Executive as he told a myriad of humorous stories. The politician was an accomplished storyteller, holding his laughter until he delivered the punch line.

John Hay sat next to Rawlins enjoying the evening.

"In Washington, Lincoln was a different person. Although always cordial to visitors, he was always reserved and on guard. When he visited McClellan, the meeting was very formal and stiff. Here with Grant, the President is very relaxed," whispered Hay.

"Grant has always been a Lincoln man. I think the two men have much in common. They both struggled in life, both are from Illinois and both have the same strong attribute—perseverance," responded Rawlins in a low tone.

At midnight, the President stood and, stretching his long legs, bade his hosts a friendly good night.

"Gentlemen, this was most enjoyable, but the hour is late and we all need our sleep."

Grant approached the President and warmly shook his hand.

"Mr. President, may we breakfast together? By then I should have an update on the success or failure of Birney and Wright."

"Sam, I'd like that very much. What time do you serve breakfast?"

"How about seven?" asked Grant.

"Seven, it is. With that settled, Mr. Hay and I will say good night. Once again thank you, Sam, for your hospitality."

Aboard the steamer Lincoln and his secretary talked until one-thirty in the morning. After three years of searching for a Commander, he had found his man. He would stand behind Grant no matter what happened. For the first time in three years the President had a peaceful sleep.

Lincoln woke at six in the morning fully refreshed. He dressed quickly and darted outside. He loved the solitude and beauty of the early morning. Standing on deck, he watched as the engineers busied themselves constructing another wharf. The ground was covered in morning dew. The smell of honeysuckle mixed with the odor of smoldering pine gave the start of the day a fresh, clean smell. He inhaled deeply. It reminded him of happier days as a struggling country lawyer and town rowdy in the growing hamlet of Springfield, Illinois.

He approached Grant's tent and was happy to see the tent flap up and his host awake. The outside guard snapped to attention and announced the President. Lincoln waited until Grant gave permission to enter.

When the Chief Executive didn't enter, Grant bolted out of his chair and ran toward the opening.

"Mr. President, why are you waiting out here? You're my boss and can enter anytime you wish."

The Illinois politician smiled and entered. Pulling up a chair he sat at the map table. Grant resumed his seat and, after ordering breakfast be prepared, he briefed the President.

"Mr. President, as I told you yesterday, Birney and Wright's Corps were ordered southwest to extend our lines. They accomplished this. We now occupy the Jerusalem Plank Road," said Grant.

"Well done, General. What's next?"

"Reports indicate some Divisions were not up to the fight. It is my plan to rest and resupply the army. I've ordered siege mortars and guns along with sap rollers. The mortars and guns will enable us to shell Lee's army and keep them under constant pressure. This worked very well for me at Vicksburg. The sap rollers are six-foot high, eight-foot wide hollow metal cylinders with handles. Taking the handle, four men get behind the roller and roll it into position. The men are protected from enemy fire by the metal cylinder. We place four or five of these next to each other and it enables the engineers to work at strengthening our position without the danger of enemy musket fire."

As the General continued his briefing, his aides set up a table inside the tent. Seeing breakfast was ready, the two men moved to the table. The President had a hearty appetite while Grant hardly ate at all as he continued his briefing. They continued to talk for another two hours. Standing, the President said good-bye and began to walk to the steamer, which was ready to leave. He was once again surprised as Grant accompanied him to the wharf. The two men shook hands warmly and leaning over, the President whispered.

"Sam, you shall have your reinforcements."

Over the next few days the front at Petersburg was quiet allowing both sides the opportunity to plan their strategies. Lee had to wait for his adversary to make a move. Grant had to give his troops rest. The hot and humid Virginia summer was upon them. If combat didn't sap the men's strength, then the weather would. The Union General had to plan a way to defeat both the Southerners and the weather.

Union engineers at City Point were rapidly transforming the sleepy hamlet into a major Federal supply depot. Navy supply ships were constantly docking and unloading supplies. Two miles from the dock, the engineers were building a huge corral to hold thousands of beef cattle. On the Southside, the engineers were constructing a hospital to house six thousand wounded—Grant anticipated a bloody campaign.

Within a few days, the men in blue would have real food and not hardtack to eat. Hardtack, or as the men called them "worm castles," were dehydrated biscuits which were so dry, the men had to use the butts of their rifles to break them. The pieces were soaked in either water or coffee to soften them. The only protein came from the little white worms which inhabited the cracker. For the last seven weeks it had been the mainstay of the soldiers' diet.

Things were worse on the Confederate side. Lee's men had to subsist on a half-pound of bacon and four ounces of flour. The bacon was from Nassau and was often rancid. The men in gray nicknamed it "nausea bacon." They would fry the pork and then mix the flour with water to make a biscuit which was fried in the bacon grease. Sometimes the men would find a pig or some corn to eat. If an unlucky mascot wandered off from his company, it was often listed as missing in action, never to be seen again.

City Point, Virginia—June 25, 9:15 PM

Meade, Burnside and Burnside's Regimental Commander, Colonel Henry Pleasants entered Grant's tent. Pleasants had a plan to get around Lee's defenses. Burnside liked it and had referred it to Meade. Although not entirely for the plan, the Army Commander decided he would let Burnside and Pleasants present their idea to Grant and let the General-in-Chief make the final decision. The light from the oil-based lamps filled the Lieutenant General's tent with a yellow hue. Outside a heavy mist hugged the ground.

"Two days ago General Burnside and Colonel Pleasants presented me a plan to breach Lee's lines. I thought about it and decided it was so daring; the final decision should be made by you," said Meade.

"Proceed Gentlemen," responded the General-in-Chief as he lit a cigar and sat down.

Burnside turned the meeting over to Pleasants

"Sir, my Regiment is the Forty-Fourth Pennsylvania. Before the war my men and I were coal miners. For the past few days, we've been taking measurements between our lines and that of the enemy. We have analyzed samples of the earth," said Pleasants.

"Colonel, get to the point. I'm sure you didn't ride here to tell me your life's history."

"Sir, my men and I feel we can tunnel under Lee's Army. We can place black powder in the tunnel and blow the rebs to hell. After the explosion, the enemy will be disoriented allowing the Ninth Corps to take advantage of the situation and attack. I calculate the enemy would be confused for at least ten or fifteen minutes, which should be enough time for us to take their breast-works."

"How long will the tunnel be? How much powder will it take? How will the men breathe?" asked Grant in rapid succession.

"Sir, the tunnel will be five hundred and eleven feet long. We calculate it will take five hundred pounds of powder. We'll construct a huge billow which will pump air into the shaft," answered the Colonel confidently.

Grant leaned back in his chair. He took a deep drag on his cigar. His first inclination was to turn it down. It had no hope of success. Its only redeeming factor was that it would occupy the men of the Ninth Corps. With that in mind, he gave Burnside and Meade his approval to proceed.

Across the lines Lee visited with Jefferson Davis, the South's Chief Executive needed to get away from Richmond. Like his counterpart in the North, Davis was not very popular with the majority of the population. Unlike Lincoln, he didn't have to worry about re-election. The Confederate constitution limited the President to one term of six years.

The people of the Confederacy were tired of war. The sacrifice in men and hardships were taking their toll. Joe Brown, a political enemy of the President, was constantly sending telegrams to Davis about his concern for Atlanta and the strategy of Joe Johnston. The Southern Congress was continually battling the President. The very concept of States' rights seemed to be the weakness of the Confederacy. Davis could only request troops from the States. Each individual Governor had the final decision of how many they would send.

At first, all the States were willing to fill quotas established by Richmond; however, as the war wore on and the Union slowly re-took control the Governors provided Richmond with less troops opting instead to keep men at home in the State militia.

"Robert, I'm concerned about Joe Johnston. He is yielding precious ground to Sherman. Each position he has yielded was considered a strong one. I have my doubts that Joe Johnston will ever do battle and will give up Atlanta without a fight."

"Jeff, I've known Joe Johnston my entire life. He is just biding his time. Eventually, Sherman will lose patience with his flanking movements and attack Joe head-on. I know you two do not get along, but I assure you he's the most capable General we have, including me."

"I wish I had your faith in the man," answered Davis.

CHAPTER FIFTEEN

Foothills of Kennesaw Mountain, Georgia—June 27, 9:00AM

Sherman had his Army up an hour before dawn. He watched the Confederates file into their trenches. Unknown to him, his adversary was watching Sherman's blue horde prepare for their assault.

At precisely nine o'clock, a single cannon was fired by Thomas' artillery signaling the assault to begin. McPherson rode behind his lines encouraging Logan and his Corps forward. The men responded without hesitation. The base of Little Kennesaw was filled with tangled underbrush causing the men to move slowly. Once through the underbrush they entered a thick patch of forest. Units became intermingled and confused. Brigade Commanders lost track of their regiments.

When they exited the forest, they encountered a swamp. Mosquitoes buzzed around the men's ears. Still they proceeded. Nothing was going to stop them. Their uniforms became caked with the red clay of Georgia. Their shoes weighed over a pound as the sticky soil adhered to the footwear.

At the end of the swamp was a deep ravine. It was McPherson's plan to have Logan's men enter the ravine and then climb to the enemy. Logan would attack the flank of Little Kennesaw while Howard's Corps assailed the enemy's front, drawing their attention away from climbing Federals.

Logan rested his men for ten minutes before beginning his ascent. The General from Southern Illinois watched as his lead Brigade under Brigadier General Morgan Smith, began its ascent. Smith was Logan's most experienced Commander. Halfway up the ravine, it dawned on Morgan the steepness of the angle would prevent the Confederates from using cannons. Encouraged, he hurried his men along. Just because they couldn't use artillery didn't mean they couldn't use their muskets.

Confederate Major General Samuel French watched Smith's men approach. The New Jersey-born Confederate had attended West Point with Grant. The two of them were close friends. Possessing the qualities of brains and bravery, French was considered by many to be one of the finest Division Commanders in the Southern Army. Unlike his peers, he took no part in politics. He met with his Brigade Commanders.

"Tell your men to remain steady. Let them come to the top. Every step they take wears them down. By the time they reach the crest, they'll be winded and we'll pour it into them. Make sure your men have plenty of ammunition," said French.

The first hundred men in blue crested the hill and took three steps when French's defenders opened fire. Five hundred muskets fired a hailstorm of lead quickly joined by artillery firing canister. The blue line fell like wheat before a thresher. In less than a minute all the men in blue laid on the ground dead, dying or wounded.

Undeterred by his mounting casualties, Smith moved his men forward stepping on or over fallen comrades. Seeing the futility of the attacks, the Union General ordered his men to lie down and use their dead comrades as human shields to return fire. Smith fought alongside his men.

"General, shouldn't we get the hell out of here while we still can?" shouted his aide Sergeant Bitters. The two men had served together since the beginning of the war. The thirty-two year old professional soldier had been in the Army since he was sixteen.

"If we can keep the rebs concentrating on us, maybe Howard and the rest of the Corps will have a chance!" shouted Smith above the noise of a thousand muskets and cannon.

On the other side of the field, French's officers were urging him to counter-attack and drive the Federals over the mountain. Their pleas were ignored. The Confederate General wasn't going to waste lives attacking. He had Smith right where he wanted him.

With Smith's men barely holding their own, Howard's Corps battled their way up the mountain. The angle of the landscape was strewn with boulders and depressions. Howard's men worked their way up by moving from boulder to boulder and from depression to depression. At first the attackers had the advantage of cover, but it was short lived. The last one hundred and fifty yards was all open terrain.

The Union's one-armed General sat on his horse and anxiously watched as his men sprinted across the open ground. They were within fifty yards of the defenders when the air was instantly filled with flying lead. The sound of musketry was mixed with the sound of screaming men as the Federals were mercilessly sacrificed in wave after wave.

Thomas and Sherman sat on their horses and watched the Army of Cumberland climb Big Kennesaw toward the rebel center. While the men ascended the mountain, they could hear the battle raging to their left. The Southern General in charge of this part of the field, Major General Ben Cheatham, watched and waited patiently.

The Tennessee-born Confederate Major General had fought with distinction and valor in every campaign since Shiloh. Although he had no formal military training, he was considered both brave and cunning. He massed all his cannon together and ordered his artillerists to fill each piece with a double load of canister and not to fire until he gave the order.

Cheatham watched and waited. When the attackers were within fifty yards of his breastworks, he gave the order for his artillerists to fire. Instantly, the air was filled with the deafening sound of thirty cannons quickly followed by continuous volley fire. It was as if the gates of hell had opened. The Federals dove for cover, reformed and tried again. Their luck was no better the second time.

Realizing the futility of further attacks, Sherman gave the order to disengage and retreat. Slowly the Union Commanders extricated their men. It was far easier for Howard's Corps and Thomas' Army to back-peddle than it was for Smith's men. The Union General requested covering cannon fire from McPherson's long-range guns. The request was approved and, within an hour, Smith had the remnants of his command safely behind the rest of the Army.

While the Union troops disengaged from Kennesaw Mountain, Schofield's Army of Ohio attacked the Confederates holding the town of Olley's Creek. The Confederate Commander positioned his defenders in a deadly crossfire. Covered by the town's buildings and their trenches, it was easily defended. Not only did the Federals have to cross the Creek with its slippery, muddy bottom under a galling fire but, once across, they would have to work their way up the muddy banks.

Schofield's little Army did the best they could. In the end, they held one side of the Creek while the Confederates held the other and the town. For two hours Brigade after Brigade crossed and was repulsed. Seeing his men lying face down in the water with swirls of blood circling their bodies, Schofield called a halt to the attacks. He knew Sherman would be seething, but he didn't care.

Sherman sadly rode back to his headquarters shaking his head in disgust, upset with himself. He should have known better. Like his friend in the East had learned at Cold Harbor, there was still plenty of fight left in the rebel Army.

While Sherman sulked and planned his next move, Joe Johnston rode along the entire length of the battlefield. He surveyed the carnage his men had inflicted. He was proud of his Army. His casualties were light. He felt vindicated. Jefferson Davis could no longer accuse him of not wanting to fight. The Battle of Kennesaw Mountain proved his strategy of retreating and biding time worked. It was a major victory for Johnston with Sherman losing seventy-five hundred men killed or wounded and fifty-two missing. The southern losses numbered two hundred seventy killed and wounded and one hundred seventy-two missing.

Foothills of Kennesaw Mountain, Georgia—June 28, 7:15 AM

Sherman met with his Army Commanders. During the night he made the decision to flank Johnston out of his entrenchments.

"Gentlemen, yesterday didn't exactly go as we planned. "Old Joe" beat us up pretty good. He has a strong defensive position. To assault him where he is now, would be suicide for us. Therefore, we'll move around his left flank.

"Yesterday Schofield's Army proved Johnston is weak at Olley's Creek. The terrain is too difficult for just fifteen thousand men. Tonight, at midnight, I want Mac's Army out of their entrenchments; re-deploying behind George's Army. At the same time, I want George to spread out to cover McPherson's vacated trenches," explained Sherman.

"Billy, wouldn't that invite Johnston to attack me and if he catches Mac on the move, the results could be devastating," interrupted Thomas.

"George, it's possible, but not probable. I'm counting on Johnston sitting tight waiting for us to attack again. He has no intention of bringing the fight to us. We'll move cautiously, extricating one Corps at a time beginning with Howard; then Palmer. When Howard and Palmer have reached Olley's Creek, I want them to take Schofield's place in the line. When that is done, I want Schofield to head to the Chattahoochee River with utmost speed; cross the river and take Atlanta," answered Sherman.

A surprised look came over the trio of field Commanders. Moving around Johnston's flank was one thing, but to make a burst of speed for the prize of Atlanta was another.

"Billy, suppose Johnston realizes our plan and attacks Thomas, or even worse, suppose he moves his Army to Olley's Creek and attacks Schofield before I arrive?" asked McPherson.

"It's possible, but highly unlikely. I hope he does attack George. The Army of the Cumberland is dug-in. It will be our Kennesaw assault in reverse. Even if Johnston discovers our plan in the morning and moves his Army to attack John, by the time he gets his Army in place both Howard and Palmer would have arrived. At the same time, as soon as George and I see him pull out of his position, we'll attack him. His Army will be caught out of their breastworks and on the march. I want to make the lunge for Atlanta no later than four days from now on July second," replied Sherman.

Kennesaw Mountain, Georgia—July 2, 9:30 AM

Johnston sent for his Cavalry Commander, Joe Wheeler. For most of the campaign the Calvary had been acting as a rear guard or used in protecting supply wagons. Twice the Army Commander had sent them on a real mission to tear up railroad tracks disrupting Sherman's supply lines. After having his campaign stalled for the second time by Wheeler, Sherman had siphoned off some of his combat troops to guard vital rail links. Since then, Wheeler and his men were virtually idle.

"General Wheeler, I have a vital mission for your Corps," said Johnston.

"My men and I are ready, sir," replied the young Cavalryman.

"Sherman has stolen another march on us. He has moved half his Army to Olley's Creek and, I believe, he intends to make a dash for Atlanta. The Army must get there before him or the city will fall. I need you to take your Cavalry Corps southeast of Olley's and buy me time. Do whatever you need to, but he must be slowed down. I need two days to get to Atlanta. You are to assume overall command of the troops at Olley's."

Leaving at midnight the Confederate Cavalry Commander and his men arrived at the creek just before dawn and quickly took control of the situation. Leaving behind those men whose horses were too weak to continue, he took the rest of his Cavalry and raced to head off Schofield.

By noon he was ahead of the Federal infantry. When he was two miles in front, he had his men fall trees across the road. Further down the road his men buried land torpedoes.

Wheeler split his command in two leaving half at the obstructions to act as snipers while he and the rest circled behind the column. When the Union troops halted to clear away the trees lying on the road, Wheeler attacked the rear of the column. At the same time, Confederate snipers peppered away at the men in blue who were attempting to clear the way.

Schofield quickly deployed his men in a defensive perimeter losing precious time in his race for Atlanta. The Union General ordered his men to charge in both directions. Wheeler broke off contact and headed further down the road to lay a new trap.

It was after five before the Federal General had his men back in formation and the road cleared. The lead column had gone a half-mile when it entered the torpedo zone. Men were blown skyward their limbs flying in opposite directions. The Army Commander had no choice but to, once again, halt his men until the roadway was cleared. With night approaching, he ordered his men to bivouac along the roadway and clear the rest of the mines at first light. Wheeler had bought Johnston a day.

For three days Wheeler and his men harassed their adversaries piling brush in the roadway and setting it ablaze when the Union lead elements approached. The thick black smoke choked the Federals and slowed their advance further. They cut down more trees across the road, and attacked the flanks and rear of the Union columns. At night they harassed the pickets causing the Federals to sound the warning of an attack, which never occurred. By the afternoon of July fifth, Wheeler and his weary men entered the Confederate fortifications across the Chattahoochee River. The red-haired General from Ohio had lost his race for Atlanta.

CHAPTER SIXTEEN

Shenandoah Valley, Virginia—July 6, 10:30 PM

The moon hid behind the dark clouds making the night as black as coal. Cautiously, a lone rider made his way through the dense forests surrounding Harpers Ferry. With every step his horse took, the diminutive rider's heart pounded faster. It was the excitement he lived for. Suddenly, from out of the brush, sprang four Confederates.

"Halt, who goes there, friend or foe?" asked one of the faceless men grabbing the reins of the horse.

"Depends on whether you're Federal or Confederate" answered the rider.

"Don't get sassy with us. We'd just as soon as skin you alive then take a piss on your dead body. Don't push our patience," retorted the solider.

"Before I know if I'm friend or foe, I need to know who you are?" shot back the rider.

"McCausland's Division of Breckenridge's Corps of the Army of the Valley," responded the man holding the reins.

"I'm a friend, take me to Breckenridge immediately," responded the rider.

"We'll take you to Breckenridge, but if he doesn't know you we'll have no choice but to hang you as a spy. You three stay here while I take this here man to Breckenridge," replied the man holding the reins.

Within thirty minutes the pair arrived at the headquarters of John C. Breckenridge. The former Vice President of the United States under Buchanan and former Presidential candidate of 1860 sat outside of his tent enjoying a nip of whisky talking to Jubal Early.

"What have you got there? He doesn't look big enough to keep," chided Early jokingly.

"I think you should throw him back," said Breckenridge chuckling.

"Sir, he must be the runt of the litter," laughed the guard.

The rider ignored their comments and dismounted. He removed the saddle from his horse and slowly reached into his boot and pulled out a small dagger. The trio's laughing suddenly stopped as the glint of the knife reflected in the campfire.

"Easy boy, drop the knife or I'll put a ball between your eyes," said the guard.

"Relax, Corporal, sewn into my saddle is my identification from Robert E. Lee and Jefferson Davis. I'm just going to slit open the saddle, reach in and remove a pouch." replied the rider.

"No you're not. One move and I'll kill you."

"Corporal, put up your weapon. Let's see who the stranger is," ordered Early.

The rider slit open the saddle, removed a small black pouch and walked to Early.

"My credentials, sir," said the rider calmly.

The General opened the pouch, removed a letter signed by both Robert E. Lee and Jefferson Davis and handed the introduction to Breckenridge.

"Corporal, you may return to your post," said Jubal.

When Early was sure they were alone, he turned to the young man.

"Mr. Stringfellow, it's a pleasure to finally meet you. General Lee briefed me on your missions before I left Cold Harbor. What brings you here?" asked Early.

"When I read in the northern papers that you're re-taking the Valley, I wanted to ride here to give you some vital information. I didn't want to chance the information not getting to you. General Early, Washington is ripe for the picking. I scouted the forts from Washington to Baltimore. Combined, both cities have less than four thousand men of all arms.

"Are you sure?" asked a surprised Breckenridge.

"Yes, sir, I'm positive," replied the spy.

Early clapped his hands and, in a joyful voice, whispered to the men. "We will march on Washington. Mr. Stringfellow, you may have just saved our cause. Please join John and me in my tent. The three of us have some planning to do," said an elated Early.

Baltimore, Maryland—July 8, 11:00 AM

Major General Lew Wallace sat at his desk. Spread before him were reams of paper. Some had notes while others were covered with words in manuscript form. Wallace was in command of the Army's Middle Department, which consisted of Maryland and Delaware. A one time close friend of Grant, the former Indiana politician was banished to the East after the Battle of Shiloh. During the battle's first day, Wallace, then a Division Commander was ordered by Grant to march his Division of six thousand men to Shiloh to help repulse the Confederates.

Wallace and his men had gotten lost in the woods and had marched in the wrong direction; away from the battle. When he realized the guide was deliberately taking them the wrong way, Wallace hung the man on the spot and moved his men to the sound of the guns. By the time he arrived at Shiloh, Grant's Army of Tennessee had been pushed back to the river for which it was named.

The Major General was interrupted by a knock on his door.

"Come in."

The door opened and in walked the General's twenty-two year old Chief-of-Staff, Major Richard Smith. Smith's uncle was an influential Senator from New Hampshire and was responsible for getting him his current position.

"How goes the book, sir?" asked the aide.

"Fine, Dick. I've finally decided on a name for the novel. I have decided to call it 'Ben Hur, A tale of the Christ'," responded the General.

"Sounds interesting, I hope you'll let me read it when it's done," answered Smith handing Wallace a telegram.

"What's this?" asked Wallace.

"It's from the Mayor of Sharpsburg. He reports Jubal Early occupies the town with a force of fifteen thousand. He says he overhead some of Early's men bragging about how they intend to take Washington.

"My contacts at the War Department said Grant is sending troops to reinforce the Capital, but they won't be arriving until the eighth or ninth. They say Rickett's Division is due in Baltimore on the eighth. What're your orders, sir?"

Wallace clapped his hands. This was his chance. He finally had the opportunity to redeem himself in Grant's eyes.

"Major, I want every man in the Department assembled. Inform the company Commanders we march immediately for Monocacy Junction. If we can delay Early, it will buy time for Grant. I want you to leave some couriers in Baltimore. When Ricketts arrives have them inform him he is to march his force to the junction. You're to telegraph me at the Monocacy the moment his force arrives.

"Begging the General's pardon, but I was hoping to march with you," replied Smith.

Seeing the disappointment on the lad's face, Wallace continued.

"Turn your duties over to one of the other aides and ride with me."

"Shall I notify Washington of our movement?" asked an excited Smith.

"No," retorted Wallace. "Halleck wouldn't approve the plan calling it risky, and Grant would say I should wait for Ricketts; but time is critical."

Wallace assembled his force of twenty-three hundred men and marched them to Monocacy Junction to hold back fifteen thousand Confederates. He was willing to sacrifice his command and career to save the Capital. He positioned his sparse force on the banks of the Monocacy River protecting the fords. He placed his eight cannon high on a hill behind some trees partially protected by the terrain. He placed snipers in the blockhouses guarding the bridge across the river and then blew up the bridge. The General sent a third of his force, under the command of Richard Smith, further north to block the Baltimore Pike in case Early attempted a flanking movement.

Just before dark, Ricketts arrived at Baltimore with reinforcements and marched with his five thousand men to support Wallace. The Department Commander warmly welcomed Ricketts and positioned his men on the defenders' left flank.

Wallace was glad to have Ricketts. The Division Commander was a career soldier who had served with bravery on several occasions. The General from New York had served in all the major battles of the Army of the Potomac. During the first Battle of Bull Run, he was shot four times and taken prisoner. He was exchanged and went back to full duty. At the battle of Antietam, he had two horses shot out from under him. Ricketts did not play politics nor did he seek glory. He was a soldier, always respectful to his superiors. His bravery was without question; however, he was not known as an independent thinker or strategist.

The two Generals talked about the upcoming battle and their respective plans to meet the rebels. They both agreed the action by their troops would be strictly defensive as any attack against Early's command would be suicide. At midnight, they said goodnight and retired until morning.

Wallace and Ricketts were up before dawn on the ninth. The two men paced behind their respective part of the line. Wallace would assume hands-on command of the center and the Baltimore Pike; while Ricketts would command the Union left.

At noon, the Confederate forces began to arrive with Jubal Early riding in the lead. The Southern General was surprised and annoyed at seeing his way barred by the Federals. He placed Breckenridge's Corps on his right while Ramseur's Division of Rodes' Corps was placed in the center. Rodes, the former Virginia Military Institute professor and friend of the late "Stonewall Jackson," took the balance of his Corps to circle around the defenders using the Baltimore Pike.

At two o'clock, Early commenced his attack. Ramseur's Division attempted to ford the river, but was cut down by Wallace's defenders. At the same time, Breckenridge's Corps was repulsed by Ricketts' entrenched veterans. On the Baltimore Pike, Smith held his own against Rodes. His causalities were light as the Southern troops were tired. Their spirit was willing, but their bodies weak. A month of marching up and down mountains in the middle of the hot and humid Virginia summer had taken its toll.

Breckenridge realized that the Union's position was too strong to be taken by a frontal assault. He sent one of his Divisions, under the command of John Gordon, further downriver to cross and flank the enemy.

On the Union side of the field, Ricketts noticed Gordon's men crossing. He shifted men to meet the threat, but it was too late. The Southerners were now on his side of the river. Ordering fix bayonets, Ricketts had his men charge. For fifteen minutes the two armies clubbed it out. Screams of pain filled the air coupled with the profanity of the dying. At the same time Ramseur kept Wallace's defenders occupied. Seeing a breach in the Union lines, Breckenridge ordered the rest of his Corps forward driving a gray wedge between the Federal defenders.

Ricketts saw his only line of retreat in danger and ordered his men to fall back. Fighting on two fronts, Wallace's men did their best to keep Breckenridge and Ramseur's men at bay; but the odds were too great and they were forced to retreat as well. What had started as an orderly withdrawal rapidly turned into a panic. The men in blue ran for the Baltimore Pike and the safety of Washington. Seeing their men break and run, the two Union Generals rode hard toward the Pike and Smith's defenders to organize a rear guard.

By four o'clock the Battle was over. Wallace had lost over eighteen-hundred eighty men with over a thousand taken prisoner or missing. Among the killed was his aide, Richard Smith. The lad, attempting to rally his men, was shot down. Recognizing a brave officer, the men of Rodes Division remembered what "Stonewall Jackson" had taught them—*"Kill the brave ones and the cowards will run away."* They took aim on the young man and fired. He died instantly, being struck in the chest ten times.

Early, seeing his men leg-weary and tired, decided to rest them and start for Washington in the morning. The small but hotly contested battle had sapped what little strength his men had left.

The tenth began just as hot and humid as the past two weeks. The Confederate lead Divisions pushed out at a quick pace raising dust, which choked those behind them. Early had no choice but to push his men without mercy. It was a race for Washington. He was still a half-day's march from the Federal Capital. The heat and dust quickly took its toll on the Southerners as some dropped along the roadside and others collapsed from heat stroke or just refused to hurry and paced themselves.

By one o'clock, Jubal Early heard the sound of siege guns being fired. The large bore cannons were the main defense around the capital. He spurred his horse forward to the front. When he arrived, he saw Gordon deploying his men for an attack. The once robust troops moved lethargically into formation. They were physically exhausted. From his horse, the Confederate Commander could see the newly constructed Capital dome six miles away. Immediately to his front was the Union's Fort Stevens.

The fortification's walls were fifteen feet high and four feet thick. In front was a lower walled enclosure for infantry. Protecting the lower walls were sharpened abattis. Timber had been placed all along the approaches to impair the movements of an attacking force. To make matters worse for an attacker, all of the approaches were covered by heavy artillery. Early positioned his forty guns on high ground even though the twelve pound cannon, named after the weight of the shell they projected, were useless against the breastworks. The artillery dual ended as soon as it had begun as the fort's defenders blew up Early's cannons, forcing him to withdraw his artillery.

Only half the Confederates were able to keep up with the rapid pace; the rest were spread along the Washington and Baltimore Pike. Of the ten thousand which kept up, only about a third were fit for duty. The Southern General had no choice but to rest his men. An hour later, the Confederate Commander noticed a large cloud of dust inside Washington moving toward Fort Stevens.

Horatio Wright led his Corps through the streets of Washington and into Fort Stevens. The Federal Capital was now safe as twenty-thousand battle-hardened veterans prepared to defend the Capital and the President. In spite of the reinforcements, the Navy kept a steamer anchored on the Potomac with a full head of steam to whisk the President, his family and the cabinet to safety in case Early took Washington. Both sides now took a watch and wait stance.

Fort Stevens, Washington DC—July 12, 1:00PM

Wright was ascending the steps to the parapet of Fort Stevens when he met the President.

"Good afternoon, Mr. President. How are you today, sir?" asked the much-surprised Horatio Wright.

"I'm fine, General, thank you. I just thought I'd see what our misguided Countrymen were up to."

"Sir, with all due respect, I think that your six-foot four-inch frame, top hat and frock coat will make an excellent target for the enemy. You must realize, Mr. President, you're not the most popular man in the South."

"Well put, General, but I'd still like to see the rebel Army," replied Lincoln laughing.

As Wright and Lincoln walked along the parapet, they were joined by the Divisional Surgeon. The three men strolled along as if they were in a park. Suddenly, shots rang out; the surgeon put his hands to his throat. Lincoln and Wright were instantly covered with blood as the man dropped dead at the feet of the President. Bullets whizzed all around the Chief Executive sending chards of concrete in all directions. Without realizing who the visitor was, a young lieutenant recuperating from wounds incurred at Spotsylvania shouted.

"Get down you damned fool! You want to get yourself killed!"

The young man reached up and pulled the President down.

"What's your name, young man?" inquired Lincoln.

Without turning the youthful soldier replied.

"Lieutenant Oliver Wendell Holmes. May I inquire what your name is?"

"My first name is Abraham and thank you for saving my life. By the way, my last name is Lincoln."

The young officer turned his head and, recognizing the President, turned pale and suddenly felt sick.

Seeing the young man's color fade, the President laughed and placed his hand on the soldier's shoulder.

"Don't worry, son. You're not in trouble."

The President crawled to the stairs and descended from the parapet.

During the night Early withdrew and headed back to the Shenandoah Valley unmolested by the Federals.

Just outside of Atlanta, Georgia—July 12, 2:00 PM

Sherman ordered Schofield and McPherson to force their way across the Chattahoochee River. The two Generals consolidated their artillery to provide the maximum punch. At two o'clock Mac gave the order to open fire. For thirty minutes the cannons hammered the defenders. The pounding did little damage physically, but had a great psychological effect on the defenders as the ground shook and spit-up basketball size chucks of dirt, clay and rocks.

Simultaneously Thomas opened with his guns and started his men toward the river's edge followed immediately by McPherson's men. While the two Armies held the enemy's attention, Schofield slipped his Army across the river and entrenched.

News of the crossing quickly reached Johnston. He ordered Hood to attack Schofield and drive the enemy into the Chattahoochee.

The crippled Corps Commander deployed his men into formation and gave the order to attack. His men stepped off quickly without hesitation. Schofield had left his artillery with McPherson. It would be musket against musket. The terrain favored the attacker. Deep depressions gave the men in gray cover as they approached. Once they exited the natural protection, it was only fifty yards of open ground to the Union lines.

From his position across the river, McPherson watched as Hood's Corps used the natural cover to move closer to Schofield. Mac acted quickly and ordered his best artillerists to concentrate their guns on the fifty yards of open ground between the attackers and the defenders; but to hold their fire until Hood's men began their assault. Taking advantage of Hood's preoccupation with Schofield, McPherson ordered his infantry across the river. Hood would be in quite a fix with Schofield on his flank and McPherson at his weakened front.

Hood's men exited the depression and sprinted across the open ground when cannons and Schofield's men opened fire. Men were blown skyward. Limbs were torn from bodies. Blood covered the ground. Hood reorganized his men and ordered them forward. The result was the same.

Johnston noticed McPherson's Army crossing the river to outflank him and ordered Hardee to pull back to the Atlanta defenses and set up a defensive perimeter. Once Hardee's men were on the road, Stewart was to pull his men back forming an inverted 'V' with Hood's Corps. Together the two Corps would slowly retreat toward Atlanta. Wheeler's Cavalry was to circle around Schofield's left flank and hold him in place until Hood and Stewart could safely withdraw.

By nightfall the Confederates were safely entrenched behind the formidable breastworks surrounding Atlanta. Sherman was pleased. The Union Commander had his adversary just where he wanted him. Sherman issued orders to rest the men and to bring up the siege guns.

CHAPTER SEVENTEEN

Atlanta, Georgia—July 13, 1:00 PM

Jefferson Davis' envoy, Braxton Bragg, met with Joe Johnston for four hours. The two military men discussed the current situation both on a military and political basis. The General from Virginia was under the impression Bragg was there to discuss the possibility of reinforcements. Instead it was more like a lengthy interrogation. Both men had quick, fiery tempers which could easily ignite. The two men had a great dislike for one another that went back to their days in the old Federal Army. Although the North Carolinian disliked the Virginian, he tried to keep an open mind. Bragg tried to get his peer to tell him his plans for the defense of Atlanta and when he would assume the offensive against Sherman. Each time the question was brought up, the cagey Virginian gave an evasive answer. Finally Bragg gave up and took his leave.

Accompanied by his aide, Lieutenant Washington, Bragg rode to the Army's telegraph office. The two men barely spoke. Bragg had chosen Washington to accompany him for two reasons—the young man was an expert telegraph operator and he kept his mouth shut.

Washington walked into the communications tent. The little office was neatly kept and well organized. Telegraph wires ran up the center pole of the tent and were hooked into the main wires out of Atlanta. In the middle of the tent were two three-foot long and thirty-inch wide tables. On top of each table was a telegraph machine. Next to the machine were four sharpened pencils and five telegraph pads. One operator sat in front of each table. The operators were both Corporals who, prior to the war, had worked as operators in their respective towns. In the corner was another small table. Seated behind the wooden desk was the Communication Officer of the day. Two enlisted men and an officer always staffed the office, twenty-four hours a day, seven days a week.

"General Bragg requires the use of this tent for a few minutes," said Washington.

The three men instantly recognized their former Commander. Incurring his wrath on several occasions in the past, they quickly scurried out.

The General reached into his pocket and pulled out a piece of paper. Picking up a pencil, he scribbled a quick message and handed it to the aide.

"Send this right away," demanded Bragg in a firm tone.

> *"To: His Excellency, President Jefferson Davis,*
> *White House, Richmond Virginia.*
> *Met with Johnston. Unable to ascertain his plans to resume offensive, I don't*
> *believe he has any. Recommend replacement with Hood.*
> *Signed.*
> *Braxton Bragg*
> *General, CSA"*

Once the message was sent, the two men went outside to have a cigar and wait for a reply. "Gentlemen, you may re-enter the tent and resume your duties," said Washington.

The faithful aide commandeered folding chairs and dinner for the two of them.

"Waiting is always the most difficult part of a soldier's life," said Bragg as the two men ate their dinner.

"How so?" asked Washington.

"A soldier is always waiting. Whether it is for his dinner or for orders to attack or for orders to withdraw. Many civilians think a soldier in the field is always fighting and killing. Actually the fighting and killing are the easiest part as they are instinctive. The body's will to survive takes over. Waiting for the next battle is the most difficult part of war. Your mind starts to think about what you just did or whether or not you'll survive the next battle and what will happen to your family should you perish. You'd think being a soldier would make you a patient person; but, believe me, I've never met a patient soldier whether he be an enlisted man or an officer."

The two men talked for several hours when Washington heard the familiar tapping of the President's special code coming in over the wire. He rushed in as the men inside rushed out.

"To: General Braxton Bragg CSA
Atlanta, Georgia
You are, hereby, ordered to relieve General Johnston of command and replace him
with Lieutenant General John B. Hood. Hood is ordered to immediately assume
full command of the Army of Tennessee and will submit his plans to this office no
later than two days hence. Once the transfer is accomplished, you are to return to
Richmond post haste.
Signed.
Jefferson Davis
President CSA"

Bragg finished his dinner, took the telegram and boldly walked into Johnston's tent. The Virginian had just finished supper and was peering over maps of Atlanta when the North Carolinian entered.

"Well, Braxton, by the look on your face you're here to tell me the President has relieved me of my command. Who's my replacement?"

"Hood has been ordered to take command of the Army," responded Bragg dryly.

"Hood! Is the President crazy? Mark my words, he'll wreck this Army. I'm out of here."

The General turned and began packing without saying another word. Bragg left the tent to inform Hood of the President's decision.

By the time Hood and Bragg returned to Johnston's tent, the General had departed for his home.

"Shit," he didn't even have the courtesy to stick around and brief me on the disposition of our Army or the enemy. Never mind I'll figure it out," said Hood in disgust.

Atlanta, Georgia—July 18, 6:00 PM

Sherman met with his Army Commanders to discuss the change in the Confederate high command. The Commanding General did not know much about Hood and he wanted to find out what he was up against.

"Johnston has been relieved and John Hood has been given command. I only know Hood by reputation. I know Lee had used his Division as his battering ram and I'm aware he was wounded at Gettysburg and Chickamauga. I need to know about the man himself," said Sherman.

"Billy, I attended West Point with Hood," responded McPherson.

"We both graduated together. Hood is an aggressive fighter. At the 'Point' he was first in the class in all physical marital arts. He is an excellent swordsman. When he was stationed out West as part of the 'old Army's' Second Dragoons out of Texas, he was always on patrol looking for a fight against the Comanche's. He's highly thought of by Jefferson Davis and Lee. At the 'Point' he was always in competition with Phil Sheridan. It was one hell of a class."

"Mac, no wonder you graduated first in your class. You had no competition, Hood and Sheridan. If you put both of them together in the same body, they would only have half a brain," teased the usually stoic Thomas.

McPherson's face turned red as Sherman, Schofield and Thomas heartily laughed. Normally it was the fun loving Mac who enjoyed a laugh at Thomas' expense. Over the course of the last few months, Sherman and his Generals had become friends. Each knew how the other thought and, more importantly, they all knew how Sherman thought. They made allowances for each other's weaknesses and idiosyncrasies. More importantly, they didn't bicker among themselves. There were no secret letters written to Grant or Lincoln. The Union Armies in the West under Sherman's immediate control were a team.

"George, at least when I graduated, we had more than thirteen stars on our flag," retorted McPherson.

Sherman allowed the bantering to continue for fifteen minutes before he brought everyone's attention back to the new Confederate Commander.

"Mac, what else can you tell us about Hood?" asked Sherman.

"Like I said, he's very aggressive. At the 'Point' he would always favor the attack over defensive tactics. Billy, in my opinion, Hood will attack just as soon as he either perceives a weakness or loses patience. He's not a patient man. He was rated in the bottom third of the class in tactics," continued McPherson.

"At Chickamauga before he was wounded, his Division's attacks were one of the fiercest of the day. He is brave. When he goes on the offensive, I'll guarantee you his assaults will be fierce and bloody. We should not underestimate him," said George Thomas.

"Good point, George. I make it a habit not to underestimate any adversary. Hood or no Hood, I intend to begin the siege of Atlanta. Mac, you and John are to move around the city proceeding south and east. Mac, your Army of Tennessee will take the position on the far right with John's Army of Ohio in the center. George, you're to move your Army around the city proceeding south and west. We'll extend Hood's lines until they break. I want to start the movements at first light tomorrow," replied Sherman.

Atlanta, Georgia—July 20, 9:30 AM

"Gentlemen, Sherman has given us a perfect opportunity. He has divided his Army in half. Thomas' Cumberlanders are on our left; while Schofield and McPherson are on our right. General Wheeler reports there is a two-mile gap between the two Federal forces. Thomas is crossing Peach Tree Creek and not entrenching. They think that we're either too timid to attack or lack the resolve to take advantage of this situation. They are dead wrong. General Cheatham, I want your Corps to feign an attack against McPherson's Army on your extreme right. At the same time, I want you to mass your cannon to cover the gap between Schofield and Thomas. If either force moves to support the other, blast the bastards to hell!" said Hood slamming his good hand flat against the table to emphasize his point.

"I want both Hardee and Stewart's Corps to attack Thomas simultaneously. Once they have destroyed Thomas they'll move in support of Cheatham and destroy McPherson and Schofield. Wheeler's Cavalry will get in the rear of the Federals and if the opportunity present's itself, he'll strike causing as much panic as possible. Any questions?" asked Hood.

Silence filled the room.

"If there are no questions, I suggest we begin our movements. I want the attack to take place by noon. We must move rapidly so we can catch Thomas while his Army is astride Peach Tree Creek."

Cheatham patiently waited for word from Hardee to begin the attack. From his vantage point, he could see the gap widening as Thomas and Schofield extended their grasp. The newly appointed Corps Commander placed his guns so they could support his infantry in the attack and, at the same time, cover the gap.

On the other end of the field Hardee and Stewart moved their respective Corps in preparation for the attack. Last minute adjustments delayed them until three o'clock. Hardee sent a courier to Cheatham telling him that at precisely three, his and Stewart's attacks would commence.

At the agreed time, Hardee's Corps began their assault. The General placed Walker's Division in the lead. Walker was a career soldier who fought against the Seminole Indians in Florida. Severely wounded, he recovered in time to serve in the war with Mexico and was so gravely wounded, the surgeons had given up on him. It was only through sheer determination he survived. His men would spearhead the assault. Depending on his success,

Hardee would then send the other three Divisions under Cleburne, Maney and Bate in support.

Union General John Newton placed his men on top of a hill covering the right flank. The experienced Army officer had his men take advantage of a slight depression on top of the hill. Even though ordered by Thomas not to dig in, it didn't prevent him from taking advantage of the natural curves of the terrain. Bending the rules a bit, he had his men dig a trench about a foot deep and pile the dirt in front of them giving his men some cover. The Virginian knew if Hood struck his twenty-seven hundred men needed every advantage to hold their position and protect the rest of the Army.

Walker surveyed Newton's defensive works. They were formidable but not impossible. His men would have to cross a hundred yards of open ground uphill all the way. The General from Georgia was confident he could break the Union line. If he wasn't successful, he knew Hardee would order Cleburne, Maney and Bate in support. Together they would carry the line by sheer force of numbers.

The Georgian drew his sword signaling the attack to begin. His men sprinted across the open field, but the steepness of the hill quickly took its effect and they slowed to a brisk walk. Their bayonets glistened in the late afternoon sun.

Newton ordered his men to hold their fire until the Confederates were within thirty yards. Sweat poured down the foreheads of the defenders as they waited for the order to fire. Their mouths were suddenly dry while their palms sweated. It didn't matter how many times a man was in combat the body always reacted the same way. A man could control his emotions and fear, but he couldn't control the body's natural functions.

Newton's men opened fire just as Walker's men let out their rebel yell. Twenty-seven hundred muskets spit forth deadly leaden projectiles. It seemed as if each one struck its target. Men in gray fell like leaves in a windstorm. Fortunately or unfortunately, depending on whether you were struck or not, the Union defenders didn't just pick out one target per man. Many times one poor soul was the target of many defenders. What made a man select one over the other will never be known. It was just a phenomenon of battle.

Walker's men quickly fell back, regrouped and charged again. Once again they were repulsed. Rather than attack a third time Walker ordered his men to take cover in the woods and return fire. The battle continued non-stop. The Georgian sent word to Hardee for reinforcements.

Unknown to Walker, while he was attacking Newton, the Corps Commander had sent Bate's Division further to the west to strike the enemy's flank. The Division Commander quickly obeyed but in order to move westward they had to enter dense woodland. Bate and his men became lost and headed away from the Federal forces. After waiting an hour for Bate to attack, the Corps Commander ordered Cleburne and Maney forward to support Walker's attacks. No sooner had they begun their movement when orders arrived from Hood ordering the Corps Commander to send a Division to support Wheeler. The Cavalry Commander had encountered a large Union force. Hardee quickly complied and sent Cleburne's Division in support of Wheeler's men.

Unknown to Hood, Sherman had ordered McPherson to send one of his Divisions to flank Cheatham and take the Western and Atlantic Railroad along with the high ground known as Bald Hill. McPherson chose Brigadier General Walter Gresham's Division to make the movement. The Indiana native had served with the Federal Army of Tennessee since Shiloh and was highly thought of.

Based on Walker's request for two Divisions, Hardee reasoned that only sending one Division to Walker would not be enough. He cancelled Maney's movements. Hardee's Corps was effectively out of the fight, leaving Stewart's Corps to take on Thomas' Army. Unknown to Hardee, the remaining seven thousand men of Walker and Maney's Divisions outnumbered the force opposing him by greater than two-to-one.

As the smoke of gunfire shrouded the battlefield, Stewart ordered his Corps forward. He would hit Thomas with the full weight of his Corps; not piecemeal like his peer. His lead Division under the command of Brigadier General William Loring started the attack. Loring, the one-armed Commander from Florida, was noted for bravery losing his arm at the bloody battle of Chapultepec during the war with Mexico.

Loring attacked the Federal right-center, while Stewart's second Division Commander, Brigadier General Edward Walthall, attacked the Federal center. The Mississippi resident was known for his coolness under fire. He had no regard for his life and was constantly in the front leading his Brigade.

Stewart's third Division, under the command of Brigadier General Samuel French, was to hit the Federal center on its extreme right. The transplanted northerner from New Jersey had chosen to fight for his adopted State of Mississippi. Although a combat veteran of the war with Mexico, he was not assigned Divisional command until the start of Sherman's campaign.

Loring hit Thomas' Army first. His men crashed into the weakly defended Federal right center, under the command of Brigadier General William Ward, with such force it caused the men in blue to recoil. Slowly they retreated toward Peachtree Creek as Loring kept up steady pressure. His men pushed Ward's Division back onto Newton's Division as the beleaguered Union men put up a stubborn resistance.

While Loring's men were breaching the Federal line, Walthall and French's men had run up against the main force of Thomas' Army. Slowly the blue coats gave way. Seeing his line faltering, George Thomas galloped across the Creek and took immediate command. Bullets flew around the Army Commander as he galloped from one point of the attack to the other urging his men to hold their ground. Seeing musket fire alone would not stop Stewart's attacks, the Union General ordered his artillery across the Creek to commence firing.

The Confederate Generals, sensing victory, continued to press their men forward. When the artillery rounds started to rain all around their men, the attacks slowed in intensity. Seeing they were caught in a no man's land, the two Division Commanders ordered a withdrawal.

Seeing his supporting Divisions pull back and receiving fire from three sides, Loring had no choice but to withdraw to his original position. The Division Commanders along with their Corps Commander were angry about the lack of support from Hardee.

As the fighting in front of Thomas' Army dwindled, it was just getting started east of Atlanta. Gresham, seeing he had only dismounted Cavalry in his front, deployed his men for an assault.

Wheeler put a Brigade at the railroad to hold the enemy in check and give him time to form a defense line on Bald Hill as Gresham moved his men forward. The Federals recoiled from the initial blast of musketry. The Union General reorganized his forces and, personally, led them back into the hailstorm of lead. This time the men in blue would not be denied access to the railroad driving the skirmishers back onto Bald Hill.

Once again, the Union General reorganized his men and attacked the defenders. This time the assault was uphill against a Division. The charging men were cut down like firewood, but still they pressed on determined to take the position. As Gresham neared the Confederate breastworks, the Federal Commander plunged to the ground. A musket ball smashed his knee. The General's aides picked him up and carried their fallen leader to the rear and safety. Seeing Gresham fall, the northerners assumed he was dead and withdrew. The attacks ended for the day.

The element of surprise was gone. Hood knew he wasn't strong enough to take on Thomas head-to-head. The Southern Commander issued orders for Hardee and Stewart to hold their positions while he erected a new defensive line just inside Atlanta's city limits.

While Hood issued orders, Patrick Cleburne and his Division were just arriving at Wheeler's front. The Confederate General placed his men alongside the tired Southern horsemen.

Meanwhile, surgeons worked feverishly in a vain effort to save Gresham's leg. The war was over for the brave Division Commander. He was replaced by his second-in-command, Brigadier General Mortimer Leggett. Gresham's replacement was a distinguished Brigade leader, but had never commanded a full Division. Prior to the war, the New Yorker was a School Superintendent.

Leggett received orders to attack at dawn. He was also told that reinforcements, under the command of Francis Blair, were on their way and would arrive before midnight. When they arrived Leggett, being the senior General, was in command.

Bald Hill, Georgia—July 21, 4:30 AM

The sky had just begun to lighten when Leggett's men started forward. The defenders waited until the men in blue were within a hundred yards and opened fire. The Northerners were surprised. They had expected dismounted Cavalry. Instead they found Cavalry supported by a Division of Infantry. The attackers paused for a moment and then continued their forward movement. Line after line of Federals reached the Confederate breastworks only to be beaten back. The defenders lips became black and cracked as they tore open powder charge after powder charge. Their dripping sweat sizzled on the overheated gun barrels.

In spite of the record heat, the Union troops kept up the pressure throughout the morning. Men dropped from heat exhaustion, but still the Federals repeatedly charged. The determination of the Federals finally prevailed and the Confederates were forced to yield the hill to the Yankees. It was a hard fought morning and men on both sides were exhausted. Cleburne and Wheeler decided to rest and reorganize their men and then retake the hill in the coolness of the late afternoon.

On top of Bald Hill, Leggett and Blair decided to have their men immediately entrench and prepare for a Confederate counter-attack. The Federal
Commanders worked their men in shifts of one hour. For one hour half the
men would entrench while the other half rested. This way they had at least
half of their men rested in case Wheeler and Cleburne decided to attack
before they were finished

At four o'clock, the Confederate Generals deployed their men in a line of
battle. The men in gray moved lethargically. They were willing to do what was
ordered, but their bodies were too broken to immediately respond. The heat
and fierceness of the Union assaults had drained them of their strength. Seeing the condition of their men, they called off the attack and for the balance of
the day rested their men. McPherson's Army now had command of the high
ground and could see the steeples of Atlanta a mere two and a half miles away.

That night Hood ordered Hardee and Stewart to withdraw from Peachtree
Creek and take new positions. Hardee was to move his Corps as soon as it got
dark back through Atlanta and join with Wheeler and Cleburne. Once he
linked up with them, he was to leave Cleburne in place and, together with
Wheeler, he was to make a wide arc around McPherson's Army coming up
behind the Federals. When Cleburne heard the sounds of Hardee's Corps
being engaged, he was to attack and retake Bald Hill. As soon as Cleburne
started his attack, Cheatham was to begin his assault against Schofield. Stewart was ordered to watch Thomas' Army. If they moved to support either
McPherson or Schofield, he was to attack and keep the Army of the Cumberland out of the fight. The plan, if executed properly, would drive Sherman
back across the Chattahoochee.

Near Bald Hill, Georgia—July 21 10:00 PM

Sherman moved his headquarters closer to McPherson. It was ten o'clock
when the Department Commander arrived at the headquarters of the Army of
Tennessee.

"General Sherman, this is an unexpected but, nevertheless, pleasant surprise. What brings you out?" asked McPherson in a genuinely warm tone of
voice.

"I missed my favorite General. I think Hood will concentrate his forces
against you in the morning and I wanted to be here in case you need help."

"I don't know if Hood will strike this far. He may order a demonstration or
feign an attack, but I doubt he'll hit me; however, as a precaution, I've ordered

Dodge to move two of his Divisions next to Blair's and cover our flank and rear," responded McPherson.

The two friends sat by the warm campfire drinking coffee and talking about the placement of troops and of friends and family. Sherman talked of his beloved wife, Ellen, and his children. McPherson talked about his fiancé and how he wished he had married her before the start of the campaign. It was almost one in the morning when they said goodnight.

The morning of the twenty-second began peacefully much to the surprise of everyone on both sides. Hood was beside himself. Hardee was the key to the attack. He was supposed to be in position by midnight and was to attack at daybreak.

Unfamiliar with the roads and in a moonless night, Hardee had gotten lost and had marched seven miles out of his way. It wasn't until eleven in the morning when he arrived. It took him another hour to deploy his men. Except for the delay in timing, everything was going according to plan. As Hardee placed his Corps, he noticed McPherson's rear wasn't unguarded as supposed. There were two full Divisions protecting McPherson from the type of attack Hood planned.

McPherson and Sherman enjoyed their coffee and continued their conversation of the previous evening. At noon the two men heard the sound of musketry coming from the area where McPherson had posted Dodge. Sensing danger to his line, McPherson called for his horse and, with only one staff member, galloped to the sound of the battle. Sherman also called for his horse and galloped to higher ground to observe the battle.

The denseness of the forest hid the men in gray. Once they exited the treeline there was one hundred yards of flat, open ground. Walker waited until his entire Division was ready. He then sent word to Bate and Wheeler to make sure they were in position. Once the entire Confederate Corps was in position, Walker gave the order for his Division to advance. The Confederate General and his men burst out of the woodland.

Sweeny's Division of Dodge's Corps were completely surprised as they dove for their muskets. Walker's men were less than fifteen yards from the Federal force when Sweeney ordered his men to open fire. It was too late. Walker's men were on the defenders before they had a chance to reload. Men in blue were instantly locked into a hand-to-hand grapple for their lives.

At the same time Bate, riding his chestnut stallion, smashed into Dodge's other Division under the command of John Fuller. Dodge thought highly of the English-born businessman turned soldier. Unlike Sweeney, Fuller had performed admirably during the campaign. While Sweeney had his good and bad moments, Fuller was consistently good.

Twenty yards from Fuller's men Bate had his horse shot out from under him. The General from Tennessee stood and, waving his sword over his head, continued to lead his men. Unlike Sweeney, Fuller had his men on the alert. They were able to fire two volleys before the men in gray smashed into their line.

Men bit, stabbed, clawed and punched one another in a desperate life and death struggle. The Confederate's bent the Union line into the shape of a horseshoe. The Federals held their ground. Dodge sent word to the Corps on his right under the command of Union General John Logan that he needed help. Logan responded immediately sending two Brigades to Dodge's assistance.

To the far right of Bate, Wheeler found the Union rear and attacked catching the Federal Division, under the command of Brigadier General Giles Smith, completely by surprise. The Union troops quickly recovered and slowly withdrew leaving behind four cannons and three Union hospitals. At twelve-thirty McPherson arrived on the scene. The Army Commander reformed Smith's Division establishing a strong defensive line. He intently watched as Wheeler's men struck the hastily constructed breastworks and were repulsed. The southerners retreated to the woods. They reformed and struck again, in vain, as the Federals held their ground.

Seeing Smith's line re-established, McPherson galloped to Dodge's area. Troops were spread all over the battlefield. It was hard to know where the Union lines ended and where the Confederate lines began. The fighting was more like a lethal brawl than a battle.

McPherson, accompanied by an aide, became confused and rode into the Southern lines fifty yards from Dodge's Corps. He was instantly approached by a Confederate patrol. They silently motioned him to step down from his horse. McPherson took off his hat and in a sweeping motion bowed to the men from his saddle as he turned his horse and galloped away. He didn't get far. The men in gray leveled their rifles and taking aim—fired. The man was dead before he hit the ground.

The aide escaped and quickly came upon Dodge. He explained the situation. Dodge was in a fight for his life and couldn't help his friend. He sent word to the Army's second-in-command, John Logan, about McPherson's misfortune and asked for orders.

Bate and Walker reformed their men and attacked again. For the next three hours Sweeney and Fuller along with the two Brigades from Logan repulsed the assaults. Bodies littered the ground. The grass was stained red from the blood of the fallen.

Hearing the fighting on his right, Cleburne ordered his men to attack Leggett's Division on top of Bald Hill. With no reinforcements available, Leggett was forced to repel the Confederate onslaught without help. Cleburne wanted that hill and he was going to get it. Five times the Southerners attacked, four times they were repulsed. The fifth time they succeeded. However, their success was short lived. Leggett reformed his men and counter-attacked driving Cleburne and his men back down the hill.

Cheatham attacked Schofield's entrenched troops. High on a hill, Sherman watched as Dodge held his ground and Leggett retook Bald Hill. Seated next to the General was Major General Oliver Howard of Hooker's Corps. The two men watched as Cheatham's men left their breastworks and started across the open ground toward Schofield. The Department Commander wasted no time. He ordered Howard to fire on the attackers with all of his artillery. The cannons did the job. Cheatham's attack was over before it began.

As the sun set, the firing dwindled down. Wheeler's men were back where they had started the day. Leggett had held Bald Hill. However, there was still enough daylight for one more attack. Walker and Bate reformed their Divisions and sprinted once more out the woods. The tired Yankees held their fire until the charging gray coats were within fifty yards. Twenty yards from the Union defenders Walker grabbed his chest and fell backwards dead. Seeing their beloved Walker fall was more than his Division could take. Sullenly, they retreated to the safety of the woods. Without support, Bate was forced to abandon his attack.

A half-hour after the battle ended, Bate sent a flag of truce across the battlefield. The General requested permission to get his wounded and recover the body of the fallen Walker. Dodge permitted the cease-fire providing he could search for McPherson's body. Within two hours the battlefield had been cleared of wounded and the two dead Generals exchanged. The rest of the dead were left where they had fallen.

The bloodiest day of the campaign was over. Sherman sat in his headquarters' office at a confiscated Plantation house. A fire was blazing in the hearth. It was the only light in the darkened room. The dancing flames spread eerie shadows across the room. Sherman sat in a chair, his elbows on the desk, his hands covering his face. The Department Commander was visibly upset about the death of McPherson. Tears rolled down his cheeks as he thought of the young man. The two had been together for almost three years. The red-haired General felt guilty about not granting McPherson leave to get married. His thoughts turned to his other friend and he wondered how Grant would take the news. The three of them had been friends for a long time.

Sitting in his Atlanta headquarters, Hood was dismayed at the failure. He was lamenting the loss of Walker and his friend from West Point, James McPherson. It was Walker who was the first to fully accept him as the Commanding General of the Army. It was McPherson who tutored him at the "Point" after lights out. He would miss them both.

Hood sat back in his leather chair and planned his next course of action. His mind raced with all kinds of alternatives. Should he renew the attacks or stay on the defensive? For now, he would do the latter.

Atlanta, Georgia—July 23, 10:00 AM

The next morning Sherman woke to the sounds of men digging entrenchments. Today he would rest his men and reorganize his Department. He had to choose a successor to McPherson. His thoughts explored the options.

"John Logan had performed well, but he didn't fully trust the Illinois politician turned solider. Hooker had experience leading an Army, but Sherman didn't trust him either. Howard had the experience and was a West Pointer. He had handled his Corps very well during the campaign. He was loyal and easy to get along with. Howard it will be."

Sherman drew up orders placing Oliver Howard in command of the Army of the Tennessee.

After receiving the news, a much surprised Howard immediately met with his Corps Commanders. Logan, although wounded in the leg during the previous day's battle, was able to walk and command his Corps. The Illinois General resented Sherman for picking Howard instead of him. The other Corps Commanders accepted the appointment without comment or jealously.

While Howard was meeting with his Corps Commanders, Joe Hooker stormed into Sherman's office unannounced.

"General Sherman, you have done me a grave injustice! I deserve to have the Army of Tennessee! I was the former Commanding General of the Army of the Potomac! I have seniority over Howard! I've obeyed your orders without question! I've put up with your tyrannical demeanor!" shouted Hooker with fire in his eyes.

Sherman slammed his fist on his desk and shouted back.

"One more word out of you and I'll have you court-maritaled and shot for insubordination!"

Hooker glared at the Commanding General. He knew Sherman would like nothing better than to court-martial him. The former Army of the Potomac Commander sat down and shut his mouth.

"General Hooker, if you feel slighted, you may take your concerns to General Grant," replied Sherman in a calm voice.

Hooker knew Grant would side with Sherman.

"General Sherman, I don't need to see General Grant; however, I, hereby, request to be relieved from command. I do not wish to serve in an Army in which rank and service are ignored," responded Hooker.

"No, General Hooker, I don't suppose you wish to serve under my jurisdiction. You are, hereby, relieved of command and are ordered to Washington to await orders from the War Department," answered Sherman.

Inside Atlanta, Hood reorganized his Army. The Confederate President ordered Lieutenant General Stephen D. Lee to Atlanta to assist Hood. Lee, a distant relation to Confederate General Robert E. Lee, had earned his rapid rise in rank for deeds performed on the battlefield and not through political appointment.

The Commanding General warmly welcomed the younger man and gave him his former Corps reducing Cheatham back to his former rank of Division Commander. Hood openly discussed the situation and the positions of both Sherman's Army and the Confederate defenders. The two men talked for most of the day before Lee went to take command of his Corps. Cheatham accepted the demotion without complaint. Down deep he felt relief. He was more comfortable leading a Division than a Corps.

As the sun set below the horizon, Sherman shelled Atlanta. He ordered his artillerists to fully elevate their guns so as to shoot over the Confederate defenders and into the center of the business district to weaken the resolve of the civilians. Every two hours cannons sent three or four shells into the district. The sky became a kaleidoscope of colors as shells struck their targets instantly igniting buildings. Atlanta's fire department raced to the scene, but instead of putting the fires out, they performed preventive maintenance to stop the flames from spreading.

CHAPTER EIGHTEEN

Richmond, Virginia, Confederate White House—July 27, 5:00 AM

Jefferson Davis sat at the breakfast table alone drinking coffee and reading dispatches from Hood, Beauregard and Lee. The South's Chief Executive liked the solitude of the early morning. Four days had passed since Hood's attacks on Bald Hill. The General had done exactly what the President wanted. He took the war to Sherman and had stolen the initiative. Unfortunately, the young officer did not have the room to operate. Davis thought if only he would have made the change sooner, then Hood would have had more of chance to maneuver.

The Confederate Chief Executive placed Hood's dispatches on the table and sipped his coffee. As the warm liquid traveled down his throat, he closed his eyes and took a deep breath. Once again, he toyed with the idea of resigning his office and assuming command of the forces around Atlanta. The Mississippian reopened his eyes and reluctantly read Beauregard's dispatch.

The Cajun General's message contained a detailed plan about how he should assume command of the South's Army of Tennessee and would bring with him the militias from the Carolinas and Florida to Atlanta giving him seventy thousand men. Leaving thirty thousand to guard the Gateway City he would put the rest on trains and attack Grant from the south. With his and Lee's army they would defeat Grant and then turn on Sherman. If Davis didn't care for the plan, then he would take the militias and join Lee, picking up at least twenty thousand more recruits along the way.

Davis put down the message alongside of Hood's and shook his head. While Johnston didn't have a plan, he could always count on Beauregard to have at least two. The problem with the Creole's strategy was that the militias

202

in the Carolinas and Florida didn't number more than five thousand. The new recruits that could flock to the General's side were already in the Army.

The President picked up a dispatch from Lee. The Virginian was pleased to notify the President that Early had turned on Crook and, in a spirited fight at Kernstown, had routed the Federal forces. The Valley was once again in Confederate control. He informed Davis that he gave discretionary orders to Early to invade the North; perhaps drawing off another Corps from Grant in the process.

City Point, Virginia—July 27, 5:00 AM

While Davis was drinking his coffee, Grant met with Meade and Burnside.

"General Grant, Colonel Pleasanton's mine is ready. I have taken the liberty to order it filled with black powder. The Colonel informed me it would take three hundred and twenty kegs of powder to accomplish what we want," said Burnside.

"Very well, please proceed," responded the General-in-Chief.

"At dawn on the thirtieth, the mine will explode. We anticipate the blast will blow a hole one hundred yards across through Lee's defensives. I calculate we have at least thirty to forty-five minutes before the Confederates regain their senses and mount a counter-attack. When the mine explodes, the Divisions of the Ninth Corps will race toward the enemy lines. Once through the enemy defenses, my Divisions will turn right and left splitting Lee's Army in half."

"What is the order of attack?" interrupted Meade.

"Ferraro's Division has been training for three weeks and will lead the assault supported by Ledlie's Division. Willcox's Division will remain in reserve."

"Ferraro's Division is made up of colored troops isn't it?" asked Grant.

"Yes, sir, it is," replied a puzzled Burnside.

"Unless General Meade disagrees with me, I'd like another Division to lead the assault. This is a new type of strategy and if it fails, I don't want any newspapermen or radicals saying we purposely sacrificed colored men in an experiment," answered Grant.

"I agree, Sam, if this fails, they'll hang all three of us and rightly so," said Meade.

"Sirs, Ferraro's men have been training for this. I think it would be a mistake to change now," responded Burnside.

"The matter is closed. General Grant and I allowed you to carry on with your plan even though we sincerely doubt its success. You have your orders," answered Meade in a terse tone.

The Corps Commander stood, saluted and left visibly upset. While he rode back to his headquarters, the former Commander of the Army of Potomac swore at the stupidity and narrow-minded thinking of both Meade and Grant. Didn't they realize that changing the order of attack could be disastrous?

Burnside called his Division Commanders together and had them draw straws to see who would replace Ferraro's Division in the lead with Ledlie drawing the short straw.

"General Ledlie, the entire Corps will follow your Division," said Burnside. "The explosion will create a gap wide enough for an entire Brigade to pass. We are going to exploit the gap one Brigade at a time. Marshall's Brigade will lead the assault followed by Bartlett's; then Griffin's Brigade from Potter's Division will follow Bartlett."

"The rest of Potter's Division will create a diversion on the right of the explosion while Willcox's Division will create a diversion on the left of the crater. Ferraro's Colored Division will be the last to go in. The Brigades are to alternate their direction and should skirt around the exploded mine. Marshall will veer to the right, Bartlett to the left and then the next one to the right and then the left and so forth," said Burnside.

Atlanta, Georgia—July 27, 5:00 AM

Sherman met with Howard as the men stirred from their sleep.

"Oliver, I've decided that Calvary alone will not be able to secure and hold the railroads leading into and out of Atlanta. The only way we'll be able to accomplish the siege is for the infantry to take the roads and destroy them. I want you to move your Army around Thomas' and take the Atlanta and West Point Railroad. Once you have secured the West Point Railroad, you are to proceed south and take the Macon and Western Railroad," said Sherman.

Howard nodded and immediately broke camp marching eighteen miles before six o'clock and was a scant four miles from his objective. Sherman, riding at the head of the Corps next to Howard, decided to make camp at Ezra Church and then, after a good night's sleep, take the railroad.

"Billy, we should push on. If we stay here, we're inviting Hood to strike us. Please reconsider," pleaded Howard.

"Oliver, Hood's men are played out. They won't attack," replied Sherman.

"Sir, at least let me entrench?

"Very well, do as you see fit," responded a perplexed Sherman.

Howard ordered his men to entrench and to take whatever logs or wood they could find and build breastworks. The men obeyed using rail fences, Church pews and fallen logs.

Sherman woke to find a nervous Oliver Howard pacing.

Smiling he asked, "Oliver, any word from Hood this morning?"

"Billy, ask me again at noon," answered Howard.

While the two Northern Generals talked, Confederates moved into position. Seeing he would be unable to hit the Federals in the rear, Stewart decided on a flank attack. Without consulting Lee, Stewart attacked just as the Union forces were beginning to break camp. Confederate Soldiers burst forth from the woodland sprinting across the two hundred yards of open ground smashing into Logan's unsuspecting Corps.

The experienced Union veterans dove behind the logs and Church pews and fired into the gray onslaught. Hearing the sounds of battle on his right flank, Howard sent half of Dodge's Corps in support of Logan driving the attackers back.

Bodies of the Southerners lay strewn across the field. Undaunted, Stewart reorganized and struck the Federals once more. This time the rebels got within fifty yards before retreating. It was now after twelve. The hot, humid Georgia weather was beginning to take its toll on both sides. Bodies were in need of water as the sweat of battle and the humidity drained precious fluids. Stewart gave his men ten minutes to drink water while he reformed for another attack.

The Federals took advantage of the brief respite to replenish their lost fluids. Logan had decided the temporary breastworks would have to hold. At twelve-thirty Stewart attacked a third time. Again it met with limited success as the rebels got within ten yards of the Union lines before retreating.

Hearing the sounds of Stewart's attacks, Lee launched his Corps in support of his comrade striking the front of Howard's Army consisting of half of Dodge's Corps along with the Army's Third Corps under the command of Major General Francis Blair. Once they heard the firing on Logan's front, both he and Dodge had their men dig in and wait.

While Stewart formed for a fourth attack, Lee hit Blair and Dodge's men getting within a hundred yards of the entrenchments before giving up the attack. They quickly reformed and attacked again. For the rest of the afternoon the attacks continued. Repulse was followed by reformation and another attack. As Lee's attacks sputtered out, Stewart's were just beginning and then as Stewart's were petering, Lee would strike again allowing Howard to shift troops from one threatened area to another.

At five in the evening both Stewart and Lee gave up the battle and dug in. Combined they had assaulted the Union lines ten times and didn't breach the breastworks. The Southerners had done their best, but there were just too few of them to win the day. Lee sent word to Hood about their failure to destroy Howard's Army. Hood was pleased that his men were successful in stopping Sherman from taking the railroad. Atlanta would survive another day.

Petersburg, Virginia—July 30, 3:00 AM

Rumors had circulated throughout the Army of the Potomac that the mine was scheduled to explode in the wee hours of the morning. Everyone wanted to see the blast. An eerie mist covered the predawn ground. It was like God had sent the Angel of death to Petersburg. In the early morning darkness a match was struck and a fuse ignited.

"How long will it take, Sergeant?" asked Colonel Pleasants.

"About thirty minutes, sir," answered the former coal miner.

"Inform Generals Ledlie and Ferraro the mine will explode at three-thirty on schedule. Remind them they are to allow five minutes for the dust to settle before commencing the attack," said Pleasants.

The courier saluted and jumped onto his mount galloping into the darkness to deliver the message. The young man rode first to Burnside's headquarters to deliver the message and then onto Ledlie's Divisional headquarters. When he arrived, he was informed the General was not there and to check the bomb-proof shelter a half-mile in the rear.

The courier found the General seated at a table in the underground shelter drinking a cup of coffee. Ledlie acknowledged the courier and then ordered him to take the message to General Bartlett. Once again the courier dutifully obeyed orders and rode away.

Fifteen minutes later he found Bartlett with his Brigade not more than a quarter of a mile from where he had started.

"General Bartlett, Colonel Pleasants' compliments, he reports the mine will explode precisely at three-thirty as planned," panted the courier.

In three years Bartlett had earned his way up to Brigadier General through countless acts of bravery. The young New Englander lost his right leg during the Battle of Yorktown in 1862. Upon his recovery, he served with Banks during the capture of Fort Hudson on the Mississippi where he was wounded twice more. Upon his recovery, he led his regiment during the Battle of the Wilderness. On May sixth he was wounded again and had just returned to duty.

"Very well, I will inform my men," replied Bartlett.

Grant looked at his pocket watch. It was now four o'clock, the time for the explosion had passed. The tip of the General's cigar became bright red as he drew the tobacco smoke into his mouth. He slowly let out a smoke ring. The sky was beginning to turn from black to dark blue as the sun rose. If the explosion didn't happen by five, he would order the assault to begin without the fireworks.

At the mine's entrance, Pleasants was consulting with his engineers. They determined the fuse must have been blown out by the wind. Someone had to go in and find where it was extinguished, relight it and get out before it exploded. Unfortunately fuses were unpredictable and for no explainable reason could relight themselves.

Pleasants asked for volunteers. Two of his experienced coal miners stepped forward, Lieutenant Harry Reese and Sergeant Jacob Douty. The men had grown up in the coal mines of Pennsylvania and were considered experts in explosives.

The two men quickly entered the mineshaft. In spite of the underground coolness sweat poured down their backs and foreheads. The duo had gone one hundred and fifty yards when they located the burned out portion of the fuse, it was spliced incorrectly. The two men corrected the mistake, ignited the fuse and sprinted for the entrance having less than five minutes to get clear.

As they dove through the entrance, the ground shook violently for a few seconds. Men and horses a half-mile from the mine wobbled unsteadily. Grant steadied his horse. Then without warning, a sound, equivalent to the firing of a thousand cannons, filled the air as the eight thousand pounds of exploding black powder erupted from the earth spiting flames and debris. The predawn sky was instantly filled with large chunks of earth, clay, timbers, guns, and bodies.

Grant's mouth opened wide causing him to drop his cigar. The man watched in awe as the dust cloud rose higher and higher then, at four hundred feet, it dropped suddenly covering attacker and defender in dust and soot.

Confederates on both sides of the mine were either blown skyward, buried alive or had run to the rear. There were no defenders as the men in blue began their assault. They quickly cleared the remaining obstructions from their path and entered the Confederate works unmolested. The men unexpectedly stopped and stared into the crater sixty feet across two hundred feet wide and thirty feet deep. They were mesmerized by the size of the hole unaware of the danger all around them.

Each Brigade entering the rebel lines stopped and gawked at the destruction losing precious time before their General got them going again. By the time the third Brigade had entered Lee's lines, the Confederates had reformed and both Marshall and Bartlett's Brigades were under heavy fire from three sides. Their Brigades, along with Griffin's men, became confused in the labyrinth of tunnels and trenches making up the Southern defensives. Brigade intermingled with Brigade. Marshall, Griffin and Bartlett did their best to sort things out to keep the attack moving forward. Their efforts were in vain as confusion ran rampant. Over five thousand Union troops were now in Lee's trenches; but, without a Division leader to organize things, they were a disorganized mob. The men in blue put up stiff resistance, but were slowly forced back into the crater.

Grant and Meade, noticing the attack had stalled, sent their aides to find Burnside to see what was going on. In less than a half hour the aides returned. They both reported the same thing—Burnside was in a panic and unable to decide what to do. The two Generals dismounted and worked their way forward through the huddled, waiting Brigades. Grant saw a full Brigade already in formation; but not moving.

"Who's in charge of this Brigade?" shouted the General-in-Chief.

"I am, sir," replied a young Colonel.

"Why aren't you moving forward?" asked Grant impatiently.

"Sir, my orders are to follow the Brigade in front of me and as you can see, it's not moving. General Grant, if you order me forward, my men and I will promptly obey," replied the officer.

"No, stay with your original orders, I don't want to muck things up more than they are now. Be ready in case I need you!" shouted Grant above the din of battle.

While Grant was talking to the Colonel, Meade had found Ferraro and ordered his Colored Division forward. They were to bypass the white troops and attack. Ferraro gave the necessary orders and then went to the rear to join Ledlie in the bunker. When he arrived, Ledlie poured a shot of rum and the two Generals sat drinking, allegedly directing the battle from their bunker a mile from the action.

Grant and Meade made their way to the front lines in time to see the Colored Division enter the rebel lines. Bullets flew around the two Union Commanders. Neither man ducked or dodged. They stood there with their eyes locked on the attacking forces.

Ferraro's men didn't stop to gawk at the crater. These men were trained to lead the assault and knew they were to skirt around the gapping hole and attack the enemy on their left. With the reinforcements; Griffin, Bartlett and Marshall led their men out of the crater and joined in the assault. Lee shifted troops from other parts of his defenses to meet the unexpected threat.

Asleep in his quarters when the blast occurred, Lee quickly dressed and issued orders to stem the attack. When Lee ascertained where the attack was taking place, he started to breathe easier. Burnside had chosen the portion of Lee's defenses under the command of one his best remaining Generals, Brigadier General William Mahone. The thirty-eight year old graduate from the Virginia Military Institute was known as a fierce fighter who would go to any extreme to win a battle. Nicknamed "scrappy" by his men, he had proven himself an able fighter and Commander.

Like Lee, Mahone was asleep when the explosion occurred. He was up in a flash and, seeing the huge dust cloud where his Division was positioned, he immediately organized a counter-attack. Without waiting for orders, he sent a courier to the Division Commanders on both his flanks asking them to be prepared to support his men. He steadied his troops and reformed his reserve Brigade. He formed a barrier to the front and left of the attackers stopping them from penetrating the lines any further. At the same time the Division Commander on his right, Brigadier General Bushrod Johnson, had formed his men as a blocking force preventing the Federals from penetrating the right of the breach. The Union troops were now hemmed in on three sides.

An hour after the explosion, Mahone and Johnson were ready. In a massive counter-attack they drove the Union forces into the crater. Cannons were repositioned and fired point blank into the flank of the attacking Union troops. Marshall was killed in the assault along with his second and third in command. His Brigade fell back into the crater for shelter. Bartlett reorganized his men and took command of the leaderless Brigade. At the same time, Griffin assumed command of Ferraro's men and, together they counter-attacked pushing the Southerners slowly back two hundred yards when fresh Confederate troops arrived from other parts of the line and threw the men in blue back into the crater. The hole was now overflowing with Union troops.

Simon Griffin, like his distant cousin Major General Charles Griffin in Warren's Corps, was a fierce fighter. He did, however, know when it was time to retreat. Being the senior General on the field, he ordered his men to dig in and wait for orders. He organized a defensive line at the rear of the crater protecting as best he could the men trapped below.

In the crater, Bartlett did his best to organize and protect his men. He ordered the dead to be used as breastworks and protection for the living. Men piled up the bodies. Even in death the departed served the Union cause.

Meade and Grant saw the Union lines falter and stall just outside the breastworks. It was now ten minutes to seven. The attack had been going on for over two and one-half hours. The dead and wounded were piling up inside and outside the Confederate lines. Meade sent his aide to Burnside with orders to cancel the attack and pull his men back. The former Commander of the Army of the Potomac acknowledged the order.

"Meade and Grant are wrong. We need to send in more men. Order Willcox to send in his Division," said Burnside to his aide.

"Sir, are you sure? It sounds like those men are in dire straits," replied the young man.

"Just carry out my orders, damn you!" shouted Burnside.

Grant's temper flared as he watched Willcox move his Division forward. It was now eight.

"General Meade, send another order to General Burnside. This time, send it in my name and order him to get his men out of there!" shouted Grant.

Once again the courier returned to the Corps Commander and gave him Grant and Meade's orders. Once again, Burnside ignored the order. This time he sent orders for Potter's entire Division to go in.

An hour had passed and still soldiers in blue headed for the breach in the enemy lines. Grant had enough. The time for action had come as he assumed direct command. He would deal with Burnside later.

"Colonel Porter, ride along the line and tell them the attack has been called off in my name. Have the men take their defensive posts!" shouted Grant.

During the entire battle, Grant observed a young staff officer running back and forth across the no man's land carrying orders to and from the assaulting troops. This time he motioned the young officer to come to him. The begrimed soldier instantly recognized the General-in-Chief and sprinted toward him.

"Major, in your opinion, do we have a chance of taking that position?" asked Grant.

"Sir, in my opinion, we should get those men the hell out of there. We have men stuck in the crater. The rebs are shooting our men in that damn hole. The Johnnies are putting bayonets at the end of the muskets and are using them as spears."

Grant threw his cigar on the ground and continued the conversation as bullets flew all around.

"What's your name son?"

"Major Powell, sir."

"Well, Major Powell, I want you to find whoever is in command inside those lines and order him to pull our men out," replied Grant calmly.

"Yes, sir. That would be General Bartlett or Griffin. If they're still alive," replied Powell.

Grant and Meade sent word for the artillery to fire every gun they had to support the withdrawal. Griffin received Grant's orders and shouted down to Bartlett inside the crater.

"Willie, Grant has ordered us to withdraw. You and your men climb up. We'll cover you!" yelled Griffin.

"It would be suicide for us to try to escape. The rebs have us pinned down. Besides, my cork leg is shot to pieces. I can't walk. Save your men. After you're gone, we'll surrender," shouted Bartlett in reply.

Griffin led the men back to the Union lines while Bartlett raised a blood stained white undershirt. It took Mahone's men ten minutes before they recognized the Union surrender. Their blood was boiling. They felt the Northerners' assault was the worst form of a sneak attack ever witnessed.

Grant and Meade watched the men in blue sprint across no man's land as artillery shells covered their run for life. At noon Griffin, being the last man, entered the Union stronghold. It was over. Grant approached the Brigadier and placed his hand on the man's shoulder and said in a low tone.

"You've done your best and I thank you for a valiant effort. Refresh yourself and then join me in my tent."

Grant and Meade sat in the General-in-Chief's tent. The two men were covered in grime and sweat. They opened their coats and rapidly drank a large tankard of cool water while cooks prepared something for the Generals to eat.

"In all my days as a soldier, I have never seen such a wasted opportunity. Why didn't Burnside get the men out when you ordered him to?" asked Grant.

"I don't know. I want to relieve him of command and have him court-martialed," answered an angry Meade.

"You have my permission. Order him to Washington to await further instructions. I assure you, they'll be a long time coming. Every commander makes mistakes, but to disregard orders not once, but twice is almost beyond belief," responded Grant shaking his head.

"I'll issue the orders immediately and I would like Major General John Parke to take over the Corps," answered Meade.

"Are you sure? Parke has no real combat experience. He was Burnside's Chief-of-Staff until I stole him away," responded a surprised Grant.

"Yes, sir, I'm sure," replied an adamant Meade.

"Another thing we must do is immediately conduct a court-of-inquiry and if need be a court-marital. We must find out what went wrong," said Grant gulping down his water.

The conversation was interrupted by Rawlins.

"General Griffin is here as requested."

"Have a seat. Would you like some water or something to eat?" asked Grant.

"Just some cold water please," replied Griffin.

"General, I want you tell us in your own words what happened today," said Grant in a fatherly tone.

Holding the glass of water in his hand, Griffin calmly relayed the course of events. Carefully explaining how Ledlie and Ferraro had issued the attack orders and then disappeared; never to be seen again. He told of the carnage and needless loss of life and how he and Bartlett assumed command. When he got to the part where Bartlett was trapped in the crater and ordered him to withdraw, his hands began to shake spilling water onto the ground as he fought to control his emotions. The two men were close friends.

Grant rose and placed his hand on the man's shoulder.

"Thank you for your report. You may return to your men. General Meade and I will deal with Ledlie and Ferraro," said Grant.

"General Grant, we could've taken that position if Ledlie and Ferraro had done their duty," replied Griffin as he left the tent.

After the Brigadier left, the two men resumed their seats and continued to talk for the remainder of the day. Grant explained to Meade his intention to give Sheridan command of the Union Armies in the Valley.

Monocacy Junction, Maryland—August 6, 11:30 AM

Grant met with Hunter and explained the change in command. He explained that although he outranked Sheridan, to avoid embarrassment for the General, Grant would give Hunter command of the Valley Department while Sheridan would have command of the Armies in the field.

Hunter thought for a few minutes and then told the senior General it would be best for the service if he resigned, thereby, giving Sheridan full command. Rather than accept Hunter's resignation, he ordered the General to Washington to serve as an aide to Halleck. As Hunter left Grant's quarters, Sheridan entered. The two men narrowly missing one another.

"Have a seat, Phil. I suppose you know why you are here?" asked Grant.

"Yes, sir, I'm to take over command of all the armies in the field in the Valley," replied Sheridan.

"You're correct, as of right now, you're, the Commander of the Department of the Valley and of all the armies herein. Your orders are simple. You are to pursue Jubal Early and his army until they are either destroyed or captured. I'll give you Custer and Merritt's Divisions. The rest of your Cavalry Corps will stay with me. As you are aware, five days ago Early burned Chambersburg. He demanded the town pay a ransom. When they didn't raise the necessary money, he torched the place. Phil, he must be stopped and now," replied Grant.

The newly appointed Department Commander agreed and the two men planned the campaign. They agreed Sheridan would need time to organize his new command before beginning his offensive. In the interim, he would keep Early contained in the Valley; being on the defensive at least through August. When he was ready, he would strike the Confederate Army of the Valley and destroy it.

City Point, Virginia—August 8, 7:30 PM

"Good evening, George. How goes the court-of-inquiry?" asked Grant.

"Very well, General, I have appointed Hancock to head the proceedings. His findings have just come in today. They recommend Burnside be court-martialed for disobedience to orders from two superior officers. They recommend Ledlie receive a court-martial for cowardice and Ferraro receive a formal reprimand," replied Meade coolly.

"I can't see a court-marital for Burnside as he was caught up in the heat of battle. He'll be assigned to Washington D.C. and stay there awaiting orders, which will never come. Ledlie will be court-martialed and be sent to Washington to await trial. Ferraro will be sent to Butler," replied Grant.

"I agree with everything you said, but don't you think that Ferraro should receive a reprimand?" asked Meade.

"If we reprimand Ferraro, the abolitionists are sure to get wind of it. They'll say we put an incompetent in charge of colored troops and an investigation will follow. I think it's best if we move Ferraro out of our way and get on with business.

"You seem upset. What's the matter?" asked Grant.

"Sir, I wanted command of the Valley Army and you gave it to Sheridan. I think I earned it," retorted Meade.

"George, it would be an insult to you and everything we've accomplished to give you a smaller Army. Besides, I need you here; we make a good team."

"How can I tell him that I am tired of his constant interference and I feel like a puppet on a string?" thought Meade.

"Sam, please forgive me. I guess I'm just tired."

"George, think nothing of it. When I met with Sheridan, I came up with a new plan. We'll extend our lines in all directions. Even Lee can't be in two places at once.

On August twelfth, Hancock's Corps will march to City Point and board steamers headed north. Confederate spies will think he's headed toward Washington to assist Sheridan, except he'll disembark at Bermuda Hundred. Butler's Army will rebuild the pontoon bridges across the James River. Hancock will then march his men across the pontoon bridge and move northeast to attack Richmond."

"If the ruse works, he'll think Hancock is on his way to Sheridan. Lee will then send reinforcements to Early, thereby, depleting the forces holding Petersburg. With the Petersburg line depleted, Warren, on the eighteenth, will strike the Weldon Railroad defenders," said a red-eyed Grant.

For three hours the two Generals went over the logistics of the campaign. Seeing his commander was not well, Meade left so Grant could sleep.

While Grant slept, two Confederate spies dressed as dock workers snuck past the picket lines. In their knapsacks they carried two time fused bombs, which are activated by setting the time for the explosion and then removing the safety pin. A month earlier Jefferson Davis had approved a covert operation to disrupt the Union high command and if possible, kill Grant.

With men working day and night, no one paid attention to the pair. The two men inspected the ships docked at the wharves and planted the bombs aboard a munitions ship which had just arrived and would be unloaded in the morning. Knowing it would draw suspicion if they attempted to leave right away; they set the bombs to explode at eleven in the morning and then bedded down with the rest of the laborers a half mile from the wharf.

Grant was up early on the morning of the ninth. A cool breeze off of the river invigorated him as he sat outside his tent drinking coffee and reading newspapers. He read with great interest Lincoln's pocket veto of the radical Republicans' bill calling for harsh measures against the States in rebellion rejoining the Union. Lincoln favored reunion without harsh penalties or malice. The radicals wanted revenge.

At precisely eleven o'clock a loud explosion shook the ground as bullets, wooden splinters, and shrapnel of different sorts flew in all directions. Comstock grabbed his thigh and fell to the ground in pain with a four inch splinter sticking out of his leg. Porter crashed to earth, his shoulder bleeding as a minie ball struck him. Most of the aides sustained wounds. Grant, unscathed, calmly rose from his chair and made sure his aides received immediate medical treatment.

Black smoke filled the sky as the ammunition ship burned. Flames leaped twenty feet in the air. The dock was ablaze. Laborers and soldiers established a bucket brigade to extinguish the fires. The ship was a lost cause and sunk beneath the waters of the river taking all hands with her. In the confusion, the two rebels disappeared making their way back to Richmond—their mission a success.

Later in the afternoon, unknown to Grant, the General's staff met and decided the day's event was an assassination attempt aimed at their boss. They decided each would take a turn during the night to personally watch the General's quarters for signs of foul play. They swore an oath of secrecy knowing if their boss found out, he would order them not to do it. In the middle of the meeting a pale, skinny man hobbled into the tent.

Overhearing the conversation he said. "Count me in."

Rawlins stared at the figure for a few seconds before recognizing the young man. He walked over and hugged him.

"Lyons, great to have you back boy, you look like shit. We've got to get some meat on your bones," said an elated Rawlins.

Richmond, Virginia, Confederate White House—August 10, 10:30 AM

Robert E. Lee met with the Confederate President discussing the state of the Armies of the South. Davis briefed his friend on the situation in Georgia. By mid-morning the conversation turned to the strategy in the East.

"Bob, if Early could create havoc in Pennsylvania and Maryland, then the people will panic. He doesn't have to bring on a battle; he just has to roam the countryside. Come election time, the people in the North would overwhelmingly vote Lincoln out and McClellan in."

"Jeff, Early doesn't have the manpower to sustain such a raid. Besides, with Sheridan in command he has to be careful not to be cutoff from the Valley," replied Lee.

"Sheridan is constantly retreating. He doesn't have the stomach for a stand-up fight," answered Davis.

"I'm not so sure. I think he's just regrouping before he strikes. So far during the campaign, he has led Grant's Calvary without committing any major blunders. When he has hit us, it has been hard," responded Lee.

As the two men ate their lunch, a courier arrived from Petersburg.

"General Lee, General Anderson reports that our spies have determined that Hancock's Corps has left Petersburg and is headed toward City Point. Warren, Smith and Parke's Corps have extended their lines to make up for the loss," said the courier.

Davis clapped his hands in excitement.

"Grant is sending Hancock to the Valley to take command. Robert, you should send Anderson's Corps to the Valley. We can pin down two Union Corps and threaten the Federal Capital until after the election," said Davis

Lee stroked his beard for a minute before speaking.

"Jeff, if I send Anderson's entire Corps away, I'll not have enough men to hold Petersburg let alone Richmond. Grant would, most likely, launch a major assault along his entire line. By just sheer numbers, his Army would overwhelm us," replied Lee.

Davis looked at his faithful Commander and realized Lee was correct. The two men discussed options for the rest of the afternoon. They finally agreed that Lee would send one Division from Anderson's Corps to the Valley to assist Early.

Just outside of Richmond, Virginia—August 13, 9:30 AM

Hancock maneuvered his men into position to attack the Richmond defenses. The Union General surveyed the battlefield. The defenders had cut down all the trees within two miles of the forts. The ground was relatively flat giving the attacking force no cover. In front of the forts were large dry moats. From his experience, the Union General knew the moats were most likely filled with sharpened stakes interlaced with telegraph wire. If this wasn't bad enough, he knew somewhere along the vast openness, his adversaries had laid land torpedoes. It was going to be a bloody fight. He gave orders for the attack to begin at ten.

Lee was surprised by the movement, but was not unprepared. When told of Hancock's departure, he suspected that Grant may be making a shift. Unsure of whether or not he was right, he decided to move only one Division from Hill's Corps; but cautioned his fiery subordinate to have the rest of his Corps ready to move if the need arose.

At precisely ten, Hancock ordered his artillery to open fire. The sound of explosions filled the air as Federal cannoneers sent shot and shell across no man's land in an effort to soften up the defenders. Little did the Union Commander realize that clerks of the War Department and convalescent soldiers manned the forts.

Hancock watched his men file into a line of battle. It was now only a shadow of itself. Gone were many of his veteran troops along with his junior officers. Many lay in mass graves along the bloody trail from the Wilderness to Petersburg. Those not dead were lying in hospital beds. Division and Brigade Commanders were having a tough time getting their men in formation. The green troops were too scared to move forward.

The Federal Commander watched as his artillery slackened and the reluctant men started forward. While the men in blue commenced their assault, the Confederate trenches were reinforced with the Division from A.P. Hill's Corps along with the Corps Commander himself.

Hill's men waited until the unseasoned Union troops were a hundred yards away, and then opened fire sending thousands of projectiles into the blue mass. Panic seized the attackers and they immediately withdrew. Reforming, they struck again and were repulsed. For the balance of the day Hancock sent Brigades along the Southern lines probing for a weakness.

Across the battlefield, Hill recognized his former adversary and reported to Lee that Hancock was on the field with his entire Corps. Lee wasted no time and ordered the rest of Hill's Corps north to meet this new threat.

For four days Hancock and Hill maneuvered troops back and forth across their front. Neither Commander was willing to yield the advantage to the other. Each day was filled with probing attacks, which were met with stiff resistance.

With Hill and his Corps north of Petersburg, the much-weakened Confederate defenses south of the city were ripe for attack. Grant wasted no time to take advantage of the situation.

Just outside of Petersburg, Virginia—August 18, 5:30 AM

Warren's Corps attacked the dug-in defenders holding the Weldon Railroad. His sixteen thousand men quickly overwhelmed the outnumbered defenders driving them back three miles. The elated veterans in blue pushed the Confederates north toward the Southside Railroad; the last supply line from the South to Petersburg and Richmond. Beauregard organized a defensive line at the Boydton Plank Road one mile from the railroad and waited for the attacking force.

As the lead elements of Warren's Corps approached the dug-in defenders, Beauregard ordered his men to hold their fire until the bluecoats were within twenty-five yards. The defenders hearts beat faster with every step the enemy took. They hated to let them get that close, but the disciplined men obeyed the order. Fifty yards behind the breastworks, the Southern Commander placed twelve cannons. The artillery pieces were hidden from view and were loaded with double loads of canister and were ordered not to fire until the infantry did.

Thinking the Confederates had either abandoned their works or had lost their will to fight, the Union troops became overconfident and broke formation. When they were within twenty-five yards, all hell descended upon them as muskets and artillery opened fire. Thousands of men were instantly transported from living to dead. The fierceness and volume of the instant resistance surprised the Yankees. Seeing their confusion, Beauregard ordered a counterattack. The surprised Federals made an orderly retreat to the Weldon Railroad.

Watching his men back peddle, Warren organized his own defensive line west of the Weldon tracks, vowing not give up the railway. He organized his thirty cannons west of the railroad supported by five thousand men. The Federals held their fire until the retreating forces were within their breastworks and then sent their own messages of death to the Southerners. Darkness brought an end to the fighting for the day. The Southern Commander was pleased with himself. With a handful of men he had driven the Yankees back to almost their original lines.

Warren was also pleased. His orders were to take and hold the Weldon Railroad and that he did. Lee's only remaining working railroad was the Southside railway. The Confederate's would now have to unload any supply trains ten miles south of Petersburg then reload the supplies onto wagons. The wagons would have to take a twenty-mile circuitous route around the Union forces to get to Petersburg. The starving Virginians had neither enough wagons nor horses to keep the defenders adequately supplied.

Petersburg, Virginia—August 18, 8:30 PM

Robert E. Lee sat in the parlor of his commandeered headquarters reading dispatches from both Hill and Beauregard. He realized Grant had no intention of sending Hancock to the Valley and had no intention of taking Richmond from the East. His adversary's main goal was to draw off forces south of Petersburg and take the Weldon Railroad. The Army Commander had no choice but to recall Hill's Corps and retake the railway. If Hill left by midnight, he could be in front of Warren by mid-afternoon on the nineteenth. If he couldn't retake the railway, then he would have to extend his lines another two miles.

In spite of the quality of the Union replacements, they were still bodies and eventually would be trained. The problem for Lee was that his losses could not be replaced. His once formidable, invincible Army was slowly melting away. The respect he once had for Grant had turned to bitterness as he wrote his son, Rooney, that Grant's only talent lay in his accumulating overwhelming numbers and then attacking. His thoughts were interrupted by a knock on the door.

"Enter," said Lee in a tired tone.

A begrimed young man entered the parlor. "You sent for me, sir?"

"Yes, Channing, I did. I need you to do your magic and get me some good intelligence on where Grant may be weak. It's going to be tough getting into his headquarters after the botched attempt on his life. The best way to get the information I need is for you to go to City Point. I want you to leave as soon as possible," responded Lee.

Just outside of Petersburg, Virginia—August 20, 1:00 PM

After traveling thirteen hours, Hill's Corps finally arrived in front of Warren's defensive line. Hill conferred with Beauregard and the two Generals decided to let the men rest during the heat of the day and to attack at four in the afternoon.

At four in the afternoon, Hill's artillery along with the twelve cannon, which Beauregard had commandeered the previous day sent shot and shell streaking across the battlefield toward the defenders. After years of fighting, the veterans on both sides had learned to dig their fighting holes deep with shelters dug into the sides where they could take cover during an artillery bombardment. When the artillery slackened, they would come out of their cubbyholes and man the trenches for the infantry assault.

The artillery continued its barrage for a half hour before the infantry began its movement. The Union men exited their shelters and manned the trenches. They watched as the men in gray came closer and closer. Being on the defensive was a unique experience for the men in blue. Since Grant had taken over command, they had been the attackers. They instantly saw the advantage of being the defender. Quickly they were filled with the anxiety of the defender as they watched thousands of men walking toward them with only one thought—to kill.

Warren had his men wait until the enemy was well within range and then gave the order to fire. Thousands of projectiles flew from the trenches into the attacking forces. Federal cannon fired canister into the gray ranks. The ferocity of the defenders caused the veterans of Hill's Corps to recoil. They reformed and attacked again. Once again, they were thrown back. Five times they attacked and five times they were repulsed. The Weldon Railroad was lost forever.

The evening of the twentieth was dark and dreary as the threat of rain once again reared. Taking advantage of the moonless night Channing Smith, donning the blood-stained uniform of a Union Captain, quietly entered the Union lines and made his way toward City Point. He carried no weapons of any kind. An hour before sunrise, the Confederate spy entered Grant's camp.

"Halt! Who goes there?" questioned a sentry.

Lyons quickly moved to the guard's side and removed his pistol from its holster. Pointing it at the Confederate's chest he waited for the man's reply.

"Captain Charles Webster, Ninth Corps. I just escaped from Libby Prison. I was captured in the crater. I'm not armed," said Smith.

Smith and Lyons stared at each other for five minutes.

"Let him pass," said Lyons reluctantly.

Petersburg, Virginia—August 24, 9:00 PM

Hill met with Lee and Beauregard.

"Gentlemen, our spies and scouts inform me that Hancock is now headed south. He could be reinforcing Warren or he could be trying to get behind us," said a weary Lee.

"If he gets behind us, then he'll cut us off from Richmond," answered Hill.

"On the other hand, if he joins Warren, then between the two of them they can make a move to completely invest us," said Beauregard.

"Grant has us in a box," responded Hill.

"Ambrose, I want you to leave one Division in front of Warren and keep your other two ready to move at a moment's notice. I'm ordering Wade Hampton and Fitzhugh Lee to put their Calvary in the saddle and patrol the railway from Globe Tavern to the North Carolina border. If they run into Federal troops, they are to delay them to the last man, if need be, and give us a chance to parry Grant's thrust.

Lee issued the orders and retired for the evening. He had just gone to bed when his aide awakened him.

"General Lee, sir," said Colonel Chilton.

"Yes, Colonel," replied a wide awake Lee.

"Sir, Fitzhugh Lee's Calvary Division has just reported a large enemy column moving south following the Weldon Railroad. He said he is shadowing them and should they attempt to cross the railroad, he will attack."

"Send a courier to General Hill and tell him he is to immediately move two Divisions to Ream's Station. Tell him time is of the essence and not to delay," responded Lee rubbing his eyes.

"Sir, I'm just curious, but why Ream's Station?" asked Chilton.

"Just a hunch," replied the General as he buttoned his coat and walked toward the entrance to his tent.

Hancock arrived at Reams Station and was surprised to see his old adversary, Ambrose Powell Hill and his Corps, dug-in east of the Weldon Railroad.

The Union General hoped to meet little or no resistance. He ordered Division Commanders to put their men in a line of battle. This time John Gibbon and his famed "Iron Brigade" would lead the assault followed by the famed "Irish Brigade" under Barlow. Both Division Commanders were highly experienced and dedicated. Gibbon, a West Point classmate of Hill and Burnside, had served in all of the major battles of the Army of the Potomac. Severely wounded at Fredericksburg, he returned to duty three months later and rejoined his Division and the Second Corps.

Barlow, the former Attorney from New York, was a civilian soldier who worked his way up the ranks. Like Gibbon he, too, served in every major battle of the Army of the Potomac. Wounded at Antietam, he returned to his Division in time for Fredericksburg. Wounded again at Gettysburg and left for dead on the battlefield, he rejoined his Division at the start of Grant's Wilderness Campaign. Like Hancock, his Gettysburg wound was not fully healed and was giving him great pain sometimes paralyzing his right arm and leg. The minie ball was too close to the spine to be removed.

Hancock held Birney's Division in reserve in case his men did not perform well. At nine o'clock the order was given to attack. Men in blue advanced toward Hill's entrenched troops. When Gibbon's men were halfway across the no man's land, Hill ordered his artillery to commence firing.

The green recruits continued forward ignoring the carnage around them. When they were within a hundred yards of the enemy, Hill's men fired sending two thousand minie balls at the attackers. It was more than the inexperienced troops could take and they broke for the safety of the rear. Seeing the men in front of them turn and run, Barlow's Division quickly followed suit.

Hill ordered his men to charge. Looking back over their shoulders and seeing the pursuing rebels, the Union troops dropped their rifles, flags and anything else that slowed them down.

Birney watched the two Divisions run toward his position. He ordered his men to let them pass through the ranks but to keep their formation. Barlow and Gibbon raced among their men trying to stop the retreat and reform for an attack, but their efforts were in vain.

As soon as the retreating men were safely behind them, Birney gave the order to open fire. The blast of five thousand muskets was enough to stop Hill's men. The Confederate General ordered the assault called off and his men returned to their line.

Hancock hung his head in shame. His once mighty Second Corps was no more. Sadly, he telegraphed Meade about the near rout of his men. Winfield

Scott Hancock, the man McClellan nicknamed "the Superb," was crestfallen. Even though he maintained his ground, it was his first failure as a Corps commander.

CHAPTER NINETEEN

Just outside of Atlanta, Georgia—August 26, 8:00 AM

William Sherman met his Army Commanders.

"Gentlemen, our Cavalry has not been successful in capturing the two remaining railroads, the Atlanta and West Point Railroad and the Macon Railroad. I intend to leave the Twentieth Corps to hold our bridgehead at the Chattahoochee and, with the rest of our forces, move against both railroads. Tonight, under the cover of darkness, we'll pull our men out of their trenches and move toward the Atlanta and West Point.

"Howard's Army will be on our right, Schofield's in the middle and George's on our left. We'll take the first railroad, destroy it and then move to the Macon Railroad. Any questions?" asked Sherman.

"Billy, what if Hood attacks us while we're on the move?" inquired Thomas.

"I don't think he will attack until after we have taken the Atlanta and West Point," responded the Department Commander.

"What makes you think that? Hood is reckless and daring. He has already struck us three times and each time came dangerously close to victory," said Schofield.

"His Cavalry is chasing ours on a meaningless mission. It will take time for him to fully ascertain our movements. By then I hope to have Atlanta completely invested.

"However, should he strike, he'll be dealt with most severely. I believe we've bloodied him a great deal more than he bloodied us," answered Sherman.

The Union Commanders continued to discuss the upcoming movement until ten o'clock and then returned to their headquarters to issue their orders.

Hood spent a fitful night tossing and turning. Something was amiss. His Cavalry had stopped the Union efforts to capture the Macon Railroad and free the Union prisoners in Andersonville. He knew he was leaving his Army blind but it was a calculated risk.

At eleven o'clock a tired Hood received a dispatch from Hardee.

> *"General Hood,*
> *It appears the Union Army in my front has left. They are nowhere in sight. I have sent out patrols and they report Sherman and his Armies are gone. They report a large Union Corps is holding the Chattahoochee Bridge. I await your orders.*
> *Signed,*
> *William Hardee*
> *Major General CSA"*

A few minutes later he received dispatches from Stewart and Lee saying the same thing. He quickly called for his Generals to meet him at his headquarters to get their opinions.

Richmond, Virginia, Confederate White House—August 27, 11:00 AM

Braxton Bragg interrupted the cabinet meeting and handed Jeff Davis an urgent dispatch from Hood.

> *"His Honorable Excellency*
> *President Jefferson Davis*
> *White House, Richmond Virginia*
> *Your Excellency,*
> *I am pleased to report Sherman's Army has retreated from in front of Atlanta. The city is now safe. I plan to pursue the enemy as soon as I can ascertain which direction he is moving.*
> *Your obedient Servant,*
> *John Bell Hood*
> *Lieutenant General CSA"*

Davis' face lit up as he passed around the message for the others to read. The news spread like ants at a picnic as Church Bells around the South began ringing. Davis telegraphed Hood with his congratulations and notified Lee.

Southern pickets along the Petersburg front taunted their foes shouting that now that Hood had Sherman on the run, Lee would put them in flight back to Washington.

Meade brought the news of Sherman's defeat to Grant. The General-in-Chief was on the wharf at City Point awaiting the arrival of his wife and family.

"George, what brings you to City Point?" asked a surprised Grant.

"Sir, grave news, the pickets report Sherman has been defeated and is retreating from Atlanta," said a distraught Meade.

"Hogwash, I know Billy Sherman better than any man alive. He would hold his ground until every man, including himself, were either killed or captured. He has not retreated. I assure you that whatever he is up to, it will spell bad news for Hood," replied Grant.

Just outside of Atlanta, Georgia—August 28, 10:00 AM

The Army of the Cumberland approached the Atlanta and West Point Railroad just outside Red Oak. Howard's Army of the Tennessee approached the railroad at Fairburn Station. Neither Army encountered enemy forces. Sherman's movement was a complete success.

Not taking any chances, both Army Commanders ordered one of their Corps to dig in and guard the other two in case of an attack. Once they secured the railroad, they gave orders for their men to tear up the tracks and cross-ties.

The Federals pried the steel rails from their cross-ties. Sherman watched as six men carried a rail to a bonfire made up of the cross-ties. They threw the rail into the fire so that the middle rested in the flames. The men would let the metal heat up for thirty minutes then, using large pincers, they removed the hot steel. With three men on each end they twisted the molten metal in opposite directions creating a spiral effect and wrapped it around a tree or telegraph pole. The men nicknamed the shape of the destroyed rail "Sherman's bowtie" in honor of their Commanding General.

Chicago, Illinois, Democrat Headquarters—August 28, 11:30 AM

While Sherman wrecked the Atlanta and West Point Railroad, the Democratic Party began its National Convention to nominate its choice for President. The outcome was a forgone conclusion. The Party needed someone who could carry the soldier vote, yet was pliable enough to seek terms for peace with the Confederates. Party leaders felt George McClellan, the former Commander of the Union Army of the Potomac, was the right man for the job.

McClellan, in his earlier years, was considered by many to be the savior of the Union. At thirty-eight years old he would be the youngest President the Country ever had. The General did not favor total war. He felt the Union should seek peace and, if possible, reunification with the South. If that was not possible, then they should become close neighboring Countries. He would be able to tell the Public first-hand how the current Administration was bungling the war.

New York Governor Horatio Seymour opened the Convention with an hour-long speech railing Lincoln for mismanagement of the war. He accused the President of being a murderer. His speech whipped the delegates into a frenzy as they smelled the end of the Republican Party. Newspapers reported the end of the Lincoln Administration.

Atlanta, Georgia—August 30, 7:30 AM

Confederate General John Bell Hood met with his Corps Commanders planning their pursuit. Without Cavalry, they didn't know which direction Sherman was headed.

"General Hood, excuse the interruption. There is a gentleman outside who says he has important information," said a young aide.

"Show him in," replied Hood.

A few minutes later, a one-legged man hobbled into Hood's office, wearing the simple garb of a farmer. His hair was uncombed and his face had a ruddy complexion. He leaned on his crutches as he spoke.

"General Hood, sir, my name is John Biggins and I have a small farm just outside of Red Oak near Shadna Church. Late yesterday morning, the Yankee's Army of the Cumberland came to Red Oak and started tearing up tracks of the Atlanta and West Point Railroad. Seeing smoke coming from around Fairburn, I saddled my horse and rode a few miles down the road. Well, General, I'll be damned to hell if I didn't see another Yankee Army tearing up tracks there. I think they were from the Army of Tennessee. I pulled a spyglass from my saddlebag and saw the one-armed Howard sitting on his horse watching his murdering thieves destroy the railway."

Hood looked at the man incredulously. He knew too much information. His report was too concise. He might be a plant from Sherman to mislead the Confederate General.

"Mr. Biggins, you seem to know a great deal about the Yankees. How is that possible?"

"Up until last September, I had two good legs. Prior to losing my leg, I was a Captain serving in McLaws' Division of Longstreet's Corps. I fought against Howard many times in the East. Then, last September, I was moved west with the rest of the Corps. My Brigade and I were reassigned to your Texas Division at Chickamauga. During our second assault against Thomas at Snodgrass Hill, I was shot in the leg. General, maybe this would help you believe me."

The young man reached into his jacket pocket, pulled out a neatly folded envelope and handed it to Hood. The General read the paper. It was a letter of commendation for gallantry during the battle of Chickamauga. The Confederate Commander quickly recognized the signature at the bottom of the letter belonging to Longstreet; he invited the former soldier to have a seat.

The Confederate Commanders were in a state of disbelief. Hood asked Hardee to send a scout to see if the reports were true. In the meantime, he ordered his Corps Commanders to ready their men to move at a moment's notice. Within an hour Hood was visited by fifteen other citizens of Atlanta all telling the same tale.

By six o'clock Hood was convinced that Sherman had not retreated and the Atlanta and West Point Railroad was indeed lost. He ordered Hardee and Lee to move their entire Corps to protect his last supply line—the Macon Railway. He then had the unpleasant task of notifying Jefferson Davis of the recent turn of events.

Chicago, Illinois, Democrat National Convention—August 31, 8:30 AM

The morning of the thirty-first was overcast and gray as railroad tycoon, August Belmont of New York, took the podium. He read the party's platform for the upcoming election. The Democratic President nominee would be for reunion and for States' rights unimpaired. By ten o'clock, the platform was adopted and the balloting begun.

By noon, McClellan had the nomination. His running mate was Senator George Pendleton, a peace Democrat. A little after two in the afternoon McClellan entered the Convention Center to rousing cheers and made his acceptance speech. He blasted the Administration for mismanagement, but praised the brave soldiers on both sides. If elected, he would extend the proverbial olive branch to his former countrymen. The center went wild. Newspapermen ran for their telegraph operators to file their stories. By evening all over the North, the Democratic Newspapers carried banner headlines predicating the demise of the Lincoln Administration. The Chicago Tribune went so far as to predict a Democrat landside.

Jonesboro, Georgia—August 31, 9:30 AM

Oliver Howard watched his men prepare to repulse the attack by Hardee and Lee's Corps. His Army of the Tennessee was the lead element of Sherman's push. The Confederates placed themselves between Howard and the Macon Railroad.

Throughout the morning, Hardee and Lee conferred with each other and, finally, after three hours of debate and last minute deployments, they were ready to strike Howard's outnumbered Federals across their entire line simultaneously preventing the Union Commander from shifting troops. At eleven o'clock, a lone cannon was fired and Stephen Lee's fifteen thousand men in gray began their walk of death across the open ground against Howard's well-entrenched Federals.

Howard gave the order for his artillery to fire on the oncoming enemy. At once fifty cannons of all sizes fired their projectiles. The artillery did its job tearing huge gaps in the gray line. Smoke from the blasts hindered the artillerists view; but, nonetheless, they kept up the murderous fire.

When Lee's men were within a hundred yards of the Federals, the Union troops fired sending thousands of missiles of death toward the attackers. Three volleys later, the Confederates withdrew to the safety of their own lines. Seeing the enemy on his right withdraw, Howard directed his artillerists to change direction and concentrate on Hardee's men, who had just begun their attack.

The Confederates under Hardee were less than a hundred yards from Howard's defenders when the infantry fired. The rebels put their heads down like a person in a fierce rainstorm and continued forward. Suddenly, artillery shells rained down on them as the Federal cannoneers redirected their efforts. The men in gray were within twenty yards of the Union position when they broke off the assault.

While Hardee's men retreated, Lee's Corps reformed and was once again assaulting the Union lines. Howard shifted his artillery back toward Lee's men. The result was the same. While Lee's men retreated for a second time, Hardee's Corps started its second assault. Howard's gunners shifted their efforts to the new attackers. For two hours, the defenders reformed and charged. Between the Union defenders and the heat, the Confederate Corps

Commanders decided to halt the attacks, rest the men and renew the contest later in the day.

At one o'clock Lee rode to Hardee's headquarters to set the strategy for the late afternoon assault. The two Generals sat in the shade of the tent; its flaps open to allow in any breeze. They discussed what had gone wrong with the morning's attacks when they were interrupted by a telegraph operator.

Sirs, I have a message from General Hood. It's marked urgent; deliver at once," said the communications solider.

"Read it," replied Hardee.

> *"To: Generals Hardee and Lee. Recent intelligence indicates Sherman plans to storm Atlanta from the direction of Red Oak. I believe Union forces in your front are a diversion. General Lee is hereby ordered to immediately march his Corps by the quickest means back to Atlanta and take position at the village of East Point. He is to hold his sector against all hazards."*

"Solider, take down this message," said Lee.

> *"General Hood, your message received and understood. I ask you to reconsider. The troops we are facing are not a diversion, but are Howard's Army in its entirety, signed S.D. Lee etcetera."*

"Mark it urgent and request an immediate reply," added Hardee.

Less than twenty minutes later the telegraph operator was back with Hood's answer. The Commanding General disagreed with Lee and reiterated his orders.

"General Hood is wrong, but orders are orders. I'll take my leave now. Good luck," said Lee.

Shoal Creek Church, Georgia—August 31, 2:30 PM

Sherman rode with Thomas and Schofield as the main force of the Army approached Shoal Creek Church ten miles north of Howard's men. Hood was right; Howard's force was a diversion. They started a day before the rest of the Armies to give the impression they were the main force. The Union Commander would now place Thomas and Schofield between Hardee and Atlanta. As darkness fell in central Georgia, Cox's Division, meeting no resistance, wrecked the Macon Railroad tracks at Rough and Ready. Sherman had divided Hood's Army.

Jonesboro, Georgia—September 1, 5:00 PM

The morning brought the promise of more hot, humid weather. Howard waited most of the day for Hardee to attack. Then at five o'clock, losing patience, he ordered his men forward. Sherman's orders were to take the Macon Railroad and he was going to do it.

Hardee watched as the tide of numbers had changed and now favored the Union troops. The men in blue, their bayonets glistening in the setting sun, marched steadily toward the now entrenched Southerners. The Confederate General waited until the lead elements of the attackers were within fifty yards and gave the order to fire. The cagey General decided to have his men fire in a series of coordinated volleys pouring a constant flow of lead into the attackers.

The men in blue recoiled, but the continuing hail of bullets quickly told them that, to pursue the attack, would be certain death and quickly retreated. No sooner had the assault ended, then Hardee received word from his scouts that Thomas' Army reinforced by Schofield's were headed south along the Macon Railroad. The Southern General realized he was cutoff from the rest the Army. He had no choice but to retreat. The only question was, which direction should he move? The dilemma was solved less then an hour later when a courier arrived from Hood informing him to move his Corps to Love-joy Station and rejoin the rest of the Army.

Just outside of Atlanta, Georgia—September 1, 9:00 PM

The Commanding General of the Union's Twentieth Corps, Henry Slocum, sat outside his tent smoking a cigar. The quietness of the evening was suddenly shattered by the sound of a large explosion coming from downtown Atlanta. Slocum sprang from his chair. In the distance he saw the sky light up as flames danced forty feet in the air against the black backdrop of the clear evening sky. The blasts continued a few minutes apart for the greater part of an hour. Slocum issued orders to his Division Commanders to have their men ready to march toward Atlanta at daybreak.

At daybreak, Slocum and his Corps marched toward Atlanta. A mile from town they were met by the city's Mayor and Town Council who officially surrendered the city. They explained that Hood had burned his munitions trains and the fire had spread through Atlanta. They had controlled the flames; but as soon as Hood's men left the town, looting had broken out. They asked Slocum's help in restoring order.

Washington D.C., Executive Building—September 2, 7:45 PM

Lincoln met with his political advisors at Stanton's office in the Executive Building next to the White House. The President sat at the head of the large, well-polished oak conference table. To his right sat the portly Secretary of War, next to him sat Henry Raymond. Raymond was the editor of the New York Times and the Chairman of the Republican Party. On the President's left sat the Secretary of State, next to him was "Boss Weed." The men discussed how they could combat the McClellan candidacy.

The meeting wore on into the late evening. Suddenly, there was a knock on the door and a courier from the war office entered. The young Lieutenant stepped lively to the President, stopping before the Commander-in-Chief; he brought himself to attention and saluted.

"Mr. President, I apologize for the intrusion. This just came over the wire and I decided it could not wait until morning," said the young officer handing Lincoln the telegram.

Lincoln read the message and, smiling, he reached for his pencil and paper. He wrote a reply and handed it back to the youth.

"Thank you, Lieutenant, please make sure General Sherman gets this as soon as possible." The young officer saluted and exited.

"God has just shown us the way to defeat McClellan and here it is. Sherman states and I quote, 'Atlanta is ours and fairly won.' By morning the press will reprint this telegram in its entirety, the Country will feel a breath of relief. My friends, Grant and Sherman will speak for us," said Lincoln smiling.

The men looked at Lincoln. They thought for a few minutes and nodded.

"I'll instruct my newspapers to drag out Sherman's victory until Election Day. Anything Grant does will be a front-page headline. We'll play down casualties and print positive stories," said Boss Weed.

"I'll meet with our party leaders and draw us all together; radicals as well as conservatives. I'll contact Andrew Johnson and have him use his influence," said Raymond.

The next day Grant, hearing the news of Sherman's victory while playing with his children, ordered his men to fire a one hundred gun salute in the Ohioan's honor. It was the lift the war effort in the North needed. Men in the trenches taunted the rebels across the lines saying that Sherman had retreated all the way into Atlanta.

Shenandoah Valley, Virginia—September 19, 4:35 AM

Phil Sheridan watched as his men went into action against Jubal Early. Unknown to the Union Commander, Robert E. Lee had recalled the reinforcements he had loaned Early.

Early was surprised by the sudden aggressiveness of Sheridan. For the past thirty days he had retreated whenever confronted by the rebels. Early came to the conclusion that the Union General lacked the stomach for a fight.

Not sensing any threat, he divided his forces and the main part of his Army was ten miles away. Jubal Early met with his Senior Division Commander, Brigadier General Stephen Ramseur.

"Stephen, I need time to consolidate our forces. You must fight a delaying action. Stop the enemy advance and then slowly retire to Winchester. You must buy me a day," said Early.

The young General had his men dig in along the Berryville Pike, a scant three miles from the town of Winchester. He posted his four artillery pieces in a crossfire covering the road. With Fitzhugh Lee and his Cavalry protecting the flanks, the Federals would have to make frontal assaults across open ground.

Wright's Corps crossed the Berryville Pike and, without hesitation, attacked the dug-in rebels. Cannon fire ripped holes into the rank and file of the attackers. Muskets filled the air with minie balls. The Federals recoiled and then resumed their assault. Twenty yards from the makeshift Confederate breastworks, the men in blue gave up and retreated.

Ramseur used the lull to withdraw his artillery back a mile. He watched as Wright shifted Ricketts' Division to the left flank of the defenders. Hidden in the woods just beyond the Pike was posted a Brigade of Fitzhugh Lee's finest horsemen. When the unsuspecting men in blue were within fifty yards of the forest, the horsemen charged. The Federals were so surprised they didn't have time to fire a shot before running away. Taking advantage of the confusion, Ramseur and Lee withdrew their beleaguered force back a half-mile.

Wright reorganized his forces and pursued the retreating Southerners. For five hours the scene repeated itself. The Union would attack, be repulsed and the Southerners withdrew to a new position. By noon Ramseur and Lee's men were a half-mile northeast of Winchester where they were joined by the remainder of the Army.

Sheridan halted his men and personally surveyed the battlefield. The Confederates had thrown up formidable breastworks supported by twenty pieces of artillery. Breckenridge's infantry and Cavalry held the flanks. Undaunted, the Union General ordered Wright and his Sixth Corps supported by Major General William Emory and his Nineteenth Corps to make a frontal assault. At the same time, he ordered his Cavalry under the joint command of Brigadier Generals Wesley Merritt and William Averell to circle around the Confederates and strike the left flank and rear of the enemy.

Wright appealed to Sheridan to allow his Corps to eat and replenish their ammunition. His men had been fighting for almost seven and one-half hours continuously and needed rest. Sheridan agreed to halt the attack for an hour and a half. At one-thirty the assault began. Emory's Corps led the attack supported by Wright.

Emory ordered his Corps forward followed quickly by Wright's men. The long-range artillery immediately fired at the Federals. When they were within a hundred yards, the infantry opened fire adding more misery to the enemy. The battlefield was quickly filled with torn limbs, bleeding bodies and disemboweled men. After an hour of punishment, the attackers withdrew.

Early took advantage of the Federal withdrawal and ordered a counter-attack. Brigadier Generals John B. Gordon and Robert Rodes gave the order to move forward. The Division Commanders had been together since the beginning of the war and had become good friends.

Sheridan ordered his cannons to fire on the attacking gray coats. The veterans of Early's Corps moved so swiftly that the Federal gunners had time for only one volley before the Confederates were intermixed with the retreating forces. The rebels breached the Union lines between Wright's and Emory's Corps.

Emory was badly shaken by his repulse and the sudden counter-attack. Wright did his best to rally his troops, but the swiftness of the attack prevented him from reforming. Sheridan ordered his reserve Corps under Union General George Crook forward to stem the tide. The thirty-six year old Brigadier General led his men into the maelstrom. Within a few minutes he connected with remnants of Wright's Corps and together they dug in. The defenders waited until Gordon's men were within range and fired, sending the rebels in a headlong retreat. Gordon reformed his men and attacked again. Three times his men attacked and three times they were repulsed. Rodes rode along his line urging his men forward for a fourth assault.

Once again, the Northerners opened fire halting the assailants. This time Rodes lay among the dead. The Confederate General had been shot five times in the chest; dying instantly. Seeing their indestructible leader struck down shocked the men in gray.

Sensing the hesitation in the enemy forces, Crook ordered his men to fix bayonets and charge the shaken Confederates driving them back to their original lines. Order was once again restored in Sheridan's front. The frontal battle had been going on for three and one half hours; however, Sheridan was not finished. He had three hours of daylight remaining and he intended to use it. He ordered Wright, Emory and Crook to form for another attack.

While Gordon and Rodes fought against Sheridan's infantry, Breckenridge was fighting desperately against Merritt and Averell. At three o'clock Breckenridge's men were attacked by the Union force. The Union Generals had their men dismount and attack on foot. Outnumbered three-to-one the Confederate General had, at first, held back the blue onslaught; however, neither Union Commander would be denied victory. Each repulse strengthened their resolve as they constantly reformed and attacked. The continual hammering wore down the defenders.

After two hours of non-stop fighting, Breckenridge's line broke. At first it was hardly noticeable as two or three men from each Brigade slipped quietly to the rear. In a short while they were followed by five more. Then five became ten. Ten became twenty and so on. By six o'clock Breckenridge's line completely broke and the Confederates ran for the safety of Winchester with the men in blue hot on their heels.

Hearing that his flank had given way and realizing he was in danger of being surrounded, Early gave the order to retreat. Gordon, along with the remnants of Rodes' Division, retired southward through the town of Winchester with the Federals in close pursuit. For two hours the fighting was house-to-house as the back-peddling Southerners begrudgingly gave ground. By nightfall Sheridan's men had taken control of Winchester with Early's men in full retreat.

At midnight the Union Commander wired Grant that he had sent Early's forces whirling through Winchester and had routed the Confederates.

Washington D.C—September 20, 7:35 AM

The following day Lincoln's political brain trust leaked a copy of Sheridan's telegram to the newspapers. The tabloids quickly picked up the phrase 'whirling through Winchester'. Headlines read "SHERIDAN GAINS GREAT

VICTORY! SENDS EARLY, WHIRLING THROUGH WINCHES-
TER!"

The diminutive Federal General was now a national hero, similar to Grant
and Sherman. For Lincoln and the North, the victory couldn't have come at a
better time. Just when the public was tired of hearing about the fall of Atlanta,
a fresh victory came from the Valley. The papers downplayed the cost of five
thousand men killed and wounded.

City Point, Virginia—September 20, 8:40 AM

Grant sat behind his makeshift desk. Sitting across was the Republican Party
representative John Eaton. Eaton, an important man in the party, was not
considered a Lincoln man. The politician was given permission from the President to call on the General. Only Eaton and Lincoln knew the reason for the
visit.

"General Grant, I want to begin by saying your campaign so far has been
brilliant. The people in the North love you," said Eaton.

"Thank you, sir, I don't intend to be rude, but I'm quite busy. How can I be
of service to you?" asked Grant.

The General was always wary of people who started off their conversations
with flattery.

"General, you can be of service, not only to me, but to the Nation as well.
As you are aware, the Democrats have nominated General McClellan to run
against Mr. Lincoln. Some of us in the party, the President being one of them,
do not think he can defeat McClellan. We do feel that if we run one General
against another; that our General would win handily. We would like you to be
our candidate. The President is willing to set aside his nomination in favor of
you," replied Eaton.

Grant sat silently and glared at the politician. His eyes turned from a gentle
warm blue to steely cold. His face turned red. Without warning, the normally
calm man abruptly stood up pushing his chair with such force it toppled over.
Clenching his fists he slammed them down on his table causing papers and
maps to fly in all directions.

"THEY CAN'T DO IT! THEY CAN'T COMPEL ME TO RUN!
LINCOLN IS THE ONLY MAN QUALIFIED TO BRING THIS WAR
TO A CLOSE! HIS SUCCESS IS AS IMPORTANT TO OUR CAUSE
AS ANY VICTORY ON THE BATTLEFIELD! YOU, SIR, SHOULD
BE WORKING FOR HIM AND NOT AGAINST HIM!" shouted Grant.

His staff was startled by the outburst. They knew better than to interrupt. Only Rawlins could break into any meeting at any time and, this time, he exercised that right. The Chief-of-Staff calmly walked into the tent and asked if the General needed anything.

Grant looked at his friend and smiled, quickly regaining his composure. He apologized to Eaton for his outburst and then politely asked the politician to leave.

Shenandoah Valley, Virginia—September 22, 6:00 AM

Jubal Early reorganized his Army and dug in at Fisher's Hill just outside of Strasburg. The Armies had come full circle. A month earlier it was Sheridan who retired from Strasburg and headed north to seek refuge at Harper's Ferry.

The Confederate Commander set up a formidable defense using the landscape to his advantage. The Massanutton Mountains divided the countryside. The Shenandoah Valley was on the right with the smaller Luray Valley on the left. Both were strategically important as together they made up the "bread basket" of the Confederacy. Early's flanks were well anchored. The Shenandoah River protected one flank while Little North Mountain of the Allegheny mountain range protected his other. From his position atop Fisher's Hill, he could watch Sheridan's movements below.

Sheridan watched the sunrise as he sat on his tall black horse named Rienzi. It was the General's favorite mount. The steed stood eighteen and half hands high, was well muscled and long-winded. Rienzi knew no fear. No matter how hot the sounds of battle, he always remained calm. The size of the horse gave Sheridan an appearance of being larger than life.

A half hour after sunrise, Union artillery began its barrage and continued on and off throughout most of the day. First the artillery would fire for an hour and then cease. The infantry then went into a line of battle. After a few hours of shifting Brigades around, the artillery would once again commence firing, followed by the infantry getting realigned. By four o'clock Early became suspicious. It wasn't like Sheridan to wait.

Without warning, Crook's men surprised the unseasoned troops holding Early's left flank. Union veterans pitched into the unsuspecting defenders with such ferocity and quickness that the Southerners had time for one volley before they broke for the rear. As the routed guardians ran for safety they shouted.

"FLANKED, WE'VE BEEN OUTFLANKED!"

The startled men holding the main line looked behind them and saw Crook's eight thousand men streaming down the mountain toward them.

Sheridan watched through his telescope as Crook's Corps descended upon the shocked rebels. He ordered Wright's Corps forward to join in the attack. Sheridan rode along his entire line, giving orders.

Seeing his only avenue of escape about to be cut off; Early gave the order to retreat. At first it was an orderly withdrawal, but the closer the Union men came, the more panicky the defenders became as their survival instinct took over. Before Early could complete the retreat, his men suddenly sprinted for the rear. It was now a rout.

Sensing a total victory, Sheridan ordered his Cavalry forward. There was still another hour of daylight. The Union horsemen pursued their fleeing foes, but were abruptly stopped by Fitz Lee's Cavalry. Custer impulsively led a charge with his Brigade. Outnumbered, unsupported and against orders he charged forward; only to be thrown back. Undaunted, the blond-haired General reformed and was about to charge again when he was ordered by Torbert, to call off the assaults. The battle of Fisher's Hill was over. In less than a week Sheridan had his second major victory. He sat inside his tent and notified Grant of the victory.

Grant immediately responded that since it was apparent the war may last into next year, he was ordering Sheridan to lay waste to the entire Valley. He was to burn crops and take livestock. He didn't want so much as an ear of corn coming into Richmond from the Valley.

Richmond, Virginia, Confederate White House—September 24, 7:00 AM,

Jefferson Davis held a council of war with Braxton Bragg, Robert E. Lee and his most trusted cabinet member, Judah Benjamin.

"Gentlemen, the fall of Atlanta coupled with Sheridan's victories gives Lincoln a good chance of getting re-elected. I called you here to ask your opinions of how we can set back the Union war effort," said Davis.

"Mr. President, my Army is not strong enough to break Grant's stranglehold on Petersburg. I need more men just to keep him at bay. I also realize the South has none to spare. I'd like to propose we draft Negroes to serve in the Army as soldiers. If we drafted only a third of the blacks, it would give us an additional one million men. Then, I'll break Grant's Army and take Washington," replied Lee.

"Robert, if we draft Negroes, we are saying they are equal to us. If that is the case, then our entire cause is wrong. Many of our men would have died in vain," answered Davis.

"Mr. President, with all due respect, drafting blacks doesn't mean our cause is wrong. We went to war to protect States' Rights. I disagree with the notion that blacks can't fight or don't have the mental capacity to learn basic military movements. General Grant has used black troops many times quite effectively in battle," said Bragg.

"Your Excellency, if you won't draft them as soldiers, can we draft them as teamsters and laborers, thereby, freeing our white soldiers for duty on the front lines?" asked Lee.

Davis looked at Lee and realized the General had given him a gracious way out. Ignoring the suggestion, he changed the topic to Early's Valley Campaign. They all agreed the Southern General had done all he could, but keeping him there would at least keep Sheridan's Army from reinforcing Grant and would minimally protect their supply of food.

"Maybe we should relieve Early and replace him with another General?" inquired Judah Benjamin.

Benjamin was considered the best legal mind in the South. He was extremely loyal to Davis. Wherever the President had problems in his cabinet, he moved the portly fifty-three year old former lawyer from Louisiana to fill the void.

"Judah, with whom should we replace him? The only two Generals who I'd trust to replace Early are Longstreet and Johnston. Longstreet is unable to take to the field and Johnston doesn't have the confidence of the President," replied Lee.

Next topic on the agenda was Hood and Atlanta.

"Gentlemen, next topic on our agenda is what shall we do about Hood and Atlanta. Any suggestions?" asked Davis.

"What about Beauregard? He has the knowledge and experience to lead an Army," said Bragg.

"General Lee, would you be willing to go to Georgia and assume command?" asked Davis ignoring Bragg's suggestion.

"Mr. President, I appreciate everyone's confidence in me and my abilities; however, when I resigned from the Federal Army, I swore I'd never pick up my sword against the Union unless it was in defense of my native State of Virginia. I must hold true to my oath and decline your offer," replied Lee.

Davis knew he could order Lee to Georgia. He also knew the honorable Lee would resign from the Southern Army rather than break his word. That would be a blow from which the South would never be able to recover.

The conference lasted past eight in the evening. It was decided Davis would visit Hood and then, based on the state of affairs in Georgia, he would either relieve the crippled General or place him under the command of Beauregard.

City Point, Virginia—September 24, 9:20 PM

Grant sat in his tent peering over maps of Richmond and Petersburg. His Army had been idle too long. The green replacements were ready. The General had taken the opportunity of the lull to reorganize his command. He placed some of Butler's men into a new Corps naming it Tenth Corps and placed David Birney in command. Birney would report to Meade, thereby, lessening Butler's span of control.

Grant decided he would, once again, attempt a two-prong attack—striking Lee just south of Richmond with Birney's Tenth Corps supported by the Union's Eighteenth Corps under the command of Major General Edward Ord.

Ord had served under Grant in the West and was considered an extremely valuable officer. Unfortunately, he was under the command of Butler. Grant decided to rectify that immediately and ordered Butler back to Washington to campaign for Lincoln, giving him a sixty day furlough. Ord was now under the command of Meade.

The Corps Commanders would strike the Southern Forts of Harrison and Gilmer, which were key to the defense of Richmond. If Lee lost those, then the Union Army could march into the Southern Capital unopposed. Grant knew Lee would have to shift forces to fend off the attacks and then he would strike south again.

As he finished writing his orders for the movement, Rawlins entered the tent with Ronald Lyons.

"You sent for me, General," asked the young spy.

"Yes I did. Have a seat." Grant said as he handed the orders to Porter to make copies and distribute.

He waited for the aide to leave and then turned his attention to his trusted source of information.

"What I'm going to ask you to do is the most dangerous mission you've ever been given. It is so dangerous, I cannot bring myself to order you to do it; so if you accept, you do so voluntarily. Is this understood?"

Lyons looked at Rawlins then at Grant.

"General, the Army is my life. I love it. You gave me back my life. I owe you a debt of gratitude that I can never repay. I accept the danger whatever it is."

Grant stared at the young man with softness in his eyes. He considered the man as a younger brother.

"Ron, I need to know the strength and disposition of the enemy forces. I have to know the number of men guarding Richmond and, if possible, how many men are facing Billy Sherman. In order to get this information you must get into Richmond. Once in, you cannot leave until we take the city. Learn everything you can and send it to me using the old Underground Railroad. Contact Miss Elizabeth Lew or Samuel Ruth, either is trustworthy and will get me the information. Be careful, I want you back alive after we take Richmond. Is that understood, Major?"

Lyons looked at Grant and replied, "Sir, I'm a Captain."

"Not any more. The General has promoted you. Congratulations," said Rawlins.

The spy smiled and standing; walked to Grant and shook his hand several times. He thanked him repeatedly with every downward motion.

CHAPTER TWENTY

Richmond, Virginia—September 26, 4:25 AM

A special train enroute for Georgia pulled out of the Richmond station carrying Jefferson Davis. No one knew he was coming. For the second time in less than a year, the Confederate President was forced to go to the front in the West in order to find out what was going on with his Army.

The train rumbled southwest through the untouched portion of Virginia. Twenty miles outside of Richmond, Davis switched trains and boarded the Weldon Railroad which would take him through Charlotte, North Carolina. He would have to change two additional times, ending his six hundred mile, arduous journey just outside of Atlanta. In spite of the difficult two-day journey, Davis enjoyed getting away from Richmond.

Davis arrived at Hood's headquarters and interrupted the General's evening meal. The startled Commander quickly offered the tired politician some food and drink. The two men talked while they ate.

"John, I know you have done everything in your power to keep Atlanta, but you didn't have enough men to hold the city or ample room to maneuver," said Davis.

"Mr. President, the men will fight. My problem is Hardee. He has performed less than one would expect from such an experienced officer. He seems more afraid of losing a battle than fighting one," responded Hood.

"Why didn't you remove him from command?" inquired the President.

"I would have removed him from active duty after the Battle of Peachtree Creek, but since he is your friend I didn't want to embarrass you. I tried to work with what you gave me. In addition, Stephen Lee is not as aggressive as one would assume with the same last name," replied Hood.

"John, what's your next move?" inquired Davis.

"With your permission, I plan to move the Army north around Atlanta and head for the Tennessee border capturing the small outposts Sherman left to guard his supply line. With his supply lines in jeopardy he would have no choice but to follow me away from Atlanta. When I have lured him far from the city, I'll turn and do battle. Sherman will have to attack or starve.

"The plan seems reasonable. Let me think on it and I'll let you know in the morning. I'd like to meet with Hardee now," answered Davis.

Hood nodded and bade the man a good night and had his aide escort the Confederate President to Hardee's headquarters.

"Good evening, General Hardee," said Davis poking his head into Hardee's tent.

The startled Corps Commander dropped the book he was reading and jumped to attention.

"Mr. President ... to what do I owe this honor?"

The Confederate President pulled up a chair.

"William, relax. Please take your seat. I want to know, in your honest opinion, what went wrong with the Atlanta campaign."

"Mr. President, with all due respect, the only thing wrong with this Army is General Hood. He issues vague orders and, during the entire defense of Atlanta, he never visited the battlefield. He has no gift for strategy. Furthermore, Mr. President, after Chattanooga when I said I didn't want command of this Army, I didn't mean that I never wanted to command it," answered Hardee.

"If you had command of this Army, what would be your next move?"

"I'd retreat southward and establish a defensive line around Peachtree City. From there I could intercept Sherman if he moves toward Macon or Milledgeville. The ground around the city affords us a good defensive position should the enemy decide to attack us head on."

"What if Sherman decides to flank you out of position like he did Johnston?" inquired Davis.

"I'd retreat further south, forcing him to extend his supply lines," replied Hardee.

Davis thought for a few minutes and then stood.

"William, thank you for your candor, but I'm afraid that the rigors of my trip have taken their toll. Can you find me a cot and tent?" asked Davis yawning.

The Corps Commander grabbed his personal items.

"Mr. President, I'd consider it a great honor if you would take my lodging. I'll find other accommodations for the length of your stay," answered Hardee as he left the tent.

The Commander-in-Chief of the South was too tired to object.

"It will only be for the evening. I plan to leave tomorrow; mid-afternoon. Thank you for your hospitality."

Shenandoah Valley, Virginia—September 27, 5:30 AM

Philip Sheridan ordered his infantry to move north and destroy the farms before the farmers could harvest their crops. The Cavalry protected the Army's flanks while the infantry went about its grisly task. The Army Commander rode with his trusted Cavalry Commander, Alfred Torbert, and his favorite Division Commander, George Custer.

Thick black columns of smoke clouded the horizon as the infantry began its destruction of the Valley. It didn't make any difference whether you were for the Union or for the Confederacy or were neutral; your barn, along with any other buildings, was set to the torch along with any crops in the field. Once the fires were started, any livestock found were either slaughtered or carried off by Union forces.

If a farmer resisted, they had orders to burn the home as well. With winter rapidly approaching, the starving masses had nowhere to go. It would be a hardship on thousands of families, but it would be harder on the forty-five thousand troops manning the defenses at Petersburg and Richmond.

Brazenly they walked into barns with no regard for a person's rights and set it on fire. They became experts on how to ignite the wooden structures and the best way to destroy crops. For the buildings, the men would pile straw and then break coal oil lamps against the sides of the structure. While the oil was dripping, they would throw lit torches against the walls and into the pile of straw. Often the barn was full of livestock. They could hear the painful whines of draft horses, cattle and pigs being roasted alive.

To burn the crops, the men would cut down stalks of corn or wheat and tie them together. Igniting the bundles; they then dragged the flaming vegetation through the rest of the fields. If the vanguard of the Army wasn't thorough in its destruction, the rear guard finished the job.

Just outside of Atlanta, Georgia—September 27, 10:00 AM

While Sheridan laid waste to the "bread basket" of the Confederacy, Jefferson Davis met with Stewart and Lee. The Corps Commanders were all in agreement with Hardee in their assessment of Hood. Stewart went as far as to suggest that maybe Hood had given all he had to give and the Army Commander was used up.

By four in the afternoon, Davis had concluded his interviews and boarded the train for Milledgeville to meet with Joe Brown. Hood shook the President's hand.

"Mr. President, if you see fit to remove me from command, I'll serve the cause in any diminished capacity you see fit. The only thing I ask is, please, do not place me in a nothing position. I'm a combat officer and that's where I can best serve our Country," said Hood.

Jefferson Davis looked at the young man, nodded and then boarded the train for his four-hour journey.

The sun was beginning to set when Davis arrived in Milledgeville. The sky was a beautiful mixture of bright orange and varying shades of blue. A gentle breeze blew through the town. It was a perfect Georgia evening. A crowd of one thousand loyal Southerners warmly greeted the President. The Georgia Governor shook the President's hand and escorted him to a platform. They all wanted to hear what was going on in Atlanta. Davis, the politician was in his element.

"My fellow citizens, thank you for this warm welcome. I have just left our brave troops outside of Atlanta and I assure you there is nothing to worry about. General Hood and his Generals have an excellent plan to move Sherman and his devils back to Tennessee. In the East, General Lee has stymied Grant outside of Petersburg. The days of the tyrant Lincoln and his demons are fast coming to an end and the day of our independence is rapidly approaching. I only ask for you to be patient and, by the grace of God in the end, the day will be ours."

The people applauded and gave him a rousing cheer when he stepped down from the platform and entered the Governor's carriage.

"Very encouraging speech if a person believes in fairy tales. Do we even have a snowball's chance in hell of pushing Sherman back toward Tennessee?" asked Georgia Governor Joe Brown.

"Governor Brown, I never said Hood would push Sherman back toward Tennessee. I said Hood had a plan to move Sherman back to Tennessee. Unfortunately, I'm not at liberty to divulge it," retorted Davis.

"I fully understand, but let me remind you that I have a State which depends on me to keep them safe," answered Brown tersely.

"And I have a Nation which depends on me to keep them safe. In order to serve both our purposes, I'm requesting you send the ten thousand men from the Georgia militia that you recalled back to Hood. He will need every man for his plan to save this State," said Davis.

"Mr. President, I will not return those troops to the Government. They are needed here to protect us in the event Sherman marches to the interior," replied Brown.

"Governor, I assure you, Sherman has no intention of marching to the interior of Georgia," retorted Davis.

"If that's the case, then why did Sherman send me a letter saying he would spare Georgia further suffering if I would secede from the Confederacy and recall my troops from the Armies in the field?"

Davis was stunned. He had no idea about the letter. If the cause lost Georgia, then Alabama, Florida, and Arkansas would quickly follow. The Confederacy would unravel from within. He tried to convince Brown that Sherman's letter was a bluff.

For the rest of the evening Davis and Brown talked strategy, politics and the cause. Over dinner, they discussed the foreign situation and whether or not France and England were going to come to their aid. The politicians conversed about the elections in the North and what the outcome would mean to the cause.

CHAPTER TWENTY ONE

Richmond, Virginia—September 28, 8:00 PM

The Union's Tenth Corp under David Birney approached Fort Clifton just outside of Richmond. The young Major commanding the defenders quickly realized he was outnumbered and in danger of being surrounded. Holding his men in position, he forced Birney to stop and deploy his Corps buying two hours for the Confederates. Using the time to his advantage, he sent word to Ewell. The eighteen-year-old officer carefully watched the enemy form for the attack.

Although young, the Officer had been with the Army of Northern Virginia for almost a year. Wounded at Cold Harbor, he was ordered to Richmond to recuperate. When Hancock first attacked, he was ordered to take command of Fort Clifton. Battle-hardened and combat savvy, he was old beyond his years. He gave the order for his five hundred men to fire at the ten thousand blue troops as they were deploying.

After two hours of preparing his men for the attack, Birney gave the order to take the fort. The Confederates continued firing and then at the last minute, the Major ordered his men to abandon Clifton and make their way to Fort Maury three miles north. Realizing he had been duped, David Birney swore at himself for being stupid. He had wasted two hours preparing for the attack and it would take at least another hour or so to reassemble his men.

Fort Maury, located at Chaffins Bluff, overlooked the James River and protected Richmond from a water attack. Situated high on the cliff, the Union gunboats could not elevate their guns enough to hit the defenders. In addition to cannons, the resourceful Southerners had placed mortars in the fort, which would shoot high arcing explosive shells over their breastworks and down on the Union Navy. Taking no chances, they also placed torpedoes all along the James River beginning a mile below the fort and continuing a mile north of it.

Ewell, placed in command of the Richmond defenses, was in his tent and had just finished a letter to his wife when the Major's courier arrived with news of the Federal movements. The Southern General wasted no time and sent word to all his fort Commanders to expect a large-scale attack on the twenty-ninth; then he sent word to Lee.

Just outside of Atlanta, Georgia—September 28, 7:30 PM

Hood met with Stephen Lee, Ben Cheatham and Alexander Stewart. Hardee was noticeably absent. The three Generals had no idea why Hood had called the meeting. In his hand he held a telegram from Jefferson Davis.

"Gentlemen, the President has reorganized the Armies in the West. Effective immediately, our Army will be under the command of General Beauregard. He will decide our overall strategy however I'll have a field command. President Davis has relieved Hardee and ordered him to take over the defenses of Savannah. General Cheatham will replace Hardee," said Hood.

The Corps Commanders looked at each other in amazement. They had expected Hood to be gone and not Hardee.

"There is no way we can drive Sherman out of Atlanta, but there is a way we can stop him here," continued Hood.

The Generals sat upright in their chairs, he had peaked their curiosity.

"How is that possible?" asked Stewart.

"Gentlemen, we're going to attack Sherman's supply lines. Tomorrow, under the cover of darkness, we move northeast circling around Sherman. By daylight on the thirtieth, we'll be north of the Chattahoochee and Sherman south of us. Once he realizes I am between him and his main supply line, he'll have to leave Atlanta and follow us. We'll capture isolated outposts and continue to move north, eventually leaving Georgia and re-entering Tennessee."

"What if Sherman doesn't follow?" inquired Cheatham.

"Then he'll starve. His supply lines will be cut. Once Lincoln discovers we are headed north, he'll order Sherman to head us off. Old Abe cannot afford to have us in Tennessee just before the elections," answered Hood.

"How are we to supply our men?" asked Lee.

"We won't have to. We'll live off the farms in Tennessee and Union supply depots," responded Hood. The four Generals continued their discussions into the wee hours of the morning.

Just outside of Richmond, Virginia—September 29, 8:00 AM

The Union troops cooked their breakfasts and waited for the beat of the long drum roll indicating fall in. They knew that before noon, some of them would be with fallen comrades of long ago. They made sure their names were pinned to their uniforms. Men threw away their playing cards and risqué French postcards. If they were killed, they didn't want their loved ones knowing their bad habits. They wanted to be remembered as righteous men. After the battle, the survivors would scour the campsite and pick up the cards and postcards.

The long roll sounded and the veterans extinguished their campfires, grabbed their weapons and assembled in ranks. Just over the horizon they caught a faint glimpse of their objectives, Forts Harrison and Gilmer.

On the other end of the battlefield, Ewell watched as Ord's Corps marched across the open terrain. When they were halfway to Fort Harrison, he gave the order for his artillery in the all of the forts to commence firing. Grape and canister struck the blue-clad troops on three sides.

Perched erect on his chestnut mare, Ord rode along his line urging his men forward. His drawn sword pointed the men toward their objective. Twenty-five yards from the enemy breastworks, he was hit by three bullets. The first struck his sword scabbard while the second smashed the General's flask. The third projectile hit him in the leg breaking the bone causing him to fall from his horse breaking his collar bone. Ord tried to stand but instantly fell to the ground. His aides carried him off the field.

Seeing their Commander shot down angered the Federals as they stormed forward and breached the breastworks. By sheer force of numbers the rebels were forced to flee or surrender.

At Fort Gilmer Birney's troops met stiffer resistance as Ewell rushed reinforcements to bolster the defenders. Twice Birney attacked and twice he was repulsed. After the second time, he sent word to Ord's second in command, Major General Charles Heckman, that he was halting his attacks.

At two o'clock Grant arrived on the scene. After conferring with both Heckman and Birney, he ordered Birney to resume his attack and Heckman to reposition his artillery on Gilmer. A half hour later the third Union assault began and, like the previous two, it was easily repulsed.

Outside of Petersburg, Virginia—September 30, 7:00 AM

Ambrose Hill ordered his men to spread out to cover the loss of Anderson's men who were shifted north to drive back Ord and Birney. A gap of three feet now existed between each of the defenders. The line was thin, but not weak. The fiery General watched as Parke's and Warren's Corps approached.

The defenders held their ground as long as possible before beginning a planned withdrawal, drawing Parke's Ninth Corps further into a trap. Warren's men, supporting the Union left, and Cavalry, protecting his right, followed suit. The men in blue pushed slowly forward. So far the resistance had been light, but the Yankee Generals knew the situation could change at any moment.

Parke watched with pride as his men crossed the Vaughn Road. The Corps Commander urged his men forward. Once across the thoroughfare, he headed north to their next objective—Squirrel Level Road another mile away. From there it was a scant two miles to the vital Boydton Plank Road, then another two miles to the Southside Railroad and the end of the war. On paper it was a short distance. In the reality of war, it was half a world away.

Just north of the Squirrel Level Road, Ambrose Hill had the main part of his Corps dug-in. He positioned his artillery on a small hill overlooking the road. The vastness of open space along the highway afforded his gunners an unobstructed view of their blue targets. He knew Parke and Warren would use the roadway to quicken their pace. On his left he positioned Wade Hampton and his horsemen. Henry Heth's Division held the right with "Scrappy" Mahone's Division in the center.

At twelve-fifteen the advance Division of Parke's Corps walked into Hill's trap. The Confederate General waited until they were within fifty yards of his position when five thousand rebels rushed out of the woods and crashed into the shocked Union troops. Men clawed, bit and kicked each other into bloody pulps. Rifles were used as clubs and the small entrenching shovels as axes. Hearing the sound of fighting, Parke ordered his other two Divisions forward at a run to support their comrades.

Seeing reinforcements coming down the road, Hill's artillerymen fired on the on-rushing Federals; sending men skyward as the shells exploded among the attackers. It slowed the Union men, but didn't stop them.

Meanwhile on the Confederate left, Wade Hampton engaged the blue horsemen. The two Cavalry units traded saber blows and shot gun blasts. The dry ground drank the blood from the wounded and dead leaving only a dark red patch. Slowly, the Federals gave way. The denseness of the forest favored the Confederates. The Union Commander, David Gregg, ordered his men to fall back one hundred yards to a clearing so that he could use his superior firepower to turn back the rebels.

Hampton noticed the Union withdrawal. Thinking they were giving up the fight, he ordered a third of his men to attack Parke's flank. Within minutes the gray dragoons struck the Union defenders putting some of the weak-hearted to flight.

Watching his line breaking, Parke ordered his men to withdraw a hundred yards to the rear. The road bent to the west sheltering the Union men from the artillery fire. His reserve Brigade dug in and gave covering fire to the with-drawing troops.

Gregg noticed that Hampton's Calvary did not follow him and ordered a counter-attack driving the reduced enemy force backward regaining the posi-tion where they had begun. Hill saw Hampton's men being pressed back and ordered Mahone to reinforce the South Carolina General. If Hampton gave way, Hill's flank would be exposed.

On the Confederate right, Henry Heth struck Warren's men. Hearing the sounds of battle from Parke's sector, Warren ordered his men to charge for-ward. The two sides collided with the force of two charging bulls. The numer-ically superior blue troops pushed the rebels backward. With the element of surprise gone, Heth had no chance to defeat Warren's Corps. The Federal General continued his push until he was alongside Parke's Corps. Together the two Generals stabilized their fronts and dug in. Hill and Hampton contin-ued their attacks, but were easily repulsed.

While Hill grappled with Parke and Warren, Dick Anderson's ten thou-sand men prepared to retake Fort Harrison. A cool breeze blew in from the James River causing the battle-scarred flag of the Confederate First Corps to flap smartly in the wind. The pennant was bullet-riddled, frayed at the ends and discolored from years in the elements. Nonetheless, the men were proud of it. The condition of the flag seemed to emulate the condition of the Corps itself. Although bloodied, worn down, barefoot and at times starved, it still had plenty of fight.

One cannon fired signaling the start of the attack. At once the men in tat-tered gray began walking across the open ground. Birney waited until the Confederates were well within range before ordering his artillery to open fire. Supporting the attackers, the cannons of the surrounding forts opened up on the Union cannoneers. Caissons were blown skyward. The air was filled with the smoke of gunpowder. Birney's guns concentrated on the infantry, while Heckman's artillerists answered the Southern guns.

When the attackers were within fifty yards of the Union breastworks, the Southern artillery ceased fire out of fear of hitting their own men. The Federal artillerists took advantage of the lull to double their efforts on the infantry.

Inside the fort the defenders stood their ground and commenced shooting. Ten thousand muskets spit flame and lead at the attackers. The combination of musket fire and artillery drove the attackers back. Anderson rested his men for twenty minutes and then redoubled his efforts to take the fort. He ordered all of his troops to concentrate on the center and drive a wedge between the Federal Corps. Once again, the Confederates were driven back. They reformed and charged a third time with the same results.

After three hours of fighting, he pulled his men back and dug in. Lee was on his way to the front. Anderson had been ordered, if he was not successful at retaking the fort, to pull back and wait for orders.

Lee arrived at Anderson's headquarters at six-fifteen and together they rode to the battlefield. As they rode, he listened intently as the Corps Commander described the day's events. Returning to Anderson's tent, he gave orders to establish a new compact line closer to Richmond. Using Gilmer as a hinge, he bent his line back towards Richmond requiring fewer men to defend it.

Washington, D.C.—October 3, 12:00 PM

Grant and Rawlins entered the White House and were escorted to the main dining room. The President was seated at the head of the table. On his right sat Stanton and on his left sat Seward while at the foot of the table sat Boss Weed. In between Seward and Weed sat the Governor of Pennsylvania, Andrew Curtin, and the Governor of Indiana, Oliver Morton. The two seats between Stanton and Weed were empty.

Lincoln sprang from his chair and walked rapidly toward Grant. Taking the General's hand in both of his he pumped it up and down like a water handle.

"Welcome, Sam. I'm glad you have come."

"I was most flattered for the invitation," responded Grant.

"How is the situation at Petersburg?" asked Curtin.

"Well, Governor, Lee has thwarted our thrusts, but his men are tiring," answered Grant.

"Do you think he will surrender soon?" asked Morton.

"No, Governor. I think the war will go on for another year. If you gentlemen can get Mr. Lincoln re-elected, then I think we'll have the time to defeat the South and reunite the States. If McClellan gets elected, he will surely let the South go its own way," replied Grant.

"We are here to plan our next move in the campaign. In order to do so, we have to know what your plans are for the next few months," said Boss Weed.

"This morning I received a telegram from General Sheridan in the Valley. He reports he has destroyed two thousand barns filled with wheat, hay and farming implements. His men have burned seventy mills filled with flour and wheat, killed three thousand sheep, burned an estimated twenty thousand acres of crops and confiscated four thousand head of stock. If you can use that information, please do," responded Grant.

"Is there anything else you can tell us?" interjected Morton.

"Yesterday, I received a telegram from Sherman reporting Hood and his Army crossed the Chattahoochee heading north and he was in pursuit."

"This is good news, but what are your future plans for the Army?" asked Curtin.

"Governor, my plans are to win the war in the shortest time possible. More than that, I will not say."

"General, besides winning the war, how else can you help us get the President re-elected?" asked Weed.

"Gentlemen, two weeks ago I began to issue sixty-day furloughs to Republican Generals, like John Logan, Ben Butler and Nate Banks, so they could campaign for the President. Furthermore, General Sherman and I have started to issue thirty-day furloughs to those soldiers whose State doesn't accept absentee ballots, like Indiana. Our war effort, particularly in the East, will be slow for the next thirty to sixty days. With winter descending upon us, I doubt any major action will take place until spring," replied Grant.

Lincoln, Stanton and Seward smiled. They knew Grant was a firm supporter and a fighting General, but this latest statement showed them that he was also extremely politically astute. The luncheon went on for another three hours before Lincoln dismissed everyone.

Cleveland, Ohio—October 3, 4:00 PM

George McClellan met with his political advisors. McClellan sat at the head of the table. To his right sat New York Governor, Horatio Seymour; next to the Governor was railroad tycoon, August Belmont; next to Belmont sat the most powerful Banker in the United States, Dean Richmond; at the foot of the table sat Industrialist, Cyrus McCormick.

"George, you must come forward and say the war is a failure. We need to portray Grant as a butcher who is just throwing away lives. Our papers in Illinois and New York are running articles once a week on the incompetence of Grant and Sherman. These are articles are no good unless you agree with them publicly," pleaded Seymour.

"Governor, I can't say something I disagree with. General Grant is fighting the war the way he sees fit. Yes, it's different than the way I fought; but, nonetheless, he has been successful. I cannot and will not call the war a failure and insult those brave lads who have died or been crippled. We can attack Lincoln and Stanton, but leave the failure piece alone," replied McClellan firmly.

"I agree with George. We should leave Grant be. He is popular with the public and if we attack him too viciously, he may come out in favor of Lincoln. So far he has remained neutral. I say that as long as he remains silent, we tread lightly on him," said Belmont.

"I think we should attack the cost of the war in manpower and money. We could also say Lincoln is a dictator who has suspended Habeas Corpus," interjected McCormick

"I think we should expand on Cyrus' suggestions," responded McClellan.

The Democrat brain trust rapidly made plans to execute the strategy. They would hit the Administration in the press and on the floor of Congress. They would hire professionals to carry the word and would employ former Democratic leaders for their support. If they were to regain the White House, the election of 1864 was their prime opportunity.

Allatoona, Georgia—October 5, 6:00 AM

Hood's plan seemed to be working as he captured outpost after outpost. The Confederate General was always one step ahead of Sherman. Noticing that the garrison at Allatoona Pass was isolated and, knowing the pass was Sherman's only supply route, he ordered Major General Samuel French to take his men and capture the lone outpost.

Sherman, back at Kennesaw Mountain, fretted over his blunder. He could lose the entire campaign if Hood captured Allatoona. To make matters worse, he had underestimated Hood and had sent Thomas and Schofield along with their armies back to Tennessee. The only troops close enough to help the garrison were at Rome, Georgia under the command of Brigadier General John Murray Corse.

Corse arrived in Allatoona with only a third of his command. Due to a mix up, the military railroad had only sent enough railway cars to hold a thousand men. The Union General rapidly deployed his troops and sent the cars back for the rest. The roundtrip journey would take twelve hours. It would be a full twenty-four hours before he had his entire command with him. Not trusting the security of the telegraph, Corse sent his aide by horseback to tell Sherman he was at the scene and had assumed command. Although outnumbered by greater than two-to-one; he would hold his position.

At dawn French started his attack. For two hours the Confederate artillery bombarded the defenders. As the cannoneers pinned down the Federals, French sent an infantry Brigade to circle around the defenders to cut the telegraph lines and destroy the railroad tracks leading from Rome to Allatoona. The outpost was surrounded.

French sent a courier under a flag of truce to Corse. The messenger handed the Union General a note.

"To: Union Commander of the garrison at Allatoona. You are outnumbered, and surrounded. Your situation is hopeless. In order to stop the needless effusion of blood, I am requesting your surrender.
Yours respectfully,
Samuel French
Major General
Confederate States of America"

The southern General from Gloucester, New Jersey would rather not waste his men's lives taking the pass. A son of Quaker parents, he had graduated from West Point a year ahead of Ulysses Grant and three years behind Sherman.

Corse read the note and showed it to his aide. Taking a pencil from his pocket he wrote his reply at the bottom of the message.

"To Major General Samuel French, CSA
Your message is received. We are prepared for the needless effusion of blood, whenever it is agreeable to you."
Respectfully,
John M. Corse
Brigadier General

Union Army"

French read the note and ordered the attack to begin. At nine o'clock, the Confederates struck the Union defenders on all sides. Corse rushed troops from one threatened point to another repulsing each assault.

Just as the fighting began, Corse's aide arrived at Sherman's headquarters and reported the General had arrived from Rome. The Union Commander smiled. His smile quickly turned to a frown when he was told of the foul up in logistics; Corse had only a third of his command with him.

French's troops continued their assaults. All along the Union lines the Southerners pressed their advantage. By nine-thirty the fighting was hand-to-hand. The defenders fired their rifles at point blank range into the faces of the attackers. Stubbornly, the blue troops began to give way. Corse raced to the front and pitched into the enemy. Seeing their General charge, the defenders counter-attacked driving the enemy out of their breastworks. Shot across the face, Corse dropped to his knees and was escorted to the rear.

French reformed his men and attacked once more. This time he concentrated all his forces for a frontal assault. When the men in gray were a hundred yards from the Union lines, the Federal cannoneers opened fire. The artillery was too much for the attackers. They halted and sought refuge in any hollow or depression they could find. Corse, his head bandaged and soaked with blood, ordered his men to lift the head log from underneath, prop it up with small logs or dirt and fire back through the opening.

At two o'clock all became quiet. Sherman stopped his pacing. He had worn a small path into the dirt. The ground around him was littered with cigars. He lit another cigar and waited for the resumption of musketry. The anxiety was taking its toll on the Union Commander. No one dared approach him for fear of being taken to task.

At Allatoona, Corse sat on a log and waited. His artillery was out of ammunition. A Corporal, not more than seventeen years old, volunteered to go to the rear and bring back more shells. It was a dangerous task as rebel snipers killed any Union soldier foolish enough to expose himself. The young man would have to cross at least two hundred yards of open territory just to get to the ammunition and then retrace his steps. Within fifteen minutes the lad returned with a bullet in his leg and an armful of shells.

Corse noticed enemy movement on his right flank one hundred and fifty yards from the Union position. French was assembling his men for another attack, this time on the Federal's right flank.

The Union Brigadier General stood, blood dripping into his eyes, ordered the dead and wounded moved aside, and a cannon brought up to the breastwork. He redeployed some of his troops from his front to his flank. He told his artillerists to make every shot count.

Twenty minutes later he ordered his sole cannon to fire. The Federals were right on target. Huge gaps were torn into the Confederate ranks, but they pressed forward. Once again, the fighting was hand-to-hand. For two hours the Southerners attacked and were repulsed. A few minutes before four they broke off the attack. To the north Corse could hear the sound of musketry. His men had arrived from Rome and were fighting their way to his aid.

Realizing he had at least a thousand enemy to his rear along with a thousand enemy at his front at Allatoona and reports of at least fifteen thousand blue troops closing in on him from the west, French abandoned his attacks and headed his Corps north to link-up with the rest of Hood's Army. As French disengaged, Corse ordered his men out of the trenches to repair the railroad and telegraph lines.

It was after seven o'clock when Sherman was handed a telegram.

> *"Major General William T. Sherman*
> *General Sherman,*
> *The enemy has abandoned their attacks. We held our position. The railroad will*
> *be repaired by end of day tomorrow. I am short a cheekbone and an ear, but am*
> *able to whip all hell yet!*
> *Respectfully,*
> *John M. Corse*
> *Brigadier General"*

As the light of the day dwindled away, Sherman retired to his tent. He sat alone at his writing table. The tent flap up allowed the coolness of the night to enter. Two lit oil-based lamps hung from hooks on the tent's poles casting an eerie yellow tint around the room. Outside, aides busied themselves with cooking dinner and preparing battle reports. The General took a clean piece of paper, picked up his pencil and began to write a letter to Grant:

> *"Dear General Grant,*
> *Today we were attacked by Hood's Army just outside of Allatoona Pass. We were*
> *able to repel his attacks, however, he never used his entire force. By his tactics of*
> *today, it is clear he does not intend to make a stand, but seems to be drawing us*

away from Atlanta. He can continue with this plan wearing down this Army as
we chase him all over Georgia.
As an alternative plan, I would like to suggest a revision to your strategy of last
March. While the destruction of Hood's Army is important, it is my opinion that
instead of chasing him, we let him go his way. With Thomas and Schofield back
in Tennessee, it would give us close to a hundred thousand men to defend the
State should Hood dare to venture there. With Howard's Army of the Tennessee
and Slocum's Twentieth Corps, I will personally, lead this Army from Atlanta to
the Sea, destroying everything in my path.
When I leave, I will burn Atlanta so it would take years to rebuild. With Hood
running around up north, there are no substantial enemy forces between the coast
and me. I am confident that even when we defeat the enemy armies, there will be
no peace until we take away the population's will to fight. By destroying their
homeland, this task will be accomplished. I know I can make Georgia howl.
Respectfully yours,
William Sherman
Major General"

Sherman called for his aide and told him to put the letter on the next military train headed for Petersburg.

Washington, D.C.—October 6, 7:00 PM

Ulysses Grant and his wife, Julia Dent Grant, entered the East Room of the White house for a Presidential reception in the General's honor. Julia tightly grabbed her husband's arm and hung on for dear life. The former Kentucky belle had been born into Southern high society, but being from a western border State, she was still considered by many to be a country bumpkin. Over the years her figure had grown and, with age and child bearing, she was now a portly matron. To Grant she was the most beautiful person on earth. Everywhere the couple went they held hands. When they thought no one was looking, they would steal a kiss. They were like newlyweds. No one would have guessed that the couple had been married ten years.

Lincoln approached the couple and took Julia's hand in his.

"Mrs. Grant, it is nice to see you again."

"Mr. President, it is nice to see you again. I really appreciate you hosting this reception in my husband's honor."

The trio continued to talk for five minutes when the President's wife, joined them. Like Julia Grant, Mary was born into Kentucky high society. Her family owned slaves and they both had relatives fighting for the Confederacy. Even though the two women had much in common and should have been friends, they disliked one another. Mary Lincoln was jealous of any woman her husband spoke to. She was paranoid, thinking they were all trying to steal him away. She loved the limelight, while Julia preferred to remain in the shadows.

"Julia, it's nice to see you again," said the First Lady.

"It is nice to see you again, Mrs. Lincoln," replied Julia.

"I love your gown. As a matter of fact, I have loved it each time you have worn it," said Mary Lincoln.

"Mr. President, I hope I didn't over-step my bounds; but, in addition to General Rawlins, I invited one of my aides to the reception. Is it all right if he comes in?" asked Grant.

"Why of course, General, please show him in."

As Grant left, Mary rolled her eyes. She was insulted the General had invited someone without informing her. In her eyes it was rude.

A few minutes later Grant reappeared. Instead of entering the reception area, he and the aide stayed at the entrance. The aide was a tall strapping young man, almost as tall as the President and powerfully built. His features were pleasant and he had a wide grin on his face.

The President caught sight of Grant and the aide and his mouth dropped open. His eyes began to water as he nudged his wife. Disgustedly, she looked at him. He pointed to the entrance. She looked up, her mouth opened.

"Robert, my son!" shouted Mary Lincoln.

Immediately she ran toward her first born quickly followed by her husband. The young man embraced his parents. For three years Robert Lincoln had badgered his father to let him join the Army. Finally, after Grant became the General-in-Chief, he relented. The General immediately took him on his staff. The young man was shown no special favors and, like other staff members, he carried the General's orders under fire to field Commanders. Like others in the campaign, his uniform was a faded blue.

"Lieutenant Lincoln has a two week furlough starting now. Please make sure he reports back on time," said Grant as he walked away.

The Grants mingled with the rest of the crowd allowing the Lincolns their privacy. In the corner of the room Stringfellow, in the guise of Elizabeth Cardwell, watched the reunion.

For the next few days, Grant met with Lincoln and Stanton on a daily basis to discuss war strategy for the upcoming winter. Sherman claimed victory over French as the Confederates had abandoned the field. All over the north, Lincoln's loyal papers printed accounts of the bloody conflict. Corse became the nation's newest hero.

Grant and Rawlins boarded the military steamer headed toward City Point. Once settled, the General-in-Chief reached into his pants pocket and pulled out Sherman's letter. He discussed the red-haired Commander's plan with Rawlins.

"John, Sherman's plan makes sense, but it's very risky. Plus, I have a few questions that need clearing up before I can give him an answer. I'm sure the answers will spark more questions. Normally I would go in person, but I have been away from Petersburg and Lee too long."

"Why not send Horace Porter in your place? He is intelligent, honest and, above all, he will tell you his own thoughts," suggested Rawlins.

"Porter it is. I'm worried about Lyons. He should have sent us something by now," replied Grant.

"I just received a message as we boarded the train. He reports Longstreet is once again in command of the First Corps. He said the enemy is on half rations."

"Anything else?"

"Nope that was all he said," answered Rawlins.

CHAPTER TWENTY-TWO

Shenandoah Valley, Virginia—October 19, 2:00 AM

"Gentlemen, I don't have to tell you how important it is for us to destroy Sheridan's Army. General Lee's men in Petersburg are on half rations. Sheridan is burning everything in sight and destroying any and all farm implements he and his band of cutthroats can find. He thinks we are finished.

"Using a back road discovered by Captain Hotchkiss and confirmed by General Gordon, I propose to send Pegram's, Ramseur's and Gordon's Divisions around the Federal camp and at dawn hit them in the rear. Since Gordon is the senior ranking officer, he'll have overall command of that section of the field. When you are all engaged, I'll strike Sheridan's front with Kershaw and Wharton's Divisions at the same time our Cavalry will strike Sheridan's left flank. Are there any questions?" asked Jubal Early

"General, how much time are you giving us to move our men around the enemy?" asked thirty-two year old John Pegram.

"From your current position I'm going to give you an hour to move your men and another hour to deploy them. If there are no more questions, I would suggest we adjourn; but before we leave, I'd like to congratulate General Ramseur on the birth of his daughter."

By four-thirty Gordon had his force in position and ready to strike. He positioned Pegram's Division on his left and Ramseur's on his right. From his vantage point he could see the Union soldiers of Crook's Corps stirring from their night's sleep as reveille sounded. Slowly the men in blue came to life as they rekindled the dying embers of their campfires. Coffee pots were filled with water as the men prepared their breakfasts unaware of the danger waiting less than two hundred yards away. Gordon's eyes lit-up as he watched the scene unfold. It was a recreation of "Stonewall" Jackson's flank attack at Chancellorsville.

Sheridan was still enroute from his meeting with Grant in Washington. In his absence, Wright was in command. Due to the lateness of the evening, Sheridan had decided to camp at Winchester twelve miles away and then press on to Middleton on the nineteenth. He sent word to Wright he planned to be back with the Army by five in the evening. In the meantime, he cautioned his second-in-command to be on the alert.

Just as the predawn sky began to lighten Gordon gave the order to attack. With his Division in the lead, the fiery General assaulted the unsuspecting Federals. The startled Union troops attempted to form ranks, but the Southerners were on them before they could fire a shot. The men in blue put up a brief hand-to-hand struggle before they bolted to the safety of the rear.

Early, hearing the sound of gunfire, ordered his artillery to open fire and the infantry to attack. The defenders in the front fared no better than those in the rear. Suddenly, the Union left flank erupted in musketry as rebel Calvary smashed into the Federals. Panic set in across Crook's entire Corps.

In spite of the heroic efforts of the Corps commander to reform his men, the surprised Federals ran for safety. Two miles away, protecting the Union right, Horatio Wright and his Sixth Corps quickly formed ranks. They held their fire to allow their comrades to enter their lines. Ten minutes later Ramseur and Gordon's men appeared. Their faces were flushed with the heat of battle as they attacked. The men in gray rushed forward, but were repulsed. They reformed, attacked again and were once again repulsed.

Meanwhile, Pegram, spotting a Division of Union Cavalry forming on the Confederate right, diverted his men and struck the blue horsemen before they could begin their assault causing the men in blue to spur their horses toward the rear.

Wright had the only Union forces between Early and Washington. If his men broke, the Valley might be lost for months. The Union General from Connecticut rode along his line encouraging his men to hold fast. The veterans of the Wilderness, Spotsylvania, Cold Harbor and Petersburg were a determined lot. They didn't spend the past five months marching and bleeding to be pushed back to Washington. The aggressiveness and determination of Grant had spread through the ranks. Wright sent a courier to Winchester to inform Sheridan what was happening.

By the time of Gordon's second repulse, Early and his Divisions had reunited. The Army Commander held a brief conference with his Generals.

"The men are played out. I'm issuing orders for them to dig in and rest. It is now ten; they'll rest until two and then at three we'll renew the assault. Gentlemen, excellent work. By this evening, the Valley will once again be ours," said Early.

Back at Winchester, unaware of Early's assault, Sheridan was meeting with his staff discussing the strategy for a new campaign. Firmly convinced the Southerner was on the defensive, Sheridan planned to push the Confederates out of the Valley and rejoin Grant at Petersburg. In the middle of the meeting Wright's courier burst into the room. He excused the interruption and quickly relayed the bad news.

"Early hit us at dawn; he has routed Crook's Corps and most of the Cavalry. General Wright is holding and is trying to rally Crook's men. The situation is desperate," panted the courier.

Sheridan sprang from his chair and ran for Rienzi, his staff hot on his heels. Without saying a word, he spurred his trusted steed and rode at breakneck speed toward Middleton. When he was two miles from Wright's defensive line at Cedar Creek, the Union General was forced to a stop as the road was clogged with the dispirited men of Crook's Corps. The moment they recognized Sheridan their spirits were lifted and they began to cheer.

"DAMN YOU ALL TO HELL! YOU ARE ALL A BUNCH OF DAMNED COWARDS, DON'T YOU CHEER ME. IF YOU WANT TO HONOR ME, THEN TURN AROUND AND FOLLOW ME BACK TO THE BATTLE. DO YOUR DUTY AS I KNOW YOU CAN. NOW CLEAR A PATH OR GET RUN OVER. I HAVE BUSINESS WITH BRAVE MEN!" shouted Sheridan as he spurred Rienzi.

The men watched in awe as the General sped away to confront the enemy. The men who could hear Sheridan looked at one another and, without saying a word, shouldered their rifles and marched back toward the battle. At first it was only two dozen, they quickly grew to two hundred, then a thousand. As word spread that Sheridan was once again in command, the entire Corps turned about and marched toward Wright's men.

Back at Cedar Creek, Sheridan met with Wright, Crook and Merritt.

"Gentlemen, we'll wait until Early hits us again. It is now one o'clock. Within an hour we'll be joined by Emory and his Corps. They'll take up position on Wright's right. They are to stay as concealed as possible. When Early strikes and is repulsed, we are to immediately counter-attack pitching into them with all we've got. General Averell, you will shortly be reinforced by Merritt and his Corps. When the Confederates hit your position, the two of you will throw them back and join in the pursuit. General Crook, since your Corps is not here, I've no choice but to hold you and your remaining men in reserve."

No sooner had Sheridan finished speaking when one of his aides pointed to the ridgeline.

"General Sheridan, Crook's men have rallied and are awaiting orders," said the aide.

"General Crook, reform your Corps and join the Cavalry on our right. We'll hit Early on three sides."

At precisely three o'clock the Southern artillery fired a lone cannon. Undaunted and now rested, the Southerners pitched into the Union defenders as if they were possessed by demons. The Union men held their ground infuriating the rebels as they stormed the makeshift breastworks and pitched into the Federals. Seeing Wright's men engaged in mortal combat and knowing the battle could still be lost in spite of his superior numbers, Sheridan altered his plans and ordered a full counter-attack along his entire line.

Instantly the tide of battle shifted to the Federals. Early's men were completely surprised at the number of attackers. Emory's men struck the Southerners in their exposed left flank; while the Cavalry, supported by Crook's infantry, attacked the outnumbered rebels holding the right flank. Noticing they were being assaulted on three sides, the men in gray at first slowly retreated, but the aggressiveness of the attackers convinced many of the Confederates that a more rapid withdrawal was necessary to survive. Men threw down their weapons and ran for the rear. The retreat quickly escaladed into a rout.

Ramseur rallied his men and had them dig in and return fire. The Southern General and his rag-tag defenders held their ground against the Union onslaught until they noticed they were being surrounded. Ramseur issued orders for his men to withdraw. While speaking, he was shot from his horse, mortally wounded in the chest. The dying General would never see his newborn baby. Seeing Ramseur fall, the remnants of the Division broke for the rear and safety.

Sheridan had turned the tide of battle. Early and his command retired toward New Market unmolested. It was now almost six o'clock and darkness set in. It had been a long day for the men in blue. Sheridan was pleased with the results of the counter-attack. Even though he lost twenty-eight hundred men killed or wounded, Early's losses were steeper. The Confederates' had lost one thousand nine hundred killed or wounded with another eleven hundred taken prisoner.

In addition to the loss in manpower, Early lost twenty-three cannons, twenty ammunition wagons and five medical wagons. If Sheridan left him alone for the winter, he would be ready to resume the offensive in the spring.

Atlanta, Georgia—October 29, 3:00 PM

Hood and his Army had left Georgia and were ordered by Beauregard to Decatur, Alabama. The Creole General had counted on Sherman following Hood into Alabama, thereby, giving the Georgians some relief. Unfortunately for the Confederates, the Union Commander did not comply.

After following the Southerners north to Resaca, Sherman lost interest in the chase and ordered Howard to withdraw back to Allatoona, while he returned to Atlanta. Anticipating his friend would ultimately approve his plan to attack the center of Georgia, he wanted to be on his way before anyone in Washington could change Grant's mind.

Waiting in the parlor of Sherman's headquarters was Grant's emissary, Colonel Horace Porter. The young officer was a favorite of both Generals. Fiercely loyal to Grant, he would defend his General to the death.

"Porter, how are you?" asked Sherman shaking the man's hand.

"Fine, sir, how are you?" inquired a surprised Porter.

"Corporal, have some coffee brought in and have a guard placed at this door. After the coffee is brought in, I don't want to be disturbed," replied Sherman to the guard at the door.

The two men entered Sherman's office. They both made small talk until the aide had brought the coffee and left.

"General Sherman, General Grant sends his gratitude and congratulations on a well-executed campaign. As you are aware, the General-in-Chief has sent me to learn firsthand more about your plan. Before he gives his ascent, he has given me some questions I'll need to have answered before I leave," said Porter.

"Horace, I understand fully. Let me assure you that you're most welcome in my camp at any time. I think that if you would allow me to fully explain my plan, it will answer Grant's questions."

Porter nodded. Sherman sipped his coffee and then leaned under his desk and pulled out a map of Georgia.

"I'll use the map for illustration purposes only. Twenty years ago when I was a young officer about your age, I was stationed in Georgia. I spent many a day walking the hills around Atlanta, Milledgeville, Columbia and Savannah. I say this to make the point that I know the countryside like I know the back of my hand. Over the years I've made many friends in this State. Many have turned against me and, I suspect, that by the time I am done I'll lose the rest.

"Hood is in Alabama. He expects me to follow him all over the land. What I'm proposing is that I cut loose of my supply lines and march from Atlanta to the sea. In my absence, General Thomas will be in charge of my Department. Between Thomas and Schofield they'll have close to one hundred thousand men to defend Tennessee should Hood be foolish enough to invade the State. I estimate the Confederates have fifty thousand men and even if Hood were reinforced with men from other Southern Armies in the field, the most he could muster would be about seventy thousand.

"I'll take Howard's Army of the Tennessee, reinforced with Slocum's Corps, and march into the interior. This will give me sixty thousand men. The troops will take five days' rations. The wagons will be filled with ammunition and medical supplies. I plan to live off the land. My Cavalry informs me the interior of the State has been untouched by the war. If they can feed Lee's troops, then they can certainly feed my men," said Sherman.

"What kind of resistance do you think you'll encounter?" asked Porter.

"I expect minimal resistance consisting of some militia and hometown guards. I'll split my Army into two wings—each one independent, yet mutually supporting one another. I plan to cut a path of desolation and destruction sixty miles wide."

"General Grant is apprehensive about your ability to feed your Army from the land. He is also wondering how you'll keep in touch with him once you leave Atlanta," replied Porter flatly.

"Ask the General when he decided to cut loose of his supply lines and feed his Army of one hundred thousand men off the land during his successful Vicksburg campaign, how he knew for sure he could do it? When he answers that question, he'll know my answer. Inform General Grant that I will not be able to keep in touch with him. He'll learn about my progress from the enemy newspapers.

In conclusion, please inform General Grant that we may defeat the enemy in the field but unless we take away their will to fight, the war will continue forever. In order to win we must fight a total war not only against the armies, but also against those who support them. I can and will make Georgia howl," answered Sherman.

"There is one question you haven't answered. We know where you are starting, but where is your final destination?" inquired Porter.

"That depends on the enemy. Since our Navy has the entire coast block-aded, it doesn't matter where I end up, just as long as it is on the coast," replied Sherman flashing a broad smile.

The two men continued to talk for several more hours. Finally, they broke for supper. Over the evening meal the young officer was bombarded by Sherman's staff with questions about Meade, Hancock, Lee and Hill. They knew Grant well. After all, he was theirs before he became the Nation's.

Atlanta, Georgia—November 7, 1:00 PM

William Sherman was eating lunch when his telegraph operator was escorted into his office.

"Sir, a message from General Grant marked urgent."

The young man handed Sherman the message and waited to see if there was a reply.

The General unfolded the piece of paper. His face beamed with the glow of excitement.

> *"Major General William T. Sherman*
> *Your plan is approved. May God protect you and your brave Army.*
> *Respectfully,*
> *U.S. Grant*
> *General-in-Chief"*

"Any reply, sir?" inquired the youth.

"Acknowledge receipt of the telegram and send him my sincere thanks," replied the invigorated Commander.

The operator saluted and left. Sherman was too busy to return the salute. He immediately issued orders to Howard and his other field Commanders. Without hesitation, he ordered Brigadier General Jefferson Davis in Rome, Georgia to burn everything of military value and to make a thorough job of it. Upon completion of the task, Davis and his Division were to return to Atlanta. Similar orders were issued to the garrisons at Kingston, Resaca, Dalton and Allatoona. The Union General was leaving nothing to the enemy.

Richmond, Virginia—November 9, 2:00 PM

Davis sat in his office and had just finished reading some dispatches when he was joined by his Vice President, Alexander Stephens.

"Alex, we have a grave issue to discuss concerning your State of Georgia. Please have a seat," said Davis.

The South's Chief Executive explained his conversation with Joe Brown. Even though the Georgia Governor was non-committal in his comments, Davis feared the State would negotiate a peace agreement which would result in the end of the Confederacy.

"Mr. Vice President, if Joe Brown negotiates a peace with the Union, it is the end of the Confederacy. Your State is the second largest in our Country in terms of manpower and supplies. If Georgia pulls out of the war and takes her troops home, Richmond and the remaining parts of the South will fall. It would be Georgia, and not the Federals, who destroy our Confederacy. Let me assure you, sir, history will not smile kindly on that sort of action," said Davis tersely.

Stephens leaned forward in his chair all the while staring into Davis' eyes.

"With all due respect, sir, I don't give a damn about what history will say. I'm only concerned with what happens to my beloved State. If Governor Brown surrenders to the Union authorities, then for me, the cause is over. I'll resign as Vice President and go home to live the remainder of my life in peace," replied Stephens coolly.

While Stephens and Davis discussed the Georgia problem Robert E. Lee relaxed by the fireplace in the parlor of his home in Richmond. With Longstreet back with the Army, he decided to avail himself of one of the perks of a Commanding General. He gave himself a two-week furlough. It had been a tedious six months for the fifty-seven year old career soldier.

His young grandchildren played at his feet while he closed his eyes and enjoyed the warmth of the fire. For the first time in over six months, he had a chance to fully relax. His wife sat next to him holding his hand. The Lees were very much in love. Married for thirty-three years, the couple had endured all kinds of hardship during their time together. Mary Ann Randolph Custis Lee was the great-granddaughter of Martha Washington. Even though a partial invalid, she managed to run a household and make a home for her family no matter where they were stationed. The Lees, like the rest of the South, had suffered greatly during the war. Their son Rooney was captured by Union troops and held prisoner at Fort Monroe in Baltimore Harbor. Their lovely

Plantation, Arlington, had been confiscated by the Federals for unpaid taxes and was now a cemetery.

The serene scene was interrupted by the sounds of wailing and crying. Robert opened his eyes, raised himself from his chair and walked slowly to the main entrance doorway. When he opened the door, he saw the street filled with sobbing women and downcast men. They aimlessly wandered in different directions. None of them looked at one another. On the ground lay newspapers. He stooped over, picked one up and read the headlines, *"Lincoln re-elected."* Lee took the paper inside. He sat in his easy chair and closed his eyes. *"The war goes on,"* he thought sighing in disappointment.

Washington D.C.—November 9, 4:00 PM

Enthusiastic crowds greeted the Union President. On his desk were telegrams from all over the North congratulating him on his victory. The one he cherished most was from his favorite General and friend, Sam Grant.

Lincoln's political machine had thoroughly drubbed McClellan. The President carried all the Union States except for Delaware, Kentucky and New Jersey. He won the Electoral College votes two hundred and twelve to McClellan's twenty-one. The popular vote was much closer, winning by a mere four percent. The soldiers had given the President the edge he needed.

It was good news for the North and Grant. The people had given their permission to prosecute the war to the fullest extent. For the South it meant more years of suffering, dying and hardship. The re-elected Chief Executive took advantage of the people's mandate and called for three hundred thousand more volunteers to put the nail in the coffin of the rebellion.

Across town, in the theatre district, sat a depressed actor named John Wilkes Booth. A Southern sympathizer, the young actor had done some spying for the Confederacy. His parents always spoiled the youngest son of their famous stage family. The youthful performer was slender and good-looking, with a disarming smile and personality. Many women adored him. His skill in acting aptly covered his hatred of the North and, particularly, of Lincoln and Grant. He made up his mind; he could no longer sit idly by and let the South be destroyed.

Atlanta, Georgia—November 16, 7:00 AM

Sherman sat on his horse and turned to his Chief-of-Staff.

"Hitchcock, make a note in that diary of yours that at precisely seven o'clock in the morning on November sixteenth, the Army of Tennessee began its historic march to the sea."

The vastness of Sherman's Army was enough to frighten anyone. Slocum commanded the left or northern wing of Sherman's strike force, while Howard commanded the right or southern wing. Each section consisted of thirty thousand men, thirty-two cannons each drawn by an eight-horse team, one-thousand two-hundred supply wagons, three-hundred ambulances and five-thousand head of cattle. Twelve-thousand five-hundred horses pulled the wagons and artillery. Each wing was an army unto itself. In addition to the supplies, the wagons carried enough pontoon bridges to cross any river. The men were in fine spirits.

The Union Commander issued strict orders on the conduct of the troops during the march and how foraging was to take place. At the beginning of each day, every Brigade was to send out a small foraging party consisting of between ten and fifteen men. Each party was to return with enough food to supply its Brigade. They were not to molest any residences or their occupants. They were to take all the food and livestock and burn whatever crops were in the fields. If the residence was not occupied, then they were to consider the home and the surrounding outbuildings abandoned by their owner and burn it to the ground. Each wing would know the approximate location of the other by the pillars of black smoke.

Howard and his men moved southeast from Atlanta toward Macon, while Slocum's troops moved on a parallel route threatening Augusta. Five thousand Cavalry, under the command of Judson Kilpatrick, hid the movements of Howard's force.

As the last of the Union troops left Atlanta, fires burned out of control. Huge columns of black smoke filled the air. Railroad tracks were destroyed for thirty miles in each direction. The towns of Kingston, Rome and Marietta were in ashes. With winter quickly approaching, many people in northern Georgia were homeless and starving. The Union troops broke their fighting spirit, but not their hatred of the Yankees.

In Milledgeville, Joe Brown organized as many troops as possible to stop the Federals. Aside from Joe Wheeler's Cavalry detachment of six thousand men, the most he could assemble was seven thousand and this consisted of young boys, old men and crippled veterans. He appealed to Davis for the return of his Georgia troops at Petersburg. He sat in his big leather chair and placed his elbows on his desk covering his face with his hands and wished he had accepted Sherman's offer.

While Sherman marched, Hood formulated a plan to invade the North. He knew Beauregard would not approve the plan, so he decided not to tell the Creole. He called his Corps Commanders together. The parlor of the Alabama mansion was opulent. Red and gold carpet covered the entire floor. The walls were covered with gilded wallpaper. A large painting of the owner of the plantation, George Templeton, hung over the fireplace. Templeton was an officer with the Fourth Alabama at Petersburg. House slaves scurried about to make the General comfortable.

"Gentlemen, as you are aware, the Yankees have split their forces. Sherman has sent Thomas and Schofield along with their respective troops back to Tennessee. He has consolidated his forces at Atlanta. This past week he burned Rome, Kingston and Marietta. I think he intends to head for the interior of Georgia," said Hood.

"General Hood, if we're going after Sherman, he'll have a huge head start on us," replied Stephen Lee.

"I don't intend to chase Sherman all over the South. Even if I were so inclined, it would mean disaster for us. His Army is still stronger than ours," answered Hood.

"The only way we can stop Sherman and, at the same time assist Petersburg, is to make sure Sherman turns back. We must force Grant to send troops away to catch us. The only way to accomplish these tasks is to invade the North. Five days hence, we'll strike our tents and move our Army north into Tennessee."

"General Hood, Thomas and Schofield still outnumber us at least two-to-one. It will be a tough road to hoe. If you're right and Sherman turns back and Grant dispatches troops from Petersburg, won't we be caught between three Federal Armies?" asked Cheatham.

"Thomas and Schofield have their troops spread all over Tennessee. Schofield is at Pulaski with eighteen thousand men. Thomas is holed up at Nashville with less than twenty thousand. We'll defeat them in pieces before they have a chance to consolidate. By the time Sherman arrives, we'll have defeated both Thomas and Schofield. His men will be worn out by their long march and they'll be almost out of supplies. He won't have enough ammunition to sustain a drawn-out fight and we'll annihilate him. By the time Grant's men arrive, we'll outnumber them and defeat them in turn. This is the same strategy "Stonewall" used in the Valley in sixty-two," responded Hood.

"I think this plan is very risky … but at the same time I don't think we have much of a choice," said Stewart.

"The fate of Georgia and the Confederacy rests with us. Sherman wrote this letter to Mayor Calhoun of Atlanta when the Mayor appealed to the Federal Commander not to order the evacuation of the residents of Atlanta at the beginning of harsh weather. I think it tells us exactly what Sherman's intentions are," answered Hood as he passed around the letter.

"To Mayor Calhoun,
My order to evacuate the civilian population from Atlanta was not intended to meet the humanities, but to win the war. You cannot qualify the war in harsher terms than I will. War is cruelty and you cannot refine it. You might as well appeal against a thunderstorm as against these terrible hardships of war. We don't want your Negroes or your horses, or your houses or your land or anything you have, but we do want and will have first, obedience to the laws of the United States. If it involves the destruction of your homes, land and way of life we cannot help it. You and your leaders have thrust this Country into this civil war. Let me assure you that war is hell and I will make my Country's enemies pay dearly.
Yours,
William T. Sherman
Major General
Union Army"

The men looked at one another and realized Sherman was going to elevate the war to a new level. It would be capitulation or destruction. He had to be stopped.

Baltimore, Maryland—November 21, 8:00 PM

John Wilkes Booth met with Stringfellow and two other Confederate agents in a Baltimore boarding house. Throughout the war, the Maryland city had been a hot-bed for rebel sympathizers. Southern spies came and went as they pleased as local law enforcement looked the other way.

The residence was located in the poor section of town where crime was rampant. At least twice a week, a person was found dead in an alley with their pockets picked and their throat cut. Movement around the streets was safe until evening.

"Mr. Booth we have need of your services," said a short, rotund man known as Mr. Gold.

He looked like a banker or railroad executive. Names were not given nor asked for. The actor knew the two men only as Mr. Gold and Mr. Red. Mr. Gold was short and rotund while Mr. Red, also short, was well muscled with a scraggly beard and short hair. His appearance, calloused hands along with his demeanor indicated he was a blue-collar worker.

"Gentlemen, how can I be of assistance?" asked Booth.

"As you are aware, the war is going badly for us and the re-election of the Ape from Illinois is not good news. He is going to keep the war going until he's thrown out of office or ... something happens to him," answered Mr. Red.

"Please go on," replied Booth.

"Because of your esteemed reputation as an actor, you are well known about Washington. On several occasions you have provided us information very few people could obtain. What we would like you to do is get five or six strong men, loyal to the cause, who can keep their mouths shut.

"When all is ready, we want you to kidnap Lincoln and bring him to Fairfax, Virginia. From there a Cavalry escort will take charge of the prisoner. We'll hold the Yankee President hostage, demanding the withdrawal of all Union troops from the South and the recognition of the Confederacy. If they refuse to negotiate, we'll kill him," said Mr. Gold.

Booth rose from his chair and paced back and forth for a few minutes. He loved the idea. It had daring, excitement and most of all a good plot. Being the actor he was, he had to play for his audience. He would pretend he was apprehensive.

"I don't know if I have the expertise for this type of caper," answered Booth feigning modesty.

"I can get you Lincoln's schedule, the rest is up to you," said Stringfellow dryly.

"Yes, I must know his movements. You can count on me," responded Booth.

CHAPTER TWENTY-THREE

Griswold, Georgia—November 23, 12:00 PM

Howard broke camp and ordered the troops of his First Division to shield the column's passage through the little hamlet of Griswold. The day before, Kilpatrick's Cavalry chased away a small band of militia. The General was taking no chances the rebels might be part of a larger group.

The Division Commander, Major General Peter Osterhaus, had chosen his finest Brigade under the command of Brigadier General Charles Walcutt to take the lead. The twenty-six year old Walcutt from Columbus, Ohio was educated at the Kentucky Military Institute. A seasoned veteran, he was considered by many to be the best Brigade Commander in the Union Army.

Brigadier General Charles Walcutt rested his men for their mid-day meal. The Brigade had been marching steadily for seven hours and needed a break. Before allowing the men to cook their meals, he had them throw up a light breastwork of logs and posted men outside his line as pickets to warn them in case of an assault. A bullet in his shoulder at Shiloh taught him to always be prepared for the unexpected. No sooner had they completed their makeshift defense when the sound of musketry filled the air. Men grabbed their new Spencer repeating rifles and dove behind their breastworks.

A deadly silence swept the field. Walcutt and his men could hear the rebel Commanders shouting orders. The Union General waited until the men in gray were within fifty yards before he gave the command to open fire. Instantly, the air rained lead as the men of the Georgia Militia fell to the ground. The force of the initial volley caused the attackers to fall back. They quickly regrouped and charged. Only green troops would charge forward in the wake of such devastation. Seven times they plunged forward and seven times they were thrown backward. Finally, after two hours of carnage, they gave up the assaults and retired toward Macon leaving six hundred dead and three hundred wounded comrades on the battlefield. Walcutt's men buried their fifty-six dead friends while surgeons tended to the thirty-five wounded.

As the fighting in Walcutt's front dwindled away, Slocum's Wing entered the Georgia Capital of Milledgeville. People closed their shutters and bolted their doors in protest as the Federals marched through the streets. Slocum sent word to Sherman that Milledgeville was now theirs.

At five o'clock Sherman and Howard arrived at Milledgeville. After six days apart, the two wings were once again reunited. The red-haired Union General met with his wing Commanders to discuss the next phase of their operation.

Sherman rested his men for two days before starting again. During this time the Union troops entered the capital building and held mock sessions. Make believe legislatures made speeches and declared Georgia back in the Union. Others broke into the State Treasury and took thousands of dollars of Georgia currency using the worthless money to light cigars and as kindling.

As the day wore on, some became drunk and began to assault the women of the town. Two soldiers walking down the street spied a Negro holding a musket sitting on a front porch.

"What are you up to there, boy?" asked one of the soldiers.

"Missy is upstairs sick in bed and ordered me to guard the house," answered the slave.

The two men looked at each other and then, smiling, hit the black man over the head, knocking him unconscious. The pair raced into the house, up the stairs and into the bedroom. Seeing the young woman alone and defenseless, they raped her repeatedly.

In the early evening the two men left the home. As they exited the front of the house, they were met by four armed soldiers on horseback. They were members of Slocum's provost guard. Upon regaining consciousness, the slave ran to the Provost Marshal's office three blocks away for help. Justice was swift. The two men admitted their guilt and were executed before sunset.

As darkness set upon the Georgia capital, the streets and front yards were ablaze with controlled campfires. While the men of Slocum's wing cooked dinner, five men approached from out of the shadows. They were thin and sickly not weighing more than a hundred pounds a piece. Their skin barely covered their bones. The men around the campfire recognized the remnants of a faded blue uniform. The five men were escaped prisoners of war from the Confederate Prisoner of War camp known as Andersonville.

The former prisoners told their new comrades how they were fed only a handful of rice a day and how the guards enjoyed torturing them. They further explained that the guards had placed string fifteen feet from the prison fence and anyone caught stepping over the line was instantly shot. The prisoners nicknamed it the "dead line." The men had escaped by tunneling under the fence. They were chased by bloodhounds as they headed west toward Sherman's Army. There were originally six of them, but one had fallen behind and was torn apart by the dogs.

While the men told their tales of horror, across town four Cavalrymen returned with slashes across the top of their necks. They told how they were captured just outside of Macon along with ten others. Even though they had surrendered, the Southerners slit their throats. Fortunately for the survivors, their captors had sliced too high on the neck.

The tales of Andersonville and the Cavalrymen spread quickly through the Army. Going forward, the Yankees would kill any dog or rebel they found.

Columbia, Tennessee—November 26, 2:00 PM

Cheatham's Corps arrived outside the Tennessee city. The Confederate General quickly positioned his men south of the city. Orders from Hood instructed him to hold his ground until the remainder of the Army arrived.

Taking advantage of the lull, Schofield ordered his troops to dig in north of the Duck River. Primarily a farming community, the town had no important military significance aside from preventing Hood from marching unopposed to Nashville a mere thirty miles away. The natural lay of the land offered an excellent defensive opportunity for the Federals. Schofield took advantage of the terrain and posted his men in a semi-circle around the town, using the rapid moving Duck River as a moat. He assigned his most senior Commander, David Stanley, to guard his northern left flank. Stanley, a West Point graduate of the class of fifty-two, was considered a hard fighter. At times he was belligerent to his Commanders, but they all respected his combat expertise. In sixty-one the Ohio-born General was offered a commission in the Confederate Army, which he promptly refused.

Hood had his entire Army in position by seven o'clock just as rain mixed with snow began to fall. The Southern General decided to rest his men and have them warm themselves. Many of the gray-clad soldiers had marched from Decatur to Columbia, a distance of sixty miles, barefoot wrapping scraps of clothing around their feet to keep warm. Before beginning the campaign,

Hood was concerned about the lack of footwear and what the hard-packed Union roads would do to his infantry. Six days of a light, warm rain had softened the ground enough to allow his men to march unimpeded without bogging down his artillery or supply wagons. At eight o'clock, Hood held a meeting with his Corps Commanders to discuss the next day's movements.

"Gentlemen, this afternoon I personally made a reconnaissance of the enemy position. Schofield has a strong defensive line. To lay a pontoon bridge across the Duck River would be suicide. It would be the same mistake Burnside made at Fredericksburg. We'll bypass Schofield and head straight for Nashville," said Hood.

"How do you suppose we do that?" asked Stewart.

"We'll cross the Duck River on a pontoon bridge; but not at Columbia. I will lead Cheatham and Stewart's Corps reinforced with Edward Johnson's Division of Lee's Corps three miles upriver. From there we'll cross the Duck River and flank Schofield. General Forest and his Cavalry will screen our movements," replied Hood.

"To speed our movements, each Corps will have only one battery of four cannons. The rest of our artillery will remain with General Lee. He will hold the enemy in place and when the enemy withdraws he will follow bringing the rest of our cannons. I'd suggest we all retire as I plan to have the Army on the move by seven in the morning. General Forrest will have his men in the saddle an hour before."

Meanwhile across the river, Schofield met with his Corps Commanders.

"Hood is before us with his entire Army. Reports from our Cavalry indicate he has been reinforced by our old adversary, Bedford Forrest. Our Army is consolidated and our position is strong. I intend to fight it out here at the Duck River. General Thomas has ordered me to buy him time to consolidate his forces at Nashville," said Schofield.

"John, what makes you think Hood will take us on head-to-head? He must realize it would be suicide. If I were him, I would circle around and strike from the rear," replied Stanley.

"General Wilson and his Cavalry will patrol our flanks and let us know of any enemy activity. If Hood tries to flank us, we'll attack while his Army is on the move," answered Schofield.

The meeting continued for another hour before breaking up. The Generals returned to their commands to issue orders.

Forrest was in the saddle just before dawn. A light blanket of snow covered the icy roads making it rough for the Confederates as horses and men slid on the ice. Marching barefoot through the snow slowed the infantry's movements. Forrest, the former slave trader from Memphis, Tennessee, split his command into three groups. Each one was to cross the river at different points. The first group was to cross three miles upriver from where Schofield's main Army was located. The second was to cross upriver four miles from the first and the third one a mile further upriver. The group furthest upriver was to cross first, drawing any Union Cavalry units away from the others. Hood planned to cross the Duck River three miles upriver, but he needed Forrest to clear the way first.

Forrest's first Brigade under his senior officer, Brigadier General James Chalmers, crossed the river at nine o'clock. The thirty-three year old former lawyer from Virginia was considered a good subordinate and a fair infantryman. Transferring to the Cavalry after the battle of Murfreesboro, he quickly became a close confident of the Cavalry Commander.

Chalmers led his men across the cold Duck River as huge pieces of ice floated by. Hidden inside the tree line less than twenty-five yards from the northern bank of the river, Union Colonel Horace Capron had his men dismount and dig in. As Chalmers horsemen crested the steep banks, the Federals opened fire. Horses and men toppled back over the edge to a cold, watery grave.

The Confederate Brigadier General spurred his horse to the front of his men and urged them to follow him. Six bullets struck his mount as he tumbled head first to the ground. Crawling back to the embankment, he ordered his men to dismount and return fire.

"Corporal Peacock!" shouted Chalmers.

A few minutes later a youthful, non-commissioned officer was at his Commander's side.

"Yes, sir."

"Corporal, I want you to re-cross the river and find General Forrest. Tell him we're pinned down and need help in order to cross. He'll know what to do."

Meanwhile, hearing the firing coming from Capron's area, Wilson determined Forrest was trying to circle the Army. Quickly he ordered his men from the banks of the river and pulled back five miles to guard the supply wagons at the Union rear. Forrest watched the enemy at the middle ford ride away leaving the crossing unguarded.

Peacock caught up with Forrest just as the General's men had finished crossing. Without hesitation, he turned his men upriver. He would flank Capron's position and either destroy or capture the defenders.

Schofield received word from Wilson that Forrest was crossing the Duck upriver from the Union forces. Undeterred by the news, he still believed the main attack would be a frontal assault; the rest were diversions.

For five hours Capron held Chalmers at bay. With ammunition running low and reports of enemy Cavalry approaching his flank, the young Colonel decided to withdraw his men and join Wilson.

Chalmers and Forrest's men galloped forward in pursuit of the Federal horsemen unaware that Federal infantry, under the command of Brigadier General John Croxton had arrived and had dug-in behind Capron. The blue infantrymen ducked their heads and let the Federals on horseback leap over. When the last of them was clear, they brought their heads up and began firing. Confederates fell from their saddles onto the rock-hard ground shattering bones as they hit.

Forrest reformed and attacked again. The blue defenders held their position forcing the Confederates to give up their assaults. The Southern Commander had his men dismount and return fire and sent word to Hood it was safe to cross. By two o'clock, Southern infantry started wading across the icy river. As the men exited on the northern bank, fires were built to dry their cloths and warm their near frozen bodies. The crossing had taken more out of them than Hood had planned. Seeing their shivering bodies, he decided to rest them at the bank and then move to Forrest during the night.

Throughout the night, couriers arrived at Schofield's headquarters. Each reported the same thing, enemy Cavalry crossed the Duck River followed by a large force of infantry. Just before dawn, Schofield sent a courier to Stanley and ordered him to place men to guard their escape route on the Franklin Pike just south of Spring Hill. He was also to take the Army supply wagons with them. If the reports were true, he had to protect his avenue of withdrawal.

Stanley had his men on the move within a half-hour of receiving the orders. If, in fact, the reports were true, then they were all in grave danger. The Union Corps Commander arrived at Spring Hill a little before nine and ordered his men to dig in. He repositioned cannons so they had overlapping fields of fire and deployed his men in a horseshoe with the open end facing their escape route.

The conditions of the roads and the raw weather slowed the Confederate advance. By four o'clock Cleburne's Division was within striking distance of

Stanley's defenders. The Southern General prepared his men for the attack. At four-thirty he struck the isolated Brigade of Luther Bradley. Cleburne's veteran troops charged up the knoll under a hailstorm of lead. Recoiling, they formed again and charged. After the second assault, the Division Commander called off his frontal attacks and repositioned his men so they overlapped the defenders' right flank.

At five o'clock the Confederates struck again simultaneously from the front and right. Taking fire from two sides, the untested Union troops panicked and broke for the rear. Bradley rode among his men in an attempt to bolster their courage, suddenly he fell from his horse, shot in the arm, and was carried to the rear. Seeing their General fall, the men in blue hastened their flight for safety.

Stanley shifted a regiment from Opdycke's Brigade to cover his now exposed southern flank. As Cleburne's men approached the Franklin Turnpike, they were greeted by the veterans of Opdycke's men, supported by the twelve cannon. Cleburne had led his men into a deadly cross-fire. The Southerners dug in and waited for reinforcements.

At six o'clock the balance of Cheatham's Corps arrived along with Jackson's Brigade of Forrest's Corps quickly followed by Chalmers and Forrest. Deciding not to take on Croxton, the Cavalry Generals simply rode west away from the Union defenders toward Spring Hill.

The lull in the battle had given Stanley enough time to rally Bradley's men. The defenders were now pressed on three sides. Using his entire Corps, Cheatham attacked. Stanley shifted men from the center to parry the Confederate thrust. The attackers were repulsed. They reformed and struck again. The result was the same. No sooner had Cheatham's attack dwindled, when Forrest hit the north and center of the Union defensive line. Stanley shifted men from Cheatham's front to bolster the areas under attack. For three hours Stanley shifted his men from threatened point to threatened point. Finally, at nine o'clock the fighting came to an end.

Schofield sat in his tent and issued orders for the Army to withdraw from the Duck River and, using the Franklin Pike, they were to proceed to the town of Franklin fourteen miles away. Stanley's men were to be the rear guard. When the rest of the Army, including the supply wagons, was safe; he was to follow. The movement would be extremely risky as the entire Army had to pass within thirty yards of the enemy. Talking, smoking and singing were prohibited. If discovered, the strung-out Federals wouldn't stand a chance.

At ten o'clock the first of Schofield's Army passed Cleburne's men. The Union troops could see the faces of the enemy as the campfires reflected across the ground. A strong, howling wind blew through the trees masking the noise of the Federals and blowing hot ashes from the campfires onto the Confederates causing them to shield their faces. By one o'clock Schofield, with the last of the blue troops, passed the southerners. He rode to Stanley, who was seated by a campfire warming himself. In his hands he held two cups of coffee.

"Good evening, John," said Stanley handing his comrade a cup of coffee. "It isn't very good, but it is hot."

"It's colder here than Jeff Davis' heart." replied Schofield taking a sip of the black liquid.

"Dave, you did a fine job today. How're your men holding up?"

"They're fine, John. I think you're making a mistake taking the wagons. They'll only slow us up. We should burn them," said Stanley

"Normally I would agree with you; but if we burn the wagons, then we alert Hood we're pulling out and he'll be all over us like a duck on a June bug," responded Schofield.

Just outside of Spring Hill, Tennessee—November 29, 6:00 AM

"What the hell happened last night!" shouted Hood.

He banged his fist on the cherry wood table causing metal plates to bounce a half-inch in the air.

"All you had to do was block the Turnpike and Schofield would have been trapped! I want the Army ready to move in one hour. We must catch him before he can reach Nashville!" shouted an angry John Bell Hood.

Schofield and Stanley hurried their men along arriving at Franklin at 8:30 in the morning. The town had formidable breastworks and a natural terrain, which favored the Federals. At Franklin they could rest their men.

Two steel bridges spanned the water. Once across the bridges, the Confederates would have to cross two miles of open, flat ground before they would reach the dug-in Federals. Stanley and Schofield positioned their cannons to catch the rebels in a murderous cross-fire. Aiming stakes were placed on the Union side of the river. Each stake had a different colored ribbon signifying the range to a target in one-hundred yard intervals, enabling the artillerists to quickly zero-in on the attackers.

At three o'clock Hood, along with his corps commanders, appeared on Winstead Hill overlooking the Harpeth River and Franklin.

"General, those works look mighty formidable," said Cheatham peering through his binoculars.

"I want our boys to cross the river. General Cheatham, your Corps will cross using the bridge nearest us on our left. General Stewart, your Corps will cross using the other bridge. General Lee will follow Cheatham while General Forrest will follow Stewart," retorted Hood.

"General Hood, let me take my Cavalry Corps and flank the enemy. This will at least divert the enemies' attention, giving the infantry a chance," pleaded Forrest.

"No, General, I'm tired of these flanking movements. The enemy must be exhausted from marching all night. We must attack before he has time to rest."

"General Hood, our artillery is at least four miles away. To attack an entrenched enemy of almost equal force without cannons is madness," replied an angry Cheatham.

"You have your orders, now carry them out or I'll find someone who will."

By four o'clock, all was ready. A lone bugle sounded and twenty thousand men in gray moved forward. Each of the battle-hardened veterans knew it was not going to be an easy day, yet they continued forward to an uncertain future. Regimental and Brigade flags flapped in the wind as the attackers proudly displayed their units' colors. The Union artillery waited until the rebels were within a half mile of the breastworks before commencing fire. Cannon balls streaked across the sky and struck the rebels with the force of a locomotive.

Patrick Cleburne raised his sword over his head and ran forward, his men close on his heels. The rebels let out their famous yell and pitched into the defenders. On Cleburne's left, Confederate Brigadier General John Brown did likewise. In less than five minutes they were on the defenders. Men swung muskets like clubs, others used them as spears. Dying men prayed while the living cursed. The trenches became saturated with blood and broken bodies. The Union troops had enough and broke for the rear, hotly pursued by their attackers. The retreating Federals created a gap. Cheatham, seeing the hole, ordered more men into the ever widening schism.

Stanley ordered his reserve Brigade under Opdycke forward to plug the gap. The Union General saw his men faltering and bolted into the fight. The sight of Stanley in the trenches fighting alongside of the defenders lifted the Federals' spirit. Suddenly he fell clutching his leg. With two minie balls in his thigh, he was carried from the field and his second-in-command, Major General George Wagner, took charge. The hand-to-hand fighting had been going on for over an hour. The Confederates were becoming exhausted. The Union's fresh troops turned the tide of battle back toward the Federals as Opdycke's men slowly pushed back the tired men in gray.

Patrick Cleburne began to rally his men when he suddenly keeled over dead. Four bullets in his chest ended the life of the man they referred to as the "Stonewall of the West." Seeing Cleburne fall, his second-in-command, Brigadier General Hiram Granbury, took over the rallying of the men.

"Remember Cleburne!" shouted Granbury

The men in gray, angered by the fall of Cleburne, counter-attacked. A few minutes later Granbury was dead with a bayonet through his heart.

Brown seeing the counter-attack led by Granbury rallied his men; but before he could lead them forward, he was shot in both legs. Brown's second-in-command, Brigadier General Otho Strahl, took over; but before he could lead them forward a bullet penetrated his brain killing him instantly. Not waiting for the rest of the Division to rally, Brigadier General "States Rights" Gist, led his Brigade in a counter-attack. He came upon a Union officer and the two of them dueled. Gist stabbed his adversary in the heart. In a final gesture, the dying men thrust his blade downward on the Confederate's neck severing Gist's carotid artery. Within minutes he lay dead next to his fallen foe.

After two hours of hand-to-hand combat, the Southerners were driven out of the trenches. The sun set, but the battle was far from over. Brigadier General John Adams rallied his men and once again, pitched into the tired men in blue. Hand-to-hand combat continued, but without Adams and his second in command, Brigadier General T.M Scott. The two men lay dead side-by-side just inside the Union trenches.

Stewart's men joined the fight attacking the Union center. Schofield personally commanded his troops and drove the rebels back. Not to be outdone by Cheatham's Corps, they attacked again and were repulsed.

While the infantry fought hand-to-hand, the two Cavalry Corps pitched into one another with an intensity never seen by horsemen in the west. Forrest's men fought with the fury of demons, but were equally matched by Wilson's men. The blue horsemen fought with saber, pistol and carbine while their adversary fought with saber, pistol and shotgun. Wounded men fell from their horses only to be trampled to death in the melee.

The fighting continued along the entire line until nine o'clock. Five hours of hand-to-hand combat had exhausted both sides. The Federals pushed the enemy back and regained lost ground as the battle came to an end. Schofield waited until midnight and resumed his retreat toward the safety of Nashville. With luck, by dawn, his Army would be reunited with Thomas.

While Schofield made his way north, John Bell Hood went over his casualty lists. Although many names would be added later, it was extensive. Over twenty-five percent of his Army was either killed or wounded. His command structure was in shambles. His losses in Generals were staggering—Cleburne, Granbury, Strahl, Gist, Scott, Adams and Carter killed. Brown, Quarles, Cockrell and Manigault seriously wounded and George Gordon taken prisoner. In all, Hood had lost twelve Generals in the ill-fated attacks.

The Commanding General went to sleep to the sounds of the screaming wounded as surgeons sawed off limbs. Outside the field hospital, the pile of removed arms and legs grew at an alarming pace.

The next morning Hood was up early. He mounted his horse and, by himself, rode the battlefield. He rode to where the breach in the Union lines had occurred. The General's heart ached as he saw the bodies of men from both sides intermingled. Some lay on top of one another. Others lay with bayonets impaled through their bodies. One Union soldier was kneeling sighting in his rifle. He looked so lifelike that, at first, he startled the Confederate Commander. As he passed the dead man, he noticed a small neat hole had replaced the eye. The projectile had entered the brain, freezing the man forever in his kneeling position.

Confederate burial details roamed the hallowed ground gathering the dead of both sides. The dead Southerners were buried in one mass grave and the Union dead in another. State's rights still existed. Hood's eyes became watery as he watched the wounded lifted onto stretchers or placed in blankets. Not long ago he was one of them.

Returning to his headquarters, he issued orders to rest the Army and bury the dead. The sense of urgency was now gone, Schofield was safe in Nashville. He had to reorganize his command structure, particularly in Cheatham's Corps.

CHAPTER TWENTY-FOUR

Washington, D.C.—December 2, 6:00 PM

"Mr. President, what is Sherman's final objective?" asked a reporter from the Washington Globe.

The President scratched his beard and stretched forward looking at the man.

"I know what hole he went in at, but I don't know what hole he'll come out of," answered Lincoln.

"Mr. President, you asked for another three hundred thousand conscripts to bolster Grant and Sherman, don't you think it's overkill given today's situation?" asked a reporter from the *New York Telegraph*.

"General Grant said he needed more men to put an end to the rebellion, and I have no reason to doubt the man," answered the Chief Executive rising, ending the press conference.

Lincoln walked outdoors along the back of the mansion. In the distance he could hear Christmas carolers. He loved this time of year. People were always so friendly and warm. Even the press seemed mellow. Soldiers roamed the gardens of the home making sure no one was lurking about.

The President mounted his horse and rode toward the old soldier's home to visit the wounded. Hidden in the shadows across from the White House, stood John Booth wrapped in a heavy cloak. He watched Lincoln ride south on Pennsylvania Avenue. As usual, he rode alone. Booth made mental notes of the route. He mounted his horse and, at a safe distance, followed the Union politician.

The weather was turning raw as thunder boomed across the horizon followed by flashes of lightning. Suddenly, Lincoln's horse reared upward and bolted toward the home knocking the stovepipe hat from his head. He gained control of the mount just as he approached the hospital.

"Good evening, Mr. President. Mr. Lamon is here and wishes to see you," said a young Cavalry officer.

"Mr. President," boomed a voice behind the Chief Executive.

Lincoln turned and saw his self-appointed protector, Ward Lamon. The man was Lincoln's best friend and had accompanied him east in sixty-one. It was Ward who first protected the President-elect from an assassination plot in Baltimore. At six foot-two inches and two hundred forty-five pounds of pure muscle, the bodyguard was not one to be reckoned with. Rumor had it that, back in Illinois, when Lincoln was just a lawyer, he successfully defended his friend in a murder trial.

"Where's your hat?" asked Lamon.

"My horse bolted when it thundered; knocking it from my head," answered Lincoln.

The body guard nodded. Lincoln smiled and walked away headed toward the wards. "Captain, I want you to send out a patrol and find that hat," said Lamon.

An hour later the young man returned. His face was an ashen color as he approached Lamon. He handed the big man the stovepipe hat. Two inches from the top was a bullet hole. The fifty-eight caliber hole entered one side of the hat and exited the other.

"Captain, from now on, the President goes nowhere without a Cavalry escort. Is that understood?"

The young man nodded as he stared at the hat in disbelief.

Booth returned to his hotel room enraged at the assassination attempt. He was too far away to see the would-be assailant. He didn't want Lincoln dead. The Union Chief Executive was worth more to the cause as a negotiating tool than a corpse.

Richmond, Virginia—December 2, 9:00 PM

Ronald Lyons made his way through the darkened streets of Richmond. People walked the sidewalks in a depressed manner. Wood and coal oil were in short supply as Grant's strangle-hold on the Southern Capital slowly drained the life from its citizens.

The Union spy was dressed in a tattered Confederate Corporal's uniform. When he went out in public, he left his wooden leg carefully hidden in his room and ventured among the masses hobbling about on crutches. Many of the city's males were either on crutches or had one arm. He fit right in. No one would ever question a solider who had given a limb for the cause. On the corner was a lady of the evening plying her trade. She spied the crippled young man and sauntered his way.

"Hey solider, are you looking for some company?" asked the attractive red-head.

The woman was gorgeous with an hour glass figure. Her face had soft features. She didn't look like a harlot.

"I may be. The Christmas season is filled with folly," replied Lyons.

"Only if you are on a trolley playing with a dolly," answered the working girl.

"Cindy?" asked Lyons.

"Ronald?" responded the redhead nodding.

"You have something for me?" he asked.

"Not here, come with me," she cooed putting her arm around his waist.

The couple walked around the block to a shabby hotel. She led the spy to her room on the second floor. Closing the door behind them, she lifted her dress. Reaching into her garter, she removed three neatly folded pieces of paper and handed them to Lyons.

"Make sure General Grant gets these pronto."

Lyons unfolded the pages and let out a low whistle.

"Where did you get this information?"

"Let's put it this way, even Confederate high-ranking officers can't resist impressing a woman, even one of ill repute," replied Cindy.

The Union spy refolded the pages and placed them inside the folded pants leg where his leg used to be.

"Thanks. I'll make sure the General gets these," he said as he prepared to leave.

"Wait, if you leave this soon, the desk clerk will become suspicious. You have to wait for at least an hour," said Cindy.

"Good idea, why don't you tell me about yourself," asked Lyons

For the next three hours the couple talked about their lives and the war.

City Point, Virginia—December 9, 2:30 PM

"Sam, this message just arrived from Lyons," said Rawlins.

Grant eagerly read the message from his spy. The young man's information was always accurate.

> *"General Grant. Shoes, socks, gloves, warm clothing and food are scarce in Lee's lines. The enemy receives one meal a day consisting of six ounces of meat and a handful of flour. When a man goes outside on guard duty, he often borrows his comrade's clothes to keep warm.*
>
> *Desertion is high among the enemy as they are receiving letters from home telling them of the hardships of the family. Men whose families are in the Shenandoah are worried over the fate of their wives and children, now left homeless and starving by Sheridan. The men from Georgia are told of stories of rape and murder by Sherman's troops. Everyday more and more men are deserting. Executions are a daily event as Lee struggles to maintain discipline. The forts surrounding Richmond are manned by walking wounded, old men, clerks and children barely old enough to shave. Jeff Davis is planning to offer freedom to slaves who fight for the South. He estimates a million slaves will eagerly join their cause. Observing the slaves forced into labor, I don't think he will get more than ten thousand, at most. I am also enclosing three pages indicating the enemy strength by regiment.—Signed L."*

The smile on Grant's face grew wider as he read the message.

"John, I don't know how the boy gets his information, but it is most welcome. We'll let the Confederates slowly starve over the winter and, come spring, we'll break Lee's Army,"

Grant picked up a telegram from Thomas in Nashville. His smile instantly vanished.

"Damn it. Thomas states Hood is digging in for the winter. For the past five days I've been strongly requesting Thomas attack the Confederate Army. Each time his reply is the same. First, he didn't have enough horses for his Cavalry and, to attack without horsemen, would spell defeat. When he finally admitted he had enough horses, he changed his excuses to bad weather. Enough is enough. John, write this down and have it sent to Thomas by telegraph immediately.

> *"To: Major General George Thomas*
> *Attack Hood at once!*
> *Signed,*
> *U. S. Grant*
> *General-in-Chief"*

Just outside of Savannah, Georgia—December 10, 10:00 AM

Sherman marched his men toward the Georgia coast. Ever since the fall of Milledgeville, the war had turned savage on both sides. Wheeler's Cavalry harassed the Union columns. When they found foragers, the Southern Cavalrymen hung them on the spot. Some of the foragers were simply tortured to death or shot. In response, the Union men no longer considered an occupied building exempt from burning.

Sherman's Army swelled in size as thousands of slaves left their masters and marched alongside their liberators. The red-haired General fed the ever-growing masses. Those who were healthy enough were used as laborers to clear away fallen trees and obstacles, while others were employed as cooks or teamsters. He met daily with their leaders to ensure they were well cared for and to make sure they understood that, sooner or later, military circumstances would dictate that he would have to separate them from the Army.

Sherman rode at the head of his troops. In the distance he could see the church steeples in downtown Savannah. His Army had marched virtually unopposed from Atlanta to Savannah. Inside the city, William Hardee assembled eighteen thousand troops to defend the coastal town. The wily Southerner flooded the rice fields surrounding the city leaving only five narrow strips of land from which the Federals could launch an attack.

Sherman surveyed the area and determined to lay siege to the city. His men had plenty of food and ammunition; however, forage for his horses was low. He had to take Savannah, but the question was how? The Navy was just off the coast. He had to link-up with them. Unfortunately, Hardee was in between, and the Navy didn't even know he had arrived outside of Savannah.

He continued to ride south to see if he could pull off one of his famous flanking movements. Everywhere he went, he saw flooded lands. He had gone fourteen miles when, in the distance, he saw a Confederate fort. He noticed the Southerners had burned the only bridge across the swamp-infested land. This was no deterrent as he could rebuild the structure in a matter of hours. When he peered through his binoculars, his eyes widened. The fields surrounding the fort were relatively dry. Once across the bridge, his men could assault the works unimpeded. With the fort in Union hands, he could establish communications with the Federal fleet and resupply his Army. The red-haired Commander organized the attack in his mind as he rode back to the Army.

Three days later all was ready. Leaving Slocum to keep Hardee from reinforcing the southern citadel, he and Howard rode south to complete their march to the sea. At four o'clock all was ready. Union Engineers, who had arrived earlier in the day, had rebuilt the bridge. Howard had chosen Sherman's former Division, now under the command of Major General William B. Hazen, to make the attack.

Hazen, a veteran of the Army of the Cumberland, was considered by many to be the finest Division Commander in the Army of Tennessee. His men crossed the newly made bridge and deployed seven hundred yards from the fort.

The Division Commander gave the order to move forward. Without hesitation his men began their assault. When they were two hundred yards from the rebels, they broke into a run. Confederate artillery opened fire, but the gunners manning the massive cannons were slow to adjust their range to the onrushing men, causing little damage to the attackers.

Suddenly, the Federals were blown skyward. They entered the Confederate mine field. Undaunted, Hazen's men continued forward swarming over the parapets. For a brief moment hand-to-hand combat ensued; but, outnumbered fifteen-to-one, the gallant defenders had no choice but to give way. At four-thirty Hazen lowered the Confederate Stars and Bars and replaced it with the Union Stars and Stripes.

"Savannah will shortly fall!" shouted Sherman.

The next day Sherman boarded the flag ship of the fleet to a hero's welcome as sailors gave him a series of rousing cheers. The normally reserved Army Commander smiled and waved. On board he wrote a message to Grant and Stanton stating he and his army had arrived safely at the coast.

Nashville, Tennessee—December 15, 4:00 PM

John Logan arrived at Nashville in the middle of a fierce rainstorm. Grant's orders gave Logan the discretion to leave Thomas in command if by the time he arrived, the slow-moving Virginian was either ready to attack or had attacked Hood.

Thomas had no idea why Logan was there, but assumed he was on a fact-finding mission for Grant. The two men met in the parlor of the mansion Thomas was using as his headquarters.

"In spite of this cursed weather, I intend to attack Hood tomorrow morning. Steedman's Corps of fifteen thousand will attack the enemy's right drawing Hood's attention. When Steedman is fully engaged, I'll attack his front. Schofield's Army will remain in reserve," explained Thomas.

At six o'clock in the morning of the sixteenth, Steedman's men waited patiently for the order to attack. A low-hanging fog hugged the battlefield. He waited an hour for the fog to burn off. At precisely seven he gave the order to attack. Men in blue surged forward. Waiting behind fallen logs and trenches four feet deep, the remnants of Cheatham's Corps took aim. When the blue coats were within range, they fired.

Steedman's veterans broke into a run and slammed into the defenders. Men stabbed and bit each other in a fury. Slowly, the Confederate troops gave way. Cheatham rallied his troops and drove Steedman's men out of the trenches. The Union Commander reformed and attacked again.

On the Confederate left, Brigadier General Thomas Wood led his men in the attack against Stewart's breastworks. Supported by Wilson's Cavalry, they charged forward pushing the outnumbered defenders back. Wood noticed the hill in front was manned by artillery with very little infantry support. The Union General ordered his men forward and, in a hail of canister and bullets, swept up and over the enemy stronghold. The ground was strewn with the dead and wounded. Seeing his left threatened, Hood ordered Lee to send two Brigades from the Confederate center to help Stewart. The fresh troops stemmed Wood's advance.

Thomas and Logan watched as Hood shifted troops from his center to reinforce the left. Just as soon as the front weakened, George Thomas ordered the main Army forward. Throughout the day, Southern troops were moved from one threatened point to another. Darkness fell bringing an end to the fighting. The Southern Army had been pushed back a mile but was still in tact.

During the night Hood realigned his army moving Cheatham's Corps from the right of the Confederate line to the left placing Stewart's battered Corps in the center where it could be easily supported.

On the other side of the battlefield, Thomas vowed to renew the fight the next day. He was determined to smash the Confederate Army of Tennessee.

Throughout the next morning, Thomas made careful preparations for his attack. As the day wore on, Wood's men became restless. Suddenly, without orders, they swarmed forward against Cheatham's men. Seeing his comrade begin his assault and thinking he missed the signal, Steedman ordered his men forward against Lee's entrenched troops. Then, like a snowball rolling down a hill, other Union Commanders ordered their men into the melee. Pacing back and forth Thomas watched his Army's attack without orders.

Hood watched as Lee's Corps melted away. He ordered Cheatham to send the remnants of Cleburne's Division, under the command of Brigadier General J.A. Smith, to reinforce the hard-pressed troops. Cheatham immediately complied but neglected to inform his other Division Commander, William Bate, to cover the gap in the line. Engaged with Union forces in his front, Bate didn't notice the redeployment of the men to his left. Through the years he and Cleburne had always communicated each other's movements, however, Cleburne lay cold in his grave and the inexperienced Smith failed to send word.

Brigadier General James MacArthur received word from Thomas to move his men forward. The young officer led his men into a hailstorm of lead. Suddenly the firing stopped. MacArthur's men reached the gap in the enemy line. The officer turned his men to their left and struck Bate's isolated Division in the flank. Noticing he had gained a strong foothold in the rebel lines, he called for his aide.

"Major, ride like all hell to General Thomas and inform him we split the enemy lines," said McArthur.

Realizing the opportunity and not taking any chances he sent two other aides with the same message.

Twenty minutes later the first aide arrived. Reining his lathered horse hard, the man dismounted and sprinted to Thomas.

"Sir, General McArthur reports he has split the enemy line and is requesting reinforcements," panted the winded young man.

"Ride to General Schofield and tell him he is ordered to send the reserves forward. You are to lead him to the gap," replied Thomas. The aide had just left when the second and third couriers arrived from McArthur.

Within ten minutes, thousands of Federals poured through the gap in Hood's line. Bate's Division taking fire from the front, flank and rear broke for the safety of Franklin. Seeing his right melt away, Cheatham ordered his last Division forward to stem the tide. The outnumbered Southerners quickly joined their fleeing comrades.

The Union troops attacked Stewart's Corps in the flank and rolled them up like a blanket. The Southerners had enough. Outflanked, out-numbered and out-Generaled the men ran for the rear. The once proud Confederate Army of Tennessee was no more. Five thousand brave rebels lay dead on the ground with another five thousand wounded and taken prisioner.

As the sun set in mid-Tennessee, Hood reorganized his battered and broken Army. He ordered his Generals to have the men on the road to Alabama at midnight. He wanted to put as much distance between his men and the enemy. He assigned what was left of Lee's Corps to rear guard action and retired to grab a few hours' sleep. As the rain beat upon the canvas, the once proud hero of the Confederacy wept. He had gone north with thirty-five thousand men. Only fifteen thousand remained.

Washington, D.C.—December 22, 5:30 PM

The Lincolns were beginning their dinner when a telegram arrived from Sherman. The President read the message and smiled.

"Send a reply thanking the General," replied Lincoln.

The courier saluted and left the banquet. Lincoln passed the message around the table for his guests to read.

> *"To: President Lincoln*
> *Your Excellency, I beg to present to you as a Christmas present, the Georgia city of Savannah together with its arsenal, seaport, one hundred-fifty heavy cannon and twenty-five thousand bales of cotton.*
> *Your obedient Servant,*
> *William T. Sherman*
> *Major General*
> *Union Army"*

The next day Lincoln sent a glowing telegram to Sherman.

> *"To: Major General William T. Sherman*
> *My dear General, I want to thank you for your Christmas present. It was exactly what I wanted. I must praise you for your foresight. While everyone advised me that you and your Army were headed for disaster, I had faith in you. In the end you have proven them all wrong. You have proven the old military saying that a General in the field knows more of the situation than a General miles away. May God watch over and protect you and those in your charge.*
> *Yours always,*
> *Abraham Lincoln*
> *President of the United States*

Lincoln sent a copy of the message to Grant knowing the two men were in disagreement on Sherman's next course of action. He knew Sherman wanted to march up the coast, but Grant wanted Sherman and his Army at Petersburg as soon as possible. Nine months earlier he promised his General-in-Chief he wouldn't interfere in military matters. He hoped Grant would read the telegram and trust Sherman's judgment. It worked. Grant relented and gave Sherman permission to resume his march up the coast to Petersburg.

CHAPTER TWENTY-FIVE

Richmond, Virginia—February 3, 1865, 11:00 AM

Jefferson Davis sat at the conference table in his office. The afternoon setting-sun cast long shadows around the dimly lit room. The Confederacy was beginning to unravel as Georgia attempted to broker a separate peace with the Federals. Jefferson Davis was losing his power in the rebellious States. At the insistence of the Southern Congress, he made Robert E. Lee General-in-Chief of all Confederate forces. The Congress felt it was working for Lincoln and there was no reason why it would not work for them.

The door to Davis' office opened and in walked three of the South's most important leaders.

"Good afternoon, gentlemen, please have a seat," said Davis rising from his seat out of courtesy; not respect.

The three men sat down at the conference table. Confederate Vice President Alexander Stephens sat across from the President. Sitting between the two men on Davis' right was the Senate leader, Robert Hunter. Across from Hunter sat the Southern Assistant Secretary of War, John Campbell.

"I have asked you here to inform you that Lincoln has decided to meet with the three of you to discuss the possibility of peace. Before you meet with him, I want to give you my instructions for the conference. Any deviation from these instructions will lead me to veto any agreement. You can tell Mr. Lincoln the South's only condition for peace is to be left alone and allowed to leave the Union," said Davis.

"Mr. President, Lincoln is not going to agree to that. We're hoping that, perhaps, we could lay down our arms and rejoin the Union, keeping our slaves and our way of life," replied Stephens.

"Mr. Stephens, if that is your opinion, then you gentlemen are wasting your time," retorted Davis.

The four men continued the discussions for five hours before adjourning.

Washington, D.C.—February 3, 4:30 PM

While Davis discussed his conditions for peace, Lincoln met with Secretary of State William Seward to discuss the up-coming peace conference.

"William, in three days we'll be meeting with representatives of the Southern Government. They are going to insist on leaving the Union and I cannot and will not agree. It has always been my position that the Union is perpetual and larger than any one State or number of States. History will say we fought this war to free the slaves. To them I say; this war was fought to preserve the Union and that the freedom of slaves was a by-product," said Lincoln.

"Abe, I agree with you. But neither one of us ever cared what history would say. We're doing the best we can for the Country in the hope of saving it for future generations."

"If they agree to lay down their arms by April first and rejoin the Union, I'm going to ask Congress to buy their slaves. Then we'll set them free. It will be cheaper than continuing the war," responded Lincoln.

Seward's facial expression indicated he was against the plan.

"Speaking of money, how is that chunk of land you insisted I buy from Russia two years ago? Has it thawed yet?" asked Lincoln.

Seward instantly recognized that his friend was subtly trying to convince him that investment in the future is not always readily seen in the present.

"You mean Alaska. One day it will be a great State," answered Seward.

"My thoughts exactly," replied the smiling Chief Executive.

Petersburg, Virginia—February 4, 10:00 AM

Robert E. Lee met with his Commanders at his headquarters in Petersburg to discuss his plans for the upcoming spring. The new General-in-Chief sat at the head of the table. Seated on his right was James Longstreet, next to him sat Wade Hampton and next to Hampton was Jubal Early. On Lee's left sat Ambrose Hill, next to him sat Fitzhugh Lee. At the foot of the table sat Joe Johnston. In the corner, away from the table, sat Channing, his normal jovial face held a dead-pan expression never seen by Longstreet, Hampton or Hill.

"Gentlemen, I have it from a very reliable source that, as soon as the weather permits, Grant is expecting to renew his campaign. We're not strong enough to prevent this; however, if we can unite our Armies in the field, we can take on each Federal Army separately and destroy it piecemeal. I've ordered Stephen Lee and Richard Taylor to each dispatch one Corps to the South Carolina Coast. They will join with Hardee giving him thirty thousand men.

"General Johnston will assume command of the coastal Army. Hardee will report to Johnston. General Hampton will command the coastal Cavalry. Generals Wheeler and Forrest will report to him. General Johnston, you have only one order—stop Sherman," said Lee.

Johnston's eyes widened at the unexpected turn of events in his favor. He would be free to command without interference from Davis.

"I have ordered Beauregard to command a new Department called the Department of Florida and Georgia. He'll be responsible for our coastal defenses in those States. At the same time, I want General Early to keep what's left of the Shenandoah open. You are to harass Sheridan and keep him from joining Grant," said Lee.

"What about Petersburg? To stay here is madness," responded Longstreet.

"Pete, I couldn't agree with you more. Tomorrow I have a meeting with the President. I'm going to request we cut ourselves loose of defending Richmond and Petersburg. This will give us the flexibility of movement. To solve our shortage of manpower, I'm going to ask the President's permission to raise regiments of slaves to fight," answered Lee.

"Robert, he'll never go for either of those ideas," replied Johnston.

"I can only try," replied Lee as pains once again stabbed at his chest.

Seeing their friend's face turn ashen, the men excused themselves and left for their commands. They knew the war had taken its toll on Lee's health, but none of them spoke of it.

"Channing, please wait," said Lee.

Sweat formed on Lee's forehead. Loosening his tunic, the older man looked at the faithful spy.

"I just wanted to say that I appreciate your contributions to our cause and I am promoting you to Colonel."

The young man responded with a polite thank you.

"What's wrong? Your mood these past few days has been very melancholy. It's not like you to be so downtrodden," said Lee.

"Sir, my fiancé is very ill and I am worried about her. We were engaged the morning of the firing on Sumter and have not seen each other since," replied the spy as his eyes began to well with water.

"She is in Richmond is she not?" asked Lee.

"Yes sir, she lives there."

"All the times you have gone through the city, you never once stopped to see her?" asked the General shaking his head.

"I was always on time-sensitive missions. We both know the cause is always more important than personal matters," answered Smith.

Lee sighed and nodded.

"That is so true. During my life, I've always put the Country above my own interests. You're, hereby, granted a sixty-day furlough. One man more or less in the trenches is not going to stop Grant. If the President doesn't honor my requests, then Longstreet is correct, our cause is doomed. Go see your girl," replied Lee as he wrote out the pass.

The next day a dejected, but determined Lee returned to the Petersburg trenches. Johnston was right. Davis rejected both of Lee's suggestions. The General would fight it out until his Army was no more. He was a soldier and soldiers obeyed civilian authority. At West Point he had been taught soldiers wage war, while civilians make peace. With the failure of the peace talks at Hampton Roads, the war would continue in the spring.

Just outside of Petersburg, Virginia—February 5, 7:15 AM

Warren started his men across the icy grass between him and the rebels. A.P. Hill watched the Union forces draw closer, holding his artillery at bay. When they were a hundred yards away, he gave the order to commence firing. The veterans of Warren's Corps were blown skyward as shells exploded among the tightly packed ranks. The Federals pushed forward through the carnage slowly driving the defenders back. Hill, on his black steed, rode along his lines urging his men to hold their ground. His red battle shirt drew the attention of Union snipers. Bullets whisked harmlessly past the fiery Corps Commander. With his line giving way, Hill turned to his favorite courier, Sergeant Tucker.

"Tucker! Ride to Pegram and tell him to bring his Division up immediately. Then ride to General Lee and inform him Grant is trying to gain the Boydton Plank Road. Tell him I need reinforcements to hold the road!" shouted Hill above the din of the battle.

Within thirty minutes, Pegram and his Division joined the melee. The thirty-two year old General and his Division had been transferred from Early's Army of the Valley to Hill's Corps a month earlier. Pegram led his men forward; stalling the Union advance. Warren threw fresh troops into the fight and the Confederates, once again, slowly gave way. After ten hours of hard fighting, the Union Corps took the precious roadway. Lee had only one supply route remaining—the Southside Railroad.

While Warren notified Meade of his victory, Hill met with his Division Commanders to discuss a counter-attack. The meeting was interrupted by Lee.

"General Lee, I didn't expect to see you, sir," said a surprised Hill.

"Your Sergeant said you needed reinforcements and I needed a break from my paper work, so here I am. By the way, I brought you another Division from Longstreet," answered Lee.

As the Eastern sky slowly turned from black to dark blue, the Southerners anxiously prepared for the assault. When the sky was completely dark blue; they struck the half-asleep Federals catching them completely by surprise. The Union men had expected a counter-attack, but not until after dawn. Lee had changed his tactics. Instead of waiting for full sunlight, he would use the partial darkness to protect his men. In the predawn light, the defenders had a hard time distinguishing friend from foe. The rebels slammed into the Federals reclaiming the precious road and pushed them back.

When full sunlight descended on the battlefield, Warren counter-attacked using the full force of his Corps along with his artillery. The men in blue pushed their gray-clad adversaries back toward the roadway. For the remainder of the day, the battle seesawed back and forth as men on both sides dropped from exhaustion. By nightfall, the Confederates were once again in possession of the Boydton Plank Road; but Warren had forced them to extend their lines two miles. Lee would have to spread his men further.

When Hill and Lee returned to Hill's headquarters, they saw the body of John Pegram being lifted into an ambulance.

"Shot through the heart leading the last charge," said the ambulance driver shaking his head.

"Pegram was a fine officer. Three weeks ago I attended his wedding in Richmond. This war has cost us dearly in future leaders," replied Lee.

Shenandoah Valley, Virginia—March 3, 12:00 PM

Sheridan commenced his attack against Early's dug-in forces. Custer's Cavalry attacked the rebel right flank. Confederate artillery opened fire on the unsupported Union horsemen, forcing them to retire. The "boy General" reported to Sheridan the road from Staunton, on the Southerners' right flank, was aptly guarded by artillery. At the same time a probe, on the Confederate left, revealed infantry was dug-in and supported by dismounted Cavalry. The probing force counted only four cannon supporting the left.

For the next three hours Sheridan shifted men from his center to the left flank of the enemy. At four o'clock, all was ready. Custer, supported by a Division of infantry, attacked the rebel right flank drawing the artillery's attention. At the same time, Crook's Corps struck the center with the intent of keeping Early's attention to the front and right. Once both attacks were well underway, Wright struck the left with his entire Corps.

The Southern cannoneers held their own against the onslaught of Custer and his men. Infantry in the trenches, supported by Southern cannon, kept Crook's men in check. On the Confederate left, Wright's men struck the defenders with such force that the outnumbered defenders had no choice but to give way. At first two or three broke for the rear, then it was one or two dozen. They were quickly followed by groups of fifty to a hundred. Like a snowball rolling down a hill, the break had begun small and rapidly increased. Suddenly, the entire left flank gave way. Like an over-flooded dam, blue-clad soldiers poured through the break capturing four cannons and thousands of prisoners. Seeing their left give way, the men in the center broke and ran. Completely surrounded by Federal troops, the men on the right had no option but surrender. Early tried to rally his men but the panic was too widespread. The Confederate General watched in horror as his entire Army melted away. The Southern Army of the Valley was no more. Early, his staff and twenty cavalrymen were all that was left. The small band made their way south to join Lee at Petersburg; while Sheridan telegrammed Grant at City Point.

"To: General U.S. Grant
Sir, I have the honor to report that today my Army completely destroyed the Confederate Army of the Valley under the command of Jubal Early. The Southern General escaped but I am pleased to report we have this day captured the following: seventeen pieces of artillery, five thousand prisoners, ten thousand arms of all types and countless stores of ammunition. As soon as we finish here, we march to Petersburg.
Respectfully yours,
Philip Sheridan
Major General Union Army"

Washington D.C.—March 4, 4:00 PM

All over the North Church bells rang in celebration of Sheridan's victory. Across the northern States the mood was one of elation as the war-tired population smelled an end to the death and destruction. Thousands swarmed to Washington to witness Lincoln's swearing-in for a second term. John Wilkes Booth sat in a boarding house planning the kidnapping of Lincoln. He decided to wait until after the inauguration. It made no sense to kidnap the man before he was sworn-in for a second term.

If they did it beforehand, the Federal government would simply wait until his term was up, and swear-in Andrew Johnson as President. Even though Johnson was from Tennessee and was considered by many to be a Southerner at heart, the authorities in Richmond felt they had a better chance of negotiating for Lincoln's release rather than Johnson's. Booth dressed and left for the ceremony.

A cold wind howled through the trees as the President stood outside on the Capitol steps. Former Secretary of the Treasury now the head of the Supreme Court, Salmon Chase, raised the bible and began the ceremony. The wind halted allowing all present to hear the speeches clearly.

Lincoln turned toward the crowd and approached the podium. The crowd applauded for ten minutes as the man basked in the adoration of the public. It had been a difficult four years. At first, no one liked him. He didn't have the support of his original cabinet and even those in his own party referred to him as an uncouth ape. Lincoln raised his right hand to quiet the crowd. A hush fell over the audience as they strained to hear the President's every word. He spoke for ten minutes. At the end of the speech, no one in the audience had a dry eye. The President's speech had touched the inner core of all present; all but one.

In the corner of a portico near a column, stood John Wilkes Booth pretending to be moved; but inside he seethed with hatred. *"Let the people cheer Lincoln now. We'll see if they will pay for his ransom,"* thought Booth as he returned to his boarding house.

Washington D.C.—March 14, 3:00 PM

Lincoln met with Stanton and Seward. In the middle of their conversation he collapsed and was carried to his room. Doctors diagnosed Lincoln's condition as exhaustion. The wear and tear of the past four years had caught up. He needed rest. The doctors forbade the man to take his nightly walks and restricted the number of visitors he saw everyday. Stanton issued an order that everyday at three o'clock in the afternoon, the White House was to be closed to visitors. Slowly, the Chief Executive's strength returned. He decided a visit to Grant at Petersburg would speed his recovery. Seward arranged the trip.

City Point, Virginia—March 27, 1:00 PM

Grant received word from Seward of Lincoln's visit and made arrangements for Sherman to attend. The red-haired General would be taken to City Point by Admiral Porter, personally. Together the three would meet with Lincoln. The men waited on the wharf for the President's vessel to tie up. The three military men boarded the ship and were led to the President's stateroom.

"Gentlemen," said Lincoln extending his hand in friendship.

The man lacked color, his appearance was drawn and worry lines now covered his entire face.

"Sam, it's nice to see you again. Please have a seat," said Lincoln in a tired voice.

"Mr. President, welcome to City Point. I'd like to present Admiral David Porter and Major General William Sherman," replied Grant

"Well done, Sherman. Where is your Army now?" asked Lincoln.

"Thank you, Mr. President. My Army is just outside of Goldsboro, North Carolina. Joe Johnston has been giving us a tough time, however, I feel confident that within a month we'll have him bagged up," answered Sherman.

"I called you here to discuss the upcoming spring campaigns and, more importantly, to get away from Washington for a while," said Lincoln.

"Mr. President, now that Sheridan and his Cavalry have returned, I plan to strike Lee within the next few days; but I've put it off because of your visit," responded Grant.

"Sam, I'm here more for a rest than an inspection. I want you to proceed as if I weren't here," replied Lincoln patting his friend's hand.

"Abe, let me give a quick update on the present situation. Two days ago Lee attempted a breakout. Perceiving a weakness in our line at Fort Stedman, he attacked with a Brigade just before dawn. At first the surprise worked. Within an hour, we counter-attacked and drove the enemy back into the trenches. From the prisoners we took, I came to the conclusion Lee's Army is starving. Thanks to Sherm's march, desertions in the rebel Army are up.

"With Hancock on medical leave, I have placed Humphrey in command of Second Corps. Keeping this in mind, I have decided to send Sheridan's Corps, supported by Humphrey's Second Corps and Warren's Fifth Corps, around the enemy right flank. Ord and Parke's Corps will replace Humphrey and Warren in the line. Sheridan will swing south toward Dinwiddie Court House, then head north to wreck the Southside Railroad. Once that is accomplished, the end will be near," explained Grant.

"What about Boydton Plank Road?" inquired Lincoln.

"Once we take the Southside, the road will fall and, with it, Petersburg and Richmond," answered Grant.

"What will Lee do next?" asked Porter.

"Without a city to defend, he'll attempt to link-up with Johnston. I intend to pursue Lee across Virginia and into North Carolina to prevent their joining forces. At the same time, Sherman will keep Johnston pinned down," answered Grant

"A well thought out plan. When does it begin?" asked Lincoln.

"Tomorrow night. I do have a question, sir. When the war is over, what do you intend to do to Lee, Longstreet, Beauregard and Johnston?" asked Grant.

The Chief Executive paused, took a sip of ice water and answered.

"If they agree to abide by our laws and lay down their weapons, I will welcome them back with open arms. Our country will need all the healing we can provide."

"What about the rest of the South?" inquired Porter.

"I intend to let them up easy, real easy. I want no hard feelings on any side. Their leaders will be allowed to live in peace, but will not be allowed to hold office ever again."

"What about Jeff Davis?" asked Sherman leaning forward in his chair.

"Sherm, that's a question I've wrestled with for the past few months. Half of me would like to hang him from the highest tree, while the other half wants him to just go away. I wouldn't be the least bit upset if Davis were to somehow slip past our patrols and escape to some foreign land. Right now he is the most hated man in the Confederacy. The people of the South blame him for losing the war. If we punish him, he'll become a martyr."

The men continued to talk well into the night. As they adjourned for the evening, Lincoln pulled Grant aside.

"Sam, I just wanted to thank you from one man to the other for everything you've done for me and the nation," said Lincoln.

"I want to thank you for all your support through the years. I know there were times when people in Washington wanted my head on a platter," replied Grant.

Lincoln looked at his friend and smiled.

"The worst time was after the fall of Vicksburg when you paroled twenty thousand prisoners. Halleck and Stanton were beside themselves claiming they would re-join the army. I told them the story of Sikes yellow dog. Have you heard the story?" asked Lincoln.

Grant shook his head.

"In Springfield there was a butcher named Sikes. He had this big old yellow dog that used to chase the boys around town. One day the boys got together and, taking some beef, they planted a lit firecracker inside the meat and threw it at the dog. It quickly gobbled up the meal. In a few seconds the firecracker exploded blowing the dog up in a hundred pieces. Sikes came running out of his store and saw his dog dead. He picked up the biggest piece, which was the tail and holding it up shook his head. A passing man looked at Sikes and said. 'Sikes, isn't that your dog?' The butcher looked at the man and replied. 'Yup, he's still my dog but he ain't worth a damn now.

"After relaying the story, they never questioned your decisions again," replied Lincoln a wide grin on his face.

Richmond, Virginia—March 29, 5:00 PM

Jefferson Davis met with Lee.

"Jeff, everyday Grant grows stronger while our Army grows weaker both in numbers and spirit. I don't know how long I can keep the Federals out of Petersburg and Richmond. I would suggest you send away any records of the government and have a train with the steam up, ready to go at a moment's notice," said Lee.

Davis realized his friend was right. It was only a matter of time.

"Robert, I'll take your advice," replied Davis placing his hand on Lee's shoulder. The two men were friends before the war and the conflict had brought them closer.

"If Grant and his Army do happen to break your lines and you cannot link up with Joe Johnston, I want you to disperse your Army rather than surrender it. Organize your men into guerilla units. We'll continue the fight for generations. We will not be defeated," said Davis.

Lee looked at his friend, but didn't reply. The tired General nodded and took his leave. When Lee was out of sight, Davis pulled a gun from his pocket and loaded it with five bullets. He then called his wife Varina to join him.

"I think the end is near. If we can't escape and the Yankees corner us, I want you to shoot your way out or at the least force them to kill you and the children," explained Davis coldly.

Varina stared at her husband and listened intently as he showed her how to load and aim the pistol. At eight o'clock, he placed his wife and children on a special train leaving Richmond headed for North Carolina promising to join them within a few days.

At the same time, Channing left his fiancé and headed to his boarding house three blocks away. A light drizzle cleaned the streets and gave the night air a clean smell. The odor of smoldering wood added to the serene atmosphere. Turning the corner, he noticed a crippled Confederate solider on the opposite side of the street talking to a lady of the evening. There was something about the man which made him seem familiar. Keeping on his side of the street, he proceeded past the couple. His sixth sense told him something was wrong.

Suddenly he remembered where he had seen the man. It was the same person who questioned him when he infiltrated Grant's City Point headquarters. The man was a spy, but for whose side, thought Channing as he remained in the shadows observing the couple.

The pair walked down the street to a broken-down hotel frequented by ladies of the night and their clientele. Channing followed the couple, remaining a safe distance behind. When the couple entered the hotel, he hailed a cab.

"Take me to the Provost Marshall's office and hurry," ordered the young man.

Ten minutes later, the carriage arrived at a red brick, colonial-style building. Outside, two sentries stood guard at the front door. Channing leaped from the cab and signaled the man to wait. He bounded up the short flight of stairs and was immediately stopped by soldiers.

"Halt, what is your business with the Provost Marshall?" asked one of the sentries.

"There's a Union spy in the Capital and I'd like assistance capturing him," responded Channing.

"Sir, we get ten people a day claiming there are Union spies in the city and requesting help. I'd suggest you be on your way," retorted the skeptical guard.

"I'm Colonel Channing Smith of Robert E. Lee's staff and I'm ordering you to stand aside or you'll be shot in the morning for aiding and abetting the enemy."

The guards looked at each other and then snapped to attention.

"Captain Archer is on duty. His office is the second door on the right," responded the sassy guard.

Channing opened the door without knocking surprising the older man.

"Captain Archer, I'm on business for General Robert E. Lee and he needs your immediate assistance."

The officer bolted upright from his chair.

"What does General Lee require?"

"There is a Union spy at the boarding house of Fifth and Main. Right now he is occupied by a woman of the night. General Lee recognized the man as a former prisoner of war exchanged in sixty-two and has ordered me to have him arrested," replied Channing.

The story was false, but the former spy was excellent thinking on his feet. It was this skill that had kept him alive for four years, the majority of which, were behind Union lines. Without hesitating, Archer ordered his clerk to pick four men to accompany him and Channing to the boarding house.

The two officers boarded the carriage followed by four soldiers on horseback. They proceeded to the hotel. Archer posted two men at the back stairwell and the other two at the front door. Satisfied he had sealed off the escape routes, he followed Channing up the stairs to the room.

The two men waited for a second and then, without warning, Channing kicked open the door. Seated at the table talking were Ronald Lyons and his contact; a shocked look was on their faces.

"Sir and madam, you are both under arrest for espionage," said the Colonel. Archer looked at Channing.

"I know this man. We have had many a drink together. General Lee must be mistaken," said Archer.

"General Lee is not mistaken and neither am I. The last time I saw this man, he was holding a pistol on me while I was infiltrating Grant's headquarters. I know he's a spy for the Union for I'm a spy for General Lee."

"I don't know what you're talking about," replied Lyons calmly.

"Enough of this nonsense, we'll sort this out in my office. Both of you on your feet," replied Archer.

"Leave the woman out of this, she is just a street walker trying to get by," responded Lyons standing.

Grabbing his crutches, he hobbled to the Confederate Colonel. Standing face-to-face he whispered in his ear.

"One soldier to another I'm asking you to leave her out of this. If you do, I'll admit to what you say. If you don't, I will produce a dozen witnesses refuting your charges."

Channing looked at his adversary and nodded.

"Leave the woman. I believe she is just a dupe," said Channing.

The three men left the room and headed to Archer's office. When the men were out of the hotel, she placed her face in her hands and wept. She had fallen in love with Lyons.

CHAPTER TWENTY-SIX

Just outside of Petersburg, Virginia—March 31, 1:00 PM

Sheridan started toward the small hamlet of Dinwiddie Court House. Confederate spies immediately notified Lee of the movement. He ordered his Calvary, under the command of Fitzhugh, along with Pickett's Division from Longstreet's Corps to Five Forks Junction while Heth's men of Hill's Corps held Dinwiddie Court House. Lee was putting a quarter of his Army in Sheridan's path. The Virginian calculated the Southside Railroad was the main objective and the only way to the railroad was first through Dinwiddie and then Five Forks Junction. He sent word to Heth to hold Dinwiddie at all costs.

Rain slowed Sheridan's advance causing him to arrive at the Court House a little after five o'clock. Blocking his way was Lee's makeshift force. Sheridan's Cavalry arrived well in advance of his supporting infantry. Humphrey sent word to Sheridan his men were two hours behind and wouldn't arrive until after dark. Sheridan fumed, he knew where Humphrey's Corps was, but he had no word from Warren. He wanted to use Warren to hold the enemy in place. Out of frustration he ordered Custer and Devin to charge. The horsemen were no match for the dug-in Confederates and were quickly repulsed, costing the impulsive Commander three hundred needless casualties. Darkness set in bringing an end to the conflict. Sheridan decided to wait for all of his infantry to arrive before attacking again. At seven o'clock Humphrey and his Corps arrived and were quickly deployed. With no word from Warren, Sheridan fretted throughout the night.

Robert E. Lee arrived at Pickett's headquarters at nine o'clock. He saw Pickett, Rooney Lee and Fitzhugh Lee seated around a campfire drinking coffee. The three surprised men immediately jumped to attention.

"Relax Gentlemen," said Lee in a tired voice.

"General Lee, would you care for a cup of coffee?" asked Pickett.

The south's first soldier nodded and took a cup of the hot liquid.

"Gentlemen, today Sheridan attacked us at Dinwiddie Court House and was repulsed. It is my belief those people will swing west and then north, here at Five Forks, hoping to outflank us and capture the Southside Railroad. You must hold this position to the last man. Today Grant's men captured the Boydton Plank Road leaving us only the Southside Railroad. If we lose this position, we lose Richmond, Petersburg and possibly the war."

The three Generals pledged they would hold Five Forks to the last man. Satisfied with their response, Lee returned to his headquarters.

The next morning Sheridan received word from Grant that Warren was on his way and should arrive by noon. The Union Commander waited, his temper rising every minute. Noon came and went with no sign of Warren. At one o'clock Sheridan had enough. He wired Grant requesting permission to remove Warren from command and replace him with Griffin who, at the Wilderness, Grant wanted arrested for insubordination. At two o'clock Warren arrived with his Corps. Sheridan explained his plan to Warren, Humphrey, Custer, Devin and Merritt.

"Gentlemen, Humphrey is to remain here at Dinwiddie holding Heth in place. The Cavalry, along with Warren's Corps, will swing east then at Five Forks turn north and capture the Southside Railroad. There is one problem," said Sheridan

"What's that?" asked Warren.

"Scouts sent out last night inform me that Lee has placed a large force at Five Forks. After reviewing our maps and, based on the Cavalry's reports, my plan is that Warren's Corps will move by White Oak Swamp Road and attack the defenders on their right flank. Devin will dismount his Cavalry and attack the enemy from the front. Custer will take his Division and attack the enemy left flank. Merritt will be held in reserve. We must move quickly before more rebs arrive," replied Sheridan.

Meanwhile, at Five Forks, Pickett, not seeing any sign of Sheridan, assumed the Union General wouldn't move for the rest of the day. Taking advantage of the lull in the fighting, the Confederate General, who Lee had left in charge, decided to have a fish bake. Rooney Lee, Fitzhugh Lee and George Pickett left their commands at two o'clock for their meal. The trio didn't inform anyone they were leaving or where they were going. Even though they would be less than two miles from their lines, the place of the picnic was surrounded by numerous large pine trees making it serene and quiet.

At four o'clock Sheridan had every one in place. Warren's Corps struck the Confederate left flank. Ayres' Division charged the lightly defended portion of the battlefield. The Confederates poured volley after volley into the on-rushing Federals. Ayres' men recoiled. Seeing his attack stall the Division Commander from New York grabbed the Division's flag and ran toward the enemy breastworks. His men rallied and joined him in the attack.

At the same time Crawford's and Griffin's Divisions overlapped the enemy flank and plunged into the rebels from the rear of their lines. The defenders were now fighting on two fronts.

While Warren's Corps attacked, Custer's Division circled around the other flank of the enemy. Dismounting his men, he hit the defenders hard causing them to recoil.

Sheridan watched as Devin's men surged forward against light resistance. Once engaged, the smoke of the muskets clouded his view. Playing a hunch, he ordered Merritt to join Devin in the assault.

Outnumbered almost three-to-one and fighting on three sides, the defenders broke and ran. Some had enough of the short rations and bloodshed and simply lay down their weapons.

Pickett and the two Lees returned from their picnic to see their commands routed. The men rode among their troops trying to rally them, but it was no use. They would not stop until it was safe.

By six o'clock it was over. Sheridan had taken Five Forks. The way was open to the Southside Railroad. The Union General attempted to organize a pursuit; but, between the darkness and the vastness of the terrain, he gave up and let his men celebrate. Still fuming over Warren's late appearance, he removed the General from command and replaced him with Griffin without Grant's permission.

Grant sat around his campfire at City Point smoking a cigar. On his left were Rawlins and on his right sat Lincoln. The men enjoyed the President's stories. At eight o'clock Horace Porter arrived in camp. He dismounted and ran to Grant.

"Sir, great news, Sheridan has taken Five Forks," panted Porter.

"How many prisoners were taken?" asked Grant.

"At last count over five thousand, but he's still counting," replied Porter.

"Colonel Porter please assemble every courier we have. John, take down these orders.

"To all Generals—upon receipt of these orders, you are to commence an artillery bombardment along your entire front. It is to continue throughout the night; spare nothing. At dawn, you are to attack the enemy at your front, never mind about your flanks. The entire Army attacks at all points at dawn.
Signed,
US Grant
General-in-Chief"

Grant drew another cigar from his pocket, lit it and inhaled deeply and then slowly exhaled.

"With a little luck, Richmond and Lee's Army will be ours by nightfall."

Robert E. Lee had just retired for the evening when the artillery bombardment began. At first it was only a few cannons, but the sound grew louder as each commander received Grant's orders. By ten o'clock, the entire sky was lit by the flame of the cannons as they spit forth tons of lead toward the rebels. Earlier, Lee received word from Pickett of his defeat at Five Forks, however, he was told neither of the fish bake nor of the extent of the rout. He ordered two Brigades from Anderson's Division of Longstreet's Corps to the Southside Railroad to reinforce Pickett's men. Lee was unaware the most Pickett could assemble was two thousand men. The fish bake had cost Lee twenty-five percent of his command with over ten thousand men killed, wounded or surrendered.

Lee tossed and turned throughout the evening. Finally, two hours before sunrise, he gave up and went outside to the smoldering campfire to make some coffee. He was greeted by A.P. Hill.

"Good Morning, General. Want some coffee?" asked Hill.

"Couldn't sleep Ambrose?" replied Lee reaching for the cup.

"No, sir, ever since we've been in Petersburg, Grant has never done an all night bombardment. I think he's going to attack us today," answered Hill.

"I fear you are correct. He'll, most likely, attack our entire front. If he does, we don't have the manpower to hold him off. This is the day I've feared ever since we came to Petersburg," replied Lee as he took a sip of the strong coffee.

For the past three years, the two men shared the life of warriors and had become close friends. Hill adored Lee and considered him his mentor. He knew Lee had his faults and made mistakes, but his loyalty for the man would always go undiminished no matter what happened.

As the sun rose, the eastern the sky turned from black to dark blue and, finally, when it reached a pale blue, the sound of battle filled the air. Hill dropped his cup and turned to Lee

"General, if you'll excuse me, I must rejoin my Corps," said Hill, mounting his horse.

Hill and his aide, Sergeant Tucker, galloped to the front. Reaching a clearing, they ran into twenty Federal soldiers. Grant's Army had breached Lee's defenses at several points. Hill drew his pistol and turned to Tucker.

"Ride back and tell General Lee our lines have been breached."

Before Tucker could argue, Hill spurred his horse and charged the Yankees firing his pistol. The red shirted Corps Commander was struck four times in the heart and was dead before his body hit the ground.

Fifteen minutes later Tucker arrived at Lee's headquarters and told the General what happened.

"Colonel Chilton and Sergeant Tucker, General Hill was correct in his assumption, our lines are collapsing. He's one of the fortunate ones, for him the war is over. However, we must continue to do our duty. Colonel Chilton, make sure this telegram goes out and is delivered immediately to the President. Sergeant Tucker, you ride with me," said Lee.

Lee mounted Traveler and, with Sergeant Tucker at his side, rode to the front to see if he could rally his men.

Richmond, Virginia—April 2, 9:00 AM

Jefferson Davis sat in church listening to the pastor's sermon when a young Captain entered. All eyes were on the young man as he walked down the aisle. He stopped at Davis' pew, bent over and whispered in the President's ear.

"An urgent message from General Lee requires your immediate attention."

Davis rose and calmly left. Once the two men were outside, Davis turned to the aide and asked.

"What's the message?"

"General Lee reports Grant has breached his line at several points and he has no choice but to abandon Petersburg. He'll make his way to Joe Johnston as previously discussed. He says he'll try to hold out for the rest of the day, but will retreat at nightfall," answered the Captain somberly.

Just outside of Petersburg, Virginia—April 2, 9:30 AM

Grant, mounted on Cincinnati, rode along the front. He watched as his men stormed the Petersburg defenses. Lee's outnumbered and badly thinned out ranks put up a valiant fight, but it was hopeless. By noon Sheridan had taken the Southside Railroad and Humphrey's Corps had pushed Heth back to Petersburg's western defenses. Parke's Corps had run into tough resistance against Gordon's Division of Longstreet's Corps. Lee pulled his men out of their defenses and consolidated them three miles back in Beauregard's original defenses. The initial success of Grant's assaults had suddenly run into tough resistance. Undaunted, Grant kept pressure all along the front. Throughout the day the Federals attacked; were thrown back; reformed and attacked again driving Lee's dwindling force a few hundred yards. Longstreet and Lee rode along the lines bolstering their men.

The day seemed to drag for both Grant and Lee. Grant wanted Lee out in the open and Lee wanted darkness to descend so he could make his escape. As darkness descended, Grant ordered his men to rest. He would resume the offensive at first light. He knew Lee would use the cover of night to retreat. Since neither he nor his Generals knew the terrain, he had no choice but wait.

The next morning Grant woke with a splitting headache making him nauseous. He received reports Lee had abandoned Petersburg and Brigadier General Gordon Wetzel had entered Richmond. Grant ordered a pursuit of Lee's Army. He wasn't going to let him get away. He sent orders for Sheridan to move his Cavalry forward and cut off Lee's retreat. He wired Sherman that Lee's Army was on the move and would probably be headed for Burkeville in North Carolina. If Lee did arrive, then Sherman would have to handle him until Grant arrived with the rest of the Army.

Richmond, Virginia—April 3, 10:00 AM

Ronald Lyons sat on the floor in his cell in Libby Prison. The converted tobacco storage house was cold and damp. Only officers were held at Libby, the other prisoners were sent to Andersonville. He thought of the woman named Lydia, his fellow spy. He didn't care if she was a common lady of the evening, he had fallen in love with her.

It no longer mattered as he was scheduled to be hung in an hour. He wondered if she would claim his dead body and see that he had a proper funeral. The young man closed his eyes and saw her face. She had the deepest brown eyes, which were enhanced by her long auburn-colored hair. They had kissed only once, but it was a feeling he would carry with him for all eternity.

Outside he heard loud voices followed by gunshots. A few minutes later the metal door to his cell was kicked open. Standing at the entrance was a young Union Lieutenant.

"Are you able to walk, sir?" asked the eighteen year old officer.

"Son, I'm damn glad to see you," replied Lyons. "What the hell is going on?"

"We broke the Petersburg line. Lee is on the run and Grant is on the chase. At dawn, my Division captured Richmond. The rebs put up some resistance, but after two hours they had enough and skedaddled faster than a dog encountering a skunk," answered the Lieutenant. "We should get going. Better be careful, Major, there're still a few rebs taking pot shots at us. Two are lying at the foot of the stairs."

Lyons hobbled down the stairs and saw the body of Archer lying facedown in his own blood. He stopped and looked at the man, shaking his head.

"He and two others tried to shoot it out," said the Lieutenant anticipating the question. "His friend next to him had a sawed off double-barreled shotgun. A second slower and I'd be lying there instead of him. We're holding the third one down the hall to the right. He was wounded in the shoulder and it took four of us to overpower him. He put up quite a struggle."

Lyons left the young officer and hobbled down the hall. Entering Archer's office, he saw Channing Smith sitting on a leather couch with a bandage around his left arm.

"You need to see a doctor. Why are you here?" asked Lyons.

"I was coming to see if you had any last wishes before you died and to tell you how much I regretted to see you hung, but war is war and we both knew the risks. I was bringing you a Federal uniform figuring you would like to be hung in the proper attire. It's ironic, isn't it? I guess now I'll be the one hung."

"Bull shit," responded Lyons turning to his rescuer. "Lieutenant, my name is Major Ronald Lyons. I'm on General Grant's personal staff. You may wire General John Rawlins or Grant himself and either one will confirm my statement. I'm taking this man with me to get his wounds properly dressed."

"Sir, I can't let you do that," answered the Officer. "He's a rebel Officer and I have orders to arrest any I see."

"Let me put it this way," responded Lyons. "Since I'm your superior Officer, you must obey my direct order. I take full responsibility."

The Lieutenant thought for a few minutes and released Channing into the custody of Ronald Lyons.

The two men walked down the street and chatted. Lyons saw a Union surgeon casually walking up the roadway. He stopped the man and asked him to tend to Channing. The doctor was tired of war and gladly administrated aid to the wounded man. When he was finished, Lyons asked him to accompany Channing to the Confederate spy's fiancé's house and tend to the ill woman. The two spies who, a day earlier, had tried to kill each other; now shook hands and parted company.

"If you are interested in seeing the woman you were arrested with, I suggest you go to one ninety eight Washington Street," said Channing.

Lyons walked two and half miles to Washington Street stopping several times to massage his stump. Turning the corner onto Washington, he was surprised to see a number of large Southern-style mansions. Each house had a large front porch. Four huge white columns supported the roof of the porch. A white picket fence surrounded the two acre properties separating them from their neighbors. Lyons walked to the middle of the block and stopped at the front gate. His hand shook as he undid the latch and hobbled to the front door. The fearless spy's mouth was dry and sweat formed on his forehead as he knocked on the large oak door.

Waiting for five minutes; he knocked again. Two minutes later the door was opened by a slender black woman. A shocked expression crossed her face as she stared at Lyons dressed in his Federal Uniform.

"My God," she exclaimed! "You're alive! The Lord be praised! Miss Mary, come quick!"

A door upstairs slammed shut as the mistress of the home raced to the staircase. Her eyes were red and her face flushed from crying. Seeing Lyons, she abruptly stopped midway down the staircase. A smile crossed her face as she ran down. The couple embraced and kissed long and hard. She took his hand and led him to the parlor. The couple, along with the black woman, sat and talked.

Mary Wentworth Gracie told Lyons how her friend Matilda, a freed slave and seamstress, was Varina Davis' dressmaker. Thinking the woman harmless, the President's wife confided in the former slave about matters better left in Jefferson Davis' office. For nearly three years the dressmaker passed vital information to Mary who, posing as a prostitute, passed them on to various Union spies. She explained how eventually each spy was caught by Archer and within a few days hung.

Outside of Petersburg, Virginia—April 4, 9:00 AM

Lee's men were exhausted as they trudged along. Gordon led the vanguard of the Army while Longstreet fought a constant rear guard action. The half-starved Confederates hadn't eaten since dawn the day before. Only love and adoration for their Commander kept them going. Every hour Lee would order a ten minute rest for his weary men. He had to keep them going. He knew if he could reach the railroad at Appomattox Station, he could resupply his men with food and ammunition. Unfortunately, the town was eighty miles away. Once again, it was a foot race. For Lee, winning meant survival; for Grant it meant victory.

Richmond, Virginia—April 4, 11:30 AM

While Grant chased Lee, Lincoln decided to visit Richmond. Lincoln ordered Admiral Porter to take him to the Confederate capital. It was ten o'clock in the morning when the President arrived at Rockett's Landing on the outskirts of the inner City. Porter and Lincoln, along with ten sailors armed with carbine rifles, left the Landing and walked two miles uphill to the Confederate White House.

The small party walked among the rubble of buildings. Bricks lay in the streets; dirt covered the once clean sidewalks. People walked through the streets in a daze, nobody paying attention to the group of men silently walking by. About halfway to their destination, an old house slave recognized the Union leader.

"Glory, hallelujah, Bless the Lord, I've seen the great Messiah," and then fell to his knees.

Lincoln was embarrassed and shocked at the reception. He told the man to get up. Within a few minutes, the Federals were surrounded by dozens of former slaves. Together they walked to the Confederate White House.

The closer they got to the Confederate Executive Mansion, the more alert people became. Word had spread that Lincoln was now in the city. The citizens of Richmond hung out of windows, stood in doorways and climbed lampposts to get a glimpse of the man who had destroyed their way of life. The onlookers were silent, not a cheer or jeer was uttered.

They had walked half an hour when they came upon Libby Prison. The converted tobacco store house was the home to many Union Officers captured during the war. Although not as bad as Andersonville, it was still a bad place. Porter and Lincoln stared at the hanging sign *"Libby Prison."*

"I'll have the building torn down," replied Porter.

"No, leave it as a memorial," said Lincoln as he continued his trek.

Reaching the Confederate White House, Lincoln climbed the stairs and began touring the Mansion. He was greeted by Wetzel.

"Mr. President, you should have sent word and I would have had a military escort meet you."

"I enjoyed the walk," replied Lincoln. "Please show me Jeff Davis' office."

In a few minutes the Union President stood in Davis' Executive Office where less than twenty-fours earlier the Confederate President had worked. Lincoln sat in Davis' chair. He closed his eyes and said a silent prayer, not for himself or Davis, but for the Nation to heal itself.

Outside of Appomattox, Virginia—April 8, 8:00 AM

Grant pursued Lee day and night. Men of both Armies were exhausted. For six days Grant kept at his adversary. Confederate stragglers filled the road hindering the pursuit. The men in gray were weak in body and spirit and had given all they had. Seeing the growing number of prisoners now under Union control, Grant called for Horace Porter.

"Porter, I want you to ride ahead and deliver this message to Lee in person. Wait for an answer," said Grant rubbing his aching temples.

Two hours later Porter stood in front of the Southern Icon and handed him Grant's message.

"Sir, I'm to wait for an answer," said the messenger.

Lee nodded and opened the correspondence.

> *"General Robert E. Lee*
> *Commanding Confederate States Army of Northern Virginia.*
> *General: The results of the last week must convince you of the hopelessness of further resistance on the part of the Army of Northern Virginia in this struggle. I feel that is so, and regard it as my duty to shift from myself the responsibility of a further effusion of blood by asking you to surrender that portion of Confederate States' Army known as the Army of Northern Virginia.*
> *Respectfully,*
> *U. S. Grant Lieutenant General"*

Lee showed the message to Longstreet. The Corps Commander read the message from his one-time friend and relative.

"Not yet," replied Longstreet.

Lee nodded and wrote at the bottom of the message his reply.

> *"General Grant,*
> *I have received your note of this date. Though not entertaining the opinion you*
> *express of the hopelessness of further resistance on the part of the Army of North-*
> *ern Virginia, however, before considering your proposal I would like to know the*
> *terms you will offer on condition of its surrender.*
> *Respectfully,*
> *R.E. Lee, General"*

Lee folded the piece of paper and handed it back to Porter.

"Please deliver this back to General Grant."

The Army of Northern Virginia proceeded on to the town of Appomattox and food. If Lee could beat Grant there, then the Confederate General could take refuge behind the James River.

Just outside of Appomattox, Virginia—April 9, 5:00 AM

Lee woke to the booming of cannon to the west. He mounted Traveler and galloped to the sound of the guns. He found Sheridan's Cavalry supported by Wright's Infantry between them and their supplies at the Appomattox train station. Gordon organized an attack in a desperate attempt to break through the Federal lines. The hungry and weak Confederates were easily repulsed. Determined to break the Union stranglehold, they reformed and struck again. The results were the same. Lee ordered Gordon to call off the attacks and dig in.

From his vantage point, Lee could see Parke's and Humphrey's Corps forming a battle line to his south. In the rear he heard the sound of gunfire as Longstreet's men fought a rear guard action against Ord's and Smith's Corps. To the north he watched Griffin's Corps approach and quickly form a line of battle. The old General knew he was surrounded. His once mighty army was reduced to a total of thirteen thousand men. One Corps of Grant's army had more men then Lee had in his entire Army.

On his way back to his headquarters, he was greeted by Longstreet.

"Pete, it looks as if the campaign is over," said a dejected Lee. "I've no choice but to meet with General Grant and I'd rather die a thousand deaths."

"Robert," replied Longstreet. "For four years we've fought a gallant fight against overwhelming odds. If it wasn't for you and your leadership, this Army would have been destroyed years ago."

"Thank you for those kind words," responded Lee. "But if you could arrange a truce along the entire line until such time as I can meet with Grant, I would appreciate it."

At one o'clock Lee and Grant met in the parlor of Wilmer McClean in the town of Appomattox Courthouse. McLean had moved from northern Virginia after the first battle of Bull Run when his home was at the center of the battle. He moved as far south as he could and still be in Virginia. He was a pacifist who hated war. He witnessed the beginning of the bloodletting in Virginia and he would witness its end.

The two commanders sat at a small table near the fireplace in the parlor. Meade, Sheridan, Parke, Ord, Rawlins, Porter and Humphrey stood against the wall listening to the conversation. The Confederate General was dressed in his finest uniform. Around his middle he wore his sword, underneath was a gold sash. Grant, on the other hand, wore no sword and his uniform was caked with mud.

"General Lee, please excuse my appearance. I mean you no disrespect, it's just that, with the vastness of my Army, I only received word an hour ago we were to meet and my headquarters is over three hours away," apologized Grant.

"I understand, General," replied Lee cordially.

"General Lee, you and I met before in Mexico," said Grant trying to ease the tension.

"Yes, I've been told that; but, for the life of me, I cannot remember when," replied Lee. "General Grant, I'm here to surrender the Confederate Army of Northern Virginia and I'd like to know what terms you're offering."

"General Lee, I would propose that the men of the Army of Northern Virginia lay down their arms and pledge not to take them up again against the lawful authority of the Federal Government. They are to be paroled and if they obey the laws of the United States; they won't to be molested in anyway. All materials of war are to be surrendered."

"These terms are most generous. Please have your aides prepare the papers and I'll sign them," answered a proud Lee.

A half-hour later, Rawlins brought in the surrender document and laid it before Grant. The Union General read it and passed it to Lee.

"One other thing which had slipped my mind," said Lee as he finished reading the document. "In the Confederate Army, our Officers and Cavalry have to purchase their own horses. I'd like them to be able to keep their property."

Grant nodded and answered. "Rather than rewrite the document, I'll give orders that any person declaring they own their horse be allowed to keep it. Is that acceptable?"

Lee nodded, "this will go a long way to securing the peace. One other item, General, you have captured my food supplies and my men haven't eaten in days. May I have some rations?"

Grant gave the order to send over enough food to feed twenty-five thousand men and to keep the Confederates fed. He also ordered that after the surrender, each man was to be given five days' rations before beginning his journey home.

Lee thanked Grant again. He stood up and shook the Federal General's hand. His head held high he placed his hat on his head and exited the building.

Standing on the top of the front porch, he called for Sergeant Tucker and the two men rode back to the Confederate lines. As they rode away, the Federals began to cheer. Grant looked at his Generals.

"I want orders issued that there is to be no cheering or carrying on, the Confederates are our fellow countrymen again," said Grant sternly.

He mounted Cincinnati and rode to his headquarters. He had gone about a mile when Porter rode up to the General.

"General Grant, don't you think that news of Lee's surrender would be of interest to the War Department?" asked Porter.

The General smiled at his loyal aide, dismounted and scribbled a note to Stanton and Lincoln

> "General Lee has surrendered the Army of Northern Virginia on terms which I have approved and will forward later. Signed U.S. Grant"

Grant stood and remarked. "Damn, for days I've had a headache; now it's suddenly gone."

Washington D.C.—April 9, 5:30 PM

Within an hour of the message being received at the War Department, the news spread all across the Capital. Bands played, people marched through the streets singing and joining hands. The Marine Corps band turned out and marched to the White House to serenade the President. Lincoln stood outside on the veranda listening to the music when someone from the crowd cried out.

"What song would you like to hear, Mr. President?"

Lincoln thought for a few seconds and shouted back.

"*Dixie* was always a favorite of mine and now we once again own it."

The crowd cheered and applauded while the band played *Dixie* and the people sang along. The Lincolns reveled in the attention. The past four years had been a living hell for the couple as the President was booed or ignored by many of his so-called compatriots. Now everything was different.

Not everyone was elated at the news. In his room at Mary Suratt's boarding house, John Wilkes Booth met with his fellow kidnappers. Seated on the bed was Lewis Payne, a Confederate deserter, who at six-foot three-inches and two hundred and forty pounds was the largest of the group. Seated across from Payne in a large overstuffed chair was David Herold who was only slightly smaller than Payne. Next to Payne sat the innkeeper's son, John. The diminutive son was enamored by the presence of Booth. Standing near the window was another large man, George Atzerodt. Missing was Benjamin Franklin Stringfellow. Realizing after the fall of Richmond the war was over and kidnapping Lincoln a fool's errand, he left Washington to resume his life with his fiancé.

"The plan has changed," said Booth in an angry tone. "It'll do us no good to kidnap Lincoln, but he must pay for his crimes against the South. I've sentenced him and his cronies to death. Once Lincoln, Johnson, Seward and Grant are dead, the Union will give us our independence. If anyone wants out, he should speak now."

The room was silent.

Booth continued, "I'll kill Lincoln and Grant on Friday while they are watching the play at Ford's Theatre. I'll sneak into the box and shoot them. While I am doing that, Lewis and George will kill Seward. At the same time, I want John and David to kill Vice President Johnson. We'll throw the Union into chaos."

"John," replied Herold. "This Friday is Good Friday. Are you sure you want to do this then?"

"David, if you're afraid of doing this, leave now. Besides, if we are successful, it will be a very good Friday for the South," answered Booth.

Washington D.C.—April 14, 9:00 AM

The President was in a cheerful mood. Sitting down to breakfast, he noticed a photograph of Robert E. Lee on his plate. His son had placed the photo there as a joke. Lincoln picked up his reading glasses and looked at the picture.

"He has a good face. I'm glad it's over."

At two o'clock he convened a meeting of his cabinet. Grant had been ordered by the President to attend the meeting. When the General-in-Chief entered the room, the entire cabinet came to their feet and applauded the military man. Grant shook hands with all of them and sat down. He told the President and his advisors about his pursuit of Lee and the terms of the surrender.

"What about Sherman?" asked Stanton.

"Sherman will have Johnston bagged within a week. As soon as Joe Johnston hears of Lee's surrender, he'll realize his cause is over. If he doesn't surrender, I'll order Meade to proceed south with the Army of the Potomac and Thomas to proceed west. Johnston will be caught between three Armies with nowhere to go."

"I think it will be over very soon. Last night I had my dream again," said Lincoln.

"What dream was that, sir?" asked Grant.

"I dreamt I was aboard some kind of a vessel floating away to a distant, unknown shore. Every time I have this dream, it is followed by some sort of a major event or disaster. I had it before Fort Sumter was fired upon, both Bull Runs, Antietam, Stones River, Gettysburg and Vicksburg. I have a feeling we shall hear from General Sherman shortly."

At the end of the cabinet meeting Grant stayed behind to chat with Lincoln.

"Sam, how about you and Julia coming to Ford's with Mary and me tonight? The play, *My American Cousin*, is supposed to be very good. It's time you reveled in the glory you have earned. Besides, the newspapers have been implying all week that you and Julia would be there," said Lincoln.

"Abe, I'd love to go, but Julia has already made plans."

"I understand," answered a disappointed Lincoln. "Sam, before you leave, I want to thank you for all you have done for me personally."

Lincoln, in a rare emotional moment, threw his arms around the unsuspecting General and gave him a bear hug.

Just outside of Appomattox, Virginia—April 14, 2:30 PM

Grant, Meade, Lee and Longstreet decided not to attend the formal surrender ceremony. The Generals on both sides faced the same dilemma. Who would they choose for the formalities? No one wanted a resumption of the fight.

On Grant's side, it had to be someone who was calm and brave, a General whom the enemy would respect and would not gloat. Grant and Meade felt they had only one man with these qualities—Joshua Chamberlain, the hero of Little Round Top.

Lee needed someone with the same qualities. He knew Early was too hot-headed; Anderson was not well known and Pickett was weak. He chose John Gordon. The one-time lawyer was respected by the Union as well as the Confederate Army.

Gordon led the Confederate Army of Northern Virginian down the road to their formal surrender. The Army followed in order of Corps numbers. Longstreet's First Corps lead the way followed by the remnants of Early's Second Corps and the remaining pieces of Hill's Third Corps. Lining the road on both sides were Union soldiers. As the Confederates passed, Chamberlain gave the command to present arms. Immediately, the men in blue brought their rifles to the salute. It was a symbol of honor and respect to a beaten foe. Gordon, surprised by the gesture and not to be outdone, ordered his men to dress right. Instantly, the men in tattered gray snapped their heads to the right in a military return salute.

When Gordon approached Chamberlain, he saluted and took his place next to the Union Commander. Each Brigade marched forward and threw their guns and bayonets into a pile, turned to their left and walked away. Some went back to their camp for a final farewell, while others headed for home. As the color bearers approached, they tossed the bullet riddled banner onto the pile. Some Brigades tore up their flags and threw the pieces onto the pile.

Washington D.C.—April 14, 6:30 PM

As Abraham and Mary Lincoln left the White House to attend the play at Ford's Theatre, the President turned to his bodyguard and said "Goodbye, Crook."

The largely built bodyguard was startled. For the past four years every night it was *"Good night, Crook."*

The President and the First Lady exited their carriage at Ford's. A large crowd gathered to catch a glimpse of the Chief Executive. The newspapers had been advertising Lincoln's attendance at the event for weeks. The man from Illinois basked in the adoration of the public as they cheered and applauded.

Inside, the entire Theatre rose and applauded as the President entered his box. He waved at the crowd as he seated himself in his rocking chair. The theater's owner had taken out a seat in the President's box and replaced it with a rocking chair for the man's comfort.

Lincoln lazily rocked back and forth enjoying the play. The third act had just begun when John Wilkes Booth silently entered the President's box. Drawing a two-shot derringer from his pocket, the man placed the gun six inches from the back of the President's head and fired. Lincoln's head slumped forward. The First Lady let out a horrified scream as Booth rushed past her. Standing on top of the railing, he jumped ten feet to the stage below. As he leaped, the heel of his right foot caught on the red, white and blue bunting draped underneath the Presidential Box. The assassin broke his right leg as he crashed onto the stage.

Pulling himself up and turning to the crowd he yelled "Sic semper tyrannis; Death to all tyrants."

He then limped off stage, down the back stairs and out the rear alley where he had a stagehand holding his horse's bridle.

Inside the theater, two surgeons examined Lincoln. He was slumped forward in the rocker as if asleep. At first they were unable to find any vital signs. After a few minutes they discovered a weak pulse. The medical men knew the wound was mortal. They decided to move the President across the street to the house of a tailor. Seven soldiers volunteered to carry the President. They gingerly lifted their leader and walked the hundred yards.

A half mile away, a lone messenger knocked on the door of Seward's house.

"May I help you?" asked the butler.

"Out of my way," yelled Payne pushing the man aside and rushing up the stairs.

The Secretary's eldest son heard the commotion and started down the stairs colliding with Payne. The assassin drew a knife and sliced the young man's forearm. The two men struggled for a few minutes before Payne pushed the smaller man down the stairs.

Rushing into the Secretary's bedroom, he saw Seward awake, but bedridden. He lunged at the helpless politician. Seward managed to raise his right arm and parry the thrust of the knife. Payne struck again and once again the thrust was parried. Before he could strike a third time, the Butler and Seward's son were on top of the would-be assassin. A struggle ensued for a few minutes before Payne broke away, bounded down the stairs, out the door and into the darkness. George Atzerodt was supposed to be waiting, holding their horses. At the last minute he panicked and fled, leaving Payne on foot.

Meanwhile, David Herold and John Surrat had a change of heart and had decided not to murder Johnson. They mounted their horses and rode into the darkness, leaving Washington in a state of turmoil.

By three in the morning Hancock arrived from Baltimore followed shortly by Grant. The two military men, by order of the Secretary of War, placed Washington under martial law. Cavalry patrolled the streets and a company of regular soldiers guarded the block around the tailor's home. Order was quickly restored and the hunt was on for the conspirators.

Stanton stayed with Lincoln throughout the night. He took charge, carefully preserving the dignity of the man and genuinely caring for the First Lady. As Lincoln's condition worsened, the Secretary limited the First Lady's attendance in the room as she was becoming more and more distraught. Finally, after nine hours of suffering, Abraham Lincoln died at seven twenty-two in the morning on Saturday, April fifteenth.

Stanton looked at his deceased friend and said, "he now belongs to the ages."

Bentonville, North Carolina—April 16, 2:30 PM

Sherman, unaware of the President's death, continued to pursue Joe Johnston. For the two Generals, the war was not over. Their forces clashed daily as casualties mounted. Johnston met with Jefferson Davis and the remnants of the Confederate Government. The men talked for several hours. The Confederate President informed Johnston of Lee's surrender and ordered the Virginian not to surrender his troops, but to organize them into guerilla bands and turn them loose into the countryside.

The meeting adjourned and Davis continued on his way. He planned to escape to Cuba then onto England. He would continue his cause in exile, waiting patiently for the North to lose interest in the guerilla war and give the South her independence.

Johnston sat in his tent listening to the rain falling upon the canvass. In the corner, a small candle burned, its flame, like the Confederacy, flickered near extinction. In the semi-darkness his thoughts raced back in time recalling those who gave their lives to the cause. The list seemed endless. Finally, after four hours of deliberation, the Virginian decided enough blood had been shed on both sides. He would surrender his Army and sent word to Sherman.

Bentonville, North Carolina—April 17, 6:00 PM

Sherman met with Johnston. The Union General was upset.

"What's wrong," asked Johnston?

Sherman looked at his adversary and handed him a telegram he received an hour earlier. Beads of sweat formed on Johnston's forehead as he read the dispatch.

> "To: Major General William Sherman
> President Lincoln died on the morning of the fifteenth. He was shot in the back of the head while watching a play at Ford's Theatre the evening before. He suffered for nine hours before expiring.
> Signed,
> Stanton"

"General Sherman," said Johnston. "You don't think I had any hand in this do you?"

Sherman looked at his adversary. "I don't think you or General Lee or any other Confederate Officer had a hand in this tragedy, but as for Jefferson Davis and his kind, I have my suspicions."

"General Sherman, I'm prepared to surrender my Army to you, I'd like to know what terms you're offering."

Sherman, remembering Lincoln's desire to let the South up slowly, answered, "I'll give you the same terms as Grant gave Lee. Your men are to lay down their weapons and return home and they'll not be bothered if they obey the laws of the Federal Government. They're never again to take up arms against the Government."

"These terms are most agreeable," replied Johnston. "Have your aides draw up the papers and I will sign them."

"One more thing," replied Sherman. "I'll have to have these terms approved by Washington and it may take several days. I'd like to suggest a truce until we receive the approval."

Johnston readily agreed. The Virginian was tired of the blood-letting. In his mind the cause was dead and the Country had to begin the process of healing.

Washington D.C.—April 18, 3:00 PM

Stanton was meeting with Grant and Union Attorney General, James Speed, when a telegraph operator brought in Sherman's telegram outlining the terms of surrender for approval.

The Secretary of War exploded. "Sherman's a damn traitor! Lincoln is murdered and he gives Johnston an honorable peace! I want Sherman court-maritaled!"

"I don't see any grounds for a court-martial nor do I think General Sherman is a traitor. He offered Johnston the same terms I gave Lee," replied Grant.

"He's probably going to march his Army into Washington and attempt a coup!" shouted Stanton banging his fist on the oak table.

"Mr. Secretary, I think you are overreacting," exclaimed Grant. "Sherman has no more designs on taking over the Government than Lincoln had at being a dictator. He's no traitor!"

"Maybe he is trying to grab the copperhead vote for the next election?" inquired Speed.

"Nonsense," replied Grant. "Sherman hates politics. He simply doesn't know the mood of the Nation right now. How could he? He's in the field. Take it from one who knows; when you're in the field, you're cut-off from all kind of news. Why don't I go to Sherman and have Johnston surrender again. What terms would you like?"

"Grant, I want the terms that made you famous, unconditional surrender," replied Stanton.

Bentonville, North Carolina—April 26, 11:00 AM

Grant met with Sherman and told his friend the mood in Washington and that Stanton had ordered that Johnston must surrender unconditionally. While the two friends talked, Federal Cavalry caught up with Booth and Herold on a farm just outside of Fredericksburg, Virginia, forty-five miles south of Washington. Herold surrendered without a fight; but Booth barricaded himself in the barn and fired on the Federals. The Cavalry Commander ordered the barn burned. While the flames took hold, one of the troopers, Corporal Boston Corbett, spotting an opening in the slats; fired, mortally wounding Booth. The Union horsemen ran into the barn and dragged the one-time actor out of the burning building. He died a few moments later.

Herold was escorted north to stand trial with the others. Only John Suratt remained at large as Atzerodt was captured the previous day in Richmond.

A heavy rain beat down on the roof of a small farmhouse. Inside Sherman and Johnston met to discuss the change in terms of the surrender. Sherman showed the Confederate General Union newspapers, which Grant had brought with him. The entire North was now crying for blood to avenge the death of the innocent President. Johnston agreed to the terms of unconditional surrender.

When he finished signing the document, he looked up at Sherman and with a tear in his eye remarked.

"The murder of President Lincoln is the worst thing to happen to the South."

EPILOGUE

Joe Johnston's statement about Lincoln's assassination being the worst thing that could ever happen to the South was prophetic. Many historians believe that, had Lincoln served out his full second term, the Country would have healed sooner.

Under Lincoln there would have been no carpetbaggers stealing land from Southerners as he was so popular after the war, he could have held the radical republicans in line. Civil rights would have been enforced 100 years earlier than in 1964. Segregation would not have occurred.

The American Civil war was one of the bloodiest conflicts ever fought by the United States. Combined, the casualties numbered over 600,000 men killed and 3,000,000 million wounded. The death toll doesn't include innocent civilians or those who, because of the war, committed suicide after the final shot was fired.

Many of the characters in the book are real; some of the aides belonging to Division Commander and Brigade commanders are fictional along with Lew Wallace's aide, Richard Smith. Some civilians like John Biggins and Mary Gracie are fictional. While Channing Smith and Benjamin Stringfellow really existed; Ron Lyons did not. The battles and strategies actually happened as Described. The Generals' personalities are based on historical records. Dates were altered in order to make the story flow more evenly. Conferences were embellished to give a dimension to the characters that is often overlooked in history books.

978-0-595-67991-1
0-595-67991-9

LaVergne, TN USA
30 March 2010
177608LV00006B/37/A